Hope's Gentle Touch

by

LAURA HODGES POOLE

FIREFLY
SOUTHERN FICTION
LIGHTHOUSE PUBLISHING OF THE CAROLINAS

HOPE'S GENTLE TOUCH BY LAURA HODGES POOLE
Firefly Southern Fiction is an imprint of LPCBooks
a division of Iron Stream Media
100 Missionary Ridge, Birmingham, AL 35242

ISBN: 978-1-64526-269-5
Copyright © 2020 by Laura Hodges Poole
Cover design by Elaina Lee
Interior design by Karthick Srinivasan

Available in print from your local bookstore, online, or from the publisher at: lpcbooks.com

For more information on this book and the author visit: laurahodgespoole.com

Brought to you by the creative team at LPCBooks: Eva Marie Everson, Yolanda Smith

Library of Congress Cataloging-in-Publication Data
Poole, Laura
Hope's Gentle Touch/ Laura Hodges Poole 1st ed.

Printed in the United States of America

PRAISE FOR *HOPE'S GENTLE TOUCH*

Poole handles the tender topic of abuse with grace and just enough tension to remind the reader that our happily ever afters are often hard won. She writes with the kind of authenticity and wisdom that transforms a sweet romance into a meaningful tale that will give readers something to think about long after turning the last page.

~ Sarah Loudin Thomas
Christy-nominated author of *Miracle in a Dry Season*

A heartwarming novel with characters you can't quit rooting for. This book is perfect for fans of small-town inspirational romance.

~ Heidi McCahan
author of *Unraveled*

Hope's Gentle Touch is a profound look at the effects of spouse/ date abuse on its victims. Heartbreaking and honest, the story weaves a realistic psychological study of the long-lasting turmoil faced by those who are trapped or have been trapped in abusive relationships. Yet author Laura Poole offers words of hope in the midst of tragedy, light in the midst of the darkness. A well-crafted novel that will bring understanding about this often-hidden evil.

~ Elaine Marie Cooper
author of *Love's Kindling, Scarred Vessels*

Misty Stephens isn't known for making prime decisions when it comes to men, and this time was no exception. Author Laura Hodges Poole crafts a page-turning and suspense-filled love story filled with twists and turns that every reader loves to sink their teeth into. Poole has put together a great inspirational novel with wonderful characters readers are easily connected to and an ending that leaves you satisfied.

~ Cindy Sproles
author of *Mercy's Rain, Liar's Winter,* and *What Momma Left Behind*

ACKNOWLEDGMENTS

To the many friends and family who have supported me in my writing journey—thank you. I wouldn't be the same writer without your encouragement, feedback, and love.

I'm eternally grateful to my Lord and Savior Jesus Christ who walks with me through all this earthly life has thrown at me—good and bad. Praise God for the gift of writing and the opportunities to develop my skills within that gift.

To my family, a huge thank you for indulging me in my love of writing—my husband James, my son Josh, my daughter Lindsay, my siblings, and my parents. I love you all.

Many thanks to my sister Trish, an RN and nurse practitioner, and my sister-in-law Robin, an RN, for guiding me through the technical aspects of nursing.

Thank you to my friend, author TC Avey for your love, support, and encouragement. I'm so fortunate that God placed you in my life "for such a time as this." Your Christian sisterhood has meant everything to me!

Thank you to my editor Eva Marie Everson for your expertise in overseeing the transition of manuscript to book.

To Theresa, my friend and confidant, whose wisdom has given me great insight into relationships, I'm forever grateful!

Thank you to my readers—without you my writing would have nowhere to go. You're truly a blessing with your reviews, emails, and notes over the years. I pray for you to have peace at a time when our nation has seen so much turmoil. May you feel hope's gentle touch as we work together to rebuild our lives. May God be blessed in all that we do.

DEDICATION

To the strong women,
who made an indelible imprint on my life:
My grandmothers
Toy and Effie Mae
My mother
Yvonne
My sisters
Teresa, Michelle, and Trish
My daughter
Lindsay Marie
and
My granddaughter
Everley Marie,
**Your dreams lie ahead—may
hope's gentle touch
guide you through life's journey.**

Chapter One

Sweat trickled down the side of Misty's face as she shoved open the bathroom window and pushed the screen out. She leaned over the ledge into the night air and surveyed the drop to the ground two stories below. Her chest heaved with jagged breaths while her mind raced through her options.

Stay and be killed—or jump.

Those were the only choices she could see. Ryan had knocked the phone from her hand when she'd tried to dial 9-1-1. Had the call gone through? Even if it had, the police would never arrive in time to save her.

Ryan's pounding on the door grew louder.

Misty snatched the wastebasket from the corner and flipped it upside down, spilling its contents onto the floor. The doorframe splintered behind her as Misty leapt on top of the wastebasket. Before it could buckle under her weight, she catapulted through the open window.

Her shoulder took the impact of the fall. The sickening sound of a bone snapping in her arm was followed by searing pain. Grimacing, she glanced up. Ryan stared down through the open window.

"Who's the crazy one?" he screamed. His face disappeared from the window.

Misty scrambled to her feet, stifling a cry. Her right arm dangled at her side. She clutched it with her other hand and tried to run. Stumbling, she fell into the bushes. Gasping for breath, she peeked out, desperately hoping Ryan would not come after her.

The back door of the house slammed.

God, help me. Don't let him kill me!

Ryan's hand reached through the bushes and dragged her out.

Misty braced herself against the pain.

A siren sounded in the distance.

"Stop, Ryan. Please. My arm is broken."

He sneered. "That's your fault, not mine. If you'd done what you were told, none of this would've happened." He shoved her against the ground and straddled her. His weight pressed against her.

She struggled to wriggle free. The pain from her arm nearly caused her to pass out.

He pulled a gun from his jacket pocket.

Misty sobbed. "I'm sorry. I won't ever disobey you again, I promise."

"Shut up! You never keep your word." He pressed the cold metal against her temple.

"No, that's not true. Please, I'm begging you."

Vehicles screeched into the driveway. Blue lights flashed against the darkening sky and footsteps pounded through the side yard.

The cold metal left her head at the same time Ryan stood. Misty rolled away from him, crying out as the earth crushed her broken arm against her stomach. She struggled to her knees but couldn't find the energy to stand.

"Move away from the woman. Drop the gun!" an officer demanded. "Now."

"I die, she dies." Ryan pointed the gun at her.

"Sir, drop the gun."

Misty cringed, falling back, wanting to scurry, but where?

The blast of a gun made her body convulse. She covered her head with her good arm, her scream cutting the air. Ryan slumped onto her. His dead weight sent excruciating shockwaves through her arm. Blood covered her. Was it hers or his?

"You're safe, ma'am. You're safe." The officer lifted Ryan's body from her.

Voices slid away as blackness enveloped her.

Chapter Two

Two Years Later

Misty's stomach knotted as she faced the stone façade of Oakview Memorial Hospital jutting in front of her. Flower beds filled with violet-and-yellow pansies dotted the pristine grounds. Yet their beauty did little to create a feeling of calm within her. Her first day back to nursing filled her with mixed emotions. Happiness. Fear. Anxiety. Hope. Employee orientation the previous week had done little to settle her nerves.

Could she go back to work and put the last two years behind her? She tried not to think of what Ryan would say if he could see her. She thrust out her chin, steeled her nerves, and climbed the hospital steps.

She'd considered leaving Oakview. Getting a fresh start somewhere outside of South Carolina was appealing, but in the end, she refused to let him drive her from her home—even from his grave.

Inside, the cool antiseptic air flooded her senses like an old friend. Any doubts she'd had washed away. Freshly painted aqua-and-cream-colored walls on the general medical floor were an improvement over the institution green they'd been when she'd worked here before. Along with a sea of pleasant faces flowing past her, the renovations created a cheery environment. She smiled. She was home.

"Misty."

Charge nurse Leah Watkins hurried down the hallway toward her. A tall, brisk, no-nonsense woman, Leah had hired Misty with no hesitation when she'd reapplied for her former position. With her graying hair twisted into a bun and firm set to her jaw, Leah looked over the rim of her glasses at Misty. Leah appeared more intimidating than she was.

"Glad to have you back." Leah hugged Misty gently, then motioned for Misty to walk with her.

"Busy day?"

"And how." Leah's pace quickened. "Sorry. I know it's your first day, but we need you in the trenches and up to speed immediately."

Misty sidestepped a pharmacy tech pushing a medicine cart. She doubled her step to match her new supervisor's stride. "I'm ready."

Leah stopped short. "Are you?"

"Definitely. Don't worry about me. Nursing's like riding a bike. You never really lose your touch." Misty hefted her purse over her shoulder. The confident voice that rang in her ears surprised her.

Leah's mouth quirked. "You're right." She picked up her pace as they continued down the hallway. "But a lot has changed. Let me know if you get overwhelmed."

They stopped in front of the nurse's station bustling with activity. Leah waved for a petite brunette nurse to join them.

"Danielle Tyler, this is Misty Stephens. You might remember her from her interview."

Danielle nodded. "Sure. Hi, Misty."

Leah turned back to Misty. "I'll leave you in Danielle's hands." She disappeared into the sea of techs and nurses in the hallway, before Misty had a chance to reply.

"Case review," Danielle explained. "Leah's on the hot seat. A patient's family has filed a complaint about his death."

"That's a tough situation." Similar episodes from her prior years on staff flashed through Misty's mind. "Some things never change. I remember going into those meetings myself."

Danielle's eyes widened. "You were a charge nurse?"

"Once upon a time." Misty laughed. "Until I discovered I'm perfectly happy working the floor."

"Well, let's get to it. You know where to find the locker room. Meet me back here after you change."

Misty pushed open the door of the locker room, and within minutes she'd changed into a set of green scrubs. She stowed her clothes and purse in the assigned locker, slipped on a matching scrub jacket, and draped her stethoscope around her neck. Tugging her strawberry-blonde hair into a ponytail, she wasted no time returning to the nurses' station.

Danielle pulled a second chair up to her computer, motioned for Misty to sit, and thrust a notepad in front of her. Misty listened attentively as Danielle showed her the computer charting system that had been updated since Misty worked for the hospital.

Nurses scurried around them, answering phones, paging doctors, and ordering medications. Danielle dealt with several interruptions while giving Misty instructions and briefing her on the patients on the floor.

"Even with a better system, it seems as hectic as ever around here."

Danielle chuckled. "Yeah, more time in our schedule is the one thing we didn't get with the improved system. If anything, the volume of patients has stretched us even thinner."

Misty pocketed her notepad and followed Danielle to the first patient's room. She went through the checklist and logged the patient's chart. When Danielle slipped from the room, Misty's pulse quickened. She prayed that charting for the rest of her patients would go as smoothly as this one.

Back in the hallway, she scrolled through the computer to review the next patient. Female with a fractured pelvis and arm. Misty pushed open the door to the room and stepped inside. The shades were closed, and the radio played softly.

As her eyes adjusted to the almost-darkened room, a man dozing in a corner chair came into focus. Misty cleared her throat. He shifted, then sprang to his feet.

"I've been waiting for someone to check on Jenny," he snapped. "I've buzzed the nursing station twice." He glanced at the young lady lying in the bed. "She finally settled down a little while ago."

Misty thought of a careful reply as she checked the vital signs monitor and switched on the light above the bed. Memories of the unpleasant part of nursing flooded back to her.

"I'm sorry. This is my first day, so I'm a little behind." She wheeled the hospital tray away from the bed then peeked under the dome cover of the dinner plate. Though the contents were scarce, nothing had been eaten. She looked up at the man. "She couldn't get any of the Jell-O down?"

He shook his head. "She was in too much pain. I think she fell asleep from sheer exhaustion. Can you increase her medication?"

"I'll make a note of it for the doctor. He'll decide whether to increase it or add another medication." Misty gently untucked Jenny's covers to get a closer look at her bandages. "Are you her husband?"

"No, I'm her brother." He ran his fingers through his disheveled chestnut-colored hair. Frustration edged his voice. "She doesn't have a husband." He waved his hand toward his sister. "Her boyfriend did this."

Nausea roiled Misty's stomach while she tried to focus on her tasks. An abuse victim. Misty's hands trembled. *Not on my first day.* A smothering sensation threatened to overtake her, but she couldn't afford to let her emotions get the better of her.

She drew a deep breath and walked over to adjust the blinds. "It's really too dark in here." The late afternoon sun seeped in, lighting the room better.

She turned back to face the man. "I'm sorry, Mr.—"

"Adam Jenkins." He extended his hand.

His rugged features contrasted with his pressed khaki slacks and button-down shirt. His face was familiar, younger than his voice had seemed in the dimly lit room. Had she seen him somewhere before?

Misty looked at his hand for a moment, then shook it. The roughness of his skin surprised her. "I'm Misty Stephens. I'll be your sister's nurse in the afternoons."

Despite his agitation, laugh lines, as her well-mannered Southern mother referred to them, edged his coffee-colored eyes. They hinted he was a man who laughed often, though she saw no sign of amusement now. More like a grizzly bear ready for battle.

"She's in a lot of pain." His words sounded deliberate, as if he weren't sure she'd comply with his request. "If you could get the doctor to write her a stronger medication, I'd appreciate it."

Misty refocused her attention on her patient. "We err on the side of caution when giving high doses of opiates, but if she's having trouble resting and eating, her doctor will take a second look at the dosage. Meanwhile, let her sleep as much as she can. And once her meds are adjusted, we'll raise the head of her bed slightly. She needs some movement."

"Thanks." He frowned. "But I'm not sure about moving her."

Misty nodded. "We won't rush her. Let's wait and see how her vital signs look after the med adjustment." Placing her stethoscope on Jenny's chest, Misty listened for signs of pneumonia. Satisfied that Jenny's lungs sounded clear, Misty draped the stethoscope around her neck and looked at Adam. "If she wakes up, try to get some of the Jell-O in her."

Adam's gaze returned to his sister.

Shaken by the bruises and lacerations on the girl's face and arms, Misty steeled herself to do her job. She checked the IV, while Adam caressed Jenny's shoulder.

He glanced over as Misty finished. "I'm sorry I snapped at you. I simply wanted a little more care for her."

Misty smiled. "Of course."

Hurrying into the hallway, she trembled at the force of the memories of her own abuse. She had to keep them at bay. Caring for her patients, especially Jenny, would be difficult if she dared think of what she'd suffered at Ryan's hands. She glanced back at the room. Rest might help heal the girl's physical wounds, but the emotional ones wouldn't heal for a long time, if ever. She quickly entered a notation into the computer in the hallway and moved onto her next patient.

An hour later, Misty had finished her rounds. Except for Mr. Duncan in room 325, everyone had been pleasant. Given the fact the elderly man battled terminal cancer, she couldn't hold his surly mood against him. Maybe she'd have a chance to talk to him more, once he got used to her.

Danielle looked up from her paperwork when Misty returned to the desk. "So how did it go?"

"Everything went well. Mr. Duncan in room 325 was the only bump in the road."

Danielle grinned. "Don't let him bother you. Nobody has been able to get through to that man. You're here to serve him, or so he thinks."

Misty slid a glance at her. "It would seem." She dropped into the computer chair to finish her patient notes. Something about Mr. Duncan seemed familiar, but was it just because he was unpleasant—like Ryan had been?

Danielle leaned over the screen while Misty worked. "When you're finished, I'll check through and initial them. That'll be one less thing for Leah to do when she gets back."

"Thanks. I appreciate your making my first day easier."

"My pleasure." Danielle picked up the phone. "Paging a doctor is the least favorite part of my job. Let's see how long it takes to get a response."

Misty groaned. "Another thing that hasn't changed."

By early evening, learning the updated system and caring for her patients left Misty exhausted. Although the new software was supposed to make the nurses' jobs more efficient, she'd spent an inordinate amount of time entering and retrieving information anyway.

Pleased to see the doctor's order for an increase in pain meds for Jenny Jenkins, Misty noted Danielle's initials next to it, indicating she'd administered the meds while Misty was with another patient. Jenny's injuries were extensive. Surviving such a brutal beating had been a miracle.

Misty breathed a prayer for Jenny when she logged off the computer a few hours later. She pushed into the locker room and changed into her street clothes. Although she'd already given report to the nurse coming on duty, she decided to check on Jenny one last time before clocking out. She opened the door to Jenny's room and stuck her head inside.

"Ms. Stephens." Adam rose from his chair.

"I'm leaving for the night. I wanted to see if Jenny's resting more comfortably." Misty stepped inside and dropped her belongings into a chair.

He smiled. "Yes, thank you. I appreciate your seeing to her medication."

"No problem." Misty tucked in Jenny's covers and brushed a few strands of brunette hair from her face. "She looks comfortable now."

Adam's searching gaze caught her attention. "May I ask you something?"

Misty faced him. "Sure."

"You seem to really care about Jenny." He paused and stared down at his hands. "I mean, all the nurses take care of her, but this seems like more than a job to you. Why?"

"Suffering people matter to me." She shrugged. "That's why I became a nurse."

"I wish everyone on staff here felt that way."

"What do you mean?"

"Some nurses do their job mechanically, as if Jenny were a number on a checklist."

Misty bristled, mainly because his statement held some truth. She'd run across a few of those in her career. "I'm sorry if that's been your experience, but that occurs in all occupations. I'm not making excuses, but some shifts are more hectic than others. We try to ensure everyone gets the attention they need." She smiled again, then softened her words. "Which may not match exactly what you're expecting."

"You're right. Sorry if that sounded rude." He rubbed his forehead. "I don't know what I'm saying, anymore." His gruff voice highlighted his exhaustion.

"Don't worry. I didn't take offense." She picked up her sweater and tucked her purse under her arm. "I'll see you tomorrow."

"Good night, Ms. Stephens." Adam opened the door for her.

She looked into his face as she stepped toward him. His dark eyes glistened, and she hesitated. The kindness reflecting not only in his eyes, but his words ignited a small spark deep within and confused her. She was sure it had everything to do with being tired.

Whatever his thoughts, he didn't voice them. Instead, he smiled. "Thanks again."

"You're welcome."

She didn't look back until she'd summoned the elevator. She shoved down the emotion welling inside her. Counseling had made it clear she'd be vulnerable from Ryan's lack of affection and putting her through the process of earning it every time she messed up. Being robbed of affection for so long made her misconstrue kindness. That was the only logical explanation for how the touch of a man's hand had sent her reeling.

The doors slid open, and Misty stepped onto the elevator and punched the lobby button. She rubbed her temples in an effort to forget the exchange with Adam. Was it possible nice men existed who wanted nothing in exchange for their kindness? She felt like a fool. Of course there were, and Adam seemed to be one of them.

The elevator settled and the doors parted. As she crossed the lobby to the entrance, Misty prayed that one day she'd feel whole again, that she'd have healthy platonic relationships with men, because one thing was certain. She couldn't risk her heart and life again in a permanent romantic relationship.

Stepping into the cool night air, she studied the constellations twinkling in the moonlit sky. "Thank you, God, for this day. Please be with Adam and his sister. Lord, they need you. And, oh, please help me get my emotions straightened out."

Peace washed over her, and she smiled. The God who numbered the stars in the sky had never let her down, not even in her deepest moments of despair.

Chapter Three

"Please page Dr. Rogers again," Misty pleaded into the receiver. She glanced at the nurse's board. The light for room 325 flashed. She groaned and hung up the phone. Although she'd only been back to work for a few days, she understood the other nurses' frustration with Mr. Duncan.

There has to be some way to get through to this man. She jumped up, strode down the hallway, and pushed open the door to Mr. Duncan's room. She pressed a smile into place. "Did you ring?"

"Get the doctor," he cried out. He clutched the self-injection medication cord with his thumb on the button. "This thing doesn't work."

As she'd suspected, he'd pressed the button too often and now wasn't getting the expected relief. He'd need breakthrough pain meds, but the doctor had to order those. The only thing she could do was stall until the doctor answered his page.

"I've paged him. He should be here shortly." Misty pulled a small book of Psalms from her pocket. "In the meantime, do you mind if I read to you?"

Mr. Duncan's eyes widened, then smoldered like hot coals. His anger seemed to blend with his short gray-blond hair that stood up on end and added to his harried look. "Are you crazy, woman? I'm in agony and you're gonna read to me?"

He yelled an expletive as his emesis basin sailed through the air.

Misty tensed. "Mr. Duncan, I understand you're in pain, but I'll have to ask you not to throw things while I'm in here." She pulled a chair up to his bed and sat. "Besides, you're not going to get rid of me that easily." She opened her book and began to read.

Within moments, Mr. Duncan's sharp cries quieted to an occasional moan. Misty had read into the third Psalm when the door opened, and Dr. Rogers stepped in with another nurse. She quickly brought them up to date and then excused herself and hurried back to the nurses' station.

"I already gave report to the next shift for the rest of the patients," Danielle said.

"I'm out of here then." Misty logged off the computer, clocked out, and headed to the locker room. She changed out of her scrubs and into a pair of khaki slacks and a burgundy two-piece sweater set before slipping into a pair of loafers. The luxury of a hot bubble bath was her only focus after the grueling shift she'd worked.

She grabbed her purse and jacket and stepped back into the hallway in a matter of minutes. Rounding the corner, she crashed headlong into a tall figure standing there. Her purse flew from her hands, its contents spilling everywhere.

Adam Jenkins.

Misty's breath caught as her hands pressed against his muscular chest. She felt the rippling sensation of his powerful arms flexing against her body as they steadied her. She pushed back, freeing herself from his grasp.

"You okay?" His hand remained on her arm.

She nodded. "Uh-huh."

He picked up her purse.

Misty stooped down and grabbed her lipstick, wallet, and other objects from the floor. She rose, clutching the items to her chest.

"I'm—I am so sorry," she stammered.

"It's okay. You're not hurt, are you?"

"No," she assured him. "I just need to learn to slow down."

The corners of his mouth edged up. "I'm on my way to the cafeteria. Care to join me for a cup of coffee?"

Misty stiffened. The brief moment she'd been in Adam's arms, against his firm chest, had sent a wave of confusion through her. "I don't think that's a good idea."

"Why?"

The man was much too attractive. He aroused feelings deep inside—ones better left buried. Besides, her feet throbbed, and her back ached.

"I'm not comfortable with that," Misty robotically recited the line she'd learned in counseling. She prayed he'd step aside and let her go on her way without more conversation.

Adam's brow crinkled. "I wanted to talk to you about Jenny. I've heard you had similar problems. Maybe you could clear up some things for me."

Warmth from her cheeks spread to her chest. *Who had been discussing her past problems concerning Ryan?*

She swallowed hard. "How so, Mr. Jenkins? How can my experiences help your sister?"

Adam shifted his weight from one foot to the other. "I guess that was kinda blunt." He rubbed his unshaven chin. "Let me start over. I'm confused, and—well, I'd hoped you could help me understand Jenny." Sincerity etched his expression. "Is that better?"

He had a way of disarming her. Misty's shoulders softened, and she smiled. He'd said the one thing she couldn't resist. "I guess we could have coffee to discuss Jenny." She looked down at his hand. "May I have my purse now?"

Adam's laughter filled the hallway as he handed the purse to her, then motioned for her to go ahead of him.

Misty grinned at his sheepish expression. She pushed down the nagging thoughts that she was allowing herself to become vulnerable to this man. Simple actions like letting her step onto the elevator first would've never crossed Ryan's mind, but she couldn't read more into Adam's gesture than existed.

In the cafeteria, Misty felt Adam's gaze on her as she filled her coffee cup. He handed her a spoon, then poured his own. After standing in line to pay, she led the way through the noisy cafeteria to a quiet table near a window. Adam held her chair while she sat. She busied herself with stirring sugar into her coffee as he settled into his chair.

"Not exactly Starbucks." He smirked.

Misty chuckled. "Hospital coffee could never be mistaken for that."

"Ms. Stephens," Adam began.

"Call me Misty. No point in being formal."

"I was raised to show ladies respect, so I don't assume anything until I'm told."

She groaned inwardly. *The man had to have a character flaw somewhere.*

Adam stirred his coffee as though he had all the time in the world. He took a sip, then set his cup down. "Misty, maybe you could help me understand why an intelligent woman puts up with a man who beats her. I mean, surely there were warning signs, verbal abuse probably. Why didn't she just leave?"

Misty's shoulders stiffened, her anger rising again, along with her exasperation. How often had she heard this statement from people who didn't have a clue about abusive relationships?

She took a deep breath and carefully weighed her response. "Adam, I'll tell you right up front your statement aggravates me."

"I didn't mean—"

"Let me finish," she interrupted. "Having said that, I also realize unless you've been abused, you don't have a clue." She stirred cream into her coffee and laid down her spoon.

"You're right, but I intend to learn because no one is going to beat my sister again." He thrust out his chin, eyes flashing.

"Well, now, I'm not sure how you're going to accomplish that." Misty was running the same hamster's wheel she'd run with her family. Weary of people's misplaced views and attempts at intervention, somehow she had to jump off. How many times had her parents tried to rescue her from Ryan, only to watch her return?

"Why?"

She smiled. "The first thing you've got to understand is you're not in control."

Adam's mouth dropped open. "I'm not trying to be."

"Actually, you are. You're trying to control Jenny every bit as much as her boyfriend." Misty winced as soon as the words left her mouth.

His cup clanked as he set it onto the tabletop. "Wait a minute."

"Okay, that was a bit of a stretch. I'm sorry. But until Jenny realizes her boyfriend will escalate the abuse until he kills her, you won't be able to get her away from him. Her mindset toward this guy began way before the relationship."

Adam leaned back in his chair. "How so?"

Misty fidgeted with her napkin. Could she share the intimate details that led her into Ryan's arms? She'd give Adam a watered-down version. "I don't want to assume what Jenny's childhood was like, so I won't even go there. It may have had nothing to do with her choice. It could be entirely coincidental she got involved with the wrong guy."

"We grew up in a very loving, Christian home. My parents have always been very supportive of all of us. Although—" He rubbed his chin. "They live on the West Coast, and Jenny is really too young to be out on her own, but she wouldn't listen to reason."

"I can only speak for myself," Misty continued. "I come from a family who loves me dearly. However, people show love in different ways. My parents were way too protective, kept me sheltered. That made me vulnerable to the first person who came along."

"Your husband?"

"Actually, he was the second. My first boyfriend had similar personality traits as Ryan—controlling, trying to make choices for me, but I was in college. My parents still had a pretty tight grip on me, so he finally gave up and moved on to someone else." Misty pressed the coffee cup to her lips then set it down.

"But I didn't learn from that." She sighed. "When Ryan came along, doted on me, lavished me with gifts, and made me feel validated, I fell hook, line, and sinker. He was smooth."

Adam's eyes reflected her pain—and likely the pain Jenny felt.

"Long story short, he didn't become a tyrant overnight. He chipped away at my self-esteem, made me believe our little spats were my fault. If I'd obeyed him as a good Christian wife would, then he wouldn't have to get mad."

Adam grimaced and shook his head. "Sick."

Misty ran her fingertips along the edge of her cup. The abuse had been a sickness on both their parts. But how could she explain that?

"After a couple of years of this vicious cycle, I began to realize he was wrong, but I had nothing left, no reserves to step out on my own." She despised herself at times for how stupid she'd been. No, that wasn't right. Vulnerable and beaten down, but not stupid. Her stomach churned at the memories spilling forth. "I kept trying to save my marriage, not do anything to anger him, trying to remake myself."

"I'm sorry if this is difficult." Adam's voice softened. "I didn't realize how much your situation mirrored Jenny's."

Misty straightened. "Don't worry about it. I've been over this a hundred times in therapy."

Adam arched an eyebrow. "Therapy?"

"Yes." Her head pounded when she thought about the years she'd wasted with Ryan and how foolish she'd been. The years she'd spent trying to undo the damage. Now she sat pouring her heart out to Adam. She felt the walls going up and realized, once again, she'd shared too much with a stranger. Would she ever learn? "I would've never gotten through all this without good Christian counseling."

"I understand."

Misty took a last sip of coffee and wiped her mouth. "No, actually you don't. But that's okay." She gathered her purse and jacket and stood. "It's been a long afternoon."

"Wait." Adam pushed back his own chair. "I'm sorry. What did I say wrong?"

She attempted a smile and met his gaze. "Nothing. There's no simple solution or answer to your questions. Only Jenny knows why she put up with this jerk. All you can do is provide her an escape along with absolute unconditional love and support. She's smart enough to see the difference between men like him and men like you. Hopefully, she'll walk away. I pray it won't be too late."

"What about the rest of your story?"

Misty shook her head. "There isn't a 'rest of the story.' I'm out of the relationship now, that's all that matters. I'll see you tomorrow."

She shrugged into her jacket and left. Once outside, she dug her keys out of her purse, happy the night was over. The sooner she got home and collapsed into bed, the better. Then she could put Jenny and Adam out of her mind.

***

Misty disappeared through the maze of cafeteria tables and chairs. Adam hadn't intended to set her off. From what he'd overheard of other nurses' conversations, she must have divorced her husband. She wasn't with him anymore, so she'd found a way to escape. How a beautiful lady like her fell for such a tyrant to begin with was beyond him.

Did Misty grasp the extent of her beauty? Her blonde hair, tinged with the slightest hint of auburn, accented her light complexion. Worry lines around her hazel eyes conflicted with her smile. Sure, she smiled, but not with her heart. A yearning graced her expression and pricked his soul every time their eyes met. It made him want to protect her from ever feeling pain again.

Adam pulled his smartphone from his pocket and checked his messages. One from his foreman reminded him he'd forgotten to order supplies for his horses. Although Adam trusted his employees, he managed the financial part of his ranch himself. He scrolled through his apps and arranged for a shipment of hay. His stock holdings had fared well in the market that day. There was nothing left to do for the night except sit with Jenny.

He stopped at the grill line and ordered a chicken sandwich. After he paid for it, he climbed the stairs to the third floor. Faced with another long night, he sighed. What else could he do but what he'd done for the last week? Until Jenny recovered, he intended to stay at her side and continue to work from the hospital.

He pushed open the door to her room. His chest tightened like it did every time he saw her lying helpless in the bed, bandages and tubes strewn across her body. No matter what it took, he'd make sure she never ended up here again.

Why, Lord? Help me to understand why a beautiful and intelligent woman would stay with a savage who continues to hurt her. Help me to help Jenny.

Adam dropped into the recliner beside the bed and opened his takeout box. He took a bite of the chicken sandwich and watched Jenny while she slept. So innocent and fragile, like the new ducklings waddling around the pond at his ranch.

His mind wandered back to his conversation with Misty. Her explanation hadn't shed much light on Jenny's situation. She and Jenny didn't seem to share any similarities in their past besides the fact they were women who trusted the wrong men.

He tossed his half-eaten sandwich into the box and pushed it aside. He grabbed his Bible from the nightstand and flipped it open. For the next thirty minutes, he alternated between praying and reading. Calmer when he laid the Book down and switched off the light, he was still no closer to an answer.

Chapter Four

Misty padded barefoot through her hallway toward the kitchen. The bubble bath she'd taken had soothed her sore muscles and spirit. How long would it take to adjust to working such long hours again? She grabbed a water bottle from the fridge, twisted the cap off, and took a sip.

She dropped onto the couch and picked up a novel she'd started reading a few nights earlier. Leaning against the arm of the couch with her feet up on the cushions beside her, she turned to the page she'd left off reading. Halfway through the page, the words began to blur. Her earlier conversation with Adam played through her mind. What was it about him that attracted her?

She'd been careful over the past two years not to let any man get too close. She vacillated between craving a man's attention, which only made her vulnerable, to going to great lengths to avoid relationships. The smartest decision she'd made was not to date again—at least until she had her head, and her life, straightened out. Who knew when that would be?

So, why had a man who'd entered her life a few days ago captured her attention? The connection was Jenny. She must be transferring her emotional tie with Jenny to Adam. It was the only logical explanation for her feelings.

Misty stared into space, absently noting the full moon that shone through the terrace windows of her condominium. She slipped a bookmark between the pages and shut the book. Pulling a quilted throw around her, she clicked on the television and surfed through the channels. Her eyelids drooped. She sank into the couch cushions, enjoying the warmth. Her exhaustion slowly drained away.

She rolled her head to one side and focused on an old photo of her parents. Warmth filled her as she thought of her dad, a first-generation American. She'd been a daddy's girl, and it suited her fine to hear her family say it. Jack and Sophia Callahan had turned heads in their day, a redheaded Irishman and a blonde Southern belle. Daddy had once been the most important man in her life.

Misty rubbed her temples. How had she let herself settle for less?

She reflected on her first week at Oakview. She'd worked diligently to renew her nursing license and get her old job back. Caring for patients fulfilled her in a way nothing else ever had. Why had she allowed herself to be persuaded to give up the job after her marriage? A shudder rippled through her as Ryan's taunting face edged her memories.

Misty roused herself and headed to the bedroom. Tomorrow was an important day. Could she go back to the shelter she'd fled to so many times over the years? Getting her life back on track made her more determined than ever to help the Jennys of the world. This time around, she wouldn't let a man derail her dreams.

***

When Misty woke the following morning, her spirit soared at the possibilities awaiting her. Humming, she quickly showered then slipped into a soft, variegated blue sweater ensemble and a pair of khaki slacks. She glanced at the clock and grabbed a muffin and apple juice from the fridge instead of sitting down to eat. Within twenty minutes, she pulled into the parking lot of the shelter.

Lord, guide my steps. Protect my heart from the awful memories of Ryan so I can help other women.

Her heels clicked on the hardwood floors, the sound echoing off the walls as she made her way through the shelter's main hallway. Her stomach knotted as she neared the director's office. She hadn't been back since that dreadful night the week before Ryan died when she had sought refuge from yet another one of his beatings.

Misty stopped in front of the office door and gripped the cold doorknob. A shiver rippled through her. Returning to the shelter to volunteer was a monumental step, but she felt a kinship to the women still trapped in their miserable situations. If she could bring some comfort to them, it was the least she could do.

She rapped on the office door, then opened it, and stuck her head in.

"Misty," an older woman with brunette hair exclaimed. "Come in." She came from behind the desk and they embraced. The center's director, Tanya Kimmel, had comforted Misty countless times over the years.

"It's good to see you again." Misty tugged at the hem of her sweater as she tried to calm her nerves. Memories flooded her senses. The air conditioner's hum, noise drifting in from the activity room, and the aroma of Tanya's chamomile tea wafting in the air pulled her back to other times she'd spent here.

Tanya rounded the desk and sat, then motioned Misty to a chair. "I've thought about you often since I read of your husband's death."

"Sorry I haven't stopped by sooner." Misty tucked her hair behind her ears and settled into the chair.

"It's completely understandable." Tanya folded her hands on the desktop. "I'm glad you're here now. What can I do for you?"

"I spoke with your new activities director yesterday. I'd like to do some volunteer work."

Tanya arched an eyebrow. "Are you sure you're ready?"

"Yeah, the time's right. The work you do is important. I might not be alive, if it weren't for this place."

Tanya leaned forward. "You're a strong woman, Misty. I knew you would pull through."

"My life's been turned upside down for several years now." Misty paused and smiled as she tried to get a handle on her emotions. "But I renewed my nursing license. I'm back at my old job at Oakview Memorial. Been there a week now."

Tanya's face lit up. "Well, now. You've been busy. That's great news." She stood and motioned for Misty to follow her. "I guess we can find something for you to do around here."

Misty trailed her through the hallway to the residential section.

Tanya opened the adjoining door slightly and leaned back for Misty to look in. "Three women arrived last night. Two have children. That brings us to a total of twelve women and five children."

The activity room bustled with children playing. A couple of women sat off to one side chatting quietly with each other.

Tanya closed the door and faced Misty, crossing her arms. "We're in desperate need of mentors and counselors."

"How can I help?"

"We have a two-hour training program for mentors in a couple of weeks, if you'd like to attend. After that, we'll put you to work." Tanya held Misty's gaze while she waited for a response.

Misty's hands tingled with excitement that crept into her soul—something she hadn't felt in a while. Could she do it? Could she reenter a world she'd tried so desperately to distance herself from?

Tanya reached out and gave her arm an empathetic squeeze. "You think you're up to it?"

Calmness settled over Misty. She'd already prayed about it. "I think so. I'd love to help these women."

"Then it's settled. Come back to the office and fill out the paperwork."

***

Misty hurried into the nurses' locker room, her chest light and warmth radiating through her. She hummed as she changed into her scrubs, draped her stethoscope around her neck, and pulled her hair into a ponytail. As Jenny and Adam's faces sprang up in her mind, a different emotion rushed through her—anticipation. How could two strangers make such an impact on her in a short period of time?

After checking in at the nurses' station and being brought up to date from the previous shift nurse, Misty headed to Jenny's room. She pushed open the door and then stopped short. Jenny's smile beamed from across the room.

"She looks good, huh?" Adam rose from his chair and set his magazine aside.

"She does." Misty crossed the room and moved Jenny's tray table away from her bed.

Adam covered his sister's small hand with his. "This is Misty, your afternoon nurse."

Jenny's smile wobbled. "Adam's told me how attentive you've been to me. Thank you."

Misty patted her arm. "No need to thank me. I'm thrilled to see you alert." She lifted Jenny's wrist to check her pulse before wrapping the blood pressure cuff around her upper arm and slipping the pulse oximetry meter onto her finger. After recording the readings, Misty pushed a button to incline the head of Jenny's bed a little more. "Cough, please."

Jenny responded with a slight cough.

"Everything seems to be in order." Misty flashed a smile. "I'll be back to check on you later. Ring if you need anything."

Adam followed her out. "Thanks, again, for everything."

His eyes sparkled for the first time since Misty had met him. She'd never seen someone so appreciative for something she'd done.

"Sure." She started to walk away, but he touched her arm. She instinctively stepped back.

"I was thinking, well, maybe you'd like to come out to my ranch. We could go horseback riding, maybe have a picnic lunch." He rocked back on his heels. "You do like picnics, don't you?"

Horseback riding? A picnic? Misty sucked in her breath. Panic spread through her like wildfire, her pulse racing along with it.

Adam is interested in me for more than his sister's care?

Her mind fumbled for an answer. "Why?"

His eyebrows creased. "Why?" he echoed.

"Why are you inviting me?"

Adam's smile reemerged. "Because I enjoy your company. Is that a good enough reason?" he teased.

Misty groaned inwardly. She couldn't do this. Not now, maybe not ever. "Adam, I like you and your sister, but I'm not interested in taking things any further."

"That's understandable, after your divorce and all. I'm not pushing for anything serious, just friends."

She took another step back. A smothering sensation pushed at her chest. "My divorce?"

His eyes widened. "You *are* divorced?"

"Not exactly," Misty stammered. "I have to get back to work. Thank you for the invitation, but I'm pretty busy right now. Sorry."

She hurried down the hallway, not daring to look back. She heard Jenny's door shut behind Adam as he returned to his sister's room.

Why can't I bring myself to talk about Ryan's death? It wasn't my fault.

Doubts nagged at her as she spent the next hour at the computer updating patient charts. Her next thought made her heart pound. Suppose Adam didn't understand Ryan's death. She dropped her head into her hands. Why did Adam's opinion matter so much ... or at all?

***

Adam ran his fingers through his hair in frustration. What was it about Misty that he couldn't figure out? She was a beautiful but complex woman—one he had come to respect through her care for Jenny. He mulled over their conversation in the cafeteria earlier in the week. She hadn't specifically said the word *divorce*, but she was out of the relationship. What did that mean?

"Adam," Jenny almost shouted.

He jumped from his chair.

"I've called your name three times." Jenny smirked. "Who are you thinking about?"

Adam frowned. "Why do you assume it's a who?"

"Well, it's either a lady or your business. Nothing else seems to consume your thoughts like that."

His laugh echoed in the room. "Okay, smarty-pants. It was someone, but nothing like that."

She smiled. "I've always loved to hear you laugh."

He took her small hand in his. "I'm glad you're awake. Maybe we can talk."

Jenny pulled her hand away, then lowered her gaze.

"What's wrong?"

She shook her head. "I can't talk about it. Not now."

"That's okay. We'll talk when you're ready."

Tears spilled down her cheeks, and Adam bent over the bed and gently pulled her into his arms. She sobbed against his chest while he stroked her hair. "Shhh," he murmured. "You're safe now."

Jenny pulled away from his embrace. He pressed a tissue into her hands and waited for her to regain her composure.

She tossed the used tissue onto her tray, picked up her water cup, and took a sip.

"He's in jail, sis." Adam stroked her arm. "That's where he's going to stay."

Her mouth quivered as she let out an exasperated sigh. "I can't believe how stupid I've been." She pinched the top of her cup with her fingertip, then set it down. "I should have listened to you."

"*Should haves* don't count. We're here now, and you're recovering. I'll take you home to the ranch as soon as they give us the green light to leave." His sister didn't like to be hovered over, but she couldn't be left alone. "You'll need extra care for a while. I don't think you should go back to your apartment right away."

To his surprise, Jenny nodded, then mustered a smile. "What would I do without my big brother?"

He planted a kiss on her forehead. "You'll never have to find out." He grabbed his jacket from the chair. "If you're going to be okay for a while, I need to run to the office."

"Go ahead. You've been stuck in this hospital room long enough." She reached for a paper on her tray. "I'm gonna fill out my menu for tomorrow and then watch some TV."

"I'll be back." He disappeared through the doorway.

He could make the board meeting at Jenkins Enterprises, if he hurried. As he rang for the elevator, he observed the activity at the nurses' station. Misty chatted with a doctor, and several other nurses bustled around.

Adam stepped onto the elevator and looked back at his phone. He typed Misty Stephens into the search engine. He scrolled through the choices and clicked on a newspaper story from two years before.

Ryan Stephens, age 35, shot and killed by police. His wife, Misty Stephens, was transported to Oakview Memorial Hospital where she was treated for a broken arm after she jumped from an upstairs window to escape her husband's attempt to kill her.

"Whew!" Adam leaned against the elevator wall. No wonder Misty had rejected his overtures. He'd been right about his feelings for her. She had more strength and backbone than she realized. He'd seen that inner strength hidden behind her tentative look. Her situation came into focus in his mind for the first time. Like a war veteran, she'd been hardened by time spent in the trenches, yet shell-shocked by whom she perceived to be the enemy. In this case, the enemy was men.

The door opened. Adam shrugged into his jacket before heading outside. He sat in his car and stared at nothing in particular. "God," he uttered his prayer, "why are there men like this? And why do women as beautiful and intelligent as Misty and Jenny stay with them?"

His jaw clenched as he thought about men like Ryan misusing their strength. Strength God gave men to protect women. The abuse nauseated him. But what could he do about it? There must be something—not only to help Misty and Jenny but other women in the community. He inserted his key into the ignition and continued to pray as he pulled out of the parking garage.

One thing was certain. Jenny's boyfriend would have to come through Adam to get to her again—and heaven help him, if he tried.

Chapter Five

"Why did you stay?"

The question came out of nowhere, startling Misty. She tucked the sheet into the side of Jenny's bed and straightened to look at her.

"I'm sorry. I shouldn't have been so blunt."

Misty waved aside her words. "No, it's fine. I wasn't expecting the question, although I should have." She smiled at the younger girl.

"I don't know why." Misty bit her lip. "That doesn't help, does it?"

Jenny's face clouded. "Not really."

Misty sobered and sat beside Jenny, patting her hand. "I guess my answer isn't entirely true. But it's the one that rolls off my tongue the easiest."

"What do you mean?"

"After two years I still find it hard to talk about." Misty twisted the end of her ponytail between her fingertips. "But you deserve an answer." She met Jenny's gaze. "I stayed because I hoped Ryan would change. I stayed because of my marriage vows, you know, until death do us part."

"Is that all?"

"No, I stayed because I believed I didn't deserve any better."

Tears streamed down Jenny's face. "Thank you," she sobbed. "I needed to hear that I wasn't the only one who's had those thoughts."

Misty reached for a tissue and handed it to Jenny. She waited while Jenny blew her nose, then leaned closer. "Jenny, you do deserve better."

Jenny sighed. "I know. I've had a lot of time to think, lying in this bed. I can't believe how stupid I've been."

"Not stupid, honey, beaten down. Your self-worth has been torn to shreds. It's just not as evident as the physical bruises." Misty motioned to Jenny's bandages. She waited for the younger girl to compose herself before continuing. "If I may be so bold, I'd like to ask you something."

"Go ahead."

"Where do you stand with God?"

Jenny's face scrunched. "With God?"

"Yes. Are you a believer?" Misty held her breath. She was going out on a limb with her patient, but she'd resolved when she came back to nursing, she wouldn't be timid about sharing her faith.

"I was at one time." Jenny laughed softly. "That sounded flaky. I meant to say yes, but I've not been to church in a very long time."

Misty squeezed Jenny's hand. "What's important is what's in your heart. I only mentioned it because I found that my faith was the only real thing I could count on, the only strength I had to draw from during those awful years." She reached into her smock pocket and retrieved her book of Psalms she carried. "Do you mind if I read to you?"

"Please do." Jenny snuggled under the covers.

Misty began reading, and within minutes, Jenny's eyes closed. Misty finished the Psalm and closed her book.

"Don't stop." Jenny's eyes flew open.

"I thought you were asleep."

"I was praying." The corners of Jenny's mouth edged up, her eyes sparkling. "I want God to be what's most important to me from now on. Maybe if I let Him lead, it'll be easier to deal with some of the stupid decisions I've made in the past few years."

Misty's throat tightened. "He most definitely will help you. I'm glad you recommitted your life to Him."

Jenny reached for Misty, and Misty hugged her.

"My mom will be thrilled." Jenny tugged at the edge of her covers. "My parents and my brother Colton came when I was first admitted, but they had to go home. My mom will be here this weekend for a visit."

Misty smiled. "That'll be real nice. I look forward to meeting her."

Jenny's face beamed. "Oh, you'll love her, Misty. You remind me of her. She's quiet but very strong in her faith."

"I'm sure I will." Misty patted her hand. "I'll check on you later. I've got some other patients to take care of. Try to rest."

Adam came into the room. "Good evening." He tossed his jacket across the chair beside Jenny's bed. "Leaving already?"

"I'll be back before my shift ends." Misty motioned toward Jenny. "Don't tire her out. She needs some rest."

"Sure, I'll walk you out." Adam held the door for Misty.

Misty glanced back at Jenny, who smiled knowingly at her. *This can't be a good sign.*

"I'm busy," Misty tried to head him off when they were out in the hall.

"I want to apologize for the other day." Adam's gaze met hers, but Misty didn't see pity. Instead, there was something different, though she wasn't sure what.

"I don't understand."

"I pushed you about coming to my ranch and about your marriage, which is none of my business." He crossed his arms, punctuating his statement. "I apologize for that."

Her cheeks warmed. Why did being around Adam make her feel so off-balance?

"But there's more." He paused, as if debating his next words.

She felt drawn to him in an inexplicable way. He had a strength about him, more than the obvious physical strength his broad shoulders represented. She waited for him to continue.

"I'm not Ryan. Nor am I anything like him."

Misty reeled from his words. "I know you're not," she stammered.

He smiled. "I wanted to get that out in the open." He took a step toward her and lightly touched her arm. "Now, would you like to have coffee with me again sometime? Maybe after your shift? I want to get to know you a little better."

Misty stepped back, breaking contact. She swallowed hard, then looked into his eyes. She realized what she'd seen earlier. Respect mirrored back at her. Could she trust that? Could she trust herself to go out on a limb and not get hurt? "I'd like that."

Adam laughed. "Wow, that was easy. I had this whole speech planned."

She laughed with him. "Well, save it for later. I have other patients to care for."

"Sure thing. See you at eleven o'clock?"

"Yeah, I'll check in on Jenny later."

Misty hurried back to the nurses' station. She shrugged off the self-doubts that seemed to needle at the edge of her mind when she tried to move forward. Staying busy for the next few hours would help drive Adam from her thoughts. She didn't think it was too soon to be dating again, but she had to guard her heart against old habits.

It would take very little for her to fall for him. She'd done the same thing with Ryan. Comparing the two men wasn't fair to her or Adam, but she had to apply the lessons from her past mistakes to her current relationships. Vulnerability to a man's affections would lead her down the wrong path. She couldn't deny the physical chemistry between them. Adam's drop-dead features combined with his gentle and caring nature were hard to resist. He'd tended to his sister's every need. But could she trust he'd do the same for any woman?

***

"Yes!" Adam pumped his fist after he pushed the door open to Jenny's room.

Jenny clapped her hands together, giggling. "She said yes?"

"About what?" Adam feigned innocence before joining her laughter. He plopped down on the bed beside Jenny. He grasped her hands in his and gave them a gentle squeeze.

"Misty agreed to have coffee with me again."

"Again?"

"Yeah, she joined me in the cafeteria to talk when you were first brought in. She helped me understand your situation better."

"You like her, huh?"

"She seems really attentive to her patients."

Jenny grinned. "She's attractive, too."

Adam made a face at her. "Yeah, she's not too hard on the eyes." He grew serious. "But she has an inner beauty, too. I wish she could see that."

"You think she doesn't?"

"I think it was beaten out of her, and she hasn't completely gotten her spark back yet." He thought about the interactions he'd had with her—and the few times he'd gotten glimpses of her with others. "But I can tell it was there at one time. She glows when she cares for her patients. I've heard her read the Psalms when she's been out in the atrium with them."

Jenny closed the magazine she'd been reading. "I agree. She and I talked. She helped me see some things."

Adam reached for the magazine and pulled the covers up around Jenny. "Hey, you're supposed to be resting."

She smiled. "I can always count on you to take care of me."

"You bet you can." His chest ached with the emotion his little sister stirred within him. He bent over and planted a kiss on her forehead.

"Get some sleep," he whispered.

***

"My farm is about thirty miles on the outskirts of town." Adam handed Misty the sugar container across the table in the bustling cafeteria a few hours later. "I mainly breed and raise horses, but I also have a hundred acres in organic crops plus apple orchards."

"Wow, that's huge." Her eyebrows shot up.

Adam shrugged. "It's modest. Several other farms in South Carolina are larger."

That's where she'd recognized him. His farm was well known in the state. She'd driven past it often. "You own Jenkins Enterprises?"

"One and the same."

"I attended a charity function hosted by your company several years ago, when I first worked for Oakview." She poured sugar into her coffee and stirred, while she digested this new information about Adam. He was still the same person he'd been yesterday. Why did his being the owner of a large enterprise make her feel threatened now?

"I try to stay involved in community functions."

"Excuse me for saying so, but you seem young to have such a big ranch."

He grinned. "It was originally my grandfather's ranch. My parents moved to California about ten years ago because Dad wanted to try his hand at ranching in the West. My younger brother, Colton, and I had practically grown up on Grandpa's ranch, so we stayed on with him. Neither of us had any desire to relocate to the West Coast. Jenny went with my parents. When she turned eighteen a few years ago, she returned here. She always considered South Carolina her home."

"I see."

Adam bit into a chocolate-covered éclair and wiped his mouth with a napkin. "When Grandpa died, he left the ranch to Colton and me. I took a mortgage and bought out Colton's interest because he wanted to go to Virginia. Jenny insisted on getting her own apartment."

Misty's vision blurred. Would Jenny's life have taken a different path under her parents' watchful eye? Misty had not fared any better with her parents nearby. She was no closer to solving the conundrum of the choices she or Jenny had made where men were concerned.

She clasped her coffee cup and looked at the steam rising between her hands. Her mind wandered to childhood when her father took her horseback riding at a local stable. She sighed.

"Why the sigh?"

"My father and I used to ride when I was a child." Misty picked up her fork. She scooted the apple cobbler around its bowl, unsure if she were brave enough to try it.

"Would you like to go riding sometime?"

"Oh, I hope you didn't think I was implying—"

Adam waved aside her words. "No, not at all. I'd love the company. I haven't had a riding partner in quite a while. Jenny used to come to the farm and ride before she hooked up with that loser."

Misty took a bite of the cobbler. How should she reply? She wanted to accept his invitation, but apprehension filled her. She wiped her mouth with her napkin. "I imagine the whole situation is difficult for you."

He leaned back, tilting his chair on two legs, and crossed his arms. "It makes me angry, yes, when I look at her in that hospital bed. But it's more than the physical damage. It's what he took from her in the process."

Tears stung Misty's eyes. How was Adam able to pinpoint the situation so accurately? That's exactly what abusers did. They took from their victims. They took their hearts, their minds, and if they could, they'd take their souls. She rubbed her arms from the chill that ran up them.

Adam lowered his chair, bringing his face near hers. "I'm sorry. Did I say something wrong?"

Fear rippled through her with his closeness. If she fell for him, it could be a disaster. Not only was he physically strong, he was a powerful, wealthy man. He would have the ability to control her in a way that Ryan didn't. She pulled back, unable to find words to express her feelings.

Swallowing her fears, she cleared her throat.

"No, you didn't say anything wrong." Misty forced a smile. "I agree with what you said."

"So, you'll go riding with me." Adam peered into his empty cup and frowned.

"Get a refill. I'll wait." She watched while he filled his cup at the coffee dispenser and returned to the table. Adam had a swagger about him that any woman would find attractive. Who was she kidding? He was incredibly appealing, and not only on the outside. Was there any reason they couldn't be friends? She enjoyed his company and had grown fond of Jenny.

God, please give me Your peace about this man—or the wisdom to walk away.

"Okay, you haven't given me an answer," Adam teased. "And I've given you plenty of time to think up some good excuses."

She smiled over the edge of her cup. "How do you know I won't say yes?"

He pounced on her statement. "So it's a yes?"

Misty groaned. "Okay, I'll come." She put her hand up. "But I've got some ground rules."

"Anything." Adam beamed.

"Friends only."

The light in his eyes flickered briefly. "Friends first."

She dropped her head into her hands. He definitely wasn't going to make this easy.

***

Misty draped her stethoscope around her neck the following evening, shoved a notepad into her pocket, and dropped into a chair behind the nurses' station. The power bar she'd eaten an hour earlier barely sustained her, but she hadn't been able to get ten minutes free to eat a decent dinner.

The floor was crowded tonight. The ER had called, requesting additional beds. Where would they put everyone, if the overflow worsened? Heading into the weekend, the situation didn't look promising. Misty scanned the patient board. All was quiet—for now.

Her mind retreated to her horseback riding plans with Adam on Sunday. She simply had to get through the crazy schedule shaping up for the next two days.

"What's up, Ms. Stephens?" One of the nighttime orderlies from Environmental Services passed by the desk, interrupting her thoughts.

She glanced up from her work and smiled. "Busy as ever, Mike."

Mike continued down the hallway. Misty was relieved to see fresh sheets had arrived for bed changes. One less thing she had to track down. She looked over the desk a few minutes later to make sure the nursing assistants were collecting linens from the cart to get to the task.

While she entered chart information into the computer, she made notations of med changes that had been ordered.

"Can we get any busier?" Danielle dropped a stack of paperwork on the desk beside Misty. "We're never gonna get caught up."

"Mmm." Misty didn't look up from her work.

The patient board flashed. Danielle groaned. "Mr. Duncan's room."

"Probably doesn't like the way his bed is being changed."

Danielle cleared her throat.

"No, it's your turn." Misty cut her off, then gave a sympathetic smile. "I've already been in there twice tonight."

"Can't blame me for trying."

Misty glanced up long enough to see Danielle disappear down the hallway amidst the techs and other nurses bustling around.

The board flashed again. Jenny's room. Misty frowned. She'd checked on her within the last half hour. "Wonder what she needs now." She tossed her pen onto the desk and crossed the hallway to Jenny's room.

"What's up?" she asked the nursing assistant.

"She started gasping for breath when I rolled her over to change the sheets," the young lady answered.

Misty's throat tightened. She ran her hand along Jenny's forehead, brushing aside her dampened bangs. "Jenny, are you awake?"

Jenny opened her eyes briefly and grimaced. "I don't feel well."

Misty frowned. "What's the problem?"

"My chest ... feels funny." She rubbed her chest, punctuating her statement. Jenny's breath came in little spurts. Tears seeped out of the corner of her eyes.

"How long have you felt like this?"

"Not long." Jenny gasped. "Oh, Misty, it hurts."

Misty wrapped a blood pressure cuff around Jenny's arm, as her breathing labored. Her monitor showed a dropping O2 saturation. Misty lunged forward and pushed the code button on the wall. The door of Jenny's room burst open. Doctors and nurses filled the room, but Jenny was already unconscious.

Chapter Six

"Blood pressure sixty over forty," Misty called out. She stepped back to allow Dr. McCarthy closer access to the bed.

Adam pushed his way into the crowded room with a takeout container in his hand. His expression grayed with unspoken questions. Misty grabbed his arm and pulled him aside, as Danielle started CPR.

"Adam, you'll have to go to the waiting room." She guided him to the hall.

"What's going on?" Adam choked out.

"We're trying to figure that out. Sorry. I have to get back to Jenny."

Misty felt terrible leaving Adam, but Jenny was the concern at the moment. She went to Jenny's bedside where Danielle continued CPR and another nurse injected epinephrine at Dr. McCarthy's command

As a respiratory therapist managed Jenny's ventilations, Misty restarted the blood pressure cuff and waited for the reading. But no reading came. She crooked her fingers under Jenny's neck. "No pressure. No pulse."

"Possible emboli." Dr. McCarthy rechecked the rhythm on the monitor and barked out an order for another med.

Misty's throat tightened. Given Jenny's rapid decline, Misty had feared the diagnosis, but she wouldn't give up hope. She grabbed the thrombolytic medicine vial, drew the ordered amount into the syringe, and pushed it through Jenny's IV line.

"Continue CPR," the doctor directed. Minutes felt like hours as the team worked feverishly on Jenny.

Dr. McCarthy shook his head at the electrical tracings on Jenny's monitor. A faint rhythm quivered across the screen.

Everyone stepped back as a technician applied the defibrillating paddles to Jenny's chest. "Clear!" Jenny's body jerked upward.

Dr. McCarthy studied her vitals. "Give another amp of epi and continue CPR."

Danielle traded glances with Misty. She leaned toward Jenny's ear. "Fight, Jenny! You can do it."

Dr. McCarthy motioned to the technician who picked up the paddles again. "Clear."

Misty stepped back and grimaced as Jenny's body jerked upward and fell like a rag doll onto the bed. The faint quivering rhythm continued across the heart monitor screen.

God, please, don't take her.

Dr. McCarthy blew out a breath. "Again."

"Clear," shouted the tech, and again, Jenny's body jerked upward and fell limp.

The monitor beeped a consistent tone as the rhythm flatlined and held.

Tears streamed down Misty's face. She braced for the inevitable declaration.

"Time of death, eight forty-five p.m." Dr. McCarthy stripped off his gloves and tossed them in the trash.

Misty squeezed Jenny's hand before placing it on top of the sheet. She brushed back the girl's bangs and stroked Jenny's cheek with her fingertips.

"Where's the next of kin?"

Misty stepped away from the bed. "Her brother's in the waiting room."

Danielle fell in line beside the doctor when he turned to leave.

"Wait a minute." Misty touched Danielle's arm. "I'd like to go."

Danielle's eyebrows rose slightly. "Go ahead. I'll call the morgue."

Misty rubbed her arm against the chill that ran up it. She'd never grow used to that word.

God, give me the right words.

Dr. McCarthy would use tremendous kindness in breaking the news of Jenny's death, but nothing would soften this blow to Adam.

Adam jumped to his feet when Misty and Dr. McCarthy entered the waiting room. The question in his eyes morphed into disbelief. His face ashen, he fell back into his chair. "What happened?"

Dr. McCarthy pulled a chair around to face Adam. "Mr. Jenkins, I'm sorry, we couldn't save her. All indications point to a pulmonary embolism—a blood clot—that dislodged from another area of her body, probably the pelvic region. We'll confirm that assumption with an autopsy. It's required by law, given the situation."

Dr. McCarthy touched Adam's arm. "I'm sorry. We did everything we could."

Adam put his head into his hands and sobbed. "No," he choked out. "God, no."

Misty inhaled deeply against the tears that stung her eyes and threatened to spill over. The fact they'd done everything possible offered little comfort now.

Face grim, the doctor stood to leave. He caught Misty's eye and lowered his voice. "I was in the middle of another case."

Misty nodded. "Go ahead. I'll take him to Jenny's room, if he wants to go."

Dr. McCarthy pulled the door shut behind him. Misty suspected dealing with deaths was no easier for doctors than nurses.

Adam continued to sob. "She's gone, Misty. What am I going to do?"

Misty rubbed his back until his anguish lessened. She grabbed some tissues, pressed them into his hands, and then dropped into the chair beside him. She waited while he blew his nose before she spoke.

"Would you like to see her?"

He raised his head. "I'm not sure."

She touched his hand. "That's a normal feeling, but you don't have long to decide."

"Why, Misty? Why did this happen?" His tormented face searched hers for the answer she didn't have.

"I could give you the medical reasons, but I don't think that's what you're asking." She held his gaze. "Only God knows why, Adam. I can't speak for Him."

His face crumpled again, and she put an arm around him. She hoped none of the other nurses would decide to join them. How could she explain that she and Adam were just friends—and that Jenny had been very special to her?

After a moment, Misty spoke. "Let's go say goodbye to your sister."

He pulled away and blew his nose again. "Stay with me, Misty."

She glanced at the clock on the wall. Other patients needed to be checked before her shift ended. In the past, when a death happened, another nurse would pick up her slack, but much had changed in the years she'd been away from Oakview.

"Of course, I'll stay." Misty squeezed his hand for encouragement then led him out into the hallway.

As they approached Jenny's room, Adam lagged behind. Misty continued her pace to the room and waited for him in the doorway. Jenny lay in the bed as she had an hour before, quiet and still. Except this time she wouldn't wake. Adam huddled in the corner as if afraid to go closer.

"Go ahead." Misty stayed near the door.

He approached the bed and then dropped into the chair next to Jenny. He lifted her small hand in his and pressed it to his cheek. "Jenny," he sobbed. "I'm sorry." He laid his head against her bed and cried. "I didn't protect you." His voice crashed with another hard, wrenching sob.

After a few minutes, Misty treaded softly across the room and placed her hand on his back. "You'll make yourself sick, Adam."

He lifted his head. "How is it possible to be numb and be in so much pain at the same time?" His tear-stained face twisted with anguish.

If she allowed herself, she'd fall apart with him. It was not what he needed. "You're in shock. I hate to do this, but I need to step out and see some other patients."

Adam clutched her hand. "Don't leave."

Misty forced a smile. "I'll be back. Take a few minutes to share what's in your heart."

She slipped away, closing the door behind her. Her whole being ached at Adam's loss but more for Jenny's—the life she'd never experience. Misty angrily swiped her tears and hurried toward the nurses' station.

Danielle looked up from the computer when Misty approached the desk. "How's he doing?"

"Not good." Misty logged on to the other computer and pulled up the doctor's orders for her patients. Somehow, she'd get through the rest of her shift, but the image of Jenny's face as she pleaded for help wouldn't wash from Misty's memory anytime soon. Determined to stay focused on her work, she made the required notations in the charts and checked on a couple of patients.

She didn't have time to deal with her emotions about Jenny's death, yet Adam wasn't far from her mind. After she'd checked her last patient, she hurried down the hallway to Jenny's room. The emptiness of the dark room reverberated around her. How had she missed the transporters from the morgue? Her stomach knotted. And where was Adam?

Misty tugged the stethoscope from around her neck and dropped it in her smock pocket. She trudged to the nurses' station—quiet, considering the shift change due in thirty minutes. She dropped into a chair behind the desk but sat idly tapping her pen on the countertop. Her notes sat untouched. If only she could escape this dreadful day. The image of Jenny lying in the bed loomed in front of her. She replayed the code in her mind, searching for clues to what went wrong. Could Jenny have been saved, if Misty had detected a problem sooner?

Leah came down the hallway talking quietly with Dr. McCarthy. Misty straightened in her chair. Her head pounded with anticipation.

"Misty." Leah motioned for her to join them.

Misty's hands quivered. She clasped her pen tighter, willing them to be still. Of course, Leah would want her version of events. Hopefully, she hadn't overlooked something in Jenny's care that would be suspect in her death.

"I'd like to hear about your participation in the code earlier," Leah said when Misty reached her side. The crease between Leah's eyebrows matched her grim mouth while she waited for Misty to speak. Dr. McCarthy shoved his hands into his smock pockets and nodded for her to begin.

"I went into Ms. Jenkins' room to assess her about five hours into my shift." Misty focused on the details. "It was after eight o'clock, I think. Of course, I checked on her during usual rounds when I first arrived for my shift and again when her dinner was delivered."

"The exact time doesn't matter. The details are recorded in the formal report. Go ahead."

"Ms. Jenkins was fine, resting comfortably. Within minutes of returning to the desk, the nursing assistant buzzed. She'd gone in to change the sheets."

Leah listened intently.

"As soon as I entered the room, I noticed Ms. Jenkins' skin appeared pale and somewhat sweaty." Misty swallowed hard at the memory. "Her eyes were closed, and I asked if she was asleep."

Leah scribbled on her notepad, nodding as Misty recounted the events that led up to her pushing the code button.

"As I suspected," Dr. McCarthy said. "Pulmonary embolism, but we'll have to wait for the autopsy for official confirmation. I'll see you ladies tomorrow."

He disappeared down the hallway. Leah put her arm around Misty's shoulders and gave a gentle squeeze. "You handled the situation perfectly."

Under any other circumstances, Leah's praise would have sent Misty's heart soaring. But today, it rang hollow.

"I was doing my job." Misty faced Leah. "But this is the part I really loathe."

Leah's eyes softened. "I know. I never get used to doing this. I understand from Dr. McCarthy that you handled Ms. Jenkins' brother like a pro." She reached out and brushed a wisp of hair from Misty's tired face. "You should be proud of that."

Misty crumpled at the mention of Adam. Sobs wracked her body, and Leah pulled her into her arms. After a moment, she stepped back and guided Misty to the locker room.

"Splash some water on your face and then meet me in the nurses' station to give a report," Leah instructed.

Moments later, Misty returned and gave all the details of her shift to Leah, who then instructed her to clock out early. "I'll update the next shift nurse. Go home and get some rest."

Misty didn't have the strength to argue. "Thank you, Leah." She paused. "I want to assure you I am up to this."

Leah's face brightened. "Of course you are. We all have bad days." She patted Misty's arm. "Unfortunately, you'll cover for someone else another day."

Misty trembled. Leah understood. Misty couldn't bear the thought of what she'd do without this job now that she had it.

"I'll see you tomorrow." Leah offered a smile.

Misty crossed the hall to Jenny's room and peeked in. She didn't expect to see Adam, but she didn't know where else to look. The room had been cleared of Jenny's belongings and prepped for the next patient. Likely he'd left the hospital.

If only there'd been something more they could've done. She shook her head, wearily turned on her heel, and left the room. She gathered her jacket and purse from the locker room and clicked on her cell phone before pocketing it.

Outside, the cool night air rushed at her. She hurried to her car across the lot. On the drive home, the roar of the city around her dulled to a hum in her haze of grief.

Dropping into bed an hour later, Misty knew Jenny's face would haunt her for weeks to come. She tried to push the evening's events down into her subconscious. Longing for rest, she cried herself to sleep.

Chapter Seven

Misty scanned her smartphone for messages before she climbed the steps in front of the hospital. In a short period of time, she'd fallen into a routine. Tomorrow she would attend the training workshop at the women's shelter, then be assigned a woman to mentor the following week.

She texted her parents about rescheduling their lunch plans on Sunday. Horseback riding with Adam was out of the question, but she wasn't up to dining with her parents, either. If only she knew how he fared.

Misty pocketed her phone. Adam came into view through the revolving doors. Her breath caught. She summoned her strength. She couldn't let herself fall apart with him, no matter how bad she felt about Jenny's death. Mustering a weak smile, she stepped through the doors and into the lobby.

Adam's face sagged, probably from lack of sleep. A crease had formed across his forehead. "Hi, Misty."

"Adam, how are you? I've been worried about you." An overwhelming desire to embrace him swept over her, but she was unsure how he'd interpret her actions.

"Rotten," he grunted and hung his head, "but I'm managing. I realized after I got home last night I'd forgotten Jenny's Bible." He lifted the little book, almost hidden in his large hand.

The fact that Jenny spent time reading it in the short time she'd been there comforted Misty. "Is there anything I can do to help?"

"I'm going to California for Jenny's funeral. Most of my family's out there. My brother, Colton, is flying out from Virginia." He glanced up. "This may seem like an odd request, but I'd like your cell number."

Thoughts raced through her mind while she tried to form an answer.

She had nothing to fear from this man, but he hadn't completely gained her trust either.

"I promise I won't bother you."

Misty waved aside his words. "Oh, no, it's nothing like that. You caught me off guard." She made a quick decision. "Of course, I'll give you my number. Please call any time while you're gone. This weekend will be rough—I know."

Adam pulled out his phone and tapped her number into the keypad. "Thanks." He slipped the phone back into his pocket. "Not only for the number but for taking care of Jenny. You'll never know how much that meant to me."

Misty swallowed hard against the ache in her throat. "No problem," she managed to get out. "Jenny was special."

"Thank you for saying that." He looked down at his feet again then lifted his head. "I can't make sense of this, Misty."

"Nor can I." She didn't know his spiritual beliefs. She only knew Jenny's heart. She had a feeling nothing she said would help right now, anyway.

"Part of me wants to go down to that jail and beat the life out of the guy who did this to her."

His venomous words made Misty recoil inwardly. Mainly because somewhere deep inside, a part of her agreed with him. She slowly nodded.

"Sorry for how that sounds."

"Anger is a normal part of grief, Adam. You feel protective of Jenny, and—" She hesitated.

"Go ahead."

"Maybe you feel like you let her down."

Tears welled up in his eyes. "You're right," he choked out.

"Oh, Adam, I'm sorry. I certainly don't believe it, but I had a feeling you do. Nevertheless, I shouldn't have voiced it."

His eyes burned with passion. "Don't ever apologize for saying what's in your heart. You don't have to hold back with me."

She forced a smile. "My shift starts in a couple of minutes. I'm sorry, but I have to go."

"I'll be back in a week." He shifted, seemingly debating his next thought. He stepped forward and gave her a quick hug.

Misty longed to hold him a moment longer, to absorb his some of his pain, and comfort him, but he turned, then walked through the revolving doors and down the sidewalk, head down, shoulders hunched.

She brushed her tears with her fingertips and walked to the elevator. Life wasn't fair, but then again, where was it promised to be? God did promise He'd be there in the midst of trials. She clung to that like a lifeline.

***

The next morning, the sun streamed through the slits in the sheer drapes of Misty's bedroom. She rolled over, checked the time, then snuggled under the covers. The class at the shelter started in an hour. If only she'd planned the class for another weekend. Her cell phone buzzed on the nightstand. She groped for it.

A message from Adam. Misty sat up and crossed her legs to read his message. The funeral was in a few hours, he couldn't sleep, and was waiting for the sun to rise. *And I thought I woke up early.* She typed a message back. "Praying for you. Hope the service goes well."

Soon after she hit send, the phone buzzed in her hand. Her pulse raced as she read his comment. "I haven't forgotten our plans for horseback riding. I feel like I need to see you more than ever now. Please don't let that scare you off, but I don't intend to waste a single day of my life."

Her heart skipped a beat. *Scare her off?* His words terrified her.

An odd excitement seized her as she traipsed toward the shower. Why did it make a difference that Adam cared to include her? She pushed down the nagging feeling that Adam could have control over her, if she allowed herself to become vulnerable to him. He'd shown no indication of doing so. Sure, he seemed a little intense, but loss often fueled a person's sense of urgency.

Almost an hour later, Misty climbed the steps of the women's shelter and opened the front door. Voices flooded the hallway as she strolled toward the conference room.

"Misty!" Tanya jumped from her chair and took Misty's hand. "Everyone, this is Misty, the newest addition to our volunteer staff."

One by one, the ladies introduced themselves. Misty tried to keep their names straight in her mind. They settled back into their chairs, and Tanya took the podium.

"Our new director, Jackie, usually leads this class," Tanya began. "But sometimes we alternate. That's why you have the pleasure of my company today."

The ladies laughed. Everyone sobered when Tanya dimmed the lights and began a video presentation showing women the shelter had served during the previous year. Misty's stomach roiled at the injustice suffered by the children in the photos. One thing she was grateful for—she'd not had children with Ryan. They would've suffered the same abuse. Did she dare hope one day she might have children with a real Christian man?

Misty refocused on Tanya's presentation and took notes. When the box lunches arrived at noon, Jackie stepped into the room.

"Hi, ladies," she greeted everyone. "Sorry I couldn't be here this morning. I had another meeting I couldn't miss. I know you were in capable hands." She smiled at Tanya. "Please enjoy your lunch. I look forward to speaking with each of you individually during the coming weeks."

Jackie sobered and stepped away from the podium toward the volunteers. Clasping her hands in front of her, she continued.

"The work you do here will serve a tremendous need within this community. As you've learned this morning, every nine seconds a woman is battered by her husband in the US. Forty-two percent of women murdered in this country are killed by a boyfriend or husband— three every day. Most are killed when they try to leave the relationship. You can see the enormous task we are faced with—the sheer number of women we serve. Yet we can't lose sight of the individual woman and her particular situation."

Misty scanned the solemn faces around her. She resisted the urge to lower her head in shame like she used to when the subject of abuse came up. She'd learned long ago she wasn't at fault for Ryan's abuse, but it had taken two years for her heart to begin believing it.

"Thank you for volunteering," Jackie concluded. "Women like you are invaluable to keeping this shelter open."

Everyone applauded. Misty opened her box lunch, lifted out a turkey sandwich, and ate while she chatted with the ladies around her. She looked forward to volunteering with them. Most were like her, either former abuse victims or married women trying to make a difference in less fortunate women's lives. By the time she finished the simple meal and tossed her box in the trash can, she'd made several new friends. With a lightened heart, she gathered her purse and slipped into her jacket. This was definitely the distraction she needed to fill her down time.

Determination flooded Misty. She couldn't help Jenny anymore, but she could help the other Jennys of the world.

Sunlight glared off the windshields in the parking lot. Misty retrieved her sunglasses and cell phone from her purse before setting it on the hood of her car. She scrolled through her text messages and read one from Adam. He was due back tomorrow from California. Her pulse quickened at the possibility of seeing him again.

Driving down the freeway moments later, Misty hummed along to the Christian radio station. For the first time in years, peace permeated her soul.

Adam's earlier text popped into her mind. He didn't want to waste a single moment. She'd given him no reason to expect more than friendship from their relationship. Yet, his intensity indicated his mind ran on a different track from hers.

She frowned. Was she prepared to spend the rest of her life as a single woman? If that were God's plan for her life, she couldn't complain. She'd been married, and it hadn't worked.

God had blessed her immensely in the past few months. She loved her job, and now the years of abuse she'd suffered would have purpose. She could help women still trapped in desperate situations.

***

Adam shifted in his seat on the plane. The funeral had been excruciatingly painful, as he'd anticipated it would be. His parents were heartbroken, though his mother remained stoic throughout the whole process. She'd clung to him at the airport, tears spilling onto his shoulder, as she struggled to tell him goodbye.

The clouds outside his window reflected the fog encasing his mind. He scrubbed his unshaven chin. Would this ever make sense to him? Never. Not as long as he lived.

The children across the way played a game on their iPad, their giggles filling the air. He remembered playing games with Jenny and Colton, though mainly outdoors. Colton had been way too restless for board games, though Jenny loved playing Monopoly. Adam almost laughed aloud. She'd insisted on always buying Boardwalk and Park Place, which usually ended up in a fight with Colton storming off.

A flight attendant came up the aisle, offering drinks to the passengers. Her long brunette hair, though pulled back, reminded him of Jenny. She stopped at his seat. "Could I get you something, sir?"

He swallowed against the lump forming in his throat. "A Coke, please."

She smiled. "Here you go. Let me know if there's anything else you need."

"Thanks." He took a sip and placed it in the cupholder beside him. Thankfully, the seat next to his was vacant, a rarity on most flights he took. A blessing from God, for sure.

Wiping his hand with a napkin, Adam realized the one thing that Jenny hadn't had throughout her ordeal. A safe place. Sure, she had him. But a place she felt like she could go and still matter. A place where she could start over—independent of her brothers and family. A place she could rebuild her self-esteem and feel like those around her understood.

He grimaced at how many times he'd uttered those stupid words. *I don't understand.* Well, too late he'd started trying. Now her death couldn't be in vain. It wouldn't be. An idea started forming. A verse his mom had chosen for Jenny's funeral came to mind: Romans 8:28.

God, please help me find a way to bring something good from Jenny's death.

***

The phone in the nurses' station rang for what seemed like the tenth time in the last hour. Misty stepped over to the desk and grabbed the receiver. "Third floor."

She clicked her pen and glanced at the clock, aware she needed to check most of her patients again before she could clock out. However, she didn't want to be rude.

"Misty." Adam's voice came through the receiver.

Her breath caught. She dropped into the chair and swiveled around to face the desk. "Adam, how are you?"

"Good, considering." He grew quiet before continuing. "Sorry I haven't called before now. I got back a few days ago, but I'm still trying to get my head together. I wasn't sure if you'd answer your cell phone at work. Since I was already on the phone with the billing department, I had them transfer me over."

"Don't worry about it." Considering the fact he'd just buried his sister, Misty hadn't anticipated him calling so soon.

"I'm going stir-crazy trying to fill time by myself at the ranch."

Misty knew the feeling. She'd been doing the same thing, working extra shifts and dropping into bed exhausted in the wee hours of the morning. But no matter how hard she tried, she couldn't rid her mind of the image of Jenny lying lifeless in her bed. Misty suspected Adam hadn't had any better luck.

"Do you have any plans for Saturday?"

"Actually, I do. I'm volunteering at the women's shelter."

"How about Sunday afternoon?"

"I'm free. What do you have in mind?"

51

"Horseback riding at my ranch, maybe a picnic dinner, then watch the sun set."

Misty fidgeted with a file folder's edge. Horseback riding was one thing, but how could she say yes to what sounded like a date?

"Are you there?"

"Yeah."

"It's not a date. I remember the ground rules," he teased.

She exhaled the breath she'd been holding. "When you put it like that, how can I say no?"

"You can't." Adam chuckled. "I'll pick you up around one o'clock."

Misty frowned. She couldn't let him come to her apartment. It wasn't safe. Wait a minute, what was she thinking? This was Adam. Yeah, but she didn't really know him, did she?

"Have I lost you again?"

"No, but I'd rather meet you somewhere else, not my place." Misty braced for his answer. "I hope you don't mind."

"That's fine." His voice fell.

She'd hurt him. "I'm sorry. It's not you."

"I know. I've learned a lot in the past few weeks. I understand, at least to the extent that I'm capable of understanding, not having been in your shoes."

She glanced at the clock. "I appreciate that. I'll meet you at the Oaks Mall out on East Brooke, if that's okay."

"That's fine. I'll see you at the main entrance at one o'clock."

"See you then."

Misty grabbed her stethoscope and hurried down the hallway to Mr. Duncan's room. She'd get the most challenging patient out of the way first. Then she could only hope the rest of the evening would go smoothly.

Chapter Eight

Misty scanned the crowd inside the mall for Adam on Sunday afternoon. Had something delayed him? She strolled to the window of Brittany's Boutique and peeked at the mannequins dressed in new spring wear. A sleeveless floral-print yellow dress caught her eye. Could she browse the little shop and still have a clear view of the entrance? She glanced back as Adam came through the front doors, then hurried through the throngs of people to meet him.

"How are you?" Dark circles shadowed Adam's eyes, but he looked better than the week before.

She smiled. "Good. And you?"

"Depends on the day." He attempted a smile. "I've had some pretty low moments, but then I try to think of the good times with Jenny. I'm pretty sure that's what she'd want me to do instead of moping around my ranch."

"Does it help?"

"Sometimes. Not always." He tugged at the hem of his jacket.

Was he edgy or just out of sorts? It was a side she'd not seen of Adam. Maybe she was oversensitive to nonverbal cues because of the years she spent reading Ryan.

"It's a little warm in here, don't you think?" Adam interrupted her thoughts.

"Actually, it is. I'm ready, if you are."

He opened one of the glass doors at the front of the mall and followed her out. She hesitated when he stopped in front of a new BMW and opened the door for her. Although he seemed low-key, his wealth showed through. And with money came power.

Her stomach knotted as her earlier fears about Adam threatened to engulf her. She prayed she would make wise choices where he was concerned. She didn't want to compare him to Ryan, but she couldn't make the same mistakes, either.

She sank into the leather upholstery of the seat. Adam pulled out of the mall parking lot onto the main road and headed toward his ranch.

"What are the plans for the afternoon?" Misty fidgeted with the gold locket hanging around her neck.

"Ride horses for a couple of hours, then take a picnic dinner up to a beautiful spot overlooking part of my ranch. How does that sound?"

"That sounds nice. I haven't ridden in years." She glanced sideways at him before continuing. "I hope your horses are gentle. I'm getting too old to be thrown."

Adam's laugh filled the car. "Don't worry. My horses are gentle. They wouldn't throw an old lady."

Her mouth gaped open. "What?"

He groaned and rubbed his forehead. "No, I didn't mean you. I simply meant they are sure-footed."

She cut her eyes at him and laughed. "You're forgiven—this time."

They rode in silence during the next few miles as they left the city. Open fields alternating with patches of woods dotted the countryside. Misty released her grip on the armrest and rested her hands in her lap. The beautiful rolling hills flew by, and her shoulders relaxed as she soaked in the natural beauty.

Adam cleared his throat. "Thanks again for taking good care of Jenny."

"She was sweet. I enjoyed my time with her. I'm sorry we couldn't do more."

He spoke softly. "There wasn't anything that could be done, I suppose."

Her eyes burned with the memory. "No, there wasn't."

Adam pulled the car up to a heavy wrought-iron gate set in a fence surrounding his property. He pressed the remote on his sun visor, and the gate swung open. His car climbed up a long winding driveway and stopped in front of a modest two-story house. Its unassuming nature surprised Misty, given the layout of the land and security measures surrounding it.

She glimpsed a five-car garage offset from the house, but Adam parked in the driveway near the front door and jumped out to open Misty's door.

She stepped from the car, slipped on her sunglasses, and looked around at the beautiful landscape from atop the hill. A sensation of belonging swept through her. The breathtaking view made her never want to leave. No wonder Jenny loved spending time here. Misty searched Adam's face. No doubt the place felt empty without his sister. Misty swallowed against the ache in her throat. She was here, but Jenny would never be again.

"Do you think Jenny's view is this beautiful in heaven?" Adam interrupted her thoughts.

Misty faced him. "Thank you for saying that."

His eyebrows creased. "Why?"

"Because I felt only sadness that she wasn't here." She mustered a smile. "God has blessed us, even in the midst of tragedy. Mostly with the knowledge that Jenny is in a glorious place now."

Adam pocketed his keys and touched Misty's back as he guided her up the front steps. "I know exactly what you mean. I've had the same feelings—wrestling back and forth with my grief, the pain I feel versus where she is."

The front door of the house opened. He motioned for Misty to step inside. "Hi, Dori," he said to the gray-haired woman who greeted them. "This is Misty, a friend of mine and Jenny's."

"Hi." Misty shook Dori's hand.

"Nice to meet you." Dori's blue eyes shone from a friendly face, though her laugh lines looked more like worry lines. A permanent crease rested between her eyebrows.

"She's my housekeeper and chef." Adam tossed his jacket onto the back of the sofa. "I don't know what I'd do without her." He flashed a smile at Dori when she came behind him and picked up the jacket.

"Oops." He grinned.

Misty giggled.

"Would you like some iced tea?" Dori opened the hall closet and hung up his jacket.

"That would be great." He strolled into the living room. An oak-paneled room, garden windows lined one wall, and mounted deer antlers and turkey hung from the other walls. A stone fireplace encompassing an entire wall accented the room. "We're going riding, so could you have the dinner basket ready in a couple of hours?"

"Yes, that's plenty of time to prepare it." Dori glanced at Misty before leaving the room. "Nice to have you."

"Thank you." Misty soaked in the comfortable feeling of the natural decor.

"Let's go out on the porch," Adam suggested. "Dori will bring the tea out."

"Okay." Misty followed him through a set of French doors that overlooked a stunning view. His depiction of it being a porch didn't do it justice. She walked the length of it, enjoying the view of the sloping valley that lay beyond the garage. Tree groves dotted the ridges surrounding the valley.

Adam pointed to a plateau beyond the hilltops. "That's my organic farm, about a hundred acres planted. The orchards are beyond it."

"Whew," she said under her breath. "What do you grow?"

"Blueberries, blackberries, raspberries, and some soybeans." He leaned against the railing, his hands in his pockets, standing with his feet spread apart. "Wait 'til you see the horses."

She laughed. "I imagine they're gorgeous. I haven't seen an ugly horse yet."

Adam snorted. "My horses are definitely not ugly."

Dori slipped through the open terrace door, carrying a tray of iced tea. She set it on a glass-and-wrought iron table underneath a window.

"Thanks, Dori." Adam handed Misty a glass.

"You're welcome." Dori stepped back through the door, closing it behind her.

Misty took a sip from the glass, then gazed again at the landscape. The enormity of Adam's property and his obvious wealth overwhelmed her. After all, he had a maid and chef, although they were the same person.

"Why so quiet?"

Misty smiled. "Just thinking."

"About?"

She shook her head. "Nothing, really." She set down her glass and clasped her hands in front of her. "I'm ready to go riding when you are."

He studied her for a moment. "Okay, follow me."

Careful of her step on the rustic path, Misty followed Adam to the stable nestled in a grove of trees adjacent to the main property of the house and garage. They emerged into a clearing in front of a red-and-white barn.

"Wow." Misty couldn't stop the word from escaping her lips.

Adam opened the double doors leading into the stable. Misty stepped over the threshold behind him and stared at more than two dozen stalls, most filled with horses.

"Oh, they're beautiful!" Misty didn't know which horse to go to first. She was drawn to a paint with a brown-and-white spotted pattern. The horse lowered its head over the stall and whinnied at her. She stroked the tuft of hair between the horse's eyes. The horse nuzzled her arm. Misty leaned her head against the horse's head.

"You can ride any of them." Adam patted the paint's neck. "Take your pick."

Misty glanced up at him. "This one."

Chuckling, he grabbed a halter from the rack. "I kind of thought you'd pick her." He unlatched the stall gate and led the paint out. Slipping the halter over the horse's neck, Adam spoke gently and stroked the animal's head. "Her name is Bella."

"Perfect." Misty stepped aside while Adam tossed a saddle onto Bella's back.

After cinching and adjusting the stirrups, he offered Misty his hand. She slipped her hand into his firm grip, placed her foot in the stirrup, and swung herself into the saddle. With her other hand on the saddle horn, she looked down into his face, unable to pull her other hand from his.

Her pulse raced against the firm grip of his hand. He had a gentle strength, one she could pull away from if she wanted—which she didn't. He took a step closer to the horse, his chest brushing against her leg.

Her breath caught as she tried to read his smoldering brown eyes that immobilized her.

Adam gave her hand a squeeze and released it. But it was too late. With his simple touch, the spark she'd felt when she first met him had been ignited into a raging fire.

Chapter Nine

After saddling a chocolate-colored gelding for himself, Adam swung onto the horse's back and led the way through the grove of trees. Misty followed close behind. Her reaction to him had come quicker than he'd anticipated. The wall she seemed to have around her made him believe she was immune to his overtures. But the research he'd done on abused women in the last few weeks had educated him on the emotional scars women carried for years.

"God," he silently prayed, "don't let me ever take advantage of Misty's vulnerability. Help me to proceed carefully with her. Don't let me say anything to her that I can't back up with my actions, and please, please, let my actions always be pleasing to you and her."

"Oh, how beautiful," Misty exclaimed as the grove of trees gave way to a brook running through a rocky terrain. Her shoulders softened, and Bella's sure-footedness allowed Misty to sit easily in the saddle.

Adam brought his horse alongside hers and pulled on the reins to steady the animal. The gelding touched his nose to Bella. She whooshed out her breath, and he whinnied and shied away.

Misty laughed and followed Adam to the edge of the brook.

He crossed his hands on his saddle horn. "This brook is one of my favorite spots on the ranch. And one of the many gems on this property."

"I couldn't imagine anything more beautiful than this." Her eyes traced the horizon. "Can we walk for a few minutes?"

"Sure." He slid to the ground and held his reins while he helped her down. Once she was safely on solid ground, Adam flipped the horses' reins over a nearby branch.

Misty crouched by the spring and let her fingers dangle in the trickling water. "Wow, it's cold." She stared up into his grinning face. "What?"

"It's nice to experience this beauty through fresh eyes."

She stood and wiped her hand on her jeans. "I appreciate you inviting me."

He reached out and smoothed a stray hair from her cheek. Her tentative look tempted him to take her in his arms and protect her like he couldn't Jenny—make her feel so secure she'd never have doubts. But it'd be a huge mistake to rush things between them. "Let's ride some more."

Misty swung up into the saddle, this time without help. She grabbed her reins and looked at him.

He laughed. "You're settling in quite nicely."

Her cheeks were a rosy pink. "I love horses, though I admit I was a little rusty at first."

"I see." Adam remounted and took the lead through the hilly terrain. Once they were out in an open field again, he turned slightly in his saddle.

"Are you up for trotting?"

"Sure."

Misty gripped the side of her horse with her legs and gave it a command to trot. She fell in beside Adam. Her hair flew out behind her in sync with Bella's mane. He smiled. What a beautiful portrait horse and rider made. The spring air cooled the sweat beads that had formed around her temples, and when she glanced at him, she radiated a glow she'd not had before. She seemed more beautiful each time he looked at her.

If only Jenny were still here with them.

He exhaled, releasing the grief, and spoke to his horse. The gelding increased his step. They crossed the field and rode for about another half mile before he signaled for Misty to walk. "You're gonna be sore tomorrow, even more if we ride too hard."

She stroked Bella's neck and spoke to her.

A steady climb took them up the side of a hill that overlooked the orchards.

Misty's breath caught when they reached the peak. "Absolutely gorgeous."

"Turn around and get the full panoramic effect from where we've ridden." He rested his hands on the saddle horn, the reins dangling from his fingertips.

His house, the stables, and the fields of organic crops were visible from their vantage point. It was one of the best views on the whole property, although he hadn't shown her half of the farm in the couple of hours they'd been riding.

With the sun at her back, she pushed her sunglasses onto the top of her head. The beautiful colors from the violet wisteria and white blossoms of dogwoods intermixed with the other native trees that gave way to Adam's orchards and crops.

"This is the most perfect place I've ever seen," she whispered.

He mentally pumped his fist and thought, "Yes!"

She led Bella to the rim of the side of the hill that had a slight drop-off. The worry lines that normally outlined Misty's eyes and sometimes tugged at the corners of her mouth had disappeared from her face. Bella whinnied and pranced. Misty pulled on the reins and brought her back to where Adam sat on his horse.

"What do you think?" he teased.

"What do I think? It's spectacular."

"Good." Adam climbed off his horse and offered his hand to her. She slipped down, but he continued to hold her hand. "Come, I want to show you something. The horses will be fine for a minute."

She allowed him to lead her to the pinnacle of the hill.

"This is why I brought you up here." He struggled to find his voice. "I want to build a women's shelter and halfway house on this hill. It's set far enough away from the main property and is accessible from the road—or it will be once a new road is built."

Misty stood silently beside him. He couldn't read her mind, though he wanted to. Would she support him in this—or even better, join him in his mission? Right now, the shelter was the most important thing in his world, but one thing was certain. Misty was the most important person. He needed her more than ever now.

***

Misty couldn't verbalize her feelings. This was the last thing she'd expected to hear from him. "Because of Jenny?"

Adam faced the meadow stretching out before them.

She swallowed hard. "That was a dumb question, I know."

He glanced over his shoulder and smiled. "No, it wasn't. And yes, it's because of Jenny … and you."

His statement stirred her emotions. "Me?"

Turning to face her, his eyes shimmered and his voice deepened. "You represent all the women who've been abused and some like Jenny who never made it."

She blinked against the tears that threatened to spill. "Thank you, Adam."

He reached for her hand again and pulled her closer. "For what?"

"For making the effort to understand." She looked into his dark eyes, brooding yet passionate. She'd never been with a man who'd committed himself fully to others, nor one who'd rattled her as much as he did. Her pulse quickened. If he tried to kiss her … Somehow, she had to get control of her emotions.

Adam's gaze traced the outline of her mouth before he stepped back. "It's been a difficult path, Misty, and I'm not there yet. Don't give me too much credit." He squeezed her hand before he released it. "Let's keep riding. I'll tell you more about the project over dinner."

Misty led Bella behind his horse, and soon they were trotting side by side over the grassy terrain in the direction of the stables. Once back in the clearing in front of the stable, they dismounted, and Adam led the horses to a water trough.

"Did you enjoy the ride?"

Misty beamed. "I loved it." She ran her hands through her hair and caught it up in a ponytail holder.

"Well, I hope you've worked up a good appetite. Dori should have our basket ready." He pulled out his cell phone and placed a call.

Misty strolled over to the trough, took Bella's reins, and led her to the stable. Inside, she found a horse brush in the supply cabinet. She stroked the horse's coat and murmured to her. The stress of the last few years melted away, and in its place, a happiness set in that Misty hadn't felt in forever. Her hand flowed over Bella's back, the animal's skin rippling with an electric sensation underneath.

"I see you found what you needed." He pocketed his cell phone and crossed the stable to where she stood. "Dori will meet us in fifteen minutes."

Misty stopped in mid-stroke and frowned. "I hope she didn't go to too much trouble for me."

He waved aside her words. "First of all, you're no trouble. Second, she loves doing it, and third, let's not forget, it's her job."

Misty smiled. "Sorry." Even the simplest hospitality extended to her seemed foreign. Ryan was the only one who'd abused her, yet she struggled to believe she deserved attention from anyone.

"Don't be sorry. I want you to feel at home here when you visit." His face reflected kindness. He reached for Bella's reins.

Adam gave instructions to a stable boy who appeared from the stables, then handed off the reins before leading Misty to a sink where they washed their hands.

"It's a short walk to the hill overlooking this side of the orchards. We'll eat there."

She followed him up a path that grew steeper as they walked. Within minutes, they reached an elevated plateau overlooking the valley, orchard, and farm from a different vantage point than the pinnacle he'd taken her to earlier.

"Wow." She clasped her hands in front of her. "How many magnificent views are there?"

He laughed. "You've seen the best two."

She turned at the sound of a utility vehicle riding up the slope. Dori deftly maneuvered the Kawasaki Mule around in a semicircle and climbed out with a picnic basket.

"Thanks." Adam took the basket from her hand. He peeked under the lid and smiled. "Just like I requested." He reached into the Mule and brought out a small cooler of drinks.

"Let me know if you need anything else." Dori pulled a quilt out of the vehicle and handed it to Misty, then climbed back into the cart. She completed the circle before heading down the hill.

Despite Adam's reassurances, Misty bristled at having someone wait on her, especially another woman. She swung her gaze to Adam. Why did alarm bells go off every time something reminded her of his power?

He reached for the quilt, then hesitated. "Something wrong?"

"Oh, no." She smiled. "That smells delicious. I can't wait to see what Dori prepared."

"I kind of figured you for a health nut," he began.

Misty laughed. "Sort of, when I'm behaving."

"Plus, I have all the resources from my personal garden, so there's no excuse for not eating well. However, it's hard not to indulge on some things, namely cheese."

She groaned. "My weak point. Along with ice cream—and pretty much anything dairy." She dropped onto the quilt next to him. "Okay, let's have it."

He chuckled and pulled out several containers. "Spinach and artichoke dip with tortillas for starters. Grilled cheese triangles on wheat bread, cucumber salad, and fresh fruit."

"Dori's amazing." She sighed.

"And you haven't even tasted it yet."

Misty cut her eyes at him. "Everything smells and looks beautiful."

He popped the lids and handed her a plate. "Yes, and I promise, everything will taste even better."

She took ample portions from each container and settled back on the quilt. Balancing her plate with the Snapple peach tea Adam handed her, she silently asked God to bless their food. She wouldn't put Adam on the spot by asking him to do so.

In between bites, he filled her in on his plans for the women's shelter. At twenty thousand square feet, it would be equipped with a laundry, gym, and daycare on site. Nodding as he talked, she tried to keep track of the endless details he cited. He'd obviously given the project a lot of consideration.

"Of course, I'll need to raise outside funds." Adam recapped his bottle of tea. "Although I have the resources to build the facility, it would put a burden on Jenkins Enterprises. The shelter needs to be a self-supporting operation. That will take sponsors."

"I can see that." Misty tried to calculate how much it would take and whether Adam could succeed, given the level of sponsorship it probably would require.

He sobered. "I've prayed about this. It's the only way I see to make sense of Jenny's death."

Her own frayed emotions about Jenny swept through her. She took a deep breath. "What can I do to help?" The words slipped out before she realized what she was committing to.

"I'd hoped you'd say that." Adam's expression lightened. "From other fundraisers I've chaired, I know I have to bring in big money to keep an operation like this running. First on the agenda is a charity ball."

"A charity ball?" Surely he didn't think she could organize something that elaborate.

"I'd like you to be the hostess."

Even worse. Her mind raced along with her heart. She'd never hosted a high-society function.

Adam touched her hand. "Don't let that scare you. Please pray about the idea before you answer. You'd be the perfect hostess."

"You must know someone else more qualified."

He shook his head. "The hostess should be someone who has a heart for the project and was close to Jenny. Unfortunately, Jenny's world had dwindled down to that loser."

He spat out the last word with such venom, Misty cringed. She knew exactly what Jenny's world had become because she'd been in the same small world two years before.

Her gaze met his. The sincerity that reflected back melted her heart. And there was Jenny. How could she let her down?

"Please." His voice softened with the simple word.

Misty gulped back her fear. "I'll pray about it."

"You'll have several assistants to help you, and of course, I'll buy your dress."

A smothering sensation fluttered in her chest. "You don't have to do that." She stood and walked over to the crest of the ridge.

Adam followed. He turned her to face him, his expression indicating he realized his mistake. "Misty, you're free to do whatever you wish. However, we're talking a few hundred dollars for a dress that will say 'hostess' to the big wallets we're trying to crack open. This will be one of the biggest events in the community this year." He smiled, punctuating his point. "It's not fair to expect you to spend that kind of money."

She looked up into his pleading face. "Of course, you're right. I overreacted. I'm not used to someone paying my way."

"I wouldn't be. You're doing this as a favor for me." He put his hand over his heart. "And for Jenny. It's only right that I pick up the expense."

Misty nodded. The sun was setting behind him, a mixture of amber, pink, and lilac streaking across the sky. "Adam, I hate to cut this short, but it's getting late. I have to work tomorrow afternoon. I need my sleep."

"You can't miss the best part." His eyes gleaming, he grabbed her hand. "Come on." He led her up a path that emerged onto the hillside with a small wrought iron and wood bench nestled under the oak trees.

She settled onto the seat next to him. They sat in silence, each in their own thoughts as the skyline shifted through its final shades of color until, at last, dusk settled around them and stars began to twinkle overhead.

Misty stirred. "Thank you, Adam. This is the best day I've had in years."

He looked down at her in the shadows, eyes glistening with tears. "Misty," he whispered. "What am I going to do without her?"

Her tears mixed with his as she slipped her arm around him and he rested his head against hers. She had no business doing so, but she was falling for the man.

Chapter Ten

M isty pulled a tissue from her pocket and handed it to Adam. She scooted slightly from him while he composed himself.

"Sorry, I get overwhelmed by my feelings for Jenny sometimes."

"Don't apologize. It's perfectly natural." Misty squeezed his hand. "You'll get through this."

He studied her face. "What would I do without you to lift me up?"

Misty straightened. Was he relying only on her to get through his grief? "Do you mind if I ask you something?"

He shook his head. "I'm an open book."

She resisted the urge to chuckle at the expression. She wanted to keep the conversation on a serious level—at least until she got her question answered.

"Are you a Christian?"

A smile stretched across his face. "If you had to ask, I guess I don't show it very well."

Misty laughed. "I'll take that as a yes." She sobered. "Actually, I don't know you that well, so don't take it too hard. All outward indications tell me you are, but I had to get it settled in my mind."

He brushed her cheek with his fingertips. The roughness of his skin against hers sent a tingling sensation rippling through her. Yearning reflected in his dark eyes. Her breath caught. He smiled, pulled his hand away, and placed it over hers.

"You're very special. Jenny said you helped her recommit to Christ. I'm grateful for that." He looked at the starry sky. "I don't know what I'd do without Christ in my life. That relationship has been my lifeline the past few weeks."

Warmth radiated through her. Those were the words she longed to hear. "I can relate." The hum of an approaching vehicle coming over the ridge startled her. "Who's that?"

Adam stood and offered his hand. "Dori always comes looking, if I don't show up by dark."

She frowned. There didn't seem to be anything Adam lacked. Why did Dori's attentiveness bother Misty? She glanced at Adam. He seemed oblivious, which was probably a good thing. She needed to sort out this hang-up in her own mind.

"She's one of a kind—kind of like a second mother." He gathered the basket and quilt. Misty held onto his arm as they walked over the rough terrain downhill.

"Thanks, Dori," Adam said when the UTV came to a stop in front of them.

"No problem." Once they were seated, Dori turned the cart around, and they headed back to the ranch house.

Misty pushed away her doubts about Adam's power. So far, he had given her no reason to think he'd be a domineering person. Her heart told her he was a kind and gentle person, one who would never hurt her. If she could only get her heart and mind in sync.

***

By Friday evening at eleven o'clock, Misty's thoughts were consumed with going home and collapsing into bed. The week had been trying, even more because of Mr. Duncan's determination to make her shifts miserable. Nothing satisfied him. His latest surgery and inpatient chemotherapy treatments were taking a toll on everyone. To make matters worse, the general surgery floor had an overflow of patients due to bed shortages in other parts of the hospital. Memories of why she'd walked away from nursing flooded back to her. Sure, it had been mostly Ryan's doing, but on nights like this, she questioned her own dedication to the field.

She clocked out, then powered up her cell phone. Several text messages popped up on the screen. She clicked the one from Tanya.

Remember to check in with the shelter office when you arrive for your assignment tomorrow.

Misty scrolled through the missed calls—two from Adam, along with a text message. Tapping his number into her phone, she whisked through the revolving doors at the front of the hospital. *Ugh, voice mail.*

"Hi Adam. It's Misty. Thanks for the lunch invitation, but Saturdays are my mentoring days at the shelter. I'll catch up with you another time. Thanks again."

She sighed. Was her life busy because she'd returned to work, or was she purposely over-committing herself to worthy causes to eliminate free time? She stood on the massive hospital steps, cell phone still in hand. Stars twinkled in the darkness, providing dim light through the clouds floating across the night sky. She shivered against the cool, damp air.

Counseling had made her self-analytical, perhaps too much. Questions with no answers. That seemed to best describe her life nowadays. She hurried down the steps and across the parking lot to her car.

When she fell into bed an hour later, she murmured a prayer for Adam. She cared for him—could even allow herself to fall for him.

Who was she kidding? She opened her eyes. She'd already fallen for him. But could she love him? Love didn't work with Ryan, and no guarantee it'd work with another man.

Misty scrunched beneath the covers and pulled them up to her chin. Perhaps the flaw wasn't with the men. Maybe it was inside her. Ugh. She was doing it again—replaying the tapes in her mind that told her the abuse was her fault.

She sat up, clicked on the bedside lamp, and reached for her Bible. Flipping it open, she read through the fourth chapter of Philippians, one of her favorite passages when discouraged. Her finger traced the words on the page, "whatever is true ... whatever is lovely, whatever is admirable—if anything is excellent or praiseworthy—think about such things ... And the God of peace will be with you."

She closed the Book and hugged it to her chest. "God, you are true and lovely. I'm your child. Please don't let my negative thoughts overtake the work you have done in me," she whispered into the stillness of the room.

Peace flooded Misty's soul. Tomorrow was important. Her mind and heart had to be in the right place in order to mentor. How could she hope to help another abused woman, if she weren't whole herself? She meant to help the women who'd been beaten down, one by one, to put their lives back together. And that goal trumped everything else in her life. Even Adam.

***

The following morning, Misty tingled with excitement when she walked through the halls at the women's shelter. She stowed a bag of gently used clothing in the bins in Tanya's office, signed in, then hurried to the activity room.

Tanya waved to Misty from across the spacious room. A young petite woman, shoulders slumped, stood next to her. Smiling, Misty took a deep breath and hurried over.

"Misty, I'd like you to meet Elizabeth Matthews." Tanya beamed. "Elizabeth joined us last week."

Misty extended her hand. "Hi, Elizabeth."

"Hi." Elizabeth stared at the floor.

Tanya patted her shoulder. "Well, I'll leave you two alone. There's a fresh pot of coffee and a box of Krispy Kreme donuts on the counter."

Misty groaned. "My weakness—donuts."

A smile brightened Elizabeth's face, then disappeared just as quickly.

"Could I pour you a cup of coffee, Elizabeth?" Misty started toward the kitchen area.

"Beth."

Misty stopped. "Pardon?"

Elizabeth cleared her throat. "You can call me Beth." She twisted a strand of her blonde hair between her fingertips. Deep-set crystal-blue eyes hinted at her emptiness.

"Okay." Misty sensed her awkwardness. If only she had an easy solution. But she didn't. Beth was at the beginning of a journey Misty

70

had spent two years muddling through.

Misty handed her a cup of coffee. Beth inhaled the trail of steam that floated upward.

"Do you have children, Beth?"

"Thankfully, no." Beth shrank back as soon as the words left her lips. "I mean—"

Misty waved aside her words. "You don't have to explain. Believe me, I know exactly what you mean. I would have loved children—but not with Ryan. I didn't see it at the time, but not having kids was a blessing."

Beth's eyes widened. "You were abused?"

"Yes."

Tears filled Beth's eyes. "I don't understand why."

"Let's take a walk outside where we can talk privately."

"I'd like that."

Misty led her out onto the terrace where cushioned bamboo sofas and chairs sat neatly arranged. The sun slanted through the ivy vines growing over the trellises. Freshly potted petunias and geraniums edged the stone patio. Beth stood inside the doorway. She didn't seem capable of making even the smallest decisions.

"I'm glad it's not hot yet." Misty patted the cushion beside her. "Please, have a seat."

Beth settled in next to her on the sofa. "The weather is nice this morning."

Misty smiled. Small talk appeared to have relaxed Beth somewhat, but she had to get back to Beth's earlier comment. Misty traced the top of her cup for a moment, carefully choosing her words.

"I didn't understand why, either. Oh, I could come up with a million excuses for Ryan, like that he was abused as a child, or that he'd been laid off from his job. I hadn't given him children, and the list went on and on." Misty paused. "They were excuses, not reasons. Don't confuse the two."

Beth nodded.

"But the bottom line is—none of the excuses answered the question why. After all, he could've chosen many other avenues to cope with his feelings or grief." Misty's stomach knotted at the memory. "But he chose to hit me instead. And it is a choice."

A sad smile hinted at the corners of Beth's mouth. "Thanks for saying that. I needed to hear it wasn't my fault."

"It wasn't."

"Coming from someone who has been in my shoes, well—" She looked down at her cup before meeting Misty's gaze again. "I feel hope for the first time in a very long time."

Misty squeezed her hand. "Oh, Beth, please have hope. That's the one thing I can assure you of. Leaving was hard—starting over will be hard. But you have a future. Let us help you."

Tears flowed unchecked down Beth's cheeks. "I want to believe you, Misty."

"You can," Misty whispered. She reached for a tissue box on the side table and extended a Kleenex to Beth. "I'm sure Tanya has filled you in on the career training and job assistance program."

Beth's shoulders slumped. "I don't know where to start. I've been here a week, but until now, I haven't had the courage to take that first step."

"And I'll be here to help every step of the way." Misty's heart ached for all that Beth had been through—and for the other families at the shelter. "Let's take a walk and get acquainted more."

Beth wiped her eyes and smiled. "Thank you."

"For what?"

"For giving me a chance to get my life back."

Misty shook her head. "Oh no, you did that when you decided your life was worth taking back."

***

"Well, dear, how are you doing now that you're back at the hospital?" Misty's mother sipped her peppermint tea and set the cup back in the saucer.

Mother glided into the Victoria Tea Room once a week, as if she'd been born in Europe. Today was no different. Misty smiled. Mother insisted on wearing tailored dresses, even to morning brunch. Clearly, Mother had been born on the wrong continent, possibly even in the wrong century. For a fleeting moment, Misty envisioned a meal with Mother and Adam at the same time. A giggle escaped before she could stop it.

Her mother frowned. "What is it, dear?"

"Nothing." Misty shook her head. "You were asking about Oakview. I love being back at my old job." She dipped her knife into the cinnamon butter, then spread it across a scone. "It's almost like I never left."

Her mother gave a terse smile. "That's good, dear."

Misty couldn't pinpoint the cause of Mother's agitation, but it began to grind on her nerves. "How's Papa?"

Something akin to a laugh escaped from Mother's lips. "Busy. He's always up to something."

"Good. Tell him I'll be out to raid what's left of his winter garden first chance I get." She pushed the last bite of the scone in her mouth and wiped her hands on her napkin. "More tea?"

Mother extended her cup and saucer. Misty refilled the cup, noting the drawn look to her mother's face.

Well, whatever troubled her would surely spill forth. Mother conformed to social etiquette, even within the family, but if Misty could count on anything, it was her mother speaking her mind—eventually.

"I'm also enjoying my time mentoring." Misty leaned back. "In fact, I'm going to work on a project with a local businessman to build a new shelter." She blushed at her thoughts of Adam, too shy to name him yet, even to her mother.

"I don't understand why you're wasting your time at the shelter." Mother stirred her tea, clinked the spoon on the side of the cup, and lifted it to her lips.

And there it was. The fact that she didn't bother to make eye contact didn't surprise Misty.

She fidgeted with the napkin beside her plate of scones. Though she'd been hungry and looked forward to brunch with her mother thirty minutes earlier, her stomach tightened in knots now. Why did she get her hopes up that something—anything—would change in their relationship?

"Mother, we've been over this. I want to give back—to help women like me."

Her mother scrunched her nose as if she'd bitten a lemon instead of her scone. She brushed her lips with her napkin. "Those women aren't like you, dear. Ryan is gone. You've returned to work. It's all behind you now."

Misty's head pounded. She leaned closer. "They are exactly like me." The words tumbled out with force, but she didn't stop. "Why can't you ever accept that I was that far down at one point? And, furthermore, it's never completely behind a woman once she's been abused."

Her mother's forehead creased. "Please don't raise your voice with me, Misty Lynn." She pushed her plate away and signaled for the waiter. "Check, please."

The waiter retrieved her check from his jacket pocket, and she handed him her debit card.

Misty waited for him to walk away before she spoke. "I'm sorry. I don't know what got into me."

Her mother sniffed. "I'll be glad to write the shelter a check. I don't think it's a good idea for your recovery to be mingling with—with those women."

Misty's pulse surged. *Those women?* She counted to ten. "I hate to cut this short, but I've got a double shift this afternoon. I need some sleep."

"Double shift? When did that start?"

"I have bills to pay." Misty put up her hand when her mother started to speak. "And, right now, I need to stay busy." She stood and kissed her mother's cheek. "I really appreciate brunch. We'll have to do it again soon."

When the waiter reappeared with her mother's debit card and register receipt to sign, Misty took the cue to leave. "Please don't worry about seeing me out. Enjoy another cup of tea." She smiled. "Love you."

Misty waited long enough to see her mother's nod before she tucked her purse under her arm and walked out of the restaurant. Swiping the tears that pressed at the corners of her eyes, she crossed the street to her car. The detachment between them bothered her deeply, but she and her mother had run on parallel tracks her entire life. She had no real hope of that changing now.

Would she ever get old enough that Mother couldn't hurt her? Better still—would her mother ever come to realize the damage she had done?

Chapter Eleven

"Sit down, Mr. Jenkins." The assistant district attorney motioned to the chair in front of her desk. Her crisp name plate matched her demeanor. Lena Moore, ADA. Several diplomas lined her paneled walls, but Adam couldn't care less. Only one thing mattered.

She closed the door against the chatter drifting from other offices amidst plea negotiations.

He dropped into the chair and inhaled deeply to steady his emotions. "I'd like to know how the case against my sister's murderer is progressing."

The ADA frowned.

Not very promising. Well, he didn't plan on being easily dismissed.

She rifled through the files on her desk until she found one marked Jenny Jenkins. Flipping it open, she peered at him over her reading glasses. "First degree battery. That's the charge."

Heat climbed the back of his neck. "Jenny's dead, Ms. Moore," he spat out. "Look again. It should say murder one."

She laid her glasses on the file and crossed her hands on the desk. "Mr. Jenkins, I wasn't aware your sister had died. I'm sorry."

Had this woman not heard a word he'd said since he entered her office? Where was the paperwork on Jenny's death? Talk about bureaucracy. Adam rubbed the back of his neck in an attempt to gain control of his emotions before he spoke. "Weeks ago! And you haven't been notified?"

"No, but it probably got overlooked by the coroner's office or mine." She waved her hand in the air as if his concerns were nothing more than a restaurant order gone awry. "I'll notify the coroner that I need the autopsy results before I can move forward."

"Then you'll press the murder charge?"

"Pending the autopsy results." She slid on her glasses, and her cold stare over the rims indicated she'd done this hundreds of times—could probably do it in her sleep.

"What does that mean?"

"There has to be a direct connection between her death and the battery."

"Why do you think she was in the hospital?"

Frustration crossed Lena Moore's face before her creased eyebrows softened and something akin to a smile crossed her lips. "Mr. Jenkins, the fact remains I have to see the report. I'm sorry about your sister's death."

She stood and began to pack her briefcase. "And I'm sorry to cut this short, but I think we've pretty much covered everything. I'm due in court in fifteen minutes."

"So that's it?"

She stopped shoving files into the briefcase and faced him. "Mr. Jenkins, I worked you into a very busy day because your sister's case is important." She tapped a stack of files on the corner of her desk. "But do you know how many cases like hers I have?"

His thoughts twisted with her words. Was it selfish to want Jenny to be the district attorney's priority?

"More than a dozen at any given time—and more than you want to know cross my desk every week. And that doesn't count my other case load." She looked at the clock, then snapped her briefcase shut. "I'm not trying to minimize what you've been through or your sister's death, but the fact remains murder is a tough charge to make stick. I'll have to look at the autopsy report before I make that judgment."

Thanks for nothing. He stood and extended his hand. "I'll wait to hear from you."

"Again, I'm sorry."

Adam pushed through the door and trudged down the hallway. He fished his smartphone from his pocket and took the stairs two at a time. Outside on the sidewalk, he pulled up Misty's number. Voice mail. He hung up, texted her, then pocketed the phone.

Crossing the parking lot, he prayed for guidance. If seeking justice took his last breath, he'd make sure the creep got what he deserved. Adam pushed aside the part of him that normally despised vengeance. He'd always believed that was God's department. With Jenny's death, he wasn't sure what he thought anymore.

Adam unlocked his BMW and climbed into the driver's seat. He roared out of the parking lot. Maybe he could catch Misty at the hospital before her dinner break. Anything would be better than going home to an empty house.

***

Misty stepped out of the elevator with several other nurses and techs on their dinner breaks. The lobby bustled with visitors and other hospital personnel. Aromas of fried chicken, onions, and roast beef wafted from the grill line in the cafeteria. Greasy sandwiches didn't appeal to Misty, so she joined the group headed across the street to Schlotzsky's Deli. There she could get her favorite—a roasted turkey sandwich on wheat.

Her pulse quickened when she caught a glimpse of Adam hurrying through the hospital lobby doors. She waved to catch his attention.

He reached her side, disheveled and breathless. "I tried to call you."

"What's up?"

Her face grew hot when the other nurses snickered like schoolgirls. "You go on without me." She stepped toward Adam and out of their way.

"I don't want to interfere with your plans."

"No, it's okay. We were grabbing a quick dinner. Wanna walk across the street to Schlotzsky's Deli?"

"Sure, that's fine." Adam motioned for her to walk ahead of him.

She frowned and stepped into the circle of the revolving door. *What was going on with him?* She'd never seen him so down—except right before Jenny's funeral.

He took her elbow when they crossed the street. His attentiveness, despite his sour mood, impressed her. Ryan would have pushed her aside. Literally. She shivered at the memory.

"Cold?" Adam stopped on the sidewalk in front of the deli.

"No, just remembering something." Shading her eyes, she searched his face. She didn't want to go into the restaurant until he voiced his problem. She'd done that scene before, too. "What's up?"

"I just came from the DA's office."

Misty's heart sank. Given Adam's mood, the news must not have been good. "I'll bet that was awful."

His face clouded. "Stupid bureaucracy."

"What happened?"

"The ADA didn't even have the autopsy report yet. They're sitting on a battery charge. She didn't even know Jenny had died. Can you believe that?" He ran his hands through his hair and began to pace.

"I'm sorry." Her words felt inadequate.

Adam stopped pacing and reached for her hand. "All I could think about was how empty my house is now with Jenny gone. I couldn't go home." His eyes reflected his pain. "I needed to see you."

"I'm glad you came." She smiled in an attempt to lighten his mood.

The corners of his mouth edged up slightly. Though his face still sagged, his eyes brooded. "I'm in a rotten mood. Sorry I bothered you."

"Don't be." She slipped her hand into the crook of his arm, and they walked toward the deli. "Are we still on for horseback riding Sunday afternoon?"

"You bet."

Misty cleared her throat and summoned her courage. "I planned to tell you Sunday, but maybe you'd like some good news."

A smile lit his face. "Please."

Her pulse fluttered at the commitment she was about to make. "I'll host the ball."

He pulled her into an embrace. "Thank you," he murmured against her hair. "It means a lot to me that you're on board for this project."

"I pray it'll be a success." She stepped back. "Now, let's go eat."

Her dinner break ended in twenty minutes, and he had to go home to his empty house, so Misty chatted about their outing on Sunday to divert his mind from the meeting. But the way Adam had handled his anger and frustration didn't escape her. Except for her father, he was the only man she'd ever seen who chose not to take it out on her. Was that something she could trust?

***

Misty had waited all afternoon on Sunday for Adam to mention her ball dress. He'd seemed content to ride horses and chat about the latest foaling mare. The fact she'd had to work an extra shift that night cut their afternoon short, or she would've worked up her courage over dinner. Maybe. She dreaded having to ask him for the money.

Now, two days later, she opened the door to Adam's office and peeked in. He balanced a phone between his ear and shoulder and motioned to her. She slipped into an oversized leather chair in front of his desk so she wouldn't interrupt his call. He tapped numbers into the computer keyboard and scrolled through the system.

"Okay, I've located the figures now. Thanks." Adam hung up. "Organized chaos."

Misty smiled. "I won't keep you long."

"No, please do. I need the distraction." He swiveled his chair and crossed his hands on his desk. "Besides, I've dropped in on you at the hospital." His face clouded. "Sorry I was in such a foul mood when I did."

"No need to apologize. Dealing with the district attorney's office is never easy."

Adam's eyebrows rose slightly. "You're right." He leaned back. "So—to what do I owe the pleasure of your company?"

She shifted. Money wasn't an easy subject—especially when asking for it.

"The fundraising ball is only a few weeks away, and I need to shop for my dress."

Adam snapped his fingers. "I'm sorry. I should've transferred some money to you before now."

"It's okay. Between work and the shelter, I haven't had time to shop until now."

He grabbed his cell phone and tapped into the keypad. "Check your messages."

She gasped when she saw the figure his app had transferred. "This would buy three dresses. I can't take this."

"Sure you can. I want you to buy the dress you like without worrying about the price tag. Whatever's left over, give to the women's shelter." He tossed his phone back onto his desktop. "Let me know if they ever need anything. I want to help support their work."

The misgivings Misty had about Adam's power pricked at her. "You're very generous." She tucked her phone into her purse.

"I've been trying to think of a name for the house and ball." He gripped his armrests. "How does Hope House or Jenny's Place sound?"

Misty tilted her head and considered the names. "I like them both."

"Me, too." He doodled on a piece of paper, writing each name.

"I'm no help, huh?"

"My fundraiser experts have advised me to go with Hope House. We can name something on the grounds, another part of the facility, Jenny's Place."

Misty frowned. "I don't follow."

"Remember, we have the main shelter building, halfway house, and daycare. I'd also like to construct a state-of-the-art job training center. I'm not sure it's doable all at once, but I want to start with those parameters in mind."

"Wow, you've really stepped up the plans."

Adam grinned. "I do have a tendency to get carried away at times."

Considering how many enterprises he had a stake in, that seemed to be an understatement. "I'm learning that. Jenny's Place sounds nice for a daycare."

"I thought so." Adam tapped his pen on the desktop. "Jenny loved children." He grew quiet as he studied the names on the pad. "Hope House it is—which means the ball has an official name now—Hope House Fundraising Ball." He scratched the name in large lettering across a clean piece of paper. He looked up and smiled. "I like it."

"Sounds lovely." Misty scooted to the edge of her seat and tucked her purse under her arm. "I really didn't intend on keeping you."

"How about lunch?" Adam stood and walked around the desk.

"You look busy, and I've got some shopping to do." She rose and found herself face to face with him—too close for her comfort. She had little control over her thoughts when she was this close to Adam—particularly the ones that could lead her into his arms. For her own safety, she couldn't allow it. She stepped back.

His eyes gleamed mischievously. "I could shop with you."

Misty snorted. "You shop? Men don't shop."

"If it means spending time with you, I will." The sincerity in his eyes pinned her where she stood.

"Yes, well ..." She cleared her throat. "Another day?"

"Another meal?"

"Pardon?"

Adam laughed. "Dinner. After you've shopped."

Misty walked with him to the door. "You're persistent. I'll give you that."

"Yes, ma'am."

She giggled at his statement. "Okay, I'll see you later."

By late afternoon, when she'd almost given up, Misty found the perfect evening dress and matching shoes in a small boutique. After making her purchase, she hurried to the parking lot to stash her purchases in the car. Adam stood on the sidewalk under the entrance canopy where they'd agreed to meet in front of the mall. A smile spread across his face as she grew nearer.

"Have any luck?"

"Yes, I found a beautiful emerald-colored satin gown. Perfect for the ball."

His eyes sparkled. "I'm sure it will be with you wearing it."

Misty's cheeks grew hot.

He grinned. "You're beautiful. Unfortunately, you've not been told that enough."

"Yes ... well." She glanced around at the people scurrying past. "Thank you. I'll admit I'm uncomfortable with your compliments.

They seem to come very easy."

Adam's eyebrows shot up, his eyes widened before narrowing again.

Misty winced. When would she learn to keep her mouth shut? She waved aside her words as if to erase them. "I'm sorry. I didn't mean that like it sounded."

He rubbed his chin. "No, it's quite all right. I want you to say whatever you feel with me. I understand your point. I've been accused of sounding flippant at times. Maybe I am too self-confident."

"Adam ..." She peered into his eyes. "That's what I like most about you."

He reached out and brushed a piece of hair out of her eyes. "You're the most beautiful woman I've ever laid eyes on, Misty Stephens. And the neat thing is you've got beauty inside." He laid his hand across his heart.

Her eyes filled with tears. This man had more weapons than she could fight against. And frankly, she didn't want to fight it. She wanted what he was offering—and it frightened her. Adam traced her lips with his gaze as he'd done before. Her pulse raced with the knowledge that he would kiss her if she gave him the slightest provocation. He cupped the side of her face with his hand. Panic swept through her like wildfire.

She stepped back. "So where are we eating?"

"Lady's choice."

"There's a new restaurant, the Jade Palace, that recently opened. It's on the far side of the mall, though."

"I don't mind walking." He caught her hand in his and led her in through the double doors.

She glanced at him. Where did his patience come from? Why hadn't he kissed her when he had the chance? She frowned. He certainly was a paradox—strength and power balanced with gentleness. She hadn't dared believe such a man existed. Determined to stay in the moment and enjoy the rest of her evening, she pushed aside her doubts. She had plenty of time to sort them out. Regardless of her feelings for Adam, she had no intention of letting him—or any other man—trap her in a binding relationship again.

Chapter Twelve

Misty looked down the line of participants at the groundbreaking event for Hope House. Though it had only been three months since Jenny's death, Adam moved at lightning speed to get the project off the ground. His fast pace went counterintuitive to how Misty thought, but she was learning to just hang on and enjoy the ride.

Each dignitary held a shovel at the ready, the mayor and police chief among them. Grateful the morning sun had not raised the temperature yet, Misty poised for the command to lift the first shovelful of dirt.

Adam grabbed the microphone from its stand and addressed the crowd. He shoved his other hand in his jeans pocket and paced the platform as he spoke.

"Ladies and gentleman, thank you for coming out today for the groundbreaking of Hope House." He pulled a drape from a large display board on the stage next to him. "This is a vision I've worked to bring into fruition to honor my sister and all the survivors of abuse in our community." His eyes lingered on Misty. "Now, without further delay, lift those shovels."

Laughter broke out, followed by applause as Misty and the others pushed their shovels into the ground. They each tossed the dirt into the same pile. Cameras shuttered as they captured the event for the local newspapers.

"Please take a few minutes to look through the architectural drawings and help yourself to refreshments." Adam returned the microphone to its stand and jumped off the stage.

He shook hands with several dignitaries. The mayor and a county council member approached.

"Mayor Barnette." Adam extended his hand.

"What a fine turnout." The mayor wiped his brow with his

handkerchief, his ample mid-section protruding from his tightly buttoned suitcoat.

"I appreciate everything you and the council did to smooth the way for the zoning change." Adam slid his hands into his pockets and rocked back on his heels.

Misty looked on as she fanned herself a few feet away in the shade of a nearby tree. It'd been a fine morning. Now, if everything stayed on schedule, the site grading would start next week, and the foundation for Hope House would be laid shortly thereafter.

"No problem. It's your land, and the shelter will be tucked away in the middle of it. Don't see where that'll hurt the neighbors any." Mayor Barnette's capped teeth showcased his smile.

Adam nodded. "Still, I'm cognizant of the effects new construction can have on the natural setting. Once the building is complete, noise and disruption should be minimal."

"What more could anyone expect? You'll add jobs and help women at the same time. It's a win-win for everyone." He clapped Adam on the shoulder.

"I agree." Adam shook their hands again. "I'll see you gentlemen later." He turned, and his face brightened when he spotted Misty standing behind him.

"Whew, what a morning." Adam shrugged out of his sport coat. "It's too hot for this." He tossed it over a chair.

Misty squeezed his arm. "I'm excited about the ground-breaking. Thank you for letting me participate."

"Of course." He frowned. "I wish the mayor wasn't so overzealous."

She glanced in the direction where the men had walked off. "What do you mean?"

Adam shook his head. "Just seems his main focus is always political."

She snorted. "That's never going to change. Look on the bright side. He backed your plan, and the council approved it. It was a straightforward proposal."

"You're right. Let's get a glass of lemonade. I'm parched."

"It is getting hot, isn't it? I can't believe summer is already upon us.

Where does the time go?"

Adam sobered. "I know. Seems like yesterday Jenny and I rode horses through here."

Misty ached every time she saw the pain reflected in his face. Jenny was never far from his thoughts. Likely, he'd mark time according to her death for years to come. "She would be pleased with this."

"I'd chuck it all to have her back. Selfish, huh?" His gruff voice broke.

She squeezed his hand. "No, human. Don't forget—God can handle our humanity. Give it to Him, and you'll feel better."

"What would I do without you?" He smiled, then lowered his voice and leaned in closer. "Now if I can get the financing in place, we'll be all set."

She searched his face. "Still short?"

"By about a million bucks."

"Whew." She shaded her eyes with her hand. "I had no idea it was that much. What are you going to do?"

He shrugged. "Like you said—trust God. Eventually, He'll bring the money to us or show us how to get it." Adam chuckled. "Too bad I can't grow a cash crop, huh?"

Misty tucked her hand into the crook of his arm, and they continued to the refreshment table. "Sorry to cut out on you in a few minutes, but I promised I'd meet Beth at the college to help her get ready for the summer session and then have lunch."

Adam handed her a cup of lemonade and took one for himself. Misty pressed the cup to her lips, grateful for the cold drink in the heat.

"Are you looking forward to the ball?"

"More like nervous. I'm still not completely convinced that I'm the best person to be hostess."

"You're the perfect person." Adam grinned, then softened his voice. "I can't wait to see you in your new dress."

Misty shot him a glance. "On that note, I've really got to leave."

"I'll call you later. Maybe we can have dinner."

She shook her head. "My shift starts at three. Another night?"

"If I didn't know better, I'd say you're avoiding being alone with me."

Guilt washed through her when she looked at the yearning in his eyes. What could she say? *Yes, I'm avoiding you.* She tossed her cup in the trash can. "I'm not avoiding you ... well, not entirely." She mustered a smile.

Adam arched an eyebrow. "At least you're honest. I'll not pressure you. I intend to keep my promise." He paused and lifted her chin. "But life is short. I want you to be a part of my life." He brushed a kiss on her forehead and whispered, "I'll wait as long as it takes."

Misty trembled with his touch. She had to get out of there before she did something foolish ... like kiss him.

She cleared her throat. "Adam, I'm going to be honest. You scare me." There, she'd said it.

He slipped his hand into hers and caressed the back of it. "How so?"

She glanced around. "Should we be having this conversation here? Where everyone and their brother can listen in?" She fiddled with the hem of her blouse.

"Perfect reason to have dinner with me." His eyes gleamed.

"Okay. Saturday night is my off night. Is that soon enough?"

"No, but it'll do."

She fished inside her purse for her keys, then dangled them on the end of her fingers, ready to leave. "Where do you want to meet?"

"Are we still doing that?"

Misty considered. His face pleaded for acceptance, trust. Her pulse raced. She took a slip of paper from her purse and jotted down her address.

"You may pick me up."

Adam's face shone like a child on Christmas morning. She giggled. "You're silly. You know that, don't you?"

"Yes, actually I do. Silly for you."

"I'll see you Saturday night. Seven o'clock?"

"I'll be there."

***

"Mr. Duncan, if you'd let me raise the head of the bed, rather than lying flat all the time, it might help your queasiness." With a heavy sigh, Misty tried to steady her voice. Nothing she'd done the entire shift had been right, in his eyes. The relaxing morning at the groundbreaking ceremony was a distant memory.

"Ms. Stephens, if you don't get out of here, I'm going to report you," Mr. Duncan hissed. "Raising the head of my bed won't do nothing— just like the other hundred things you've tried. Now get!"

Misty trudged from the room, allowing the door to swing shut behind her. "Lord, help me," she breathed her prayer.

This was the man's second admission in three months, this time for testing to see if his cancer was in remission. Meanwhile, his doctors couldn't seem to get his side effects to the meds under control. Her heart broke for patients caught in these dilemmas. That sympathy was the only thing that made her shift bearable on these nights. Especially since this irritating man reminded her more of Ryan every time she dealt with him.

She dropped into the chair behind the nursing desk and rubbed her temples. Tomorrow night off—and her date with Adam. Spending time with him had grown easier in the past few weeks. Jenny's death had brought them together, but the relationship was maturing beyond that.

Even so, nightmares of Jenny pleading for help continued to plague Misty. During the middle of the night, she often slipped to her knees beside her bed and prayed for the women trapped like she'd been— women she couldn't save—women like Jenny who died, despite help. Adam's nights couldn't be any easier.

Misty logged onto the computer and entered the patient info for the evening. When she finished, she sorted the paperwork on the desk. Danielle and another nurse on duty, Nita Sanchez, returned to the station from their dinner break.

"How're things on the floor?" Nita dropped into the chair beside her.

Misty smiled. "Everything is fine except—"

"—for Mr. Duncan," the other two ladies chimed in.

Misty groaned. "He's in a particularly foul mood tonight. I'm looking for the lab results now to see if we have some good news to share. I didn't see anything in the computer."

Nita shuffled through a stack of paper until she found the labs. She handed Misty the form. "Here's what you're looking for. All indications are he's in remission."

Relief flooded Misty as she looked over the lab sheet. "Why isn't it in the system?"

"I called the lab and they said there's a glitch with their entries so they gave me a verbal report," Nita replied.

Misty glanced up. "And the PET scan results?"

"Clean." Danielle leaned on the computer monitor. "Now if Dr. McCarthy will hurry and get here to deliver the news, maybe we can get some peace."

"That would be nice." Misty placed the labs with the others in the tray.

The patient board flashed, indicating two patients needing assistance.

"Well, we're off." Danielle followed Nita down the hallway where they separated at the first patient's room.

Misty refocused her attention on Mr. Duncan. Her throat tightened, and she swallowed to keep her emotions down. What was it about him that made her care so much?

Thank you, God, for your mercy toward this man.

Maybe once the meds wore off, Mr. Duncan would return to some semblance of normalcy, and maybe, just maybe, he would take some time to reflect on his good fortune. She had tucked a prayer card into his personal belongings with the name of her church on it. Dare she hope he might visit at some point? Well, God was in the business of the impossible.

***

Misty rolled her necklace between her fingertips and peeked through the blinds of her condominium window Saturday evening. Maybe she'd been hasty in allowing Adam to pick her up. After all, they'd only known each other for a few months. Her hands tingled as she kept her gaze trained on the street. Not that he was a serial killer or anything. Her shoulders softened. He was actually the nicest guy she'd ever met.

She grabbed her purse when his car rounded the corner and met him on the curb when he pulled up.

"I would've been glad to come to your door." Adam jumped out and hurried to her side of the car to help her.

"No problem." Misty waited for him to climb in. "I happened to see your car coming down the road."

The skin around his eyes crinkled, matching his smile. "While you were watching for me?"

She glanced sideways at him, then joined in his laughter. "Maybe."

"How are things at the shelter?" Adam maneuvered onto the main road and headed downtown.

"They're great. Beth registered for classes. I'm proud of her willingness to stay on track." Misty faced Adam. "So many women feel they have to go back to their situations, whether for economic reasons or emotional ones."

He shook his head. "I don't claim to understand the attachment when someone has tried to bash your head in, but I can see feeling trapped because you have no money to start over."

Her head pounded at statements like his, but she didn't voice her frustration. The emotional attachment was the harder one for a woman to break at times. She looked out the window while she tried to gain control of her feelings. She mustn't blame Adam for not understanding something he hadn't experienced himself.

"Why so quiet?"

"The beaten-down feeling a woman experiences is difficult to explain, Adam. I'm stronger now than I ever imagined I could be."

He smiled and placed his hand over hers on the seat between them. "I see your strength. I don't doubt that for a minute."

"Where are we going?" Misty didn't want to continue to discuss abuse. It nauseated her and had controlled too much of her life—in the past. She didn't intend to let it dominate her present or her future, except to the extent she could help others escape.

"Morelli's, a quaint Italian restaurant down on the riverfront." Adam maneuvered into the downtown area.

"Oh, I've never been there."

"You'll love it."

Within a few minutes, he pulled into the parking lot. Misty soaked in the charm of the old rock-and-stone building nestled by the water. Dimly lit faux candles glowed in the windows, and lanterns lighted the sidewalk leading up to the door and around the side trailing down to the riverfront.

"We can take a walk afterwards, if you'd like." Adam held the door for her.

"I'd love to."

He stepped inside behind her and gave his name to the maître d'. Misty followed Adam and a waiter to a corner table.

An hour later, after Adam paid for their meal, he escorted Misty out through the terrace doors.

"It's simply beautiful." She scanned the horizon, filled with boats in the distance and ducks offshore. Japanese lanterns lined the edge of the path.

Misty slipped her hand into Adam's as they started down the trail toward the river. If only life could be this perfect all the time. She glanced up at him. He smiled and squeezed her hand. They strolled in silence for a moment before they stopped under a persimmon tree on the riverbank.

He looked into her eyes. "Now, what's this about being scared of me?"

She could see his effort to be lighthearted. How could she answer him without minimizing her feelings or ruining such a beautiful evening? Her feelings for Adam were deepening. As much as his power still scared her, she wanted him in her life. "Not you specifically. Men in general." She smiled. "Makes a lot of sense, huh?"

"Actually, it does, considering what you've been through." Adam sobered. "I'll never hurt you, Misty. I'd swear it on a stack of Bibles, but that won't change what's in your head—or your heart."

His plea for acceptance broke her heart. How could she doubt him? "I believe you."

He smiled and brushed a wayward hair from her cheek. His fingers traced the outline of her chin. Her pulse raced, panic sweeping over her as he gently kissed her. What was she doing? Just as quickly, he pulled back, seemingly aware of her need to not rush things.

"I meant what I said at the ground-breaking ceremony," Adam murmured, "I'll wait as long as it takes."

"Thank you." Her brow crinkled as the meaning of his words sank in. "I want to be completely honest with you." Her stomach knotted as she considered how to voice her feelings. She didn't want to hurt him. "I don't know if I'll ever be able to commit to a long-term relationship again. It's only fair you know that."

Adam's mouth soured. "God doesn't intend for us to go through life alone, Misty." He held up his hand when she started to object. "But I'll wait for you to come around to that way of thinking."

"And if I don't?"

"God's in the business of the impossible."

Misty's mouth gaped.

"What?"

"Nothing. Except I had that very same thought this week."

Adam chuckled.

"But not about you."

He grimaced. "Ouch."

Chapter Thirteen

"I'll race you back to the stable."

Misty shot a sideways glance at Adam, dug her heels into Bella's sides, and commanded her to run. She'd grown comfortable riding the mare over the last few months, so she didn't fear pushing the horse faster.

"Hey, no fair," he shouted behind her.

Misty leaned forward, urging Bella into a gallop across the green pasture. Only when she came up on the trail to the stable did Misty ease the horse into a trot. Laughing, she looked back through the dust trail she'd kicked up. Adam was catching up, but he wouldn't make it in time. She pulled hard on the reins, and Bella came to a stop in front of the horse barn.

Their Sunday afternoon rides were becoming routine, though Misty didn't take a moment of it for granted. Joy filled every fiber of her being when she was on the ranch.

"You're a cheater, I'll have you know," Adam exclaimed, out of breath and indignant when he arrived thirty seconds later.

"You challenged me to a race."

"To which you didn't reply."

"Sure I did."

Adam couldn't continue to feign indignation. He snickered as he swung his leg over the saddle and dismounted. Misty followed suit and led Bella to the water trough where Adam's horse drank.

"Careful, don't let her drink too much." He pulled his horse away and headed to the stables.

"I won't." Misty pulled gently at Bella's reins, tossed them over the hitching post, and grabbed a brush. When she finished, she led the horse inside where Adam was securing the gate behind the stallion. "My absolute favorite part of the week is coming out here to ride."

He beamed. "Good."

Bella whooshed out her breath toward Misty as she led her into the stall. She giggled when the warm air hit her face. "Silly girl, you don't like it when the ride ends, do you?" She pulled a carrot from her pocket and held it while Bella's lips pulled it in then leaned across the stall to nuzzle her. Misty stroked the horse's dark head and neck. Her big eyes flickered in understanding as she lifted her head up and down.

"You're gonna spoil her," Adam called from across the stable. He grabbed a pitchfork and tossed a load of hay into the stable with his horse, scooped another forkful, and moved to Bella's stall.

"I'm not out here that often." Misty rubbed Bella between her eyes. "Besides, a girl could use a little spoiling."

Adam leaned on his pitchfork. "Is that so?"

"What? I'm not here that often or she could use spoiling?" Misty feigned ignorance.

He smirked. "Both." His cowboy boots thudded against the wooden floor as he thrust the pitchfork into the haystack and crossed the stable to where she stood.

"I do seem to be here a lot these days."

"Which is the way I want it." He followed her out and closed the stable door behind them.

"Oh, Adam, I love it here. I don't feel this relaxed anywhere else." She pulled her hair from its ponytail, shook it, and then ran her hands through it.

"I'm glad you enjoy it." Catching her hand in his, he whistled as they walked up the path toward the house.

"The last few months have been stressful. Here I can be completely stress-free."

"I know what you mean." Adam drew her into his arms. "The more you're here, the more natural it seems. The ranch is lonely when you go home."

Misty grinned. "The ranch or you?"

"Same difference." He kissed her gently. "I love you."

Misty's heart flopped. It wasn't the first time he'd said that to her. Why couldn't she bring herself to say those three little words back to him? She did love him. Or at least she thought she did. But there was the rub. She didn't trust her feelings. They'd always gotten her in trouble in the past.

She leaned her head against his chest and allowed him to hold her. He didn't press her for a response. He never did. Where did his patience come from?

He roused her. "Come up to the house before you leave. I've got some initial architectural drawings to show you for Hope House."

"Wow. That was fast."

"We can continue to clear the site, but the blueprints have to be finalized before we get too much further into the project." Adam opened the terrace door and waited for her to step inside. He looked around. "Good, Dori left a pitcher of tea on the sideboard. Help yourself. I'll be right back."

Misty poured herself a glass of tea and one for Adam. He reappeared with a long roll of papers.

"I don't have the official blueprints yet. We'll get those in a few weeks, but this is a mockup of my ideas."

His strong, rough hands unrolled and then pressed out the scrolls onto the tabletop. He grabbed a paperweight to hold one of the ends down while he leaned a hand on the other side. "Here's the main building."

Misty leaned over his arm and studied the different features he pointed out. "I love the spacious day room." She grew serious. "On bad weather days, the moms are stuck inside with their kids, who can get rambunctious. If nerves are already shot, it doesn't help to have restless little ones underfoot."

"I can imagine." He stripped away the top copy and showed her the plans for the daycare center. "We'll have to see how it works out, but I'd like to have field trip days where the older kids can come down to the stable to ride."

She looked up from the prints. "Oh, Adam, they would love that—and I'd love to be part of that."

He beamed. "I kind of thought you might."

A knock at the door caused him to look up. "Come in."

Adam's foreman, Ted, popped his head in before he entered the room. Something about the man always gave Misty the willies, though she couldn't say what.

"Ms. Stephens," Ted's voice drawled. He nodded in her direction, then focused his attention to Adam.

"What can I do for you?" Adam plopped another paperweight on the edge of the paper and raised up to face him.

Ted extended a handful of papers to Adam. "Need your signature on some purchase orders."

Adam reached for a pen from his desk. "What're these for?"

"Need some extra medical supplies for Willow. She'll be foaling any day now. Two other mares are close behind." He lounged against the desk and stole a glance at Misty. She turned back to the drawings.

Adam rifled through the paperwork, affixing his signature where Ted indicated. He gathered them up and handed them back to Ted. "Make sure I get copies of the invoices."

"Yessir," Ted drawled.

Adam recapped his pen and tossed it on the desk. "And call me as soon as Willow shows signs of foaling. I want to be there."

"Sure thing." Ted tipped his hat to Misty and left.

Adam tossed his pen onto the desk and joined Misty at the table. "Is there anything you'd change?" He stared intently at the sketches.

She shook off her feelings of misgivings about Ted and refocused her attention on Adam and Hope House. "No, everything seems perfect the way you've planned it."

"What?"

Misty studied his face. "The talk about Willow made me think of Jenny."

He sat on the edge of his desk and crossed his arms. "Yeah, she looked forward to Willow having her colt. Probably won't sell that one."

She rubbed his arm. "Sorry I brought it up."

Adam patted her hand. "Don't be." He smiled, slid off the desk, and rolled up the architectural sketches. "It won't be long now until the ball. Another week. Excited yet?"

Excited wasn't the word. More like scared half to death, but she couldn't voice that. "I'm *excited* about raising the money for Hope House."

His laugh echoed off the walls. "Smooth."

She put her hand on her hip. "Now what does that mean?"

He reached out and tweaked her nose. "Just that you always manage to skirt around what you are really thinking." His face clouded. "Actually, that's not a good thing. I shouldn't be laughing."

"How so?"

He lifted her hand in his and drew her close. Her breath caught. "You don't have to sugarcoat your feelings—your thoughts—always trying to put your best foot forward. Not with me, anyway."

She pulled away, walked over to the window, and looked out. What could she say to that? He'd seen through her statement, as usual. "It's habit, I guess. One I'm finding hard to break."

Adam strolled over to the window and stood beside her. They were exact opposites. He was an open book. She was a closed vault—at least where men were concerned.

"I understand," he murmured. "But we'll get through this. One day you're going to trust me enough that the first thing out of your mouth will be exactly what's on your heart. You won't stop to gauge my reaction."

Tears pooled in her eyes as she looked up. "You have a lot of faith in me," she whispered.

"And don't you forget it." He kissed her forehead then pulled her into his arms.

She leaned her head against his chest, savoring the feeling of security when she was in his arms—like the outside world and all their problems didn't exist. Finally, she stepped back, breaking the spell. "Time to go. I'm scheduled to work an early shift tomorrow. I need to get some sleep." She grabbed her purse from the chair and slipped it over her shoulder.

"Okay." He caught her hand in his and walked her to the front door. "You're still planning to meet me at Jenny's midweek to help clean out her apartment?"

Misty's throat tightened. She'd sorted Ryan's things after his death. Not a pleasant job, regardless of the circumstances. "Sure, call me and let me know when."

When she dropped into bed an hour later, she recalled Adam's words. He had so much faith in her and their future together. It scared her. But even more concerning was his foreman. What was it about Ted that set off her alarms?

Chapter Fourteen

Wednesday morning Misty lugged a bag of toys and books into the activity room at the women's shelter. Tanya lifted her head from the children she played with on the floor, then rose to her feet.

"Oh, good, fresh supplies." Tanya beamed. She lowered her voice. "The kids who've been here a while are tired of the same ol' toys."

Misty tucked her hair behind her ears. "It's not much. I picked up most of them secondhand at the Goodwill store. Don't worry. I washed the toys and wiped down the books."

"No problem. I shop there myself for the good deals." Tanya unloaded the bag, stacking the books on their shelves and tossing the toys into the bins.

Misty's heart soared as the children gathered around to see the new toys.

"Miss Tanya will be back this afternoon to play." Tanya tousled the hair of a little red-haired boy next to her.

Misty followed her down the hallway into her office.

"Have a seat." Tanya motioned to the taupe-and-floral sofa under the window. "I have a minute to chat. Can I get you a cup of coffee or tea?"

"Tea would be great." Misty sank into the plush sofa cushions. She waited for Tanya to pour the tea.

Tanya handed her a cup and sat next to her. Misty let the steam rise and inhaled the aroma before taking a sip. "Just what I needed."

Tanya laughed. "I couldn't get by without my afternoon peppermint tea." She wrapped her hands around her freshly poured cup. Her smile faded.

Misty sensed her friend was troubled. "What's up?"

"We're overcrowded. I'm worried about the day when we have to turn someone away."

"It's that bad?"

Tanya nodded. "How soon will Hope House be open?"

Misty frowned. "Not until the first of the year—and that's if everything goes according to schedule."

"We'll continue on as we have been. The Lord has provided everything when we've needed it." Tanya patted Misty's hand. "How're things with Adam?"

Misty shrugged. "I'm not sure."

"What do you mean?"

"He's so confident—so sure of what he wants."

Tanya tilted her head, her forehead creasing. "And that's a bad thing?"

"He says he loves me."

Tanya's eyes widened, then narrowed. "How do you feel?"

Misty chuckled. "My feelings are what've always gotten me into trouble in the past." She lifted her cup to her lips and sipped the fragrant peppermint liquid.

Silence hung between them for a moment. Tanya finally spoke. "I can't advise you on what to do. You're intelligent. You've been through a lot in the last few years, not the least of which was your husband being shot in front of you."

Old feelings from that night rose up and smothered her again. This wasn't what she'd hoped for when she ventured into the conversation with her friend. Misty shook her head. "You're right, but more than that, I need to be sure of my feelings before I act on them. I want to get it right this time."

Tanya set her cup down and leaned toward Misty. "Go with that. Adam seems like a great guy. If he's the one for you, he'll respect your pace."

"He's the greatest." Misty sniffed back her tears. "He hasn't pressured me at all, but I feel his intensity."

Tanya reached for a tissue and pressed it into Misty's hand. "We both know that's not unusual after someone experiences the death of a loved one."

"I can't match that intensity—not yet."

"Then don't even try. Be you. After all, that's the Misty who Adam fell in love with." Tanya glanced at the clock and rose. "I'm sorry, but I've got a new arrival due any moment."

Misty clutched her purse, stood, and gave her friend a hug. "Thanks, Tanya. I always feel encouraged after our chats."

"No problem. Hang in there. I'll see you Saturday."

Outside, Misty fished her car keys from her purse. One chore complete. Next, Jenny's apartment. After tossing her purse onto the passenger seat beside her, Misty adjusted the volume on the Christian radio station and pulled from the parking lot.

God, help me get through the next few hours.

Memories of Ryan flooded her mind. Tears stung the corners of her eyes, and she blinked them away. Not today.

And God … be with Adam … help me to be a blessing to him through our work.

***

That afternoon Misty folded the last of Jenny's shirts and laid them on the pile she'd stacked on the bed. Jenny had impeccable taste. Misty could almost imagine her strolling through the apartment dressed in the beautiful clothing. Unfortunately, she never got to see that side of her.

Almost four months had passed since Jenny's death, yet sometimes the pain was as fresh as if it had happened yesterday. The only other death Misty had ever experienced was Ryan's, and her emotions, while out of control, had been on a different plane.

"Grab the door, will you?" Adam called out. He shouldered a massive box of books.

Misty ran to open the front door and stepped back to allow him through. She followed him to his cherry-red Chevrolet pickup.

He tossed the box into the truck bed, then brushed his hands on his jeans. "That's the last of it. Now I have to figure out what to do with

Jenny's furniture."

Misty shaded her eyes from the afternoon sun. "May I make a suggestion?"

He turned toward her. "Sure."

"Donate it to the shelter. We're always looking for household items to help the women get a fresh start in their new homes or apartments."

Adam snapped his fingers. "Now why didn't I think of that?" He slammed the tailgate of the truck shut and walked back to Jenny's apartment with Misty in tow. "I have something for you." He held the door open and waited for her to enter.

"Of Jenny's?" She tucked her hair behind her ears.

He retrieved a box from the mantel top. "A pair of earrings I bought for Jenny when she graduated from college." He opened the box, revealing the emerald-and-gold jewelry.

"Oh, they're beautiful," Misty whispered. She ran her fingertips over the fine jewels.

"Go ahead. Try them on." He set the box in her palm.

She slipped the earrings out of the box and affixed one to each ear. She tossed her hair back and grinned. "How do they look?"

His eyes glistened. "Stunning—the earrings and the lady."

She resisted the urge to banter with him, as she usually did when he paid her a compliment. "Thank you. You have exquisite taste."

"Jenny would be happy you have them now."

Misty touched the tip of her finger to one of the earrings. "I'll think of her every time I wear them. In fact, they'll match my ball gown."

"Even better." Adam surveyed the apartment. "If you'll arrange the pickup of the furniture, I'll leave the key with you."

"I'll give Tanya a call this week."

"That'll work. I've paid the rent until the end of the month." He pulled his cell phone from his pocket. "I'll schedule a cleaning crew for next week, then."

Misty cleared her throat. "Did you ever hear anything from the DA?"

Adam's face sagged, his mouth grim. "Yeah, in fact, I talked to their office Monday. They made a plea agreement. I wanted him charged with murder, but they said we'd never make it stick. I was going to tell you, but it puts me in such a foul mood to talk about it."

Heat rose in Misty's chest and spread to her cheeks. She took a deep breath to rid her body of the anger that threatened to engulf her. "I understand. It makes me angry when that happens, which is more often than it should."

"Angry and disgusted." He pocketed his phone. "As long as I live, I'll never understand making plea agreements with thugs."

"What counts is that Jenny's life mattered to her loved ones. Hope House will help many other women. We'll never let anyone forget that she's the inspiration behind it."

Adam put his arms around her. "I love you, Misty. I don't know what I'd do without you."

Again, the words that came easy to him refused to come from her mouth. Instead, she did what she always did—she laid her head against his chest. What would it take for her to feel whole again?

***

Adam slung the last hundred-pound fertilizer sack into the pickup bed. He clanged the tailgate shut, pulled a handkerchief from his pocket, and wiped his brow. The sun loomed overhead, oppressive in its warmth.

"Go ahead and get started. I'll meet you at the orchards in an hour." Adam handed Ted the truck keys. Though they were about the same age, their similarities stopped there. From the slouching Levi's, tan Brogan boots, and tattered hat, Ted's work was nevertheless impeccable. Adam couldn't wrap his mind around stark differences between the man and his appearance. He shook his head.

"Sure thing, boss." Ted's drawl matched his stride. He slid into the cab of the truck.

Adam held his tongue. He didn't know anybody could move as slow as Ted. The man's work superseded this annoying trait, so Adam tolerated it.

He fished his cell phone from his pocket as Ted drove off. Scrolling through his messages, Adam searched until he found the anticipated text from his buying agent.

No-go on the Appaloosas. Went to a higher bidder.

He shoved the phone back into his pocket. How could he have been outbid? His stride matched his irritation as he trudged up the path to the barn. He'd counted on the horses to start a new line in his stock. The Appaloosas were strong show horses. Losing the bid would set him back eighteen months or more in his plans to branch out his horse business to sell to larger stables.

Pitching a rake and shovel into the back of his UTV, he fought his frustration. He doubled back to the barn and pushed open the wide door. He stepped over the threshold and went to Jenny's favorite horse, Willow. Foaling any day, the mare's belly sagged. She paced around the wider stall Adam had given her. Willow approached and nuzzled his arm.

He rubbed her between her eyes. "You're definitely Jenny's horse. No one has your spunk."

Willow reared her head and neighed before shying away.

Adam chuckled. "Thank you, God, for reminding me what's truly important." He saddled a charcoal stallion and led him from the stables. Ted had bottled water in the pickup, but Adam stopped to fill a canteen. Maybe he'd go farther up the path from the orchards and check on the outer ranch pastures.

He punched in Ted's cell phone and waited for him to answer. "You know what to do. Don't wait on me. I'll be a little later than I anticipated." Adam hung up, then swung into the saddle.

He put the horse into a gallop and covered the terrain at a fast clip. The wind dissipated the perspiration on his forehead and dried his sweaty shirt. The horse's hooves pounded underneath him, drumming out his thoughts.

The ground grew rocky, and his horse carefully picked its way through the rough patches before coming into a plateau of pastureland. Adam tightened the reins and came to a stop on a pinnacle. He swung the horse around. This was the best view on this side of the ranch. One day he'd bring Misty up here. He crossed his hands on his saddle horn, his gaze taking in the expanse of his property.

Could he secure funding for Hope House separate from his ranch, while at the same time increasing the capacity of his business? He frowned. Ultimately, the ranch's financial success linked to the shelter's stability. At this point, with no major donor in sight, he couldn't rely on fundraisers each time they needed capital. Jenkins Enterprises had to be strong enough to carry Hope House should the need arise. Expanding his horse breeding was the answer, or so he thought.

Adam rubbed his chin then crossed his hands over his saddle horn. He'd lost so much in the past few months. With his family spread out across the country, Misty had become the most important person in his life. Her reason for spending time with him had been Jenny. Then it was Hope House. Even though they had a good time, she'd grown quiet each time he'd told her he loved her. Would he lose her, too, if the project failed?

He couldn't let that happen.

Warmth seared him at his memory of holding her body against his. Her soft skin, the lingering scent of her Gardenia perfume, and her silky hair flowing through his fingertips assailed his senses. He ached when they were apart. The sooner she became his wife and joined him on the ranch, the better. With the fundraising ball on Saturday night, he prayed his plans would fall into place.

Adam twisted in the saddle. Debris from the latest storm lined the ranch's perimeter. Ted would need to get a crew up here and cut the limbs and haul them back for firewood. Eventually, Adam would fence and cross-fence the open pasture for more horses—when that day came. He bristled when he thought again of the lost bid.

Pulling a handkerchief from his pocket, he scanned the rest of the countryside. He wiped his forehead and the back of his neck, then tugged the reins to his right and spurred the horse.

Back at the stables, he swung out of the saddle and handed the reins to his oldest and most reliable ranch hand, James. "Thanks."

James pulled the horse toward him, then stepped aside to face

Adam. He lifted his hat and scratched his salt-and-pepper hair. "We'll need more feed before the end of the month."

Uneasiness stirred inside of Adam. "Didn't we get a shipment?"

The older gentleman's eyebrows creased. He resettled his hat atop his head. "A couple of weeks ago. Wasn't as large as usual."

"Hmmm." Adam clapped his hand on James's shoulder. "Thanks for telling me. I'll ask Ted about it when I get to the orchards. I'm sure there's a reasonable explanation."

"Sure thing." James made a clicking noise to the horse and ambled toward the stables.

Adam jumped into the Mule and rumbled up the path to the orchards. He parked, grabbed the shovel and rake, and joined Ted, who'd already spread most of the fertilizer. "Good thing you work faster than you walk and talk, or you would've been out of a job long ago."

A half-smile slid onto Ted's face. He leaned against his shovel. "Yessir. A smart man knows where to apply his energies."

Adam laughed aloud as he strolled up the rows checking the trees for signs of disease or weakness. "Looks good this year. We're on track for a bumper crop."

Ted's whistling mixed with the sound of the rake scratching the ground.

After checking the trees in close proximity of their work, Adam retraced his steps and climbed into the Mule. His hand draped over the steering wheel, he paused before starting it. "I understand we're running low on feed."

Ted straightened from his work. "Already on it, boss. Called the company this morning. They shorted the last order. It's on the way now."

Adam threw the vehicle into reverse. "Thanks for staying on top of it."

Ted waved in response and began loading the tools into the back of the pickup.

Satisfied with the work accomplished and excited for the week ahead, Adam lumbered over the bumpy terrain toward the barn. He couldn't shake the concern emanating from James. The man rarely displayed emotion. After all, they'd been shorted on a feed order. Wasn't the first time. Adam rubbed his chin.

Maybe he'd spread himself over too many projects. With Jenny's death, the need to stay busy overrode everything else. Did that include his common sense? Thankfully, the feed issue had been a minor oversight, and he had men like Ted and James to rely on. Once the fundraising ball was behind him, he would take a closer look at the management of the ranch. Even though Ted was the foreman, and a good one at that, it wasn't fair to shove so much onto his shoulders.

Maybe I need to back up and reassess everything I'm trying to accomplish.

God would provide the extra horses at the right time. The only thing left to do was be ready when the time came. He had enough to worry about ensuring his orchards and crops produced through the fall. Soon after, Hope House would near completion.

He had to do better at living in the present and quit pushing beyond what his human capabilities—and everyone else's—were.

Lord, help me to remember that you are sovereign. Your timing is perfect. Don't let me lose sight of that.

Chapter Fifteen

Misty glanced around the room at the local dignitaries who had trickled in during the last thirty minutes. As much as she'd grown accustomed to being around people in the nursing environment, social events remained uncomfortable. She twirled the diamond pendant from her necklace between her fingers. Beth's familiar face appeared in the doorway. Misty hurried over to her.

"Oh, Misty, I'm nervous." Beth twisted her purse strap in her hand. "I can't believe I let you talk me into this."

Misty prayed her own fluttering stomach would settle down. "I need the moral support myself." She clutched Beth's hand. "It'll be okay. There'll be dancing later after the meal. Right now, I have to mingle."

Beth's forehead creased, and her eyes dimmed. "You're leaving me?"

"No, you're going with me."

"Actually, I'm fine here by the hors d'oeuvre table." Beth stepped back.

Misty smirked. "I kinda thought you might say that. Be back as soon as I can."

She felt terrible leaving Beth on her own, but she'd shown tremendous growth over the last couple of months. The wide-eyed, beaten down woman who'd presented at the shelter had disappeared. In her place, a woman determined to find her place in the world.

"Misty." Adam gestured for her to join him. Two salty-haired gentlemen in black-and- white tuxedos stood by him, clutching drinks.

"I'd like you to meet Mr. Perotti and Mr. Henk." Adam touched his hand to her back when she reached his side.

"Nice to meet you." She extended a hand to each gentleman. "I'm glad you could attend tonight's function."

"Our pleasure." Mr. Perotti's teeth sparkled against his olive skin, though his smile didn't extend to his eyes. "Adam has told us about your connection to his venture."

Misty's pulse tripped. *To what extent had Adam shared her story to further his cause?* She guiltily dismissed the thought as soon as it arose. Tonight was about Jenny—and the other Jennys out there, the ones who would survive because a facility and staff existed to intervene on their behalf. Besides, Adam had never been anything but discreet.

"I'm very passionate about seeing Mr. Jenkins's plan for this facility come into fruition." Misty clasped her hands in front of her. "May we count on your support?"

Mr. Henk laughed. "Straight shooter you have there, Jenkins."

Adam laughed with him. "That's why she's the hostess of this event. Nothing like a pretty lady to twist your arm."

Mr. Perotti nudged him. "Or our wallets."

Misty shifted with the banter. Why did she feel like she was on the market block all of a sudden?

"If you gentlemen will excuse me, I see some other guests who have arrived." Misty hurried to the entrance, her satiny emerald dress swishing around her ankles.

Adam appeared at her side.

"Sorry if that made you uncomfortable." He touched her shoulder. "They're the two biggest wallets to crack in here."

She waved aside his words. "That's what I'm here for—to loosen up the wallets. I hope I didn't offend them by excusing myself."

"Not at all." Adam glanced at the other guests. "You're doing a beautiful job, but I want you to enjoy yourself." He frowned. "You're not to do anything you're uncomfortable with. You're here to host—not to put up with foolishness."

"I overreacted." She glanced at Mr. Perotti and Mr. Henk standing across the room with a group of local businessmen. "Are you sure they don't think I'm rude?"

He flashed a smile. "You're handling everyone perfectly." He started to walk away, then turned back. "Save a dance for me."

She grinned. "I'll try."

She refocused on the guests trickling in. A half hour later, when the band began to play, she welcomed the reprieve. Misty made her way to where Beth stood at the hors d'oeuvre table. She slipped her arm around her friend's shoulders.

"Are you having fun?"

A smile lit Beth's eyes. "I am. I was terrified when I first came in, but I can't remember when I've had such a good time."

"Then I'm glad I invited you." Misty faced her. "Several of the guests have made commitments to funds for the shelter. We'll tally up the silent auction later."

"A good night." Beth searched her face but didn't voice her thoughts.

"A terrific night," Misty gushed. "I'm so excited that we're going to make a difference in women's lives—women like you and me—women still trapped."

Tears trickled down Beth's cheeks.

"Oh, honey, what's wrong?"

Beth shook her head and attempted to gain control. Finally, she spoke. "What would I have done without you? The women in this community don't know how fortunate they are to have you in their corner."

"You've done this yourself—with your own strength, and the strength of God." If only she had the ability to instill confidence in Beth, but time and hard work on her part would do that. "If anything, all I've done is help navigate." Misty smiled and gave Beth a gentle hug. "Let's get some sparkling cider and enjoy the band, okay?"

Beth dabbed her eyes with a napkin. "Yeah, let's enjoy the evening. No more tears."

"I agree." Misty looked around for a waiter and flagged one down. Lifting two glasses off the tray, she handed one to Beth. "To tomorrow—and not looking back."

"Tomorrow," Beth echoed and took a sip of her sparkling cider.

"I have to mingle again. I'll catch up with you later."

"Actually, I'm leaving. It's late, and there's church in the morning."

"I hope to get out of here at a decent hour myself." Misty held Beth's purse while she draped her wrap around her shoulders. "I'll call you later in the week, and we'll have lunch."

Misty blended in with the crowd and made her way through the assorted groups, stopping long enough to chat and explain the necessity of the shelter and training center. She danced with more than one patron before finally taking a rest on the sideline. Adam appeared at her side with a glass of ginger ale.

"Thank you." She took the glass from his hand and sipped. "Whew! I needed that."

"I kinda thought you might."

"How are we doing with donations?"

"Not as good as I'd hoped." He tugged at his collar. "The economy is too unstable right now. Lots of folks looking for support. A women's shelter is a hard sell when other crises appear more pressing."

Tears stung at the corners of her eyes. "The hidden epidemic."

"Hmm." Adam took another sip from his glass. "We're not going to solve it all in one evening. How about that dance you saved for me?"

His sparkling eyes erased the screaming from her feet. She could dance all night as long as he looked into her eyes like she was the only woman in the room. She glanced around. She almost was the only woman left. Many of the attendees trickled out.

"This has been a tremendous evening." Adam led her onto the dance floor.

"Yes, it has." Misty tried to focus on the dance steps, but the closeness of his body against hers sent a ripple through her—one she could get used to. She could feel the pounding of his heart. Her breath caught as he nestled against her hair.

"Thank you," he murmured.

"For what?"

"Everything you've done in the last several months." He raised his head and looked down at her. "I couldn't have gotten through Jenny's death without you, nor did I have the fortitude to host this fundraising ball by myself."

"I'm glad to be an encouragement to you." Misty held his gaze. "It's been rough, but we've made it."

"Yes, we have." Adam twirled her around, then pulled her close again. "Let's go outside on the terrace."

Misty's pulse raced. "Whatever for?"

"Still don't trust me, huh?" He grinned.

"Don't be silly." She glanced outside. "Although it is kinda dark."

His laughter echoed through the room. "Who's being silly now? I'm not the boogeyman."

She looked sideways at him. "No, but I think I'll keep my eye on you, just the same."

"Please do." Adam's eyes teased back.

Misty grinned and followed him through the French doors leading outside to the terrace. The country club grounds were immaculate. The full moon's beams danced off the golf green in the distance. The clear night sky dripped stars almost within reach. Discreetly placed landscaping lights added to the ambiance of the outdoor setting.

Adam gestured to the wrought iron cushioned loveseat underneath a rose trellis. The aroma of gardenias and roses assuaged her senses. Misty closed her eyes, relishing the moment. "I don't know when I've seen you so relaxed."

"This has been a perfect evening." She sank into the cushions. Nothing could make this night any better.

Adam lifted her hand in his and caressed it with his other hand. Her pulse flitted. She opened her eyes. What was on his mind? She couldn't read his expression.

"I love you." He'd said it before but not with such intensity.

Misty's breath caught. "Adam—"

He brushed her lips with his. "And that's not all." He pulled a small jewelry box from his pocket.

A smothering sensation pushed at Misty's chest.

No, he's not!

Adam slid off the loveseat and onto one knee.

Chapter Sixteen

"Marry me, Misty."

The cold golden ring slipped onto her finger. She held it up, and the diamond sparkled in the moonlight.

"I—I don't know what to say." Misty swallowed hard to catch her breath.

"Say yes." Determination burned in Adam's eyes. He loved her.

Her heart didn't doubt that. It was her mind that screamed "no." Misty came back to her senses. "Isn't this kind of sudden? We've only known each other a few months."

"Life is short." Adam clutched her hand. "I've never met a woman like you—kind, encouraging, strong, beautiful—tell me when to stop."

Misty smiled. "No, go on."

His eyes glistened, the laugh lines on his cheeks relaxed into a smile. "I love you, Misty Stephens. I want you to be my wife."

Tears traced her cheeks, and she cupped Adam's face in her hand. His sincerity gave her courage. "I love you, too," she whispered.

"I'll never push you to do something you don't want."

"I believe that. I need time—to think—to make the right choice. I can't afford to be hasty." She held her hand up and looked at the ring.

"Keep the ring." Adam slipped into the seat beside her again.

"Oh, but I couldn't." Misty shook her head.

"Are you saying no to marriage?"

"Not exactly."

"Then keep it. When you're ready, give me an answer."

Adam sounded very matter-of-fact. Why did that bother her? Was she simply another acquisition? She groaned inwardly. If only she could shake the negative thinking.

"I'd love to be your wife." She looked down at the sparkling ring.

"But not right now."

"Fair enough." His smile faded. "There's something more, isn't there?"

Adam read her too well. She hesitated. The only way marriage could ever work would be complete honesty. Might as well find out now if he could truly handle her—baggage and all. "Your decisions seem to come easy. I don't want to be another acquisition," she whispered.

He gathered her into his arms, then buried his head in her hair. The warmth of his breath caressed her neck. "No. Never. I love you. I'm sorry if I gave you that feeling."

"I'm being silly," Misty murmured against his chest. Her pulse raced with the closeness of his body to hers.

He leaned back and lifted her chin with the crook of his finger. "You're never silly for sharing your feelings. These are the kind of things we need to get ironed out, if we're going to be husband and wife. This isn't a business deal, but we do have to think with level heads. Maybe my approach was not romantic enough, but—"

Misty put a finger to his lips. "Shhh, your proposal was perfect."

He captured her fingertips and kissed them, then pulled her into an embrace. His lips met hers with a fiery passion. She felt herself melting into him, terrified and excited at the same time. The emotion wasn't merely physical but a symbiosis of energy that transcended what her mind could grasp.

She pulled away. His eyes searched her face.

Adam stroked her arm. "I understand more than you realize."

"Do you?"

"Yes."

"I'm not being difficult?"

"Absolutely not, but—" He hesitated, as though choosing his words carefully.

"Go ahead."

He ran fingertips along her chin, sending a tingling sensation through her. "My feelings will never change. I love you. Except for God, you are the center of my universe." His eyes burned with passion.

She had nothing to fear from this man. God had brought them together. She had to trust that. She twisted the ring on her finger and considered. Peace flooded her. The life they'd have would be unlike the turmoil she'd experienced with Ryan.

"I'll marry you, Adam."

His eyebrows shot up. "Really?"

She giggled. "Really."

"Woo-hoo!" He scooped her up and swung her around before pulling her into another embrace.

"You won't regret this. I promise."

She stroked his hair. "I do love you."

***

The following week Adam flipped through the invoices on his desk a third time. No mistake. Someone had forged his signature on the purchases. How many other things had gone on right under his nose while he'd been preoccupied? He'd always prided himself at being able to multitask, but his life had been upended in the last six months.

He slammed the papers onto his desk and leaned back in his chair. How could he have been so stupid?

He pressed the intercom. "Dori."

His office door opened. Dori stuck her head in. "Is anything wrong? You sound stressed."

"You might say that." The heat in his chest spread to the back of his neck. "Have you noticed anyone around my office in the last few weeks?"

Dori considered for a moment. "Ted, James, you know, the usual."

Adam drew a deep breath. "Okay, anyone more often than the others—or more often than usual for them?"

"Ted seemed to be around quite a bit during Jenny's, um, death and afterwards." Dori shifted uncomfortably.

"It's all right, Dori." Adam's tone softened. "You can mention Jenny. In fact, I encourage you to." He ran his fingers through his hair. "Okay, do me a favor. Don't breathe a word of this conversation to anyone."

Her shoulders relaxed. "Sure thing."

He forced a smile. "I've got something to take care of, and then Ms. Stephens will be here to ride horses. If you could pack us a lunch basket, that'd be great."

"I'll do that now." Dori walked to the door.

"I'm calling Ted now. Show him to the office when he arrives."

"Yes, sir."

Adam picked up the phone, called his foreman, and asked him to report to his office. Where had he gone wrong with the man? He'd been very generous with his salary package and perks to go with it. Was there a logical explanation for the missing money? He shook his head. Maybe he wanted to see the good in people to the extent that it colored his discretion.

Adam paced the office, stopping to look out of the window that overlooked his ranch. Ted pulled up in a utility vehicle and climbed out. Adam took a deep breath and returned to the desk.

Within moments, a light knock came at the door before it opened, and Ted looked inside. Adam waved him in.

"Have a seat." Adam seethed inside that this man had attempted to take advantage of him during a very difficult time in his life.

Ted dropped into the chair in front of the desk.

***

Misty pulled her hair in a ponytail and then looped the tail back inside to form a loose bun. She double-checked her makeup, grabbed her purse, and locked the door behind her. Being free on a weekday meant working Saturday, but it was a good tradeoff on a beautiful sunny day. As she drove down the freeway, memories of the ball from the weekend before flooded her mind. She smiled. The decision to marry Adam had been surprisingly easy. The difference between him and Ryan was night and day.

Guilt nagged at her when she looked at the light glistening off the diamond on her hand. She hadn't told her parents about the engagement and dreaded doing so. She could hear her mother's voice warning her about acting in haste.

She swung her car into the winding road that led to Adam's ranch. The horses were in the main pasture as she wound up the driveway. If it weren't for Adam inside waiting on her, she could've sat there all day as they ran and pranced. Sighing, she parked in front of the house and hopped out of the car.

She rang the doorbell, and Dori promptly appeared. Misty pushed down her concerns about having this woman wait on her one day. Why did that still make her uncomfortable?

"Ms. Stephens, come in." Dori smiled and held the door.

"Thanks, Dori." Misty stepped across the threshold. "How are you today?"

"Great. Thanks for asking."

Misty twisted the bracelet on her wrist. Where was Adam? He always greeted her at the door.

"Mr. Jenkins is in his office. He said for you to wait for him. He's dealing with a personnel problem, but he'll be out shortly." Dori motioned to the sunroom off a porch. "May I bring you something? Tea or coffee?"

"No, I'm fine, thank you."

Dori hurried down the hallway toward the kitchen.

Misty settled onto a loveseat overlooking a view of the ranch. After fifteen minutes, she glanced at a sunflower-shaped clock on the wall. If she ran to the restroom, she'd be ready to ride when Adam came out of his office, and he wouldn't have to wait on her. Surely he wouldn't be much longer. After all, their afternoon was already dwindling away.

She slipped softly down the hallway in her tennis shoes. As she rounded the corner, raised voices echoed from Adam's office. They grew louder. She checked her step and stopped outside his office door.

"Is that the best explanation you can come up with for these expenses?"

"You weren't here. I couldn't reach you on the phone. You have animals, not to mention crops, that have to be taken care of," a familiar voice answered Adam.

Misty's heart pounded. Sweat broke out on her forehead. She leaned closer to the door.

"The emergency fund has always covered my absences. None of these invoices match the inventory in the computer," Adam said. "I've been through each one."

The reply was inaudible.

"You've given me no logical explanation for any of these excess charges."

Again, the other man answered, but Misty couldn't understand. She jumped at what sounded like Adam's fist striking the desk.

"That's the lamest excuse anyone has ever given me. You took advantage of my distraction over my sister's death. That's inexcusable, Ted. Pack your bags. I want you out of here."

Misty gripped the doorframe. *Pack your bags!* Where had she heard that before?

Ted's voice rose in response, but she wasn't listening. Her mind zeroed in on Adam's voice.

"You may not like the way I run the ranch, though heaven knows, I've been very generous with you, and this is how you repay me—by cheating me. I'm the boss. Seems you forgot that, at least temporarily."

I'm the boss. I'm the boss. Ryan's voice mixed with Adam's in Misty's mind. She took a couple of steps back before turning and running to the sunroom. She pulled a notepad from her purse, hastily scrolled a message telling Adam something unavoidable had come up, then propped it against a vase. Glancing back to make sure Dori wasn't around, Misty slipped out of the terrace doors. Picking her way around to the front of the house, tears stinging her eyes, she fled to her car. A sob escaped her throat as she pulled down the drive and onto the highway.

How could she have been foolish enough to trust a man again after what Ryan had put her through? Her tears hampered her vision, so she pulled onto a side road and put her car in park. Sobs wracked her body as she wept into her hands. Anger at her naivety in being caught up in another relationship flooded her.

"God, am I ever going to be whole again?" Almost to the point of nausea, crying did her no good. She gulped in a few breaths of air and pulled tissues from her console. After blowing her nose, she grabbed a bottled water from the floorboard.

She took a drink and recapped the bottle. The reflection in the rearview mirror startled her. Misty barely recognized the swollen eyes staring back. More than that, when had she become this woman? And why couldn't she escape her poor choices?

The tiniest spark of hope kindled inside her as a verse from Psalms came to mind. *He who dwells in the shelter of the Most High will rest in the shadow of the Almighty. I will say of the LORD, "He is my refuge and my fortress, my God, in whom I trust."*

God was the only One she could truly trust. Adam was a fallible man. He wasn't like Ryan—she wouldn't put him in the same category with that monster, though she'd been foolish to believe Adam would never show anger. He had—and in a very demonstrative way. He might have had a very good reason—in fact, it sounded like he had. But she wasn't ready for that. Her emotions were still too raw.

The engagement ring glistened on her finger. She slipped it off and dropped it inside the inner pocket of her purse. The engagement had to be broken—for both their sakes.

***

Saturday afternoon, Misty forced herself to drive to the ranch. Now that she stood in the den, she almost lost her courage. Even worse when Adam came through the door and halted at the sight of her.

Misty extended the ring between her fingertips to him. The pain etched across his face seared her heart. It couldn't be helped, but she could try to explain—perhaps soften the blow. She took a deep breath.

"Adam, you and I are at different places in our lives," she began. "With Jenny's death, you've realized how short and unpredictable life is. You're on a fast track moving at lightning speed with an urgency I can't match. I accepted your proposal because I got swept up in the excitement the other night at the ball."

"Tell me what to do—what you want." He spread his hands out, palms up in exasperation.

Misty shook her head emphatically. "No, Adam. I won't—because it's not right. Whether or not we ever end up as man and wife, we have to leave that in God's hands and in His timing."

Adam thrust out his chin. "I've prayed about our relationship and the proposal."

"I'm not saying you didn't. In fact, I believe you did, or I wouldn't have accepted the ring to begin with."

"So, where's the problem?"

"Like I said, everything happened too quickly." She dropped her gaze. It was the truth—just not the whole truth. How could she tell him that she'd overheard him, and he sounded like Ryan? She looked into his eyes. The pain reflecting back sent a shudder rippling through her. She loved this man. But she couldn't trust him—not completely—not yet. Anger bubbled inside her for what Ryan continued to rob her of, even from the grave.

"There's something more."

"Nothing," she whispered and swiped the tears before they could fall. "My shift starts in an hour. I have to go."

"Misty," Adam pleaded. "Talk to me."

She shook her head, afraid to speak or she'd start crying.

He reached out and pulled her into his arms. "I'll give you as long as you need," he murmured against her hair. "I love you. Nothing will change that."

Every time he held her she could believe anything he said. And that was the problem. She couldn't let her heart cause her to do something her head knew wasn't quite right. All men had the potential of being like Ryan. And she couldn't—she wouldn't do that to herself again. She had to be strong.

Misty wriggled out of his embrace. "I can't promise you our relationship will ever change. Please don't hinge your dreams on my being your wife, because the reality is—" She paused. "It may never happen." There. She'd said what she came to say.

She tucked her purse under her arm and walked away, not daring to look back. She couldn't bear the pain she caused him. But better to break the engagement now than try to escape later when she was trapped by a very powerful man. She had done the right thing. So why did it feel so rotten?

***

As Misty disappeared through the door, Adam slumped into the chair behind his desk and ran both hands through his hair. None of her explanation made sense. Would he ever understand her?

He didn't think he'd been hasty in asking her to marry him. The connection between them was strong. They'd been together every free minute over the last few months. They'd spent long hours talking about life, riding horses, and planning for the future. He knew her as well as he knew himself—or so he'd thought.

He placed the ring in its leather box before unlocking his safe. One day—hopefully soon—he'd slip it back on her finger, this time for good. Until then, he'd be patient.

He prayed for guidance. His future was intertwined with Misty's. He knew that in the depth of his soul. For whatever reason—and he'd tried desperately to figure out why—she didn't see it. Or perhaps didn't trust it.

Rousing himself from the desk, he left the house to check Willow's colt. He climbed into the utility vehicle and rode over the rough terrain to the stables. Stopping briefly, he checked the colt, then continued on to the construction site. The work was on schedule, according to plan. Hopefully, they'd hold a dedication ceremony by year's end.

Adam picked his way through the scattered boards and mounds of dirt until he reached the top of the hill. His throat ached as memories of Jenny resurfaced from their childhood. Every place he looked, he saw her. The times they went horseback riding, grooming their animals for the county fair, working side by side in the garden, and chasing Colton with water balloons.

The ranch was hollow without her spark to fill it. She would've been thrilled about Hope House and the ladies it would serve.

But why did she have to die? He kicked at a tuft of grass in frustration.

Misty had asked for space. Could he honor that request when she was his heart and soul? He had to—that much he'd figured out. The only way he'd win Misty back was to prove to her he had no intention of exercising any control over her life. Although he didn't know the specifics of why she'd returned the ring, he guessed it had something to do with that one hang-up.

"Lord, why can't everything come together at the same time?" he prayed. "First, I lost Jenny, and now—well, who knows about Misty?" He dropped to his knees. "God, give me strength."

Adam relied on the same faith that had shouldered him his entire life. The God who'd seen him through every scrape, disaster, and loss would get him through this trial. He looked heavenward. Ultimately, this wasn't about him. More than anything, he wanted Misty to be whole. "Whatever Misty's struggle is, Lord, please help her."

Chapter Seventeen

From beneath the covers, Misty fumbled for the alarm clock snooze button and pressed it. How could she face the world? She'd made such a mess of her life, broken the one rule she'd made after Ryan's death and her own recovery. No men. A mere six months after meeting Adam, she'd been swept off her feet in a whirlwind of romance and had become engaged. Well, romance faded. She'd learned that the hard way.

Yesterday had been brutal. Adam's face had reflected the agony she'd put him through. But it was nothing compared to what her heart felt. Or how her dignity had been hurt by rushing into an engagement, after she'd pledged not to be foolish again.

The alarm clock buzzed again. This time, she threw back the covers. She'd be late for church, if she didn't make herself get in the shower. All motivation had drained from her, except for the fact Beth needed her guiding hand.

Who was she kidding? How could she guide Beth to do anything when she'd almost made a mess of her own life—again?

Misty climbed into the shower and began to suds her hair. *God, help me. I can't keep making the same mistakes over and over. Adam is not Ryan, but I rushed things. Please help him to see that so we can get back on an even keel in our relationship.* Water dripped unchecked down her face as she had another thought. What if they couldn't go back?

"This isn't getting me anywhere." She stepped out of the shower, toweled off, and got dressed. There was only one thing to do—push the whole incident as far from her mind as she could.

Thirty minutes later, she was en route to church. Relieved she'd managed to arrive a few minutes early, she hurried inside to look for Beth.

Misty glanced around the sanctuary. Would Beth show before she had to take a seat? The choir was overdue to enter. *Everyone seems to be running late this morning.* She resisted the urge to scan the crowd for Adam. She'd hurt him terribly, and he needed time to come around to her reasoning. If he ever did. Her heart ached at the idea of sitting in church week after week without him. Well, she couldn't have her cake and eat it, too, her mother would say.

Misty perused the Sunday bulletin, noting small group and volunteer opportunities. Good. The ad for the women's shelter had been included. Her church had long been a supporter of the shelter and the women who cycled in and out. Maybe Pastor Kenny would support the shelter's fall festival, as well.

She breathed a sigh of relief when Beth's face appeared amongst the throng of people entering through the foyer. Misty smiled and waved to catch Beth's eye. Beth responded with a little wave and hurried over.

"Sorry I'm running late," Beth said.

Misty smiled. "Don't worry. It appears you have plenty of company this morning."

Beth opened her purse and dropped in her sunglasses. "Couldn't seem to get going."

"Let's find a seat." Misty led Beth halfway up the aisle. They slipped into a pew as the choir came in and took their position in the choir loft. Misty glanced around at the other parishioners and spotted a few familiar faces. Seemed more and more visitors filled the pews each Sunday. Ahhh. God's house brimming with worshippers. She smiled, warmed by God's comforting spirit in her.

Together, she and Beth rose for the first hymn and, shortly thereafter, greeted those around them during the fellowship moment. Beth's face reflected her timidness. Misty's heart ached at the path Beth traveled—the slow one to emotional recovery. She hadn't reached the end of it herself.

Misty pulled out her Bible and settled in for the sermon. Adam's face rose up in her mind briefly, but she shrugged off the image. Instead, she focused on jotting sermon notes until they rose to sing the final hymn.

She grabbed her purse, tucked her Bible under her arm, and

followed Beth out. They made their way through the line of people trickling up the aisle.

"Feel like some lunch?" Misty whispered.

"Why are you whispering?" Beth whispered back.

Misty lightly nudged her with her elbow. "I don't know. Why are you?"

Beth giggled. Misty looked away so they wouldn't start laughing. She and Beth got along too well sometimes, almost like sisters. She remembered her mom admonishing her and her sister for giggling in church. When Savannah announced she was becoming a missionary years later, Misty had been shocked. Now she missed her sister more than ever. She'd give almost anything to be able to talk to her, but Savannah hadn't answered her last call.

Beth fidgeted with her purse strap, seeming impatient with the crowd in front of them. They'd managed to lag behind and be the last ones up the aisle. Misty started to speak but then checked herself. Whatever troubled Beth would surface soon enough.

"Tim called," Beth blurted out. "He wants to reconcile."

Sliding her arm around Beth's shoulders, Misty leaned in closer. "What did you say?"

"I can't." A small sob hiccupped from her throat.

Aware of the people in front of them who could possibly hear their conversation, Misty chose her words carefully. "Would you like to talk about it over lunch?"

Nodding, Beth opened her purse and pulled out a tissue to dry her eyes. "I can't go back."

"You don't have to. We'll discuss some strategies over lunch. Above all else, you have to be safe."

"Thank you, Misty."

Misty gave her a squeeze before releasing her. "That's what I'm here for."

There wasn't time for further conversation. They reached the church foyer, and a couple of elderly women stopped to greet Misty. She excused herself as quickly as she could without appearing rude.

"How does the steakhouse sound?"

The creases on Beth's forehead relaxed. "Actually, it sounds great. I'm famished." She glanced around guiltily. "And more than ready for some quiet time."

"I agree."

Misty glimpsed the profile of an older man before he blended in with the crowd leaving through a door on the opposite side of the church. Her breath caught. Could it have been who she thought it was? Adam's voice rang in her head. She smiled. *God is in the business of the impossible.*

***

Misty hurried through the hallway on the third floor of the hospital, sidestepping other nurses and technicians along the way. Her stomach rumbled in protest from her late dinner break. At least the salad bar and grill line would still be open in the cafeteria.

She punched the elevator call button and waited as the digital light paced through the floors. The doors parted, and Adam stepped out. His eyes widened upon seeing her, then narrowed.

She cleared her throat. "Hello, Adam."

"So, you're speaking to me?" Pain edged his voice.

She shifted uncomfortably. "Of course, I am."

He rubbed his chin. "I just met with a couple of doctors about volunteering at Hope House when we open. I'd hoped to see you … maybe talk to you … but I realize now it wasn't a good idea with you working."

She glanced around. He was right. This wasn't the place to have this particular conversation, but she had avoided Adam for almost a week, and that had been unfair.

"I'm headed to the cafeteria for a quick dinner." She motioned toward the elevator. "Would you like to join me?"

Adam stepped back inside without a word and held the door. She stepped on, and the doors shut behind her. A painful silence hung in the air.

"I'm sorry." She shifted uncomfortably. Such a lame statement explained nothing. An apology was not what he wanted. He wanted a wife.

He faced her. "Misty, I love you. I've never once raised my voice or threatened you in any manner—even by implication."

She shook her head. "Oh, no. It's nothing like that." *Well, not exactly. Why was it all so hard to explain?* This was why she had avoided him. Her mind got jumbled in his presence.

"Then what is it?" His eyes pleaded along with his voice.

"I can't completely trust you. Agreeing to marry you was a hasty decision, made in a moment of emotion." She cringed at how awful her words sounded.

"I see." Adam turned back to face the doors as they opened. He motioned for her to step off first.

They made their way through the crowd of people and around the corner to the cafeteria. Misty stole a glance at Adam. She couldn't tell by his profile whether he was angry or hurt. She groaned inwardly. Of course, he was both. Who wouldn't be?

Moments later, they sat at a corner table and Adam reached for her hand to say grace, as he'd done countless times over the last few months. She slipped her hand easily into his—a strong, sure hand, one she hoped would never hurt her. But did she truly know that? How could anyone ever know that for sure about another person?

Adam stirred his coffee, took a sip, and set the cup down. "Misty, no matter what it takes or how long, I'll do what I can to erase your fears. However, I'm not perfect. I don't know what I did wrong, but you can't hold me to a standard of perfection. I'll never be able to prove I deserve that kind of trust." A smiled stirred at the corners of his mouth.

"What?"

"Until we've been married maybe sixty years." He leaned forward. "And that's how long I intend to stay married—at the least. Raising our kids and grandkids—"

She raised her hand. "Okay, I get the picture." His persistence was hard to defend against. "You seem to have a lot of patience."

"I have faith in God to work this out for our good. Right now I believe that includes marriage. And yes, you're going to learn that I have the patience of Job."

She couldn't help but chuckle.

Adam sobered. "But that doesn't mean I'll never get upset. And yes, I'm sure I'll get angry. But I can make you a promise you can take to the bank. I will *never* strike you or abuse you emotionally. That's not me."

Misty fidgeted with her napkin. His words made sense. But then his words from the week before echoed in her mind. Impatiently, she shrugged them off and looked into his eyes. Could she confide what she'd overheard? Would it help straighten things out between them or perhaps he'd think she'd been spying? Ryan had accused her of that more than once. Her head throbbed from the thoughts wrestling in her mind. These were two different men. Why couldn't she just accept that and move on?

"I believe you." Misty looked at her plate before lifting her gaze again. "But can we not talk about this anymore? I can't do this and be back at work in fifteen minutes. I want us to go on as we did before you proposed." She reached for his hand. "Can we back up a little bit? I don't want to marry you—or anyone else right now—maybe not ever."

Ugh. Why did I say that? How hateful that must have sounded. Every time she attempted to explain her feelings, it came out wrong.

Adam pulled his hand away, leaving her question unanswered. His eyebrows scrunched as he lifted the top of his bun and squirted ketchup onto his hamburger. No doubt he'd hoped for some kind of resolution, but he didn't push it.

Her stomach churned, but if she didn't eat, her shift would be a disaster. She had three hours before she could clock out. Inhaling, she tried to rid her body of its tension. She pushed around the salad with her fork before finally lifting it to her mouth.

Adam bit into his hamburger and then gulped the last of his coffee. He wiped his mouth with his napkin.

"Will you pick me up for church on Sunday?"

He scooted back his chair and tossed his napkin onto the tabletop. "Actually, I'm going out of town for a rancher association meeting, then to Virginia to look over some horses and spend time with my brother."

Misty laid down her fork. She'd been pushing for space but not this kind. "When will you be back?"

"In a week—or so. Haven't decided on a definite return date." His eyes narrowed, matching the grim set to his mouth.

Misty had caused that pain. Silence hung between them until she finally cleared her throat. "I hope you have a good visit with Colton. Will you call me when you get back?"

"Yeah." Adam stood. "I've gotta get back to the ranch now. Take care of yourself, Misty." He walked away through the cafeteria, disappearing into the crowd.

Misty swallowed hard against the ache in her chest that had worked its way up to her throat, choking her. She brought her napkin up to her mouth and sobbed. She didn't care who saw her. She'd let the most important person in her life walk away.

Chapter Eighteen

Fifteen minutes later, Misty deposited her empty tray on the conveyor belt leading into the kitchen and walked out of the cafeteria, determined to put Adam out of her mind. She'd demanded her space, and he had given it to her. She had no one to blame but herself.

Stepping off the elevator, she paused. It was too quiet. Except for an occasional technician or orderly who passed her, she didn't see any nurses. Hmmm. Where was everyone?

The unit clerk was on the phone when Misty arrived at the desk. She began to double-check all the doctor's orders in the computer.

The patient board lit up like a Christmas tree. Where had Nita disappeared? Misty pressed the speaker to each room, telling the patient she would be there shortly. She grabbed her notepad, jotted the room numbers, and hurried down the hallway to the first room.

She'd worked half the list before Nita appeared. Misty tried to maintain her patience as the younger lady walked toward her.

"I've looked all over for you. Several patients have buzzed for help."

"Sorry, Dr. McCarthy stopped me in the hallway and quizzed me about Room 225." Stress tugged at the corners of Nita's mouth.

Misty shook her head. "We can't have patients buzzing the board repeatedly with one nurse on the floor." She held up her hand when Nita started to retort. They were spread thin with two nurses who had called in sick. A relief nurse promised from another floor had not shown up yet. No use wasting time debating the issue. "I know it wasn't your fault. Just help me with the rest of these patients."

Within an hour, Misty returned to the nurses' station to organize the rest of the shift. She'd given up being a charge nurse in prior years because of the stress, but at times like this, she questioned her desire to nurse at all long term. She grabbed a juice from the fridge and popped it open while she pored through the charts.

Who was she kidding? Not many career nurses stayed in one department. The general surgery floor was one of the busiest at Oakview. The number of younger nurses surrounding her on a daily basis had changed, even since she took back her old job six months ago. But they were also very green. She rubbed the back of her neck. Was she making a difference in anyone's life here?

Misty glanced at the clock. She'd managed to stay busy enough not to think of Adam in the last hour. She gulped the last bit of juice and tossed the container in the trash can. Nita hurried into the station.

"Why does it have to be busy when we're short-staffed? If the board will stay quiet for five minutes, maybe we can get organized." Nita plopped down in front of the computer. The phone rang, and she groaned.

Misty flashed a sympathetic smile. "You were saying?"

She leaned forward and picked up the receiver. Her mood lightened when Beth's voice came through the line.

"Beth, how are you?" Misty glanced at the patient board and prayed it wouldn't light up. "I'm great. I'm sorry to bother you at work, but I have a quick question. My cell phone is so old, it won't stay charged long. Otherwise, I would've just texted."

"You're not a bother. Go ahead."

"My court date came in the mail." She hesitated. "I'd hoped you would go with me."

Misty had never gone through the drawn-out process Beth faced with her divorce. But Misty couldn't say no. She was Beth's mentor. More importantly, they were friends.

"Of course I will. When is it?" She grabbed her cell phone and tapped the date into her calendar. "Wow, they didn't give you much notice."

"I know. My mail is forwarded to my new address, and the paperwork arrived today. That's why I called you right away—to make sure you're gonna be available." Beth's voice strained. "Will you be able to make it?"

"Yes, working second or third shift frees up my days." Misty didn't point out she often slept during that time. Instead she assured Beth they would work it out and said good-bye.

Satisfaction swept over her. Beth knew she could count on her. Their bond of trust had been almost effortless. Misty chewed on the end of her pen and compared it to her relationship with Adam. She'd spent much more time with him than Beth, but the trust wasn't there with Adam. Yet. She prayed one day it would be.

She longed to be married. To have a real marriage. What she had with Ryan wasn't marriage. More like a dirge she had constantly sung. To share Adam's life, stand by him through thick and thin, maybe have children—the possibility sent a shiver through her. Tears stung the corners of her eyes.

Why can't I have that? As quickly, another thought took her breath away. It was as if God had spoken aloud. "You can—reach out and take it."

A smothering sensation pressed at her chest, as it always did when she came close to telling Adam she'd changed her mind. But then she would have to confess to overhearing his conversation and wondering if he were like Ryan, even in a small sense. Acknowledging that would hurt Adam even more. Would he think she'd spied on him—regardless if he voiced it? No, she couldn't risk his condemnation.

The board flashed, and Misty hurried down the hallway to the patient's room. The busier she could stay the better. She had no resources to keep bouncing around the what-if scenarios in her head.

***

Adam paced the length of his terrace. With the construction crew behind schedule, it didn't help that rain had delayed his building plans more than once. Already into autumn, and with a January first dedication ceremony, overtime would have to be logged to get the project finished.

He leaned on the railing and peered across his property. Longing filled his soul for the day Misty would be beside him as his wife, discussing some project, and perhaps planning a family. He smiled. He definitely would enjoy that. Even the touch of her hand on his in the cafeteria had practically sent him over the edge.

Waiting on her would take patience only God could give him. He'd confidently proclaimed he had the patience of Job, but who was he to make such a claim? No man did. The last week had tried his patience terribly. He couldn't keep thinking about her or she'd drive him nuts. He resumed pacing as he steered his thoughts back to the ranch.

Losing Ted had been a blow. He'd been careful in hiring a new foreman. He was thankful for his longtime ranch hand James. The older man went about his work methodically and missed nothing. More than once, he'd helped Adam out of a jam.

Adam blew out the breath he'd been holding. No one had seen the situation with Ted beforehand. That didn't keep him from chastising himself. He understood Misty's issues with trust, now that he'd been burned by his right-hand man.

He'd foolishly allowed his finances to be jeopardized. The community leaders had been more than generous with their donations to Hope House, and he didn't intend to waste any of it. Nor did he want to dip too deep into his own funds. It was imperative Hope House be financially independent.

If only things would progress faster with Misty. "God, help me to trust Your perfect timing," he prayed. "I can't live without her in my life."

He grunted. How lacking in faith his words sounded. He'd lost Jenny and managed—albeit poorly. All his life he'd heard the phrase "God doesn't give you more than you can handle." It sickened him now more than ever to hear it, mainly because it was usually spoken by someone who didn't take the time to think of something genuine to say to comfort.

He leaned against a terrace pillar. If Misty wasn't the one to share his life, God would provide someone else. As much as that hurt, this period of darkness and walking alone with God had a purpose.

But there was the rub. He hated the dark, lonely nights in his empty bed. When it came right down to it, he saw no evidence of the patience he'd glibly claimed an hour before.

Dori stuck her head out of the terrace door. "Mr. Jenkins, are you ready for me to take you to the airport?"

He stirred. "I'll be right there."

She started to close the door.

"Hey, Dori." He motioned for her to join him.

She crossed the terrace. "Is there a problem?"

"No. Everything's fine." The back of his neck grew warm. How desperate could a man get? Now he was seeking counsel from his housekeeper. He cleared his throat. "I have a question."

"Sure."

"Do you feel I'm ever short with the staff here?"

Dori's laugh lines scrunched. Was she confused or amused?

"I mean, generally, I'm okay to work for, right?"

"Of course." She spread her hands out palms up. "Have I done something wrong?"

This is going from bad to worse. "No, certainly not." He faced the ranch, gripping the terrace railing. He rose up again, mustering his courage. "Okay, here's the deal. I need a woman's perspective."

Dori's face softened. "Why didn't you say that?" She chuckled. "What about?"

"I asked Ms. Stephens to marry me."

Eyes wide, Dori clapped her hand to her cheek. "So soon?"

He crossed his arms over his chest. "That's the problem. I didn't think it was soon. I consider myself a patient man."

Dori's laugh radiated across the terrace. "Do you want my honest opinion?"

Adam's stomach knotted. "I think you just gave it to me."

"You're the kindest man I know. Yes, you're patient with your employees and with Ms. Stephens—from what I've seen." She sobered. "But when it comes to getting things, horses, the best price for your crops..." She looked at her hands. "The construction schedule for Hope House ... well, you're very impatient."

"I see." He paced the length of the terrace before returning to where Dori stood. He inhaled deeply then sighed. "I appreciate your candor."

"It's gotten worse since Jenny's death." Her fading smile quivered.

Her honesty was almost more than he could bear. "I rushed Misty, and now I've probably blown it with her."

"I wouldn't be so sure," Dori began.

Adam shook his head, cutting her off. "You didn't see her face when she gave me back the ring."

Dori's eyebrows lifted. Another piece of news she didn't know, and now he'd blurted it out.

"I don't know what happened between you two, and it's none of my business, but I think she needs time. Women don't like to be rushed. Marriage isn't like buying horses."

Adam rolled his eyes. "Tell me about it."

Dori's face softened into a smile. "If we're going to get you to the airport in time to catch your flight, we need to leave now."

"Thank you, Dori."

"You bet." His housekeeper shut the door behind her.

Adam took one last look out onto his property before going inside. Maybe the time away would help him get his head together. Dori's words encouraged him, but she didn't know the whole story. He frowned. For that matter, he was sure he didn't, either. If what Misty said was true—she really had no plans to ever marry—he didn't have much to come home to. With Jenny gone and his future with Misty up in the air, the emptiness at the ranch was only matched by the longing in his soul.

Chapter Nineteen

Adam strolled through the Roanoke Regional Airport clutching his black-and-gray carry-on and pulling his matching suitcase. He hadn't reconciled in his mind how long this trip would take, but rushing home after the Rancher Association meeting didn't appeal to him. Unless Misty came to her senses.

He cringed at his childish thinking, but his hurt feelings overrode his sensibility. If he could only figure out what had spooked her into giving back the engagement ring.

Adam caught a glimpse of someone waving in his direction. When the crowd thinned, Colton's sandy-blond disheveled hair came into view. Good. He'd managed to get away from his ranch for the afternoon. Adam quickened his step. After his connecting flight had been delayed twice, he had assumed he'd have to rent a car.

Spending time with his brother and looking over horses was the distraction he needed right now. No one he'd rather have by his side than Colton, when it came to buying horses.

Two years older than Colton, Adam's affection for his little brother outweighed Colton's stubbornness and constant effort to get the upper hand in the relationship. Adam tired of the antics he hoped Colton would outgrow one day.

Now that he saw Colton, Adam's anguish about Jenny's death rose to the surface again. Colton had never dealt with adversity well. He hoped Colton hadn't hardened in the months since the funeral.

Adam crossed the space between them in easy strides and clasped his brother's hand. Dressed in jeans and a T-shirt, Colton squeezed Adam's shoulder with his other hand.

"Easy there." Adam winced, then tightened his grip on his brother's hand. "I'm not one of your roping steers."

"Good to see you, bro." Colton's wide grin spread like wildfire across his tanned face, replacing his usual gruff disposition. He reached for Adam's carry-on, which Adam gladly relinquished.

"Whew! Good thing you were able to get away on such short notice." Adam slid his sunglasses on as they walked through the glass doors at the terminal entrance. "Saved me the hassle of renting a car."

"I'd already planned to spend the afternoon in Roanoke, so picking you up was no problem." Colton tossed the carryon bag into the back seat of his blue Ford F-150 cab, and Adam slid the suitcase in beside it.

Adam rested his arm on the frame of the open window as Colton pulled from the parking lot. The cool breeze blew into the warm cab, drying the perspiration beading on his forehead and refreshing him from the long plane ride. "Nothing can compare with the beauty of the Appalachians."

Colton crooked his hand over the steering wheel and glanced over. "You could move. There's a three-hundred acre farm a couple miles from mine."

Adam shook his head. "Nope. I love to visit, but South Carolina is home—for now."

"Does this have anything to do with the lady you've been seeing?" Colton slapped his hand across Adam's chest.

"Man, why do you do that?" Adam rubbed the sting radiating across his chest. "Good thing Mom's not here, or she'd put you in your place."

Colton's laughter echoed through the cab. He sobered. "Seriously, I'm glad you called. Ever since Jenny's funeral—" His voice trailed off. Silence hung between them until Colton regained control. "I'm glad you're here."

"Me, too, bro." Adam looked out across the landscape rushing past. "I can't leave South Carolina. Not only because of Misty. Because of Jenny. Everything about her is still there."

Colton nodded. "Still can't believe she's gone."

They rode in silence for several miles until Colton pulled onto a dirt road that wound a quarter of a mile through his ranch to a sprawling two-story home atop a hill. Oaks, elms, and dogwoods angled for space surrounding it. He threw the truck into park in front of the house.

"Looks like nothing's changed." Adam climbed from the cab and reached for his bags. He liked the unhurried feel of Colton's ranch. Except for the spot he'd cleared for his home, the rest he'd left unspoiled. A blue merle Australian Shepherd and a black-and-white-splotched border collie raced toward Adam, with a little tan Corgi stretching to keep up in their dust.

"Whoa." Colton planted a boot in front of Adam to stop their progress.

Adam braced himself against the doors and laughed as a sea of fur engulfed him. He petted each one before picking up his bags again. "A couple of new ones since I've been here."

"Rescue dogs." Colton led the way up to the front steps. "My two hounds were hit by cars last winter." He waved toward the road, then opened the front door. "Want something to drink?"

"Sure. Whatever you have is fine." Adam pulled back the curtain and looked out over Colton's farm. They'd had little rain compared to Oakview.

He strolled into the living room and studied the family portraits lining the pine-studded walls. Colton had never been much of a decorator and liked the sparse, rugged look, but family photos were always front and center. Jenny's ten-year-old face smiled from an oval frame on the wall. Adam swallowed hard.

"Here's a Coke." Colton handed him a bottle, dropped into a recliner, and opened a bottle for himself. He took a swig, then looked at Adam. "How long are you here for?"

Adam eased into an oversized leather armchair. "A couple of days." He didn't want to mention the spat with Misty and his lack of desire to rush home.

"Too bad you can't take a real vacation. We could go camping, maybe do some hunting."

"Hunting never has been my thing." Adam took a long drink of his soda and recapped the bottle. "But throw in some white-water rafting, and you might convince me."

Colton pointed his bottle at him. "Now you're talking." He set the bottle on the side table and leaned back in the recliner. Stress lines creased his face and settled around his eyes.

Normally, Adam didn't pry, but something troubled his brother. Colton never had been one to open up and share. Adam cleared his throat. "Hey, remember the time you talked Jenny into climbing into the trees over the driveway?"

Colton's face brightened. "And we would've jumped onto old Mr. Finley's pickup truck bed when he drove up, if you hadn't told on us."

Adam snorted. "Mom tanned your hide for that."

"I can still feel it." Colton grimaced. "What about the time you cut Jenny's hair? Mom wasn't too happy about that either."

"She'd gotten gum stuck in it. Gum she wasn't supposed to have— that I gave her." Adam shook his head.

"Jenny always managed to get what she wanted from us."

Adam's throat constricted. "That she did." He took a swig of his Coke. "How have you been since the funeral?"

A frown creased Colton's face. "Just tryin' to take it a day at a time. I'd rather not think of Jenny—lying in that—casket." His voice broke off, and he scrubbed his hand over his face. He raised the recliner and jumped to his feet. "Let's go to the stables. I have some colts to show you."

Adam followed his brother out through the mudroom and down the path to the stables. Colton's pain was palpable. Pressing him to talk would be futile. Adam ran his hands through his hair. Leaving South Carolina didn't give him the solace he sought—at least not in Virginia.

Colton pushed open the stable door, stepped over the threshold, and flicked a light switch. He waved his hand toward the first stall. "Take a look at the newest arrival."

Adam leaned over the stall gate. A chocolate-colored foal with a white splotch spilling over its side whooshed her breath at him. He chuckled. "Beautiful colors. She ought to fetch a good price when you're ready to sell."

"Remember you said that."

Adam laughed aloud at his brother's prediction. "I didn't say I would pay it, though."

In total, Colton had five colts that would be ready for auction in the next year. The discussion turned to the ranch they'd visit the next day. After seeing Colton's horses, Adam yearned to add more to his ranch. His herd needed new blood, and he still rankled at the loss of the Appaloosas at the earlier auction. If only Jackson Howell would sell at a reasonable price.

The brothers strolled outside and leaned against the fence. Colton plucked a long stalk of grass and settled it between his lips. He rested one boot heel against a board in the fence. "There's ten ranches within a hundred miles of here. From what I've heard, they'll all have horses at the auction next week, if you can stay that long."

Adam listened attentively to Colton's description of the nearby ranchers, their stock, and the prices he believed they'd seek. Adding to his current stock was paramount to keep it strong, but Adam wouldn't pay exorbitant prices. Not when he had the long-term upkeep of Hope House to consider. Nor could he commit to staying a full week.

Colton tossed the blade of grass to the ground. "Steakhouse for dinner?"

"Well, I'm certainly not going to eat your cooking." Adam punched him in the arm.

"Not unless you want beans."

"I don't."

***

Misty scrolled through her messages. None from Adam. He'd been gone almost a week. Could she really expect him to check in with her after the way she'd hurt him? She pocketed the phone and went into the church office. Meeting with the pastor topped her to-do list for the day. He'd promised the church would host the fundraising festival for the women's shelter, and she wanted to discuss the details before she went any further in planning.

"Hi, Misty," Nancy Simmons, the receptionist, greeted her. "He's expecting you. Go right in."

"Thanks, Nancy." Misty stepped into the pastor's office, the adjoining door propped open with a doorstop. His office reminded her of Papa's study. Bookshelves lined the oak-paneled walls behind his imposing desk. Fresh-cut flowers sat on the edge of his desk, no doubt Nancy's touch.

"Misty." Pastor Kenny Crayton rose and extended his hand. His black hair, graying at the temples, offset his blue-gray eyes and dark suit, his usual attire. "Have a seat."

She shook his hand, then took the seat he'd gestured to in front of his desk. "Thank you for working me into your schedule."

"Always have time for a parishioner." He crossed his hands on his desk. "What can I do for you?"

Misty foraged in her purse for the list of items, then straightened. "Since you promised to host the fundraising festival, I'd like to run some ideas by you."

"Certainly."

She extended the list. "You'll note a few commitments for some of the smaller items, but we'll have to rent the jump house and slide. We need a few strong volunteers to help set up and break down the events after we're done."

Pastor Kenny perused the list. "All doable." He scribbled on his open notebook. "I'll be sure to make the announcement at Sunday morning services." He capped his pen and leaned back. "I'd like for our church to become more involved in activities such as these. According to the statistics you've given me, likely some of my parishioners deal with abuse in their homes. That's not acceptable." He frowned. "Pastors must be more proactive in reaching the abused—and the abusers."

Misty shivered at his last statement. He was right, but she hadn't reached the point of wanting to work with abusers.

She shook off her thoughts. Everything was falling into place for the festival. "I don't want to take up any more of your time." Smiling, she stood to leave. "I appreciate everything you're doing."

He waved her back down. "Please, don't hurry off."

Confused, Misty sank into the chair and laid her purse in her lap. "Okay. Is there something more you needed to discuss?"

Smiling, he leaned his head against the chair's headrest. "Just curious as to how you're doing. You scurry about, involved in one thing or another, but how much time do you take for yourself? Downtime."

Misty returned his smile. "I do better when I stay busy."

He sobered. "We can become too busy."

She nodded. "I agree. It's just—well—." She looked at her hands clasped in her lap. How could she explain about Adam? Would Pastor Kenny think she was flaky? She looked up into his eyes, which sparkled with kindness. Before she could stop herself, she'd spilled the story of Adam's proposal and their breakup, minus the vivid details of Adam's office conversation with Ted.

Kenny leaned forward. "God gives us intuition for a reason. To protect us. You were wise to trust yours, whatever prompted it. Marriage entered into quickly is often regretted. You have all the time in the world to make sure it's right—for you and Adam."

Misty sighed, releasing the tension in her body. "Thank you, Pastor. I needed to hear that this morning."

"You're welcome. Let's pray before you leave." Pastor Kenny bowed his head and Misty followed suit.

After his short prayer, he raised his head and smiled. "Perhaps you would like to write a blurb for the weekly bulletin about the festival."

"Thanks. I meant to ask about that. It would be great."

He stood. "I have another meeting shortly. Ask Nancy for paper and pen, then give your write-up to her when you're finished." He motioned to his receptionist's desk outside the open door.

Misty gathered her purse and sweater and extended her hand. "Thank you again, Pastor Kenny. You don't know how much this meant to me—getting the situation with Adam off my chest."

He smiled. "That's what I'm here for. I've seen your growth over the past few years. You'll make the right decision."

"I appreciate your saying so." She went into the receptionist area, got a pen and paper, and sat to compose a bulletin insert. After a few attempts, she was satisfied with her results and handed the paper to Nancy.

"Okay. I'll get this in the Sunday bulletin." Nancy placed it in her top tray. "I'm sure you'll get lots of volunteers."

"From your lips to God's ears." Misty tucked her purse under her arm. "Thank you. Have a good day, Nancy."

"You, too, Misty. See you Sunday."

On the sidewalk in front of the church, Misty slipped on her sunglasses, then looked heavenward.

Please, God, show me how to reach Adam. I don't want to lose him.

Chapter Twenty

With the first item on her to-do list completed by midmorning, Misty climbed into the car and headed to her parents' house. Mother had been after her to rehang their drapes.

A few minutes later, she pulled into her parents' driveway and hurried inside. She dropped her purse into a living room chair. "Mother, I'm here," she called out.

Her heart sank when she saw the massive drapes spread out over the sofa. Why didn't Mother hire someone to do her annual cleaning? Sending the curtains out to the cleaners was an ordeal, as was rehanging them afterwards. The job had fallen on Misty's shoulders as her parents grew older.

Mother hurried into the room, wiping her hands on a dishtowel. "Ladies don't yell from one room to another."

"Sorry." Misty suppressed the urge to laugh. "Are you ready to work on the drapes?"

"Yes." Mother slipped the towel over the back of a chair and picked up the first set.

Misty climbed onto the stepladder and took the drapes while Mother talked about her bridge club meeting the day before. Half-listening, Misty wrestled the drapes onto the rod and placed it back in its hooks. When they finished the living room, they moved to the next room.

At the mention of Adam's name, Misty snapped back to reality. Her mother's small talk had been too good to be true. Maybe she could act as if she hadn't heard Adam's name, and Mother would go on to another subject.

Misty straightened the last panel of the curtains she'd rehung for her mother and stepped down from the ladder. "Do they look okay?"

Her mother stood back and assessed Misty's work, the firm set of her mouth indicating she was measuring to the quarter inch.

Misty sighed. "Well?"

"They'll do. Thanks, dear." Mother untied her apron and hung it on a peg. "Would you like a drink?"

"Yes, I'm parched. Hanging draperies gets more difficult every time I do it." She bit her lip to keep from suggesting hiring help. Mother would think it a big waste of money.

"Iced tea?"

"Yes, please." Misty took the glass offered. "Your tea is the best in the South."

Something like a smile edged the corners of Mother's mouth. "Now, have a seat. I want to hear more about Adam."

Misty couldn't tell her about the botched engagement. Mother's reproach would be more than she could handle. And it would be followed by her usual lecture about how to find the right man.

"Well?"

Misty set her glass on a blue-and-white lighthouse coaster on the coffee table. "There's nothing much to tell. The ball went great. Adam's an amazing man."

"And?"

Groaning, Misty leaned against the cushions in the chair. She had to steer her mother onto a different path. "We've broken ground on the women's shelter and halfway house."

"That again?" Her mother stood and carried the iced-tea pitcher back to the refrigerator.

Choosing to ignore her mother's statement, instead of walking into it as she usually did, Misty plunged ahead with the details. "Hope House will give women hope for their future. A place for them to start over, have daycare for their children, and enter a vocational training program, if they'd like."

Mother turned and faced her, hands on her hips. "How do you always seem to get involved in these types of endeavors? Wasn't hosting the ball enough?"

"Because I want to." Misty stood, crossed the room, and reached for her mother's hand. "Mother, I can help these women. I was one of them." She raised her other hand to stop her mother's retort. "Adam's sister died from abuse. He's very passionate about helping others in similar situations."

Mother withdrew her hand. "I guess I can see the good of his philanthropy."

"If you want to look at it that way, yes." Misty gathered her courage to press forward. "Why can't you see that I have to be involved, too?"

For the first time, a sparkle danced in her mother's eyes. "Whatever makes you happy, dear."

Misty threw her arms around her mother's neck. "Thank you."

Mother disentangled herself. "Enough melodrama. I'll find your father and tell him he's buying us lunch."

Misty waited in the living room while her mother went upstairs to get her wrap and purse. Contentment swelled inside her chest. Progress.

If only she knew what Adam was doing—or how he was doing. She'd thought about calling Dori, but how lame would that seem? Not a single logical reason existed for calling with Adam out of town.

She shook her head. No, best to keep putting one foot in front of the other and pray that Adam would come back in a better frame of mind after spending time with his brother. Then maybe she could hope to tackle the building project without the engagement looming over them. Start fresh. She sighed. Was that too much to hope for?

***

Adam leaned over the corral fence at Jackson Howell's ranch the next morning with Colton beside him. Stallions pranced and pawed the ground on the other side. One broke into a run and the others followed. Adam kept his eye on the ringleader, an all-white horse that towered over the others. He hoped the price wouldn't be too high, but he meant to have that horse. He glanced over at Colton, who appeared to have similar thoughts. Adam traced his gaze back to the lead stallion. He rubbed the back of his neck. Would Colton try to beat him out of the sale?

Adam walked away from the fence and reconsidered the wisdom of adding to his stock right now. Hope House and Misty were never far from his mind. He pulled his cell phone from his pocket and checked for incoming messages. None. He shoved it into his pocket and rejoined his brother. Jackson Howell had made special accommodation for him before opening his stock to the general public. Adam prayed he'd make the right decision.

"What's up, dude?" Colton turned toward him.

"Just trying to decide what I want."

"Well, you better get it straight fast. Here comes Jackson." Colton gestured to the older farmer making his way down the path to the barn.

Adam met Jackson with outstretched hand.

"Adam." Jackson shook his hand and then Colton's.

"The herd looks good, Jackson." Adam leaned against the fence again, the other men on either side. "Guess we need to discuss prices."

Jackson tucked his hands into his pockets and rocked back on his heels. "Always have been a straight shooter."

"There's no other way." Adam pulled a piece of paper and his cell phone from his pocket. He quickly went through some figures on his calculator app and came up with an estimate of the three horses' values. He jotted them on the paper and extended it to Jackson.

Jackson studied the figures. "Seems fair."

Adam straightened as he considered the man. Had he missed something about the stallions? He glanced at Colton. His brother had given no indication he'd seen anything out of the ordinary, yet he'd remained uncharacteristically silent. "What gives?"

Jackson shook his head. "Need the money." He surveyed the stable yard, his profile rigidly set.

"What about the auction next week?" Adam rolled the piece of paper through his fingertips, waiting for the man's response.

A smile spread across Jackson's face. "You know as well as I do there's no guarantees at auction. Likely to be more like these." He motioned toward the stallions. "Lot of ranchers hurting right now. Hard to pay for feed, and we need even more with this drought."

Adam had hoped for a good price but never dreamed it'd be this low. "Well, I'll take them off your hands. Say the word."

"Be sure of what you're doing, Jackson." Colton lounged against the fence. "Might hate yourself in the morning."

Adam shot him a pointed look. He'd given Jackson ample opportunity to consider other possibilities. Now that he'd brought him to the brink of a deal, he didn't need Colton messing it up.

A grin tugged at the corners of Colton's mouth. "Like you said, never know how much you could get at auction." He lifted his boot and clanged its heel against the fence as he shifted his weight.

What was his brother doing? An image of Cain and Abel flashed in his mind. Or was that Jacob and Esau? He frowned deeper, hoping his brother would read the message he telegraphed to him: *Be quiet.*

Jackson's eyebrows arched. He looked from Colton to Adam, then rubbed his chin. "Just what are you two up to?"

"Nothing. I assure you." Adam extended his hand to Jackson. "Do we have a deal?"

Colton guffawed, slapping his leg. "Go ahead, Jackson. Just trying to rile big brother here a little."

Jackson's shoulders softened. He extended his well-callused hand. "Deal."

***

Adam followed Colton and the waitress as they wound through the country-style buffet restaurant to a back table. After spending the afternoon at Jackson Howell's signing paperwork and arranging for delivery of his stallions, kicking back and enjoying the evening was Adam's only priority. Except for trying one last time to get Colton to open up before Adam left for home.

As much as he dreaded going back to the empty house, being in the same town with Misty was better than being hundreds of miles away. Besides, he'd been childish, and he prayed for an opportunity to make amends with her. Maybe start over.

If it were possible.

He waited for the waitress to bring their iced tea before he attempted conversation. Colton's mood had flip-flopped, and he'd withdrawn into a sullen silence as the afternoon wore on. Perhaps it was the heat. Adam certainly had been worn down by it.

"If we keep eating like this, we'll have to shop for husky jeans before the weekend is out."

Colton set his already half-empty tea glass on the table. "I eat like this all the time." He leaned back and slapped his stomach. "Don't get leaner than that."

Adam shook his head. "Yeah, I see."

Colton pushed back his chair. Adam followed him to the buffet, filled his plate, and then returned to the table where Colton shoveled through his chopped steak with mushroom gravy like it was the last meal on the planet.

"Must have been a good choice based on how empty your plate already is." Adam forked an edge of the broiled salmon from his plate. "Do you eat here often?"

Colton's right eyebrow lifted slightly. "Small talk? Even for you, that's not much of a lead-in. What's on your mind?"

"And Jackson said *I* was a straight shooter."

"Guess we're cut from the same cloth."

"Yeah, Dad taught us well." Adam took a long drink of his iced tea, then plunged ahead. "I'll listen, if you want to talk about Jenny."

"I don't." Colton stabbed the last bite of steak and stuck it in his mouth.

"Will you listen while I talk?"

Colton scowled his response.

Adam pressed forward. "It's been rough the past few months. Working on Hope House and having Misty by my side has made a difference."

"Well, if you haven't noticed, wise guy, there's no lady here to help me forget." He shook his empty glass at the waitress when he caught her eye.

Praying for the right words, Adam waited for the waitress to refill their glasses and move to another table. "Like you, I'll never forget. But I'm gradually working my way through the grief. Misty is only part of the solution. I'd never have gotten through without the strength God gives me daily."

Colton rolled his eyes. "Now you're gonna bring *Him* into it?"

An uneasiness filled Adam. This wasn't like Colton to be so—so anti-religious. He steeled his voice. "He's a part of everything I do—every breath I draw—every decision."

"Sounds like a lead-in to a country song." Colton snorted at his own joke.

Heat rose up through Adam's chest and spread to his face. "Bigotry doesn't suit you, bro."

"Hey, what's that supposed to mean?" Colton stopped eating and clanked his fork down. He leaned across the table. "Well, I'm waiting."

"Do we have to do this?" Adam winced. The conversation had deteriorated quickly. He'd never have started it in the restaurant, if he'd realized the vitriol Colton felt toward God.

"You started it." Colton picked up his fork and began eating again.

"Well, like Mom would say, I'm finishing it. You used to be a believer—"

"Used to being the key phrase there."

"Why?"

"He didn't answer my prayer. Simple enough."

Adam ran his hand across his neck. "I prayed that Jenny would live, too. I don't know why God said no, but I have to accept it."

"Maybe you do. I don't." Colton tossed his napkin onto his plate. "I'm finished with this conversation. Either we can visit the dessert bar and drop it, or—"

Adam blew out a breath. "Or?"

"Let's leave it at that."

Adam eyes met his brother's glare. He didn't like to be threatened, even in a subtle way. Better to meet the challenge right now. "I'll drop it out of respect for your feelings, which you are entitled to."

Colton's eyes narrowed. "What's that supposed to mean?"

"You couldn't beat me when we were ten and twelve. Won't happen now, either." He laughed to punctuate the foolishness of Colton's statement and hopefully relieve some of the tension.

Disbelief flashed across Colton's face before he broke into laughter. "As if. Let's get some pie."

Adam exhaled. Colton had always been wound a little tight. Turning his back on God wouldn't make his disposition any more pleasant, but Colton was his brother, and Adam loved him. Nothing, not even Colton's surly mood, could trump that fact.

***

The next morning, Adam rolled his suitcase into the foyer and dropped his carry-on bag beside it. The aroma of breakfast wafted through the hallway. Considering he'd eaten pastries the last two mornings, the smell of freshly cooked food was a nice surprise. He went into the kitchen where Colton had a hearty breakfast of eggs, bacon, pancakes, orange juice, and coffee already on the table.

"Thought you didn't cook." Adam snitched a piece of bacon before pouring a glass of orange juice. He pulled out a chair across from Colton's place and sat.

"Don't usually, but it's a peace offering." Colton reached for the juice. "Sorry about last night."

Adam's stomach unclenched for the first time in twenty-four hours. "I'm sorry, too."

Colton pointed his fork toward Adam. "But, please don't bring up religion anymore to me, okay? Truce?"

Adam wouldn't promise something so serious as his brother's eternity, but he'd postpone the argument for another day. Colton had an impenetrable wall up at this point. Only prayer and intervention by God could break it down. Adam didn't know if that included him or not. For now, he'd back off.

"Truce."

A smile spread across Colton's face. "Good. So, when does Hope

House open?"

Adam forked a bite of egg into his mouth. "First of the year, if we can keep it on schedule. Will you be there?"

"Of course. Wouldn't miss it for anything. Besides, I wanna meet Misty." He shoveled the last of his pancake down and reached for his coffee.

Adam tried not to squirm at the mention of Misty's name. He hoped and prayed things would be settled between them—maybe even engaged by the first of the year. But that would be up to God's timing and will. He couldn't voice that to Colton. It was too complicated.

"You'll meet her. Try to be on your best behavior, okay?"

Colton's mouth gaped. "Me? Of course."

Adam didn't buy his innocent routine. "I've seen you in action. Mom and Dad will be there. So will her parents and maybe her sister."

"Well, then, I'll be there with bells on. I'll be the best-behaved brother you could ask for."

Adam snorted. "I'm sure."

Colton took a drink of coffee and motioned toward the food. "Eat up. Your flight leaves in three hours. I don't want to get a ticket trying to get you to the airport."

Thirty minutes later, they were en route to the airport, Adam's luggage stowed behind the seat of Colton's pickup.

"Thanks again for putting up with me for a few days." Adam double-checked his e-ticket on his smartphone and stashed it in his pocket.

Colton looked sideways at him from the driver's seat. "Any time."

"First week of January, don't forget."

"I'll be there."

Chapter Twenty-One

Misty scanned the steady stream of people coming into the courthouse. Where was Beth? Court started in less than an hour. They'd agreed to meet on the courthouse steps at eight a.m. Misty dug her phone from her purse and tapped Beth's number. No answer.

What is going on?

She texted Beth before pocketing the phone. Nothing to do but wait. Misty slipped her sunglasses on against the morning sun.

By eight-fifteen, she began to grow alarmed. Another fifteen minutes passed and still no sign of Beth. Misty ran up the steps, pulled open the front door, and walked to the security station. A gray-haired, stockily-built guard stepped out. The squeak in his shoes matched the squeak of his gun belt.

"I'm meeting a friend for a divorce hearing that starts at nine o'clock. She's never late," Misty explained. "I'm concerned for her safety."

The guard frowned. "What do you want me to do about it?"

Misty pushed down her exasperation. "Could you notify the judge my friend might be late? I'm going to her house now."

"Name." He pulled the clipboard from under a counter.

"Beth Matthews."

He ran his finger down the list until it rested on Beth's name. He clicked his pen and made a notation next to her name.

"We'll be back as soon as possible, or I'll phone," Misty called over her shoulder as she ran from the building.

"Please, God, don't let anything be wrong." She backed out of the parking space and pulled onto the road. She fought the urge to speed, but more than once, the speedometer needle crept upward. Finally, she turned onto Beth's street. In the distance, she saw Beth's silver sedan and a black SUV parked behind it. Misty pulled past the vehicles and rolled to a stop at the curb. She glanced out her passenger side window at the house. A slight movement behind the curtain caught her attention. She punched Beth's number into her cell phone. After six rings, Misty hung up.

"God, show me what to do." Misty fumbled through her purse for her pepper spray, the only defense she had. She couldn't call the police when she didn't know for sure whether or not Beth was in real danger. Her stomach knotted. She drew a deep breath.

Leaving her keys in the ignition and the car unlocked, Misty climbed out and hurried up the sidewalk.

She pressed the doorbell and stepped back. Rustling noises came from behind the door before it opened a crack. Beth's face emerged, frightened and wide-eyed.

"Hey, did you forget our appointment?" Misty forced a smile. Someone behind the door prevented Beth from opening it.

Beth cleared her throat. "I'm not going to be able to go, Misty. Something came up." The calmness in her voice belied the fear on her face.

"They're expecting us." Misty stalled. Should she walk back down the sidewalk and call the police? It could potentially create a hostage situation, and Beth might not come out the victor. Experiencing Ryan's death at the hands of police was one death too many. She had to try to save Beth without anyone getting hurt.

The door opened a fraction wider. Beth smiled to punctuate her point. "I'll call you later, Misty, okay? I'm really busy right now."

Misty made a quick decision. She mouthed her words to Beth. "Does he have a weapon?"

Beth's eyes widened. "No," she mouthed back.

Misty cocked her head toward her car as a signal and then said aloud, "I'll see what I can do to reschedule." She pulled the pepper spray from her purse and shoved the door hard.

"Run!" she screamed at Beth.

Beth charged down the sidewalk with Misty close behind. Footsteps pounded close behind her. Misty twisted and sprayed the pepper into

Tim Matthews's eyes, then ran to her car. Expletives filled the air as Tim stumbled, tripped, and fell, before struggling to his feet again. Beth was already in the passenger side with the door locked.

Misty jumped in, started the car, and sped away from the curb. She fumbled in her purse for her cell phone and pressed 911.

"Oh, Misty," Beth cried. "What just happened?"

"Victory," Misty uttered the single word. Though her violent shaking matched Beth's, for the first time in her life she felt empowered. She rolled to a stop two blocks away and completed her call to the police while Beth watched for Tim's SUV.

"We're safe." Misty gathered Beth into her arms and tried to comfort her sobbing friend. "The police are on the way."

She wasn't sure what the ramifications would be of what had happened, but she sensed it was a turning point—for both Beth and herself. She pressed tissues into Beth's hand. Sirens sounded in the distance, and Misty pulled her car forward and did a U-turn. Panic filled Beth's face.

"No, Misty. Don't go back." She clutched Misty's arm.

"We have to give a statement and make sure he's arrested." Misty retraced their route and pulled in behind a police cruiser.

A police officer met her on the lawn in front of Beth's house. Tim was already in the back of a squad car. Brave two minutes before, Misty couldn't bring herself to look in his direction now.

"His wife is in my car." Misty motioned behind her. "Can you take her statement over there?"

The officer smiled. "Sure can. I'll need to get statements from both of you."

"Start with her. I have to call the courthouse. They had a divorce hearing scheduled for nine o'clock. Obviously, we won't make that." She fumbled for her phone. "She'll have to reschedule."

After the officer walked away, Misty walked toward her car while she called the magistrate's office. Once she had explained the situation and assured them Beth would reschedule, Misty tucked the phone in her purse.

Beth's voice drifted over as she talked to the officer. Misty's heart pounded when she reflected on what she'd done. *What was I thinking? I could have gotten both of us killed.* A cold chill ran over her. Somehow, she'd found the courage to do what had to be done. Ryan's death had shaken her to the core. She had not realized how much, until she was faced with walking away from Beth's door and leaving her inside with Tim.

Tears spilled down her cheeks. She quickly swiped them away and gulped down a sob before it escaped her throat. She pushed Ryan's image out of her mind. Dwelling on the past would do her no good. Her mind flitted to Adam. She needed him. She wasn't a superwoman, nor did she aspire to be one.

Would Adam even be back from Virginia? And how could she call him—after she'd ruined things between them? She sighed. That wasn't entirely true. She realized now she'd been looking for an escape hatch. Ted's firing had provided it.

Misty rubbed her temples. Adam said she could always count on him. It wasn't a test—the fact was she needed a shoulder—and not any shoulder.

***

"Misty! What's wrong? Adam jumped up from behind his desk and came around to where Misty had burst into his office moments before.

She stood trembling, trying to get control of her emotions. Finally, Misty recounted the incident with Tim Matthews that morning.

"You did what?" Adam drew her into his arms. "You could've been killed."

She buried her head against his chest, soaking in the comfort of his embrace. "I don't want to think about it," she murmured. "Just hold me."

He stroked her hair, allowing her time to compose herself.

Misty pulled away. "It's weird. I never felt so empowered as I did when I made the decision to push that door and save Beth." She laughed. "Then I shook like the cowardly lion when it was all over."

"I can imagine." Adam crossed his arms in front of his chest. "What am I going to do with you?"

"Don't worry—I don't plan on making a practice of rescuing women—at least not like that."

"I hope not." He rubbed his chin, his eyes still filled with disbelief. He grinned. "Though I wish I'd been there to see it."

She began to giggle, the nervous tension flowing from her body.

"It's not that funny." His brow creased.

"Oh, Adam," she wailed. "I don't know what to feel—how to act—what to say to you anymore."

"Shhh." He held her again. "You don't have to do anything. I'm sorry I've acted stupidly. I let my male pride get in the way of my common sense."

She stepped back and met his gaze. "What do you mean?"

"The day in the cafeteria." He captured her hands in his. "Can we start over?"

"What do you mean? From the beginning?"

The corners of his mouth edged upward. "We can't do that. But we can go back to before I let my wounded ego get in the way."

She tilted her head and pondered his words. "I'm sorry I hurt you, but I honestly think it was for the best to take our time."

"I know, and I was insensitive to your needs."

Cupping her hand to Adam's cheek, she leaned in and kissed him. "I love you. That never changed."

His eyes gleamed. "So, may I court you, Ms. Stephens?"

Misty smiled. "Yes, you may."

Adam slid his arms around her. She drank in the woodsy scent of his cologne. His lips touched hers, softly at first, then deepened as he drew her close. His fingertips traced her cheek, sending a tingling through her that scared and excited her at the same time.

"I think I'm gonna savor the slow pace, after all," he said when he lifted his head.

"The tortoise instead of the hare?"

"Hmmm … something like that," he murmured before he kissed her again.

Misty quivered as his lips trailed to her neck. Her skin flushed with the warmth of his breath as he nuzzled against her hair, and his hands slid down her back to pull her even closer.

She struggled against the wave threatening to sweep her under. "I-I should let you get back to work."

He brushed a final kiss on her cheek and released her. "No, in fact, if you've got time, I want to show you something."

"Sure." She smoothed her hair, then reached for her purse. "Lead the way."

Ten minutes later, Adam guided a utility vehicle over the rough terrain of the ranch with Misty beside him. "It's been a long couple of weeks without you."

She smiled up at him. "It sure has. How was Virginia—and Colton?"

"The trip was productive. Bought three stallions to increase my herd. They'll be delivered by week's end."

"And Colton?"

"Angry and disillusioned."

Misty frowned. "I'm not surprised. Jenny?"

"He blames God for letting her die."

"Oh no. Did you try to talk to him?"

Adam nodded. "It was no use. God's gonna have to work on his heart for a while. It's impenetrable—at least to me."

She rubbed his arm and leaned against his shoulder. "I'm sorry."

He kissed the top of her head. "All we can do is pray—and I know you'll do that."

"Certainly."

"The ground's still a little damp, but I wanted to show you how far we've come with Hope House." He parked the Mule and hurried around to the other side to help Misty out.

"Are we on track to meet the deadline?" She shaded her eyes with her hands and looked out over the construction site.

"We've had so much rain, hard to say." He stepped over scattered debris with Misty close behind. "With the dedication planned for

January first, I'd hoped we'd be furnishing and hanging drapes before Christmas."

Misty shook her head. "We've got some serious praying to do to accomplish that."

He laughed. "That's what I love about you. You never concentrate on the roadblock but rather the path around it."

"It's the only way to live." She surveyed the structure. The outside walls were intact, as well as the roof. Perhaps, even with the bad weather, the indoor construction could be completed on time. "Besides, it looks like we're not that far off from our plans."

"You're right—as usual." Adam slipped his hand into hers, and they picked their way back down the hill, avoiding muddy puddles as they went. "If you're not pressed for time, you wanna take a spin around the ranch?"

"I'd love to." Misty stepped into the vehicle, and Adam climbed in beside her. He turned the cart around and lumbered back to the gravel road the construction crew had laid.

She glanced at him. His brow creased like he was a million miles away. She put her hand over his.

His face softened into a smile. "Just thinking about Jenny."

"She'd be proud of Hope House."

The trail grew bumpy, and Misty clung to the edge of the cart. Sun streamed in between the darkened clouds and created a silver edge around them. The light morphed into a rainbow as the cloud moved. Her breath caught. Almost like Jenny was smiling down on them.

Adam pulled the Mule to a stop at the edge of the apple orchard and jumped out to help Misty.

She followed close behind as he led the way through the rows of trees. Little nubs of fruit clung to the branches.

"Believe it or not, these will be ready to pick in a few weeks." He ran his fingertips over an apple. "Looks like a bumper crop this year."

She tried to suppress a giggle.

He turned quickly. "What?"

"I've never actually seen an apple growing on a tree."

Adam's laughter echoed through the valley. "Oh, for Pete's sake. Are you serious?"

"It's not that funny." Misty tried to sound indignant but gave in and laughed with him. "I'm not a farmer, you know."

"Well, yeah, I'd forgotten that." He gave her a mischievous smirk. "Maybe one day."

She rolled her eyes, then sobered. "I have to admit your ranch brings out a lot of emotions in me. I feel such a deep level of serenity and security, and at the same time, excitement."

Adam's face shone. He shoved his hands into his pockets and waited for her to continue.

"You never know when a mare is going to foal, or one day the apples will be ready to pick."

"That's why I'm here. There's security in knowing I'll wake up every day and all of this is here." He spread his hands to emphasize his point. "Yet life happens. Nothing is stagnant."

Misty snapped her fingers. "You've put it into words perfectly." She grew quiet, contemplating what he'd said. Crossing her arms in front of her chest, she looked out over the valley. No doubt, she loved this place.

***

Adam stepped toward her and rested his hands on her shoulders, looking over her head toward the orchards. He longed to tell her that one day this would all be hers, as well. They'd raise a family here. He choked back the lump that formed in his throat and cleared his voice.

"Are you ready to ride some more?"

Misty shook her head. "Actually, it's about time for me to leave."

Disappointment crept into his soul. He didn't want the afternoon to end. Didn't want her to leave. "I'd hoped you'd stay for lunch."

"That wouldn't be fair to Dori."

"Dori has the day off. I'm cooking."

Her eyebrows shot up. "You?"

Adam feigned indignance. "I'm a good cook. Actually, it's leftovers, or you may have a sandwich."

"Well, in that case, how can I say no?" She tucked her hand into the crook of his arm and smiled up into his face.

That smile almost sent him over the edge. His pulse raced, and he longed to pull her into his arms when she teased him like that. The companionship she seemed satisfied with was highly overrated. He rolled to a stop behind the house and helped her from the electronic Mule. They walked to the terrace.

Once inside, she followed him into the kitchen. "Have you selected interior colors and patterns?"

"Hmmm, I knew I'd overlooked something." He washed his hands at the sink.

She nudged him. "Hey, make room for me."

"You look like you need cooling off." He splashed water onto her arm.

She giggled and threw up an elbow. "No fair."

He laughed, reached for a dishtowel, and extended it to her. "Sorry, you're hard to resist teasing." He nestled a kiss onto the nape of her neck.

She shrugged him off and dried her hands. "Seriously, I'd love to help with the interior decorating, if you'd like my input."

"I would love your input. Decorating is not my forte." He reached into the fridge and brought out containers of sandwich meat and fried chicken.

Misty layered turkey and cheese on slices of wheat bread. "I'm no expert, but I'll be glad to make suggestions. We'll need to start considering ideas pretty soon."

Adam set potato salad and fresh fruit on the table. "I'll get some brochures sent to us from the various stores in High Point, North Carolina. That'll be the best place to shop for interior furnishings."

"I agree." She set the sandwiches on the table.

He frowned. "Then we'll have to deal with the elephant in the room."

Misty slid into a chair and reached for his hand. After Adam said grace, she spooned some potato salad onto her plate along with a generous portion of fruit salad. She waited for him to heap his plate before she spoke. "Money?"

"Always." He lifted a sandwich and held it midair. "But I'm not going to worry about it anymore. I prayed about the shelter before I started the project. I'll trust God to work out the details." He took a bite and reached for his iced tea.

***

Stretching dollars was nothing new to her. Misty mulled over his words. She'd worried about the power his money represented. She'd never stopped to consider the worry that went with having money and the responsibility of running big operations like Jenkins Enterprises and Hope House.

"Maybe we could pop over one day and talk to Tanya at the shelter. She might have some suggestions." Misty scooped strawberries onto her spoon.

"Great idea." Adam leaned back in his chair. "Could you arrange that?"

"Sure. I noticed the pumpkin patch while we were riding. Maybe next year, we could host a fall festival and let the kids pick apples and select small pumpkins to decorate at the shelter. And if we open it to the public, there's good potential for income."

"Another great idea." Adam reached for his sandwich again. "I knew I was keeping you around for something."

"Hmmm. Is that why?" She quirked a smile at him.

"Why else?" He laughed between gulps of tea.

The easy banter contrasted with the crease that seemed to have permanently settled between his eyebrows. Another thought came to her mind she hadn't considered before. Would this easygoing Adam eventually give way under the stress of juggling so many projects to the Adam she'd heard fire Ted? Money issues had been the final blow to her marriage—despite the fact she'd begged Ryan to let her return to work to help out. Adam had displayed no such narrowmindedness.

In fact, he'd encouraged her to be a part of the project, to shoulder the work, and welcomed her ideas. She breathed a prayer that Adam—that they—could hold up under the stress.

Please, God, continue to bless our work with Hope House—and help me to shake off the chains of my past.

Chapter Twenty-Two

"We're always at capacity and sometimes overflowing." Tanya walked with Misty and Adam through the women's shelter. "The sooner Hope House is up and running, the better."

"We're pushing as hard as we can, Mrs. Kimmell." Adam held the door for the two ladies as they came back into the main building.

Tanya flashed him a smile. "Tanya. Mrs. Kimmell is my mother-in-law."

Adam laughed. "Tanya."

Crossing her arms in front of her chest, Tanya faced Adam and Misty. "Have you given any consideration to staff?"

"Actually, I have a few ideas, but nothing solid," Adam admitted.

"We have several qualified women who've graduated the shelter's retraining program you could interview for your office staff." Tanya started walking again. "I'll be happy to share some resumes. If nothing else, it'll give them interviewing experience."

Adam nodded.

"I'd be very careful about your choice for director," Tanya continued. "It needs to be someone you trust explicitly and who is well qualified. Someone with a heart for these women."

"I agree." Misty appreciated the care she'd received with Tanya at the helm. "Someone who understands that they're not dealing with statistics but people."

Tanya exchanged a look with Adam. She stopped in front of her office.

What was that about? Misty leaned against the doorjamb. "By the way, Tanya, Beth's rescheduled divorce hearing went splendidly. I was proud of the way she handled herself."

Tanya patted her arm. "Looks like you've done a good job with her."

"I've done very little." Misty shifted. "She's amazing. I wonder if I could've done the same in her shoes. I know it wasn't her first choice, but Tim refused to seek help and eventually would've killed her."

"We find the strength to do what we have to when we must." Tanya smiled. "But I don't need to tell you that."

Adam slipped his arm around Misty's shoulders. "Gave me a scare, the chance she took."

Misty shivered as she remembered the incident at Beth's house. He pulled her closer. "The important thing is Tim's locked up, and Beth's divorce is final."

"Very true."

Adam cleared his throat. "Sorry to break this up, but I've got a meeting in forty-five minutes."

Tanya extended her hand to Adam. "It was very nice to meet you. Anytime I can answer more questions for you, let me know."

"I appreciate you taking the time to do so." He shook her hand.

Misty brimmed with contentment. The plans for Hope House were falling into place, and the folks at the shelter, Tanya in particular, were willing to lend their expertise to make it a reality.

Adam pushed open the double glass doors that led outside. "That was very productive."

"Isn't it exciting how everything is coming together?" Misty slipped her sunglasses on while Adam opened the car door for her.

"I'm beyond excited." He climbed in on the driver's side, and within moments, they raced down the highway.

She glanced over at him. He wore a very satisfied look on his face, almost to the point of being giddy. Like he had something up his sleeve. She shrugged. Maybe it was her imagination.

"Now if I can only find the right director."

***

The following morning, Misty stood and slipped her hand into Adam's as the pastor delivered the benediction from Psalm seventy-three. "Yet I am always with you; you hold me by my right hand. You guide me with your counsel, and afterward you will take me into glory ... My flesh and my heart may fail, but God is the strength of my heart and my portion forever."

God's spirit moved in Misty's heart as it often did when she heard a Psalm. Always present, God was her strength. She closed her eyes and basked in the spiritual peace filling her soul.

Adam rustled beside her, and she roused herself. They inched their way up the aisle. Along the way, she recognized people and waved across the church or mouthed hello to them.

"The announcement for the festival looks nice." Adam clutched his bulletin along with his Bible.

"I noticed everyone seemed attentive when Pastor Kenny pointed it out." She tingled with excitement. Everything was on track. She glanced toward the entry and something caught her eye. "Oh, look, Adam."

Across the church, making his way to the door, was Mr. Duncan.

"Hurry," she whispered.

Adam laughed. "I'll see what I can do." He maneuvered through the sea of people. "Who exactly are we chasing down?"

Misty gripped his hand and murmured, "Excuse me," as they brushed past.

Mr. Duncan had reached the outside door when Misty hurried up to him. "Yoo-hoo, Mr. Duncan."

The older man turned, his eyebrows creasing with obvious distaste for being discovered.

Misty refrained from embracing him. Instead, she extended her hand. "I'm glad to see you."

Mr. Duncan slipped his gnarled hand into hers as if he saw no way to escape. "Yes, well," he grumbled.

"And this is Adam." She motioned toward Adam, who extended his hand. Mr. Duncan shook it. Misty bubbled on. "Did you enjoy the service?"

"It was okay."

Adam rested his hands on Misty's shoulders. She caught the signal and relaxed. "I'm glad you're here. How're you feeling?"

The man's countenance relaxed a little at the mention of his health. "Surprisingly well. I guess all those treatments during my miserable weeks at Oakview did some good after all. At least y'all managed not to kill me."

Misty bristled at the description of his care. "Well, I'm glad you're better. Hope to see you next week."

Mr. Duncan shot her a dismissive look and turned to leave.

Misty glanced at Adam, who always seemed to guess her thoughts nowadays. He nodded.

She touched Mr. Duncan's arm. "Would you like to join us for lunch?"

His eyebrows rose before plunging into a frown. "I prefer to eat alone, thank you."

Six months ago, his answer would have stung. Misty was stronger now—and she knew the man. That was as close to polite as he would get.

"Maybe another time." She smiled. "Good to see you."

Mumbling something unintelligible, Mr. Duncan walked through the open doors leading outside.

"A little progress at a time, my dear." Adam squeezed her hand.

Misty watched the older man walk down the sidewalk, head down, and her heart was heavy. But Adam was right. Baby steps. Mr. Duncan had shown up for church.

She flashed Adam a smile. "Lunch?"

"I won't say no." His eyes teased.

Locking her hands around his arm, she leaned in. "You're one man I can count on."

"And don't you ever forget it."

***

Thursday afternoon, Misty glanced at her phone a second time. It wasn't like Adam to be late. Since she had the evening off, she'd agreed to take a look at a temporary office with him at a strip mall centrally located between the hospital and his ranch. He sought her input more and more regarding Hope House, and he insisted the office he rented be convenient for both of them.

Adam's blue BMW pulled into the parking lot. Misty smiled. She was out of her car by the time he parked next to her.

He pushed his sunglasses on top of his head and gave her a quick kiss on the cheek. "Sorry I'm late."

"Fortunately, this is my day off, so I'm all yours."

Adam's eyebrows raised.

Her cheeks warmed. "You know what I mean."

He tucked his arm around her waist, and they walked up to the office building. "The owner has made a very generous offer on rent for three months. He's desperate because of the economy. Even though the timing will overlap with the opening of Hope House, we need office space now."

"That's good. Not the economy part, but the other. We have to be careful about how we spend Hope House funds."

"I'm paying for this." Adam peeked through the office window. "I don't want to touch Hope House funds for anything except the actual property expenses."

"Oh." Misty studied him.

He met her gaze. "Problem?"

"I thought Hope House needed to be financially independent. Will this jeopardize Jenkins Enterprises?"

He smiled. "No chance. I've got everything under control."

Did he? Or would he risk everything to make Hope House a reality? She wished she shared his confidence.

Adam pulled a key from his pocket. "The owner said to take our time looking around and then I can drop the key back to him or sign the lease. He's fine either way."

"It's nice that he trusts you." Misty pocketed her sunglasses and stepped inside while he held the door.

"We've had a long working relationship. I've rented other storage space from him in the past. We've typically never had a problem with a handshake deal." He paused. "Of course, after Ted…"

She touched his arm. "You don't have to explain to me about trust issues."

"Let's look around." Adam put on the lights in the two rooms and looked at the bathroom. "Kind of small, isn't it?"

She crinkled her nose. "I'd hoped for something larger." The walls were institution white and the carpet a dull gray.

"There are other places we can check out. This was the best location, though. And it's temporary." He shoved his hands into his jean pockets and waited for her answer.

"You're right." She considered for a moment and looked at the second room and restroom again. "At least there's a window in each room."

"It's only the two of us, until we get more staff."

Misty smiled. "We ought to be able to make this work. Likely we won't even be here at the same time."

"So, we're agreed? This is the place."

"Definitely. Now what about furniture?"

"Dori can pick out a few pieces from storage and have James and the new foreman bring them over."

She imagined what the rooms would look like filled with furniture. The walls were bare and the air stuffy from the room being so small and closed off for a while. "We need better airflow. A healthier environment. I'll bring a few plants from home."

His mouth quirked. "Whatever you'd like."

Was he teasing? "I want to be as much help as I can, but I don't want you to feel like I'm being pushy."

He waved aside her words. "Not at all. I need your help. This place needs a woman's touch. In fact—"

"What?"

"I want to ask you something, and before you answer, I'd like you to pray about it, because I have."

Misty's heart raced. *Please don't bring up marriage again.*

"I need someone to help me oversee hiring of staff, be a sounding board for ideas, and make sure I leave nothing out when it comes to this shelter." Adam paused. "You're already doing most of these things. I want you to be director of Hope House."

Misty exhaled the breath she'd been holding. "I kind of figured that's where you were headed." She grinned. "In fact, you and Tanya didn't fool me with your coded lingo the other day."

Adam laughed. "You're smart. I'll have to be careful around you from now on. You're gonna always keep me on my toes."

She slid a glance at him.

"In all seriousness, will you pray about it?"

Misty sobered. "I have been, but I haven't arrived at an answer. Whether or not I formally accept the position, I'll continue to help you through this process."

"I'll need someone on board full time pretty soon. It might mean giving up your nursing position."

Misty shook her head. "I could probably go to a PRN schedule."

Adam frowned. "I don't follow."

"Sorry. On an as-needed basis. Maybe only work one shift a week." She tucked her hair behind her ears. "I want to keep my license. I like my job, but I've discovered I don't like it full time. I'd love to help run Hope House, but—"

"But?" He crossed his arms and faced her, his feet spread slightly. The firmness of his biceps bulging against his chest and chiseled line of his jaw lent to his commanding presence.

Misty chewed the corner of her lip. She had to be completely honest about their expectations of each other. Exhaling, she squared her shoulders. "This is separate from our relationship—regardless of where that heads. Can you live with that?"

Adam nodded. "Absolutely. Hope House is completely separate. I believe we will be husband and wife one day." He put his hand up when she started to protest. "Having said that, even if we go our separate ways romantically, it will not jeopardize your position as director. I'm not the kind of person to put personal conditions on someone's employment—and definitely not yours. You are free to oversee the staff of Hope House as you see fit. The only thing I ask is that you don't make decisions unilaterally that differ from the mission statement or rules that the board of directors will set up."

A weight lifted from inside her. She hadn't considered the fact there would be a board of directors. Why did she feel she needed that protection? The scene from Adam's office with Ted came rushing back to her. She faced the window overlooking the parking lot.

"What is it?" Adam put his hands on her shoulders.

Her pulse raced at the memory of that day outside his office. He'd sounded like a different person—like there was another side to him. But didn't everybody have two sides? Everyone got angry. Perhaps she'd overreacted by holding Adam to such a high standard.

As a boss, Adam had every right to be angry and fire an employee who'd not only cheated him and violated his trust but also had broken the law. He could have easily had Ted arrested but chose not to.

Her insecurities clawed at her anyway. What if Adam raised his voice to her? Would she ever make a mistake that could get him as angry as he was with Ted?

Misty turned and looked into his smoldering brown eyes. "Adam—"

A buzzing from Adam's pocket interrupted her. "Hold that thought." He fished his phone from his pocket and scrolled through his messages. "Sorry to have to do this, but something important has come up on the ranch."

Misty's heart sank. When she'd mustered her courage to bare her soul—an interruption. "We can talk later."

He reached out and took her hand in his. "Whatever is troubling you, we can work through. Trust me on this, okay?"

Trust me. He didn't realize how difficult it was for her to process those two little words. She groaned inwardly. She didn't want anything coming between them—like her eavesdropping. They'd never really had a serious disagreement. "Sure. Go ahead."

He kissed her on the cheek. "Good. I'll call you as soon as I'm finished."

Adam locked the door behind them and walked Misty to her car.

"Dinner later?"

"Sounds good." Misty smiled. "Are you going to sign the lease?"

He leaned against his BMW. "Yeah, the location is perfect." He dropped the key into her hand. "Go ahead and bring your plants over. Feel free to fix up the place like you want."

She chuckled and pocketed the key. "What time are you picking me up for dinner?"

"Seven o'clock?"

"Perfect." Misty kissed him again.

"Mmm." He pulled her closer.

"And don't forget the festival on Saturday." She patted his arm, then climbed into her car.

"No way." He gestured with his cell phone. "Even if it weren't on my calendar."

She waved as she pulled out of the parking lot, still reveling in the warmth of his embrace. Adam was always so reassuring, deferring to her wishes. But that was now.

If their relationship soured, would he let her walk away as easily as he'd indicated? Her stomach tensed. Ryan had been amicable about her nursing career—until they were married. She wanted the position of director, but she didn't want to be faced with starting over again, if it didn't work out. Leah had accommodated her when she wanted to return to the hospital. Maybe she would tire of Misty making repeated mistakes when it came to her career—and men.

Misty shook her head. *God, you're the Father of peace. Remove this chaos from my mind and help me make good choices.*

Chapter Twenty-Three

Adam unlocked his door and slid into the driver's seat. Something troubled Misty and weighed heavy on her heart, yet she refused to share it. Was it the money? She'd bristled at his mention of paying for the offices himself.

Maybe this was part of the process God wanted them to overcome. As hurt as he'd been with her rejection when she returned the engagement ring, he now saw the wisdom of the breakup. Misty was the woman for him, but unless she could open up and share her feelings, the relationship wouldn't work.

He frowned. He knew nothing about her parents' marriage. The only other marriage she'd witnessed was her own. Misty was much wiser than he'd given her credit for. He'd only felt his own pain in her rejection. He wanted to be married. But there was the catch. He had thought with his heart at the time—and not his head. Misty obviously saw something in the aftermath of their evening at the ball he hadn't.

Adam steered his BMW onto the road leading to the ranch. As he shifted through the gears, he noticed the leaves on the trees beginning to change colors. Summer faded fast, and he, for one, was glad. Fall was one of his favorite seasons. Jenny's, too.

His mind lingered over his memories of Jenny. She'd always been his sounding board. Now he had no one to confide in about Misty. He had a few friends he played golf with on occasion and attended regional farmers meetings with, but no one he could bare his soul to. Well, at least no earthly person. He rolled to a stop in front of his ranch house. The afternoon sun streamed through the trees and beat down on the car.

Adam's mind flitted to his brother. The chasm between him and Colton couldn't last. It felt unnatural, especially with Jenny gone. How could they allow their relationship to become this superficial? They had a lot to work out. He ran his fingers through his hair. Colton, Misty, Jenny—his mind needed a break.

"Thank you, God, for your provisions and mercies to me. I've been a bonehead when it comes to this marriage thing. Thank you for giving Misty the insight to put on the brakes." When he climbed out of the car a couple minutes later, Adam still had no answers, but he trusted that God did.

Now if he could only figure out what troubled Misty. If they couldn't reach a level of complete honesty with each other, the relationship was doomed.

***

Misty hurried through the crowd scattered on the church grounds Saturday morning. The wind blew gently through the oaks and pines, making the heat more bearable.

All the festival stations were in full swing. She shaded her eyes, anticipating the arrival of the fire truck promised from Oakview Station 3. No use worrying. It would arrive soon enough.

She smiled as children scurried from the face painting tent to the merry-go-round, and others played in a sprinkler. For those from the shelter, this reprieve was exactly what they needed.

"Misty!"

She glanced around to see who'd called her name.

Tanya waved to her from the hotdog stand. She cupped her hands around her mouth. "We need more buns."

Misty changed course and headed inside to the kitchen. She grabbed several bags of buns and refills on the condiments and returned to the hotdog stand.

"We're running of out supplies quicker than I expected." Tanya slathered ketchup and mustard on a hotdog and handed it to a little boy. "Here's a napkin." Wiping her hands on a dishtowel she faced Misty.

"You're a mess." Misty laughed and reached out to push a scraggly hair from Tanya's face.

Tanya chuckled. "Well, it's for a good cause. With this being our biggest fundraiser of the year, I'm pleased with the turnout. Thanks to you, we have this lovely new venue."

Misty brushed aside her words. "No problem. Glad to help." Misty heard her name being called again. "Sounds like Adam has arrived. See you later."

"Sure." Tanya turned her attention to the new customers approaching.

Misty reached for two red Solo cups filled with iced tea while she waited for Adam to jog across the lawn. He dodged two boys and a stray soccer ball before reaching her side.

"Thanks." Adam planted a kiss on her cheek and accepted the tea she offered. "Turned out to be a hot day after all." He took a long drink. "Just what I needed."

Misty giggled. "Well, lucky for you, we have a vacancy at one of the booths."

He grunted. "Why don't I like the sound of that?"

She slipped her hand into the crook of his elbow. "Come on."

They strolled through the church grounds, stopping occasionally to check on the progress of the booths and see if anyone needed supplies. When they arrived at the dunking booth, Adam tried to bolt.

"Oh, no, you don't." Misty grabbed him with both hands.

"I don't have a change of clothes." He stalled.

She loosened her grip. "Dori dropped off a change of clothes for you when she brought the baked goods."

"What you're saying is you two conspired against me?"

Misty laughed. "You're so melodramatic. But yeah, something like that. You said you'd help in any way we needed—and you're needed here. Besides, show all these other men how it's done."

"When you put it like that." A smile eased across his face. He slipped off his shoes and climbed into the booth. He leaned out. "Hold my wallet, will you?"

"Are you sure you trust me with this?" She waved it in the air.

"I guess if I trust you with my heart, my wallet is safe enough." He winked and settled onto the seat.

Misty tucked the wallet into the pocket of her dress, then unlatched the chain blocking the booth. She motioned for the first person in line, a brown-haired middle-school boy, to step up and select a ball from the basket. "What's your name?"

"Samuel." He tossed the ball from one hand to another and sized up the target. After two attempts, the ball hit the center of the bulls-eye. Adam plunged into the water.

The crowd that had quickly gathered cheered and applauded.

Misty patted Samuel on his shoulder. "You've got quite an arm there. Why don't you try again?"

"Hey, one turn each." Adam scrubbed the water from his face with the palm of his hand.

"No talking from the peanut gallery." Misty smirked then handed Samuel another ball and turned back to Adam. "Your paying customers are waiting."

Adam climbed back into the seat and held onto the wire cage in front of him. He began to heckle Samuel to miss. After two tries, the boy squarely hit the target, and Adam plunged into the chilly water once again.

Misty leaned in and whispered. "I guess twice is enough. A line is forming behind you."

Samuel beamed as he collected his prize, a diecast car. "Thanks, lady." He ran toward his mother and his little sister. She toddled forward, and he caught her hand and pulled her to him protectively.

Misty recognized the family from the shelter. Beth had spent time with them. They were one of the newest arrivals.

She sent up a silent prayer and turned to the next little girl, whose mother had been at the shelter more than once. Misty handed her a ball. "Okay, Sarah, let's see what you can do."

"I'm good at playing ball." Sarah wiped her nose with the back of her sleeve.

Misty ignored the gesture. It wasn't her place to correct the child.

Instead, she flashed a smile at her. "Aim at the loud man sitting on the seat in there." She pointed to Adam.

He gripped the wire in front of him. "Hey, I'm not loud."

Sarah giggled, then whispered. "He kind of is."

Misty grinned. "Go ahead."

After several missed attempts, Misty squatted in front of Sarah. "Want me to show you an easier way?"

Sarah's headed bobbled up and down. Misty reached for her hand and they walked to the dunking booth.

"Hey, no fair." Adam redirected his appeal to Sarah. "You don't really want to dunk me, do you?"

As they grew nearer the booth, Sarah suddenly wriggled her hand out of Misty's grasp and hid behind her.

"Hey, what's wrong?" Misty bent down and put her arm around the little girl.

"I'm afraid."

"Oh, honey. I'm sorry." Misty's heart broke for what Sarah must have gone through in her short little life. "Mr. Jenkins is loud, but that's because he doesn't like to get wet. He's really a teddy bear."

Adam had remained silent through the exchange. "Actually, I'm pretty hot up here. Maybe some water would cool me off."

Sarah peeked out from behind Misty's dress and looked at Adam.

Misty patted her shoulder. "It's up to you."

"Okay."

Misty lifted her up, placed her little hand on the lever, and pushed. Adam dropped into the water.

Sarah gasped when the water sprayed her. She giggled again. "That was fun."

Misty set her on the ground. "Mr. Jenkins agrees. Here's your prize." She extended a mini plush rabbit.

Sarah's face lit up. "Thanks!" She ran back to her mother who was in line with her other children.

Adam climbed back onto the seat and leaned toward Misty. "You okay?" He kept his voice low where only Misty could hear him.

"Yeah. I hate seeing these kids go through this." She glanced through the line of kids, some observing her interaction with Adam intently. Was it possible they'd never seen healthy bantering between a man and woman?

"Which is why we do what we do." A determined look crossed his face. "Little girls like Sarah shouldn't have to worry about being safe."

Misty swallowed hard against her constricting throat. She reached into the bucket of balls, then motioned for the next child to step forward. She processed through several more children before time to close the booth for an afternoon break. The festival had been a great success so far. Children were a blessing from God. Maybe one day she'd have some of her own, but when she looked at the broken families and the wide-eyed fear of the little ones, again, she was glad she hadn't had any children with Ryan.

God, please be with these families, and guide us in our efforts to help them heal.

***

Moments later, Adam toweled his hair while Misty hurried to the church driveway where the red-and-chrome fire truck had rolled in moments before. Some kids pushed to get a closer spot. Despite Misty's efforts to organize them, the smaller children scrambled when the fire horn blew. Adam watched, mesmerized by Misty's doting on them to calm their fears. She seemed a natural with kids.

They'd agreed to meet in thirty minutes, after Misty finished the fire-safety activity with the children. He hurried inside to the restroom to finish toweling off and change clothes. He tucked the wet clothes into a plastic bag and placed it next to Misty's belongings. As he was leaving, Tanya came into the building.

"Adam, I hear the dunking booth was the hit of the day." Tanya laughed.

He winced. "Something like that."

"When we tally the profits for today, I fully expect them to exceed our expectations." She motioned for him to follow her into the kitchen.

"If you've got time, I need some help restocking the booths."

"Sure, anything to help out." He tucked his bag under his arm and reached for the cooler she'd refilled with Coke, Sprite, and Dr Pepper.

She grabbed a pot of cooked hotdogs and led him outside. At the hotdog cart, she set the pot on the cart and pointed to a spot under the table for the cooler.

"Need any help?" Tanya asked the volunteer working the booth. She waited only long enough for an answer, grabbed two Cokes from the cooler, and motioned for Adam to follow her to a shade tree.

She handed a can to Adam and popped open hers. "Hot day considering it's already fall."

He leaned against the tree. "Perfect for a festival. How many fundraisers do you have during the year?"

"A couple of smaller ones. This is the main one." She smiled. "I'm thrilled Misty secured this venue for us. Pastor Kenny has been a joy to work with."

Adam mulled over the information. How much would he have to personally fund Hope House in proportion to what could be raised annually? And realistically, could he manage both? He continued to pray God would provide an answer.

A young mother with a crying baby on her hip captured his attention. She ruffled through a diaper bag and withdrew a bottle. The baby's wails stopped as his mouth latched onto the bottle. Adam chuckled. He couldn't let these women and children down.

"Of course, endowments are great, if you can secure them. Grants, as well."

"Yeah, I'd heard that." He drank the last of his Coke and tossed it into a nearby receptacle. "So far, I'm the only one with any money."

Tanya nodded. "You've done very well with the fundraising. The ball was a success. Misty has been a tremendous asset to you, I'm sure."

"That she has."

"Well, I'd better check on the other stations." Tanya took a couple of steps and then turned back. "Give her some time, Adam. She'll come around. You didn't know Misty when Ryan was alive. It was a horrible time for her—just like Jenny and the others you're hoping to serve through Hope House. Healing doesn't come easy, nor overnight."

His chin dropped to his chest and he rubbed his forehead. His mind grasped her words. Why couldn't his heart understand something this obvious?

She touched his arm. He raised his head and met her gaze.

"She loves you. She'll get there."

"Thanks."

With an encouraging smile, Tanya hurried away.

Laughter and squeals reached his ears from the driveway and the fire truck. He snorted when the truck gave a blast on the siren and the kids shrieked and jumped. One little boy huddled against Misty, and she knelt down to hug him.

Longing filled Adam for a life with Misty which included marriage and children. Again, he wrestled with his anger toward Ryan for what he'd robbed her of. And Jenny and the children she'd never have. His own pain hadn't completely healed. He couldn't expect Misty to move at a faster pace. And when it came down to it, how could he be angry with Colton? His brother had his own grieving process. If only he weren't trying to go it alone.

At one point, he and Colton hadn't been so different. Both were lifelong bachelors, absorbed in making their ranches successful—even somewhat competitive in doing so. Except for brief relationships, neither had felt compelled to get married. That all changed for Adam when he met Misty. He'd grown closer to God in the process, and because of that, he'd begun to grieve in a healthy way.

Adam rubbed his chin. Why had Colton chosen a different path? One that included rejection of God.

Adam reached the driveway and helped Misty keep the children back while the fire truck edged out. Once the truck was into the street, she helped the children to disperse to their families.

Misty wiped her neck with a napkin, then fanned her face. "It's supposed to be fall. What's up with this hot weather?"

"Are you gonna melt?" Adam quirked a grin at her.

"I might." She rolled her eyes. "Behave yourself."

He kissed her on the cheek. "Yes, ma'am. Let's get back to the dunking booth then." He suddenly had an idea. "Since you're hot, why don't you get inside it this time?"

Her face clouded. "I don't think so."

"Yes, I think so. I don't want you to melt."

"Hmmm."

Would she do it?

Then she looked down at her clothes. "Sorry, I have a dress on. It'd be an awful mess climbing up and down." She grinned. "Not to worry. We have a volunteer for the rest of the afternoon."

"Okay, let's go for a walk, down by the pond before we have to start breaking down the festival and cleaning up." He slipped his hand into hers, and they crossed the lawn under the shade trees. Marriage could only make life better, but more than ever before, Adam counted on God's perfect timing.

"My parents leave on a cruise this week." Misty's words broke into his thoughts.

Adam glanced over at her. "Sounds like fun."

"I'm happy to see them getting away. Ever since Dad retired, he's content to sit at home. I actually think that's part of why Mom's always grouchy."

"Is she?" Adam frowned. "That doesn't sound like a good combination at all."

"Mom's a hard one to figure out. She's not big on explaining her feelings—or even sharing them, for that matter." Misty stopped and leaned against an oak tree. Acorns scattered down around them as squirrels chattered overhead.

"Well, right now, I'm more interested in her daughter." Adam placed a kiss on her lips.

"Mmm. I'm sure." Misty's eyes sparkled up at him as she slipped into his arms. "I could get used to that."

"I'm counting on it."

Misty relaxed against his chest, her silky hair nestled against his chin. He lowered his head and drank in the scent of gardenias that flowed from her soft skin.

Lord, give me strength.

Chapter Twenty-Four

In church the next morning, the pianist tapped out the final stanza of the closing hymn. Life had not been kind to the elderly gentleman. Much of that had been his own doing. Mr. Duncan looked across the church at Misty alongside her boyfriend, Adam. The lady on the other side of Misty was with her every Sunday, as well. Thought he'd heard Misty call her Beth. Timid little thing, but it was none of his business who Misty had for friends.

Misty was about as perfect a lady as anyone could hope to meet. The preacher's sermon had been about Second Corinthians thirteen—the love chapter, the preacher had called it. As far as Mr. Duncan could see, Misty was the epitome of St. Paul's definition of love.

She'd brought life to him when he'd had none. When he'd discovered her significance to his life, he'd immediately discounted the idea of sharing it with her. No matter how perfect she was, he doubted she could forgive him.

The sun shone through the stained-glass window depicting Jesus ascending into heaven. He sighed. One day, his time would come, and he'd have a heavy heart if he hadn't made peace with her.

His gaze was drawn back to the overhead screen, but the song came to a close. The pianist played the last note as the congregation sang, "Amen."

The preacher stood to deliver the benediction. That was Mr. Duncan's cue to duck out. He didn't need to run into Misty and her boyfriend. Making small talk wasn't his strong suit—nor did he intend to master it at his age. He'd gotten along fine with no one for years, but solitude had been a hard way to live.

He slipped through the back doors and glanced over his shoulder long enough to catch a final glimpse of Misty. The doors swung lightly against each other before coming to a stop. He twisted his hat in his hand. Did he have the right to pray Misty would forgive him? He wasn't even sure he deserved forgiveness—from her or from God.

He clapped his hat onto his head. In the sunlight, where summer's heat ebbed into cooler days, he climbed into his pickup truck, slipped on his old wire-rimmed sunglasses, and backed out of the parking lot. He had no answers, nor did he have the patience to continue mulling over his conundrum. When his time came, likely he'd get what he deserved and nothing more.

***

"What are you carrying in here, a body?" Misty lugged the last of her parents' luggage to the front door on Monday morning.

"Not amusing, Misty Lynn." Mother checked her passport again and tucked it into her purse.

Misty glanced at her father whose lips quivered along with his belly. He'd crack up, and they'd both be in trouble, if she gave him the slightest provocation. Considering he was the one riding to the airport with Mother, Misty resisted the urge.

"The idea of being delayed going through customs draws on my nerves as it is." Her mother looked into the hall mirror and smoothed her hair before facing Misty. "Water my plants twice a week and get the mail."

"Yes, Mother. You'd better get going or you'll be late for your flight." She reached up and brushed a kiss on her mother's cheek. Her mother bristled slightly before patting Misty on her arm.

Misty threw her arms around her father and squeezed. "Papa, take care of Mother, okay?"

"Melodrama." Her mother rolled her eyes and walked through the open front door.

Misty and her father burst into laughter.

"Ah, lassie, you almost got me in trouble." Her father wiped his eyes with his handkerchief.

"I don't know how you do it, Papa." Misty reached for his hand

and held it between hers. "Be careful. I couldn't take it, if something happened to you."

"Nothing will." He pulled her into an embrace before reaching for the luggage. "Lock up, will you?"

"Sure, Papa." Misty stood at the door while their car pulled away from the curb. How could two polar opposites bring out the best and worst in her at the same time?

She had time to stop off at Hope House offices before heading to work. Hopefully, she'd catch Adam there, and they could discuss the personnel she wanted to hire.

When she pulled into the parking lot fifteen minutes later, Adam's BMW was parked beneath a shade tree. Her heart fluttered.

"Ah, now my day is better," Adam greeted her when she came through the door.

She tossed her purse onto the desk and gave him a hug.

"Is that all I get?"

Misty giggled. "For now. If you're lucky, I'll let you take me to lunch before I have to get ready for work."

He smirked. "I'll behave then."

"My parents are winging their way to Florida to meet their cruise ship." Misty dropped into the desk chair and swirled around to face him.

"Sorry to see them go?"

Misty crinkled her brow. "Actually, no. I'm happy they're having a good time. It's the way life should be at their age."

"I agree." Adam spread the blueprints on the desk and Misty leaned over to look.

"Never tire of looking at those, huh?"

"I had the architect tweak them some, and he just got around to sending over the new copies." Adam traced the lines of the building with his finger. He stopped on what appeared to be a gymnasium.

"This is where the gym will be in the back. I decided to add an outdoor basketball court." He tapped the spot on the blueprints. "I wanted the front of the building to be offices and the activity room."

Misty nodded. "Beautiful views."

"Exactly." Adam chuckled. "Great minds think alike, huh?"

"Hmmm, something like that."

Adam pulled her into his arms. "You know I love you?"

"Yeah, I think you mentioned it a time or two."

"Silly." He brushed a kiss onto her cheek before growing serious again. "Listen, I've meant to talk to you about the holidays."

"What about?"

"Thanksgiving's right around the corner. Every year, I host a meal for any of the ranch employees who don't have family to share the holidays with." He paused. "Jenny used to help Dori prepare it."

Misty cupped his cheek in her hand. "The holidays will be rough."

"I know." His dark eyes dimmed. He kissed the back of her hand. "But I have you to help me through."

"It's not the same."

Adam shook his head. "No, it'll never be the same, but Jenny wouldn't want me moping around. So, I'll try not to. Join us for Thanksgiving—unless you're spending it with your folks."

"I haven't checked with them." She pulled her day planner from her purse. "My sister is in China on a long-term mission trip. It's possible they'll fly over there during the holidays. It's been quite a while since they've seen her."

"No point in spending the day by yourself." A smile stretched across his face. "We can start our own traditions. You could help Dori with the meal."

Misty smiled. "I'd be glad to help her."

"Good, then it's settled. You'll spend Thanksgiving at the ranch?"

"After I've checked with my folks about their plans." She jotted a note in her planner and slid it back inside her purse.

"Of course."

"I'll do that as soon as possible so Dori knows how to plan."

Adam turned back to the blueprints.

Misty strolled to the window and looked out. The cool weather made her restless. Autumn was her favorite season with the leaves changing. But it also reminded her no matter how constant everyday life was, the earth turned, life changed, and eventually, like the leaves that fell, her earthly time would end.

She nibbled on the edge of a hangnail and contemplated everything that had happened in the last six months. Adam's hands rested on her shoulders. She reached up and pulled them around her in a hug.

"I needed that." She savored the feeling of his embrace.

"Why so quiet?"

"Just life." She didn't want to get into a long discussion about the thoughts that bounced around in her head, because, in truth, she had not sorted them out. She turned in his arms.

Adam's eyes glistened and a smile brightened his face. He didn't press her, which was one of the things she loved most about him.

He kissed her forehead before releasing her. "Any suggestions as to how we're going to pay for all this?"

"We've already held a ball. We can't go to that well twice."

Adam exhaled. "True. We can't expect the same people to continue to write checks."

"The challenge is coming up with new money."

Sitting on the edge of the desk, he twirled a pen between his fingers. "I wish I could sign on the dotted line for all of this, but it would be too risky. Doing so would put the shelter and the ranch on shaky ground."

"No one expects you to exhaust your personal resources." Although he probably would, if it came down to it. "Besides, I happen to know you've already chipped in quite a bit of your own money."

"It's important that no matter what happens to Jenkins Enterprises or me personally, Hope House is financially independent. With the economy like it is, it'd be foolish to intermix the two entities."

Misty frowned. "Is everything okay with the ranch?"

"Yes, and I want to keep it that way." Adam walked around the desk and opened his top drawer. "Although—we've had a significant donation in the last week." He slid a check in front of her.

She gasped at the amount. "$100,000?"

"Largest donation to date."

She flipped the check over and then back to the front. "I don't recognize this organization."

Adam exhaled. "It's a holding house—a front to cover for whoever is donating."

Misty looked up, her stomach tightening. "Is that legal?"

"Perfectly legal. The person apparently wants to remain anonymous." Adam dropped the check back inside the bank pouch in his desk. "But that doesn't solve the shortfall. Which means more prayer time for us, Missy."

She giggled. "You mean Misty?"

He drew her into his arms and buried his face in her hair, which tickled her even more. "No, I mean Missy," he murmured, as his lips trailed to her mouth.

She was swept under by the passion ignited between them. Passion that made her knees weak. Adam lifted his head. The love reflecting from his eyes took her breath away. Before she could stop herself, those three little words escaped from her lips.

"I love you." Her eyes brimmed with tears.

"What's the matter?" He cupped her cheek gently. "What is it?"

She leaned her head against his chest. "I don't want to talk. Hold me."

He smoothed her hair with his strong hand as he held her. After a moment, she pulled back. His eyes held questions he didn't voice.

She cleared her throat and smiled up at him. "Sorry I'm flaky sometimes."

"Not at all. I want to share all your moments, regardless of how you feel or whether or not you can voice your feelings."

"I can't right now. You overwhelm me."

He grinned. "Good."

She cut her eyes sideways at him, though a smile tugged at the corners of her mouth. "You're terrible, you know that?"

"I've been told." He smirked. "The question is—terrible good or terrible bad?"

She resisted the urge to join his banter. Instead, she stroked the side of his face. When he kissed her, she savored the feeling of his closeness, her heartbeat melting into his, and knowing what their passion would become, if she found the courage to marry him. A shiver rippled through her.

"Ah, Misty," Adam murmured when he released her. "I don't know how much longer I can go on like this."

If only her mind could trust what her heart felt.

Chapter Twenty-Five

Misty relaxed on a chaise lounge in her sunroom and tried her parents' number. Time had flown while they were on their cruise, especially since she'd worked a few double shifts in the last two weeks. With a rare day off in the midst of a hectic week, she'd lain around most of the morning. The mockingbirds tweeted to each other on the other side of the window. Robins and blue jays flitted from limb to limb, taking turns dive-bombing each other in the birdbath.

The view from the sunroom overlooking her rustic flower garden was her favorite. She'd have to find a day soon to clean the fall flowers and rake the leaves. She loved the feel of crackling leaves underfoot. Childhood memories of Dad with rake in hand, surrounded by massive piles of leaves, flooded her mind. She'd jump into the piles, then he'd hand her a rake and say, "Lassie, if you're going to mess up, you have to rake up." They'd laugh as she tried to maneuver the rake that overwhelmed her in size.

Her throat ached at the memories. Life had been simple as a child.

"Mother?"

"Hello, dear."

"How're you doing?" Misty gathered the knitted throw around her feet to ward off the cold.

"Papa and I are doing great. How about you? I'm sorry we haven't called since we returned."

"I'm equally guilty. Staying too busy, all of us."

"Savannah is getting furlough to Europe next month."

Misty's heart filled with contentment. She was proud of her sister and equally pleased her parents were in the position to travel when her sister got time off. Not to mention she wouldn't have to haggle with Mother about spending Thanksgiving with Adam. "Does this mean you're packing?"

Her mother's gentle laughter came through the phone. "You know me well. We've barely unpacked from the cruise."

"I don't blame you." Misty adjusted on the seat and tucked the throw in closer. "I'd be going, too, if she were my child." As soon as the words left her mouth, she cringed. She couldn't talk about her past or future with her mother. The children she didn't have—might never have. The subject sparked too much pain. To her surprise, Mother didn't press.

"Your day will come." Mother changed the subject. "What will you do for Thanksgiving since we won't be home?"

"I'll celebrate it with Adam—at his ranch." Misty gripped the phone tighter and bit her lip.

"Good."

Misty exhaled, her tense muscles relaxing. Was it her imagination or did her mom sound pleased with her admission? "Is Papa there?"

Mother's voice drifted away, and after a muffled exchange, Papa got on the phone.

"How's my lassie?"

Misty chuckled. "I'm fine, Papa."

"What's this I hear about a man—Adam's his name?"

"He's a friend." She loved her dad more than life itself. She could tolerate a little prying from him.

"A boyfriend?"

Misty smiled at his high school term. She felt like she was getting ready to ask permission to go to the prom. "I guess you could say that."

"Does he treat you right?" Her father's voice tightened. No one would come in and mistreat his daughter again—ever.

"Papa, you'd love him. He's a perfect gentleman." She paused, then said the one thing she knew would win him over. "He's a lot like you."

"Well, then," her father said gruffly. "I guess it's okay."

She suppressed the giggles bubbling inside. Her father came from a generation whose blessing meant something. Many people her age brushed off the wisdom of their parents. She treasured her father's opinion above anyone's. Too bad she'd not listened to him about Ryan. She exhaled to rid herself of the knot forming in her stomach. Her life was about Adam now. She wouldn't give Ryan any more headspace.

Her smartphone flashed an incoming message. She scrolled over it and frowned.

"Papa, that means everything to me. You're gonna love Adam when you meet him."

"I love you, lass."

"Love you, too, Papa. Look, I hate to cut this short, but something has come up I need to take care of."

"I've talked long enough anyway."

Misty laughed aloud. "Yeah, this is the longest conversation we've had in a while."

After saying goodbye and promising to call on the weekend, Misty tapped Adam's number into her phone. "What's up?"

"Could you meet me at the office in, say—an hour?"

Misty's heart fluttered. "Anything wrong?"

"Nothing. I didn't mean to scare you." Adam's voice sounded agitated. "I'm in the middle of ten things right now, but someone wants to meet us. I don't have time to get into it over the phone. I'll explain when I get there."

"Sure thing. I'll see you in an hour." Misty placed the phone back in its base and tossed off the knitted throw. *What could be so important?*

***

"Why does Mr. Duncan want to meet us here—both of us?" Misty paced the length of the room. "I mean, he barely knows you, except in passing at church, and me—well, he barely tolerates me."

Adam fiddled with a stuck drawer in his desk. "It's a mystery all right." He reached for a screwdriver and wedged the drawer out. "Now, how come a brand-new desk has a flaw like this?"

Misty smirked. "I don't know. Good thing you're so handy."

Adam slid a glance at her, which made her giggle. Misty walked over to the window to look out. An old Chevy pickup lumbered up the road and into the parking lot. Butterflies filled her stomach.

"We won't have long to find out."

Adam raised his head. "He's here?"

"He just pulled in."

He parked the truck and the driver's door popped open. The older man gingerly climbed out, his age reflected in each step he took.

"Oh, Adam, for some reason, I'm nervous."

He came around the desk and put his arm around her. "Don't be. I'm here. Besides, he's never threatened you or anything, has he?"

"No. Nothing like that."

A knock at the door interrupted their conversation.

Adam opened it. "Mr. Duncan, please come in." He extended his hand to the older gentleman.

Mr. Duncan nodded at Misty. What was that in his eyes? His subdued demeanor sharply contrasted with his usual grouchy disposition. He twisted his straw hat between his hands. "Ms. Stephens."

"So good to see you, Mr. Duncan." Misty motioned to one of the leather chairs in front of Adam's desk. "Have a seat." She turned the other chair slightly to face him before she sat.

"Would you like a cup of coffee?" Adam offered.

Something like a half-smile tugged at the corners of Mr. Duncan's mouth. "That would be good. I take it black."

Adam poured a cup and put it in the man's hand before taking a seat behind the desk. "Now, what can we do for you?"

"I've got something to say to Ms. Stephens—something she should've known long ago."

Misty's pulse raced. She couldn't bear more upheaval in her life. What could this man possibly say that would have any impact on her? Nothing she could think of. She relaxed her shoulders and waited for him to continue.

Adam's smile faded.

Mr. Duncan cleared his throat. His hand shook as he set his coffee cup on the desk in front of him. "First off, I have something to give you for your new shelter." He reached into his pocket, pulled out an envelope, and handed it to Adam. "I heard you were up against the wall with your financing. I wanted to make it a little easier for you—and the ladies you're gonna help."

Adam opened the envelope and withdrew a check, eyebrows arching. He slid the check across the desk to Misty. Her hand trembled as she picked it up. She couldn't believe her eyes.

"Mr. Duncan," she gasped. "Am I seeing this right? Did you mean to give us a quarter of a million dollars? Where—how?" She couldn't finish her sentence.

Mr. Duncan grunted. "I meant to give it to ya. As for how—I've had a very successful dairy farm for the better part of the last four decades." He looked down at his hands before looking back at Misty. "Ever since the docs gave me that cancer diagnosis, I've begun to reevaluate my life. I couldn't keep up the farm. I sold most of my land and the dairy operation. I kept a small interest in it, but I don't oversee the actual operation anymore."

Misty's heart broke for the older gentleman, though she still didn't see what any of it had to do with her. "That makes sense, given your health over the last year."

"And, we both know where I'm headed. The cancer is in remission, but mostly you don't beat cancer. It eventually beats you."

Misty refrained from arguing his point—mainly because, in his case, there was some truth to what he said. And it would do no good to start an argument or cite statistics when he'd clearly come to discuss something else.

"I was fortunate enough to make good choices in the stock market over the years. Pulled out a good bit right before it tanked a few years ago. I'm sitting on more money than I can possibly spend. I want to put it to good use."

"It'll certainly be put to good use, Mr. Duncan. I can assure you of that." Adam slid the check back across the desk and studied it.

"There's more where that came from." Mr. Duncan's wrinkled face morphed into a half-smile.

Misty's stomach inexplicably twisted as tension rose in her. Old feelings of mistrust flared. Her mind ruminated on the comment he'd made when he first sat in front of her. She studied his eyes, his face. Did he want something in return? They would promise him nothing.

"You've answered the how. I'm curious about the why." With effort, she kept her voice steady. "You said there's something I should know."

He twisted the straw hat between his gnarled hands. "I gave the money because I wanted to do something decent for someone before I die. No strings attached."

"But there's more." Adam leaned forward, his expression stern. Misty had seen that expression before, the day she first entered Jenny's room, and he'd demanded better care for his sister.

Mr. Duncan looked Misty in the eye. "What I'm about to tell you—maybe it'll give you peace. Maybe it won't."

She braced herself. Adam's gaze darted to Misty and back to Mr. Duncan.

"You see, I don't have any other family to speak of. It won't surprise you to know what little I had, I ran off."

Misty believed it, but she didn't voice her feelings.

"And, well—I kind of consider you family. Thought maybe I could make amends before I die."

Misty's mouth gaped. "I—I don't understand."

The older gentleman swallowed hard. "There's no easy way to say this, and I don't believe in beating around the bush. I'm Ryan's daddy."

Chapter Twenty-Six

The room spun like she'd stepped off the tilt-a-whirl at the state fair and didn't have her land legs yet. Misty clutched the side of her chair, her nails digging into the fabric. "That's impossible," she choked out. "Ryan's father is dead. In fact, he told me both of his parents were dead. Is that a lie too?"

"No. His mama died years ago. She married me when Ryan was little. His biological father died when he was a baby." Mr. Duncan rubbed his neck. "I raised him. You might say it's my fault he turned out like he did. I left way before he was grown, but once he had a say-so, he wanted nothing to do with me."

Bile stung the back of Misty's throat. She was going to be sick right there in Adam's office. Hot, angry tears coursed down her cheeks. Why hadn't Ryan told her about his father?

Adam stood, grabbed some tissues, and handed them to her. He poured her a glass of water. She wiped her face and took a sip.

"Ryan only talked about his father dying when he was too young to remember him. He seemed awfully bitter about it, but other than that..." Misty's voice caught.

"I'm sorry this is such a shock to you." Mr. Duncan softened. "I considered writing you a letter, but you deserved for me to tell you in person. You deserve to have your say."

"I appreciate that," Misty choked out.

"I want you to know I never hit his mother."

Misty shot him a glare. *Some comfort.*

"But I taught him how to disrespect women, that's for sure. It cost him his life, and it cost me his mother. Some might refer to that as poetic justice."

"There's no justice in the fact that Ryan lost his life and came very close to killing me in the process," Misty spat out.

Mr. Duncan shook his head. "Didn't mean that, just meant the fact that I'm alone now."

Adam cleared his throat. "It's none of my business, but it seems to me Ryan had a choice. He could have rejected your upbringing, could've gotten help."

Mr. Duncan's voice held steady. "True, but I sowed the seeds."

Misty's head spun. This was her father-in-law. She rubbed her temples to try to get the throbbing to stop. *God, please, help me. I don't know what to say to this man.*

She took a sip of water and fidgeted with her tissue. She cleared her throat. "Mr. Duncan, I appreciate your honesty. I think Adam is right, though. Ryan had abuse modeled for him, but he was educated. He could've sought counseling. Lord knows I begged him to go enough times. And he had to have felt some outrage for how you treated his mother. Yet, when it came right down to it, none of that drove him to save our marriage. His problems went deeper than simply blaming his behavior on you."

Adam nodded. "I think you're on to something, Misty."

She mustered a smile she didn't feel. "You don't owe me anything, if that's what this check is about." She tapped the slip of paper to drive home her point.

Mr. Duncan put up his hand. "No. Nothing like that. I have nothing else to do with the money. I feel like since I was part of the men who drove women to places like this, the least I could do is try to help the women now in what small way I can."

"It's no small way, I assure you that." Adam picked up the check. "Misty, it's up to you. Do we keep the check?"

How could she turn down the money? She couldn't make Hope House about her. Hundreds of women would cycle through over the next few years, and the shelter needed the funds to take care of them. In a roundabout way, Mr. Duncan was right. He did owe the cause of abused women. It was time to break the cycle. If one abuser could see that, maybe hope existed for others.

"We'll keep the check." Misty wiped her eyes.

Mr. Duncan's lips quivered as he attempted a smile. "Everything will be yours when I pass. In the meantime, if you need more, let me know."

Misty shook her head fiercely. "No. I don't want your property or your money. But the shelter does need it. If you really want to make amends, leave it to Hope House."

Mr. Duncan's eyebrows creased. "I understand your anger, Ms. Stephens. I didn't expect forgiveness."

Forgiveness? She almost choked on the word. Her mind couldn't even grasp what he'd told her, much less her heart or her soul.

"Can I tell ya something else?"

Adam stared at Misty, waiting for a signal from her.

How much worse could it get? She nodded. "Go ahead."

"Once I realized who you were—when I was lying in that hospital bed and your name finally registered in this old brain—I didn't want to own up. I had no intention of it. After all, you probably thought I was half crazy anyway. I knew Ryan had passed—read it in the paper." Mr. Duncan's voice wavered. "But then I saw that little prayer card you slipped into my belongings."

Misty smiled. Her prayer had been that this man would seek God before he died.

"I think God worked on my heart because of you." He straightened. "My soul was so restless, I couldn't stand myself. Finally, I snuck into church one Sunday. Started listening to what the preacher was saying. Before long, my old hardened heart started softening a little."

"God will do that." Misty relaxed her rigid posture.

"This Jesus you'd told me about, the preacher spoke about. A man could forgive me, make me whole again? At first, I figured it was a joke. I didn't want to believe it."

Misty exchanged a glance with Adam. She gulped back her tears.

"Then I knew if Jesus would come into my heart and save me, I had to come here and make a clean breast of things."

Misty put her hand over the man's gnarled hand. "Jesus will forgive you of anything. But I'm glad you came and confessed all of this. One day, it will make sense to me, perhaps."

The older man cleared his throat. "I don't have no right to ask this, but I wonder if some day you'll find it in your heart to forgive me."

Adam leaned forward and clasped his hands in front of him. Misty held his gaze. He gave her a smile of encouragement. She had to forgive Mr. Duncan. Forgiveness was the premise of everything she believed in and stood for. If she couldn't forgive this man, she had no business calling herself a Christian. So why couldn't she open her mouth and say those simple words? *God, help me,* her soul cried.

"I'll be completely honest with you. You've blindsided me. My emotions are raw. I'm hurt, angry, and numb all at the same time—if that's possible." She paused. "But Christ has forgiven me more times than I can count. And, as a Christian, I believe He has forgiven you, if you've asked for it. I'm not above Him, so I forgive you." She was surprised at the peace that washed over her when she said those simple words. The aching in her soul and mind hadn't lessened and probably wouldn't for a while, but aside from that, she could forgive this man. God's grace astounded her sometimes.

A smile beamed from Mr. Duncan's face—the first real smile she'd ever seen from him. One that, a few months ago, she'd been sure wasn't possible. Somehow, she must find a way to separate the man she'd grown to know from the one she'd just learned helped shape Ryan into a monster and, in turn, robbed her of her marriage and several years of her life. She had to, for the forgiveness to mean anything. Weariness pressed against her from all sides.

Adam cleared his throat, breaking the silence that hung between them. "Did you make an anonymous donation a few weeks ago, Mr. Duncan?"

The older man lowered his eyes and twisted his hat between his hands. "Yeah, that was me. I wanted to come here then, but I was sick, and—well—I chickened out every time I considered it." He looked at Misty. "When I started to send another check, I realized I wasn't no kind of a man, if I couldn't own up to everything in person."

"We're glad you came now." Misty looked to Adam, who stood, signaling the meeting was over.

Mr. Duncan eased up from his chair and slipped his straw hat back onto his head. He extended his hand to Adam, then to Misty.

"Thank you, Ms. Stephens." His eyes reflected the closest thing to kindness she'd ever seen from him.

"Thank you for the check—and for sharing. I appreciate both. I'm glad you found the courage to come clean." Misty meant it. Hopefully, this new knowledge would lead her to a better understanding of what had happened in her life—perhaps lead her to forgive Ryan, as well.

Adam came around the desk and opened the door. "Thanks again, Mr. Duncan. Best wishes on your health." He patted the older man on his back.

Mr. Duncan slipped out the open door, down the sidewalk, and climbed into his truck. Adam closed the door, turned, and opened his arms. Misty rushed to him, sobbing from the depths of her soul.

***

Misty dumped the old soil from the flowerpots, one by one, into the corner of the tiny yard her condominium afforded her. She thrust her spade into fresh potting soil, scooped some dirt, and shoveled it into an empty pot. Plants didn't survive under her care for more than a season, yet she couldn't bear the empty plant shelves, especially during the winter months.

She settled a purple African violet into the center of the soil and gently pressed around it. After repeating the process several times, a row of pastel-colored pots sat on her terrace ready to be taken inside. She grabbed the hose and spritzed each plant. The sun peeked over the terrace wall, but she felt safe leaving the pots outside for a short time, since the sun wasn't directly overhead yet.

Toweling off her hands, she stepped back inside and went to the kitchen for a glass of iced tea. She leaned against the kitchen counter, replaying the scene with Mr. Duncan in her mind. Her temples pulsated with anger. She'd been naïve in her belief that she would be free of Ryan's grasp when she buried him. She was beginning to think that would never happen.

The doorbell's chime a couple of minutes later surprised her. She groaned. She'd forgotten Beth was coming by to chat.

She hurried to the front door. "Beth, come in." She stepped aside and motioned for her friend to enter.

"I hope I'm not early." Beth glanced at Misty's soiled slacks.

Misty laughed. "My head's not in the game today."

"We can do this another day." Beth gave a tight smile that didn't reach her eyes.

Misty shook her head. "Absolutely not. If you can put up with a little dirt …" She gestured to her clothing.

Beth brightened. "I don't mind at all."

"Good, then I'll put you to work." Misty motioned to her. "Come with me."

Beth followed Misty onto the terrace. "What can I do?"

"Grab a couple of those pots." Misty picked two African violets and led the way into the sunroom. "Put them anywhere you can find a shelf."

Beth carefully arranged the plants she'd brought in and stepped back. "I love your sunroom." Wistfully, she looked around the room. "Ooh, I've always wanted a chaise lounge." She ran her hand over the velvety floral print on the headrest.

Misty smiled. She'd never felt a particular attachment to any material item, probably because she'd lost so much over the last few years. Attachment wasn't part of her vocabulary—or her life. But the lounge was the nicest piece of furniture she owned. "Have a seat."

Beth's face clouded. "I hope you didn't think that was rude."

"No way." Misty plopped down in a recliner and motioned to the lounger. "I'm serious. Have a seat. I want to talk."

Beth giggled and settled into the plush cushioned seat. "I feel like royalty."

Misty snorted. "Well, you're in the wrong palace for that."

"It's nice to have this girl time."

"I know what you mean. I've missed it." Misty jumped up. "I forgot to offer you a drink. Iced tea?"

"Sounds great."

Misty returned moments later carrying a tray with a pitcher of tea, glasses, and a plate of cookies. She set it on the coffee table, poured Beth a glass of tea, and then one for herself.

"You know, I cut myself off from so many people during my marriage. Then one day, I discovered I had no friends." Misty sank down into the recliner.

Beth nodded. "I know exactly what you mean. When you finally escape, you feel like you're damaged goods—like you can't go back to the friendships you lost. You're not the same."

Misty longed to argue Beth's point, but she couldn't. It'd taken almost two years to reach the place where she could hold her head up and go back to work. Perhaps that's why she and Beth had formed such a bond. She was thankful she'd helped rescue Beth out of the vicious cycle she'd been trapped in for too long herself.

"No, we're not the same. But somehow we have to figure out how to go on—to become better in spite of it all."

Nibbling on the edge of a cookie, Beth stared out the window. The sun's rays streamed through the sheer drapery fluttering back and forth in the wind that flowed through the open window.

"It's the becoming better part that has me stumped," Misty finally spoke.

"How so?"

"Just when I think I'm past the anger and starting to feel whole again, something happens to trigger the past."

"What happened?"

Misty set her glass down. "You're very astute. I had a visitor a few days ago—Ryan's dad."

Beth's hand flew to her mouth. "Oh, no."

"Actually, the man who raised him. His biological father died when he was a baby." Beth's face softened. "That must have been awful."

"Like a blow from a sledgehammer." Misty rubbed her temples. She didn't really want to talk about Mr. Duncan when she hadn't processed his news, but she found she couldn't keep it inside. Beth would be the one person who could understand. "You'll never guess who it is." "I know him?"

"Mr. Duncan."

Beth clunked her glass onto the coffee table. Her eyebrows arched. "Mr. Duncan? Our Mr. Duncan?"

Misty laughed. "Is he ours?"

"You know what I mean. The one you introduced me to at church, your former patient."

Misty sobered. "Yeah, that's the one." She stood and paced the room. "It blindsided me, Beth."

"I can imagine."

"Of course, I forgave him for being the vile person he is, for teaching Ryan how to abuse women—"

"But?"

Misty spread her hands in front of her. "I'm angry."

Beth's eyes glistened. "Of course you are."

Misty moaned. "That's just it. I was past that stage—you know the five stages of grief you hear about. I'd gotten past the anger. Why now? Why did he have to come forward now?"

Smiling, Beth patted the chaise lounge and scooted over. Misty dropped down beside her. "You put me back together after I left my husband. I wish I had an answer for you, but I don't—not a simple one, anyway. With any grief, sometimes the hurt is fresh, like it happened yesterday."

Tears seeped down Misty's cheeks. "That's it exactly. I keep feeling myself falling from that window. Ryan sneering down and telling me I was going to die." She began to sob.

Beth put her arms around Misty. "But you didn't," she whispered. "You didn't die. Evil didn't win that day."

Misty snuffled one last sob and reached for a tissue. Wiping her cheeks, she determined right then she'd had enough of the past.

"Don't let it win now," Beth said emphatically.

Misty shook her head. "I don't intend to."

"That means letting go, once and for all, and—" Beth paused.

Misty turned to face her. "And?"

"And holding on to the good—moving forward."

"Like Adam?"

"Like Adam. He's a good man. Don't let him slip away. Don't let Ryan take your future, too." Beth smirked. "I hope I have a wedding to attend at some point."

Misty elbowed Beth playfully, and she giggled.

"Thank you, my friend."

"You're welcome."

Misty excused herself and went to the restroom to freshen up. She changed into a fresh pair of khaki slacks. It was time to get on with her life. At the top of that agenda was hiring an administrative assistant. And she knew exactly who it would be.

Chapter Twenty-Seven

Returning to the living room, Misty made a quick decision. "How about lunch? My treat."

"Sounds great." Beth beamed. She reached for her purse. "I don't get to eat out much on my budget."

"I have something to show you first."

Beth's eyebrows creased. "What?"

"Come along." Misty led her out and locked the door behind them.

Fifteen minutes later, they arrived at Hope House's temporary offices. Inside, Misty felt for the switch on the wall. The room flooded with light. Beth stepped into the office behind her.

"There's not much to it." Misty swept her hand in the air. "Just these two rooms, a bathroom, and a small storage closet outside, which we're not really using."

Beth peeked inside the other office then the bathroom.

"What do you think?"

"It's cozy." Her eyes twinkled with excitement as she ran her fingers over the leaves of a peace lily perched on a wrought-iron plant stand in a corner. "You've fixed the place up nicely."

Misty crossed her arms and waited while Beth surveyed the room. She would be the perfect assistant. "Only one problem."

"What's that?" Beth lifted the window blind and looked out. "View's not bad either."

"I need an assistant."

"I can see where there's probably too much work for one person." Beth retraced her steps to where Misty stood.

"Right now I can't give you more than about twenty hours a week."

Beth clasped her hands in front of her. "Oh, Misty, you mean work for you?"

"That's exactly what I mean. Would you like to be my administrative assistant?"

"I'd love it!" She threw her arms around Misty.

Laughing, Misty disentangled herself. "You haven't worked for me yet, so you don't know if you'll love it."

"Of course I will."

"Will the hours suit you?"

"It's more than zero, which is what I have now."

"You can work full time once the shelter opens." Misty dropped into the chair behind the desk and motioned for Beth in front of her. "Will you be able to handle that with your course load?"

"I'm almost finished with my degree." Beth bit her lip. "I need the paycheck more. I'll cut back my classes to part time, if need be."

Made sense. Beth would handle the job well. Misty had considered a few other applicants, but Adam had been adamant about finding a person she trusted above all else. She'd weighed the position carefully in her mind and examined her motives. Her employee choices included two other staff members whom she'd never met before. But for this particular position, Adam was right. It should go to someone she trusted to manage the daily functions of the shelter in her stead.

"Here's the salary and benefit package we can offer." Misty pulled a computer printout from the folder on her desk and placed it in front of Beth.

Glancing over the particulars, Beth nodded. "Looks good."

Misty smiled. "Then you're on board?"

"Absolutely."

Standing, Misty closed the folder. "Now let's go eat."

Beth grabbed her purse. "This is my kind of meeting."

***

Misty glanced through the new admissions the following week and noted Mr. Duncan's name. She scanned his admitting diagnosis. Internal bleeding. His cancer had returned. She draped her stethoscope around her neck, grabbed her notepad, and headed to his room.

Regardless of their history, she intended to give the man top-notch medical care. He was her brother in Christ. She refused to think of his role in Ryan's life.

Mr. Duncan's expression was flat when Misty pushed through the door of his room."How are we feeling today?" Maybe a cheery disposition would help his usually surly mood.

"I don't know about you, but I'm feeling poorly," he grumbled.

She inserted the ear thermometer and recorded his low temperature. Wrapping the blood pressure cuff around his large arm, she noted sores running along the length.

"Don't think I'm gonna make it this time."

"Hmm." Confirming his fears wouldn't help. She recorded his vitals in the chart.

"Is that all you got to say?"

Misty smiled. "I'm sorry. I was recording your vital signs." She tucked in his covers and rose to face him. "To be honest, I don't know how much time you have. Neither do you. I'd rather think positively about your chances with the medical care here at Oakview."

Mr. Duncan scowled. "Well, when you put it like that." He loosened the covers and reached for his cup of ice water.

Misty drew a chair closer to his bed and sat. "I don't want to discount your feelings, Mr. Duncan. They're valid, but I don't like to give in to pessimism."

He rolled his head toward her and attempted a smile, which ended up crooked. "You don't ever give up, do you?"

"No, I don't." Misty fished a small book from her pocket. "I've got a couple of minutes. Would you like me to read to you?"

"Out of the Bible?"

Misty smiled. "Yes. Psalms?"

He closed his eyes and settled his head on the pillow.

Misty began to read. She had managed to forgive this man. Her attempt to disconnect him from Ryan had succeeded. She glanced over the top of the book. He rested comfortably. Now if she could figure out how to disconnect herself from the past once and for all so she could get on with her life.

***

"Did you ask your parents about Thanksgiving?" Adam led Misty onto the dance floor at the country club. Slipping her hand into his, she glided in rhythm to his step.

"They're going to Europe, so I'm all yours."

Amusement danced in his eyes. "You don't say?"

Misty's cheeks grew warm. "You know what I mean."

"I'm a little dense. Why don't you explain it to me?" He twirled her around, before pulling her back into his arms. He gently maneuvered her through the maze of other couples on the dance floor.

She smiled. Adam's mood was contagious. Although she'd been resistant to spending a Saturday evening at the country club, she'd been pleasantly surprised by the laid-back atmosphere. High French doorways surrounded the brightly lit dance floor and led into the dining area and onto the terrace outside.

The band played softly. Misty leaned her head against his shoulder. She loved this man. More important than his rugged good looks, his quiet calm had attracted her. Calm she craved in her own heart. Why couldn't she get past her silly fear that he would hurt her?

Did she dare hope one day she'd have her head—and heart—straightened out enough to marry him? More importantly, would he wait for her or lose patience?

He kissed her forehead. "You seem a million miles away."

"You look different in a suit than your jeans and cowboy boots."

"That was random. But good to know you're fantasizing about me." His eyes sparkled.

"I didn't say that's what I was thinking about."

"You got me there. If I could get away with it, I might wear them here sometime." He gave her a crooked grin and another twirl.

"I believe you." Her own blue swoop-neck taffeta dress was modest compared to the other women in the club, but Adam had insisted she not overdress.

The music faded between numbers. Several other couples left the dance floor.

"Let's sit the next one out. I'm exhausted. I've worked every night this week." Misty glanced around. "I could use a cold drink."

Adam stopped a waiter and ordered two ginger ales. "Let's take our drinks and go onto the terrace. It's not too cold yet."

Misty followed him outside and sat by him on the loveseat. She sipped her soda, the bubbles tickling her nose. The starry sky reminded her of the night Adam had proposed. Her chest tightened. How many chances would she get to make the right choice? If only she could manage to choose wisely on the first try.

"Clear skies." Adam's gaze followed hers. "No rain to delay the construction."

"Hope House is never far from your mind, is it?"

He shook his head. "I guess not. Speaking of which, do you want to ride up to High Point to help me select furniture and flooring?"

"Is it already time to do the interior?" She swirled the drink stirrer around and fished out the cherry. "They have the best ginger ale here."

"Nice segue." He slid his arm around her. "Scared to leave the state with me?" He nestled close, his breath warm on her neck.

Her pulse tripped, and she snuggled closer. "Should I be?"

"Could be dangerous." He brushed a kiss along her chin, sending a tingling sensation rippling through her.

She pulled away, breaking contact. "Behave yourself. So, when would we go?"

"Yes, ma'am." He reached for his drink. "When's your next day off?"

"Wednesday."

"Is that too soon?"

Misty tilted her head and considered. "That'll work."

***

Monday morning Adam shuffled through Hope House paperwork his attorney had sent via courier. He pulled up their expense spreadsheet and ran figures through his calculator based on what he knew they were expecting to receive. Still short a hundred and fifty grand. He grimaced. Where would he get that kind of money?

He clicked on the file of his financial holdings for Jenkins Enterprises and pored through the stocks his company held. Maybe one or more could be sold without jeopardizing Jenkins Enterprises' strength. He clicked on the icons of his largest holdings and read through the specifications.

An hour later, a knock at the door interrupted his work. He swiveled forward and dropped the file onto his desk.

Dori stuck her head in. "Mr. Bowen is here to see you."

"Send him in."

Adam rose and shook hands with his attorney. "Good to see you, Max." He motioned to the chair in front of the desk then settled back into his chair. "Thanks for sending over the info." He leaned against the headrest. "Might as well get right to the point. The only thing left to do is to sell a few holdings."

Max shook his head. "Not a good idea, Adam. You'll jeopardize everything you've worked to build in Jenkins Enterprises. That company is your future."

"I disagree." He tapped the folder in front of him. "Hope House is my future. We've come too far to lose it. Besides, I think it's worth the risk. We're not talking that much in the scope of what my company is capable of earning. I'm branching out, breeding more horses than ever."

"Which means less liquidity until those horses actually get bred and colts are sold." He fished his smartphone from his pocket. "Let me make a few calls and see if I can get additional CEOs on board with funding."

Adam raised his hand. "No, Max. We've begged as much as we're going to." He relaxed again. "This may seem strange, but I feel like this is on my shoulders. This is for Jenny. I have to pay for this myself."

Max frowned. "Okay, if you insist. I'll shoot Ms. Stephens an email."

Adam drew a deep breath. "We're not going to tell her."

Max's eyes narrowed, pinning Adam with his stare. "Not a good idea, either. Why don't you borrow the additional funds?"

"I refuse to borrow against a charity, even if the bank would give me the funds, because there's no way to make money to pay it back. I'd use JE funds and borrow against the ranch, if need be."

Max's eyes widened. "What if your crops were to fail? Or an epidemic sweeps through your stock?"

Adam laughed. "Wow, I don't know how much more of your optimism I can stomach." He sobered. "That's in God's hands." He tapped his pen on the desktop. "The bottom line is, with the economy like it is, the stocks may take another tumble in value. It would probably be better to liquidate than borrow, anyway."

Max nodded.

"And we can't ask community leaders to pitch in any more than they have. I've managed to scale down the cost of this project by subcontracting things like landscaping and interior decorating. Misty and I are going to High Point to select interior designs and find subcontractors to install them. My parents chipped in a substantial donation, as did Colton."

He swallowed against the ache in his throat. The decision had not been easy. "This is on me, Max. Even with Mr. Duncan's donations, we're still a hundred and fifty grand short. I've found a way to solve the problem. Sell the stock."

Resigned, Max lifted his briefcase into his lap and clicked it open. He deposited the file Adam gave him. "I'll get on it right away." He stood and moved to the door.

"And another thing."

Max turned back. "Yeah?"

"Don't put it in all at once. Make several deposits."

Max's lips pursed. "Why?"

"It'll buy me some time with Misty."

Max shook his head. "You're treading on dangerous ground. She's your director. If she doesn't discover it, her assistant will."

"I have nothing to hide. I merely want time for the dust to settle and by then ..." Adam rubbed his chin.

"By then it'll be too late to talk you out of it." Max grinned.

Adam chuckled. "Something like that."

Chapter Twenty-Eight

Misty tried to focus on anything but the blur of the landscape as it flew by her window. Adam had picked her up half an hour before, and they had clocked good time en route to High Point, North Carolina, early Wednesday.

"Could you take it a little easy?" Misty clutched the door as Adam changed lanes on the interstate for the third time in the last quarter mile.

He grinned. "Sorry, I'm used to riding by myself."

"I see that." Her shoulders softened. She fished inside her purse for a pack of gum. "Care for a piece?"

"Sure."

"Don't be surprised by how the warehouse looks when we get there." Adam set his cruise control and settled back in his seat. "It's very stripped down, dusty floors, the whole nine yards. But in operating that way, they have little overhead. And believe me, we'll get the best prices within a 200-mile radius. I used them when I built my house."

"Well, I'm dressed for anything." Misty looked down at her tennis shoes and jeans. Adam smirked. "I see that."

Misty pulled her phone from her purse and made note of schedule changes from the hospital. She looked forward to switching to a PRN schedule. She couldn't continue to be divided between the hospital and Hope House. Though she loved nursing, the profession had become even more stressful during the years she was away. And she yearned to make a difference on a greater level than mentoring at the women's shelter on her days off.

"Anything important?" Adam glanced over at her.

"Schedule changes and a message from Beth." She slid her phone back into her purse and dropped it onto the floorboard at her feet.

Adam smiled. "You've done a good job with Beth."

"She's an amazing woman—which is why I hired her to be my assistant."

"You'll get no argument from me on that."

Misty tucked her hair behind her ears. "Her skills transcend what I expected."

"Always a nice surprise in an employee."

The traffic thinned, after they rounded the bustling city of Charlotte. Leaves still clung to the branches of the oaks and elms that dotted the sides of the road. The palette of crimson, auburn, and yellows blended like a Picasso painting as the cars brushed past.

Misty glanced at Adam. He rested his hand on the top of the steering wheel, gazing at the road. She was glad she'd agreed to come on the shopping trip. They were comfortable with each other. She frowned. And what was wrong with that? Did they have to ruin things by getting married?

Her breath caught. Where did that thought come from? Marriage wouldn't ruin their relationship. She firmly believed the Biblical concept of marriage, that it would strengthen them as a couple in a way they had not experienced before.

Misty rubbed her temples. Every time she made progress in her thinking, ugly precepts from her past life crept in.

"Why so quiet?" Adam's gaze fixed on her before looking ahead again.

Misty managed a smile. "Not to worry. Just thinking." One thing was certain. If she ever intended to be Adam's wife, she had to get her thoughts under control. Her strength after Ryan's death had surprised her. God's strength, really. When she reflected over the last year, her return to work, the success she'd enjoyed at the shelter with Beth, and working side by side with Adam to establish Hope House, she marveled at how her life was coming together. If she could only get over that last hurdle.

"We're a great team, aren't we?"

Adam's eyebrows arched as he stole a glance at her. "Yes—we are."

"I mean, Hope House is becoming a reality."

"Where is this headed?"

She looked at her hands. "Do you pray for me?"

"Where's this coming from?"

Misty shrugged. "Just wondering."

"Hold on." He carefully maneuvered his BMW off the exit ramp and into a travel center parking lot. He clicked off the ignition. Lifting her hand, he looked into her eyes. "I'm sorry I didn't tell you this sooner, but yes, I pray for you every day. Is there something specific that's wrong?"

"No. I needed to hear that." She caressed the top of his hand. "I know this sounds wishy-washy, but I'm still trying to figure out our relationship—what I want, who I am to you."

Adam shook his head. "Not wishy-washy at all. All of these things are important. We can't possibly hope to be husband and wife one day if you don't get these issues straightened out in your mind."

Her shoulders softened. Adam actually understood what she'd been trying to get across to him since she'd returned the engagement ring.

He chuckled. "Surprised you on that one, huh?"

She stroked the side of his face, brushing his hair back slightly with the tips of her fingers. He caught them in his and kissed them.

"I love you, Misty Stephens," he murmured. "You'll get everything sorted out, and then we'll talk marriage again—when you're ready."

"I don't deserve to have you wait on me."

"Deserving has nothing to do with it. Kind of like our salvation."

She listened, trying to follow his reasoning.

"Not that I'm so cocky to think I'm in the same class with our Savior, but I firmly believe the Bible when it says that man is to pattern himself after Christ." He paused. "That's especially important in the marriage relationship."

Misty's pulse raced with the realization of Adam's words. And she believed him. He was ten times the man Ryan had been. Despite that, her sense of inadequacy had not been overcome. Ryan had not taken her strength, but he'd taken her sense of security. Robbed her—like an identity thief.

"I believe you. The trouble is—I'm not quite there yet."

He gave her hand a final squeeze then restarted the car. "You'll get there, my love, don't worry."

Would she?

***

"We've looked through twelve different shades of green, Adam," Misty almost wailed later that afternoon. "Can we go with this one?" She plopped the sample onto the counter.

"Yes."

She laughed. "After all this going back and forth—yes? Just like that?"

His eyes glimmered. "Now will you settle on the floor sample so we can get back on the road before the five o'clock traffic hits Charlotte?"

Misty groaned. "Definitely." She walked back over to the assorted wood flooring samples. She picked up a light oak piece and motioned to him. "The hardwoods are the way to go. Trust me. You don't want linoleum." She was glad she wore her tennis shoes, but her feet ached from standing too long on the unfinished floors. And this her day off.

"Won't hardwoods be harder to maintain?"

"They're more durable."

He glanced at the time on his phone. "Okay, I'm going to let you win this argument, too."

"You." She started toward him.

He backed up and put his hands in the air in defeat.

"You didn't let me win anything." She smiled smugly. "You finally saw the light."

"Speaking of lights ..."

Misty dropped her head into her hands. "We haven't even been to the lighting department."

Adam waved his hand in the air to attract the salesman's attention. "These are the flooring and color samples we've agreed on. We're headed to the lighting department."

The salesman smiled, hurried over to the counter, and began jotting down their selections on the order form.

"I'll race you," Adam egged her on.

Misty raised her chin and sniffed. "Ladies don't race."

Adam shoved his hands into his jeans, his smile fading.

Misty glanced around. They were still the only customers in the showroom. She broke into a run.

"Hey! You cheated." He ran after her, their laughter filling the factory warehouse as the salesman shook his head.

When Adam caught up to her, he grabbed her and pulled her into his arms. "I guess silly ladies race." He kissed her. "That's your prize for winning."

She wriggled free. "You're the silly one. Now let's select the lights and get out of here."

Within the hour, they were climbing back into Adam's BMW with the invoices for the interior supplies for Hope House.

"This is exciting." Misty clicked on her seatbelt as Adam backed out of the parking lot.

"I agree. To see this come into fruition is a dream come true." He maneuvered his car onto the freeway and took the interstate ramp headed back to South Carolina.

"For Jenny."

Adam glanced over at her. "Yes, for Jenny."

"I'm not one for ignoring grief. But in this case, you've not really ignored it. You've turned it into something positive."

He nodded. "The holidays will be tough. But staying busy will be therapeutic." He grew quiet for a moment. "I want to open Hope House on January 1, Jenny's birthday."

Misty's throat tightened. "I didn't realize it was her birthday."

"It's okay." He glanced over his shoulder and changed lanes. Semis and travel trailers roared past.

"You know, this year, with work, meeting you guys, her death, it all feels like a blur now."

"I agree. These last few months I've been in a fog. A functioning fog, but a fog nevertheless. And nothing could ever fill the void left by Jenny's death. But she would be happy if she could see all the women we're helping."

Tears blurred Misty's vision, but she choked them back. "You're right, Adam."

They rode quietly for a few miles before Adam pointed out several billboards for restaurants. "We're not going to make it around Charlotte before five o'clock, and this traffic is already crazy. What say we pull into a Cracker Barrel and have an early dinner?"

"That's a great idea. I'm famished."

Adam took the next exit and found a convenient parking spot at the Cracker Barrel, jumped out, and got Misty's door for her. Joining hands, they walked inside.

She prayed the challenges with Hope House finances and finishing the project on schedule would come together in the weeks ahead. Adam's mood had changed decidedly in the last few miles. Was it just Jenny?

Misty glanced over at his sober expression as they reached the door of the restaurant. She didn't know where the money for Hope House's future would come from, but they only had to trust God.

With Him, all things were possible.

Surely, Adam believed that too.

***

They were seated right away, ordered iced tea, and then looked over the dinner menus. The fire crackled in the fireplace behind them. After the waiter placed their drinks on the table and took their order, Adam leaned back. Misty traced the top of her glass with her fingertip. He didn't know what he would have done, how he would have gotten through Jenny's death without her—without the promise of a future. He couldn't go it alone. At times, Misty seemed whole, but then she'd pull back. Something stood in her way—something she couldn't talk about. Well, he'd wait—forever, if he had to.

"Should I get with Dori about Thanksgiving?" Misty interrupted his thoughts.

"That would be a great idea. I'll leave the menu to you two." He reached for his Coke.

"I don't want her to go to a lot of trouble for me."

Adam sighed. He had to get Misty's hang-up with Dori straight, once and for all, or there would be a real problem when they married and Misty came to live at the ranch. If they ever married. He ran his hand through his hair.

"Dori is paid to take care of my house and cook for me. And she seems to really enjoy it."

Misty nodded. "Oh, I know. I guess I'm not used to having someone wait on me."

"Look at it this way. Dori has a job that maybe she wouldn't otherwise have with the economy like it is. The job's flexible—I'm flexible. I put no demands on her. She's free to run the house and the menu the way she sees fit." He covered Misty's hand with his own. "I don't want you to worry about it."

"I'll try harder."

"Good." He unwrapped his silverware from the cloth napkin. "Now, let's talk about Thanksgiving afternoon."

Misty's forehead crinkled. "What about it?"

"Let's plan to go riding. It's not very cold yet. I think if we ride after noon we should be back before dark. It may be our last opportunity for a long ride before winter sets in."

"Sounds like a plan."

Adam smiled. Horseback riding was the one activity where Misty seemed completely free. "Dress warm and casual. I want to take you to a new spot on the ranch, one I don't go to often because it's isolated. But it's well worth the ride."

Misty's face brightened. "I'm always up for an adventure."

Chuckling, he leaned back as the waiter arrived with their dinner plates. After he thanked the man, Adam said grace.

"This grilled salmon looks delicious." Misty forked the edge of the fish and lifted it to her mouth.

"Almost as good as my sirloin." Adam sliced through his steak.

"Mmm, it's as tasty as it looks." Misty closed her eyes as she chewed. "This was an excellent idea."

"The best one I've had all day, huh?" He lifted his iced tea glass.

She groaned. "Don't remind me of those warehouses. I don't want to see another carpet sample or paint swatch for the rest of my life. By the way, how are the donations coming along?"

"I think we'll be okay." Adam's heart pounded like a drum. He hadn't done anything wrong. Well, not technically. He owned Hope House and Jenkins Enterprises. He could do what he wanted. So why the guilt?

He rubbed his temple. He should tell her about the money. Sooner rather than later. But no sense in ruining the afternoon by talking about it now.

"When I looked at the budget a couple weeks ago, we were short quite a bit." Her eyes narrowed as she studied him.

"Nothing to worry about." Adam wiped the corner of his mouth with his napkin. "Let's get back to Thanksgiving. If it makes you feel any better, I always give Dori and the other employees the afternoon off, so we'll be on our own."

"I'm glad she'll have some time off. Does she have family?"

He shook his head. "Not around here. She's incredibly tight-lipped about her private life—at least with me. So, with the staff off, that means—"

Misty looked up from her plate. "Yes?"

"We'll have to get our own supper and clean up."

She clasped her hands to her cheeks. "Oh, no."

"Of course, my specialty is cold turkey sandwiches." He winked.

"Another one of my Thanksgiving favorites." She balanced her vegetables on her fork. "With little dill pickles?"

He rolled his eyes. "Yes, I'll make sure we have little dill pickles."

She grinned. "Great."

This woman would drive him nuts if he had to wait much longer to propose again. Silently, he prayed for God to intervene, do something—anything—to hasten his plans. Because, from the looks of things, Misty seemed perfectly content to carry on as companions—indefinitely.

Chapter Twenty-Nine

Misty flipped through the files in Hope House's temporary office. Moving to the new site would be wonderful, once it happened. She glanced at the calendar. Within the next month, they could anticipate moving the office over. A tingling sensation rippled through her. She smiled. Things were coming together perfectly.

She scanned the budget. Everything in and out appeared in order. Adam was right. The account held plenty of money. She stared out the window at the trees swaying in the blustery wind. Why had alarm bells gone off at Adam's response to the budget question during dinner the week before? They'd had a wonderful day on the road. Maybe he was simply tired of dealing with the money issue and that's why he'd blown her off. She chewed the end of her pen. Probably her lack of trust rearing its ugly head again when Adam was innocent.

God, forgive me.

Humming a hymn from yesterday's church service, Misty pulled a Post-It from the pad and jotted a quick note to Beth. The bank statements needed reconciling. With Beth's bookkeeping background and coursework, it'd be the perfect task to delegate. Misty dropped the tagged file into the tray. With everything in order, she had enough time to run to the produce market before her shift at the hospital began.

Thirty minutes later, she stopped at her house long enough to toss the produce into the refrigerator and change into her work clothes.

At the hospital, Misty hurried to the nurse's station to take report from the previous shift nurse. Perusing the patient roster, she noted Mr. Duncan had been sent home. She smiled. Good news, she hoped.

"You're perked up after having a few days off." Danielle slid into the computer chair beside her.

"It was wonderful." Misty twirled the end of her ponytail between her fingertips. "High Point was beautiful, and it's always fun to spend time with Adam."

"I'll bet." Danielle chuckled and turned to the computer.

Misty laughed. "How did things go here?"

"Busy, as always." Danielle glanced over and smiled. "I'm glad you're back, though. I miss your efficiency when we're training the new hires."

"Thanks." She hadn't told anyone except Leah about her plan to scale back her work hours to part time. The frown lines settling around Danielle's eyes told her this wasn't the time to share the information. Instead, Misty stood. "I'll be back."

Danielle nodded her response and continued checking patient data.

An hour later, Misty had completed her rounds and hurried back to the desk. Maybe she could squeeze in a short phone call while the floor was quiet. Danielle must still be with her patients. Misty dropped into a chair and reached for the phone.

"Hi, Dori." Misty frowned. Adam normally answered his own phone. "Where's Adam?"

"Hi, Ms. Stephens. He's in with his attorney. Said not to disturb him."

"Nothing serious, I hope."

"No. He's been here a few times this week. Something to do with Hope House. But you know more about that than I do." Dori gave a soft chuckle.

Misty's heart skipped a beat. Was there something going on with the project she wasn't privy to? She nibbled at the edge of her fingernail.

"Are you still there, Ms. Stephens?" Concern laced the housekeeper's voice.

Misty straightened. "Oh, I'm sorry. Yes. Would you let Adam know I called and I'll catch up with him later?"

"Sure thing."

Misty dropped the receiver into its base and felt an uneasiness stirring inside her. Was her God-given instinct trying to steer her away

LAURA HODGES POOLE

from trouble or was her overactive imagination trying to derail her life? She rubbed her temples and replayed the conversation with Dori in her mind. Mr. Bowen had been there several times on Hope House business. If Hope House was in jeopardy, shouldn't she know?

Her stomach flopped.

What was Adam hiding?

***

"What do you feel like for lunch?" Beth stacked the folded moving boxes into an office corner out of the way.

"Is it already that time?" Misty glanced at the clock.

Beth grinned. She grabbed a dust cloth from the small closet and wiped the window ledge where dirt had spilled from a plant. "No, I'm thinking ahead."

"You make me hungry when you do that." Misty dug through her purse for a pack of gum. She withdrew two sticks and extended one to Beth. "Here, that'll get your mind off food."

"Thanks." Tossing her wrapper in the trash, Beth sank into a chair next to Misty. "The bank statements are balanced. Is there anything else I can do?"

Misty considered. "You've caught up everything." She snapped her fingers. "I meant to ask. How did the account look?"

Beth's smile spread to her eyes. "It looks great. We actually have a surplus now. Not much, but it's better than being in the red like last month."

Misty arched an eyebrow. "So we received extra donations?"

"I guess. Funny thing is several of the deposits were similar."

Misty's pulse skipped. She studied her friend. "All the same amount?"

Beth's face clouded. "Basically. What's wrong?"

Misty forced a smile. "Nothing. I hope." She glanced out the window. Adam's BMW pulled into the lot and rolled to a stop under a shade tree. Her mind twisted with questions. "I think I'm ready for lunch after all. Since you're current on everything around here, why

235

don't you run pick us up something?"

Beth's gaze followed Misty's to Adam walking across the parking lot then back to Misty, questions filling her eyes.

"Hi, ladies." Adam dropped his briefcase on his desk and kissed Misty on the cheek.

Beth reached for her purse. "Sorry to run out on you, but Misty's hungry."

Adam's eyes twinkled. "Already?"

"I'm getting there." Misty fished a twenty-dollar bill from her wallet and extended it to Beth. "A veggie sandwich on wheat from Schlotzsky's Deli, if you don't mind."

Beth pocketed the money. "Sounds delicious. I'll be back shortly."

"No rush." Misty swiveled to the computer and logged onto the Hope House accounts.

Adam's eyebrows creased. "What's up?"

"Does anything have to be up?" She straightened.

He perched on the corner of her desk and crossed his arms. "I've had warmer receptions."

She attempted a laugh. "I'm going over the bank account for Hope House." Did she imagine it or did he flinch?

Adam slid from the desktop and leaned over her computer monitor. "Is there a problem?"

She leaned back and looked into his eyes. "Hope not. We seem to have a surplus where we didn't a month ago. Where did it come from?"

His smile tightened. "Jenkins Enterprises."

Tossing her pen onto the desktop, she frowned. "I thought you felt intermixing the two would jeopardize JE."

"I changed my mind."

"Just like that?"

His forehead creased. "It had to be done. The contractor has to be paid regularly. I couldn't let the project fall behind. It would end up costing me more in the long run."

Her stomach churned. "Why didn't you tell me you were transferring funds to make up the shortfall?"

He shrugged as if the answer were so simple it was hardly worth mentioning. "I figured it would come up soon enough."

She pushed her chair away from the desk and walked to the window. Trying to get control of her emotions, she finally faced him. "How many times have we brainstormed about where to get the extra money?"

"Several."

"Exactly." She didn't like the way he was forcing her to drag the information out of him. Her chest burned with anger. "Stop playing games with me, Adam."

His eyes narrowed, his smile vanishing. "I don't know what you mean. I transferred money from my company." He paused. "It's legal, and I have the right to do what I want with my money."

The flames radiated from her chest into her neck and spread to her face. "I'm your director." She held his gaze without blinking. "You don't get it, do you?"

His forehead crinkled. "No, I guess I don't." He raked his hand through his hair. "I mean, I knew you would try to talk me out of taking more money from JE, but I didn't think you'd be angry. I didn't want you worrying about the money anymore. I took care of it."

Misty shook her head. "Oh, Adam, you're not that foolish."

His eyes widened. "Foolish?"

"Yes, this has to do with respect ... and trust. And the fact it was such a small thing makes me wonder what you'd do if something major came along. I'm your director." She tapped the desk to drive home her point. "I should be included in all decisions. Don't you respect me enough to let me voice my opinion and know I'd acquiesce to you in the end? As you said, Hope House is your project."

Adam rubbed the back of his neck. "I'm sorry. And to answer your question, yes, apparently I am that foolish."

She winced. "I'm sorry I used that word."

He reached for her hand. "You were right."

Her hand felt small and cold against his. He'd hurt her. She longed to slip into his embrace, for him to tell her everything would be all right. But would it?

She pulled her hand away. "Is there anything else I don't know?"

Her words were like arrows stinging as they hit their target and he flinched.

His eyes reflected remorse. "No, there isn't. I convinced myself shielding you was the right thing to do, but I get it now. I really do. And I won't keep anything else from you. I promise." He laid his hand across his heart.

Her shoulders softened and her gaze dropped. Could she trust that? "Well?"

She lifted her head. "Well what?"

"Do you forgive me?"

Tears moistened her eyelashes. "Yes."

"Can we put this behind us and move forward?"

Misty slipped into his arms then. "Of course," she murmured against his chest. She squeezed her eyes shut against the memory of his firing Ted a few months earlier. And worse yet, the sickening familiarity of betrayal that Ryan had imprinted on her heart. Every time she and Adam managed to take a few steps forward something knocked them back a step. She prayed nothing else would materialize to undermine her trust in Adam.

Somehow she had to get over this obstacle that stood in the way of their happiness.

***

Adam looked at the calendar. The third week in November, with Thanksgiving in a few days and Hope House opening soon after Christmas. His heart ached at not having Jenny to spend the holidays with for the first time in his life. Colton had refused to come to South Carolina. Adam was sure it had everything to do with his unresolved grief and anger toward God.

Adam sighed. Some days his own grief was as fresh as if Jenny had died yesterday. How could he expect Colton to do any better, especially when he insisted on going it alone?

Tossing his jacket over the back of the couch, Adam glanced around for Dori. It wasn't like her not to greet him when he came in. Footsteps sounded in the hallway.

"Mr. Jenkins, I didn't hear you. I was in the pantry rearranging for Thanksgiving." Dori wiped her hands on her apron and reached for his jacket.

He motioned her away. "Don't worry about it. I'm going to the stables to talk to James. Has Misty called you?"

Dori smiled. "Yes, we've got the meal planned. I'm looking forward to spending time with her."

Adam nodded. "Good. I'm glad it's worked out."

"She was a little shy at first." Dori opened the hall closet. "Would you hand me that box off the top shelf?"

Adam slid the box down. "Misty shy?"

"Quiet?"

He closed the door and followed her back to the foyer. "Well, whatever it was, I'm glad you two are growing closer."

She opened the box and began to unpack the Thanksgiving decorations. "I'll pick up fresh squash and gourds from the store to accent these."

"Do what you want, Dori. The finished product is always beautiful." Adam turned toward the living room. "I'm headed to the stables."

He shrugged into his jacket and stepped outside. The least of his problems—Dori and Misty's relationship—had flourished. If he could solve his own stupidity … How could he have made such a blunder with the funds from JE?

Lord, help me to see beyond my nose when it comes to money and Misty. She was right. My decision didn't show her the respect she deserved—as director or as my future wife.

He'd hoped to give her the engagement ring again during the holidays. Had he totally blown that?

James came through the stable doorway and pulled the heavy wooden door shut behind him. "Mr. Jenkins."

"James, would you make sure the white stallion and Bella are both groomed and properly shod before Thanksgiving morning?"

"Yes, sir. Going riding with Ms. Stephens?" James flashed a rare smile.

"Up to the north ridge."

James's smile faded. "Kind of a long ways for an afternoon ride."

Adam shook his head. "We probably won't ride to the top of the ridge, but I haven't been to that part of the ranch since the last storms blew through. I thought I'd combine sightseeing with a little reconnaissance. I'd hoped to get up there this week, but it hasn't happened."

"Do you want me to ride up there and check it out?" James shoved his hands in his jeans pockets and squinted at Adam.

"No, it'll be fine."

James nodded. "I'll make sure everything is in order with the horses then."

Adam clapped his hand on the older man's shoulder. "What would I do without you?"

"Probably wouldn't ever want to find out."

Adam's laugh echoed through the valley. "You're in a good mood this afternoon."

"Just life. It's treating me well." He reached for the pitchfork. "Gotta finish feeding now. Anything else?"

"No. Thanks, James." He faced the valley as James disappeared inside. His orchard sloped up the hillside toward the blueberry and strawberry fields. A bumper crop of apples had reenergized his bottom line at JE. Now the trees rapidly fading in color would lay bare until the following spring. The last storm did little damage to the blueberries and strawberries. He'd keep a close eye on the fields over the winter and cover them if temperatures grew severe.

Adam rubbed his chin. If only life were as simple as farming. Storms passed through, he cleaned up afterwards, he moved on. Farmers anticipated problems and planned accordingly. Outcomes weren't guaranteed, but he still cycled through the same basic challenges year in and year out.

How could he have misjudged a decision so horribly when it came to Misty? He would never make the mistake of violating her trust again, but was it too late? Could the damage be undone?

Chapter Thirty

Misty ran her hand over her hair to smooth it from the blustery November wind. Clutching her large tote bag laden with a broccoli casserole, cherry cream dessert, and macaroni salad, she pressed the doorbell and waited. Dori answered and stepped aside to let Misty in. The aroma of turkey and dressing, as well as freshly baked pumpkin and apple pies, teased Misty's senses. Different shades of small orange and yellow pumpkins and squash surrounded by an array of autumn decorations dotted the foyer table.

"Happy Thanksgiving, Ms. Stephens." Dori flashed a smile and motioned Misty in. She reached for Misty's bag. "Wow, did you bring the kitchen sink?"

"Almost. I'm sure it won't compare to what you've prepared." Misty joined in Dori's laughter. "Happy Thanksgiving to you, as well, Dori. My, you're chipper today."

"My most favorite holiday. Let me take your coat."

Misty slipped out of her jacket and handed it to the housekeeper. Adjusting the burgundy sweater over her camisole blouse, Misty hoped she didn't look as windblown as she felt. She noticed Dori wore a beautiful short-sleeved dress with little cornflowers dotting the light auburn print. Her hair was pulled back fashionably. Casual flats completed her outfit.

"Dori, you look beautiful." Misty's cheeks warmed. "I mean—you always look beautiful—but, today—"

Dori beamed and clasped her hands in front of her. "Thank you. I told you this is my favorite holiday." Her smile wavered. "Really the only holiday I enjoy."

Unsure how to respond, Misty looked down at her own casual outfit. "I feel a little underdressed."

Dori waved aside her words. "You're not. I get a little carried away sometimes. Besides, Mr. Jenkins is wearing jeans."

"Good." Misty followed her into the kitchen and unloaded her bag. "I'll help you put the food on the table later."

"There's time yet. The turkey isn't quite finished. I'm kind of at a standstill for a few moments until the potatoes finish boiling."

"Let's see what Adam's up to, then." Misty tucked her arm into Dori's. They walked into the living room where Adam was seated in front of the fireplace.

"Well, don't you two look chummy?" He stood, kissed Misty on the cheek, and motioned for her to have a seat on the sofa.

"Do you need anything?" Dori asked.

He glanced at Misty, who shook her head. "How about a pitcher of water for now?"

"Okay, I'll be right back."

"No rush." Adam sat next to Misty on the sofa. She slipped her hand into his.

"After I drain the vegetables then." Dori grinned and left the room.

"Have I told you that I love you?" Adam's eyes teased down at her.

She tilted her head. "Maybe once or twice."

"And that you're absolutely gorgeous?"

"Keep going." She grinned.

He cupped the side of her face with his hand and gently kissed her. "I'm thankful I have you in my life."

His expression broke her heart. She loved him more than life itself, so why couldn't she commit to a lifetime with this man? She snuggled up to him, and he put his arm around the back of the sofa.

"Especially with this being the first holiday without Jenny."

Misty searched his face. "I imagine it's pretty difficult."

His eyes glistened. He'd not cried in her presence since the night under the moonlight out on the ridge. She leaned her head against his.

"It's okay to be sad," she whispered.

He drew her into a hug, clinging to her like a lifeline. After a moment, he spoke. "Jenny being gone makes me very sad, but the emptiness is softened by you."

Adam pulled away and brushed a wayward hair from her face. "Now, let's talk about happy things, not the sad times. That's what Jenny would want."

"I agree. Let's check out the view." Misty stood and walked to the terrace window.

Adam followed. "Beautiful day, isn't it?"

"Hmmm." A few colorful leaves still clung to the branches of the elms and oaks, but most lay in piles, crisp and brown. An invisible dust devil stirred a pile, gently lifting the leaves before settling them back down.

"Wanna take a walk before lunch?"

Misty smiled. "Let's."

They strolled arm in arm through the terrace gardens and down the path leading to the stables. Adam opened the large barn door, and Misty stepped over the threshold. She went straight to Bella's stall. The paint whinnied and nuzzled Misty's arm, making her giggle. "Oh, I've missed you." She leaned her head against Bella's and ran her hand through her mane.

"Still your favorite, I see." Adam grabbed a couple of carrots from the bin and handed them to Misty.

She held one out to the horse. Bella's lips drew the carrot in as she chewed.

"Sometimes I think you come to the ranch to see her." Adam winked.

Misty extended the other carrot to him. "Bella will share."

He snorted with laughter. "But will she share you?"

"Why don't you ask her?" Misty laughed with him. She gave the carrot to Bella and dusted her hands in the air.

"I'm glad you wore jeans and tennis shoes." Adam closed the bin. "Although you'll need a heavier jacket."

Misty frowned. "It's not that cold."

Adam took her hand, and they stepped over the stable threshold outside. He shut the barn doors behind them.

"It will be by early evening. I don't venture far from the ranch without being prepared. We might not get back to the stables before dusk, since we're not leaving until later in the afternoon."

"Is it that far?"

Adam nodded. "Almost two miles over somewhat rocky terrain. Plus, we want to take our time and enjoy the scenery along the way."

"Wow, I had no idea."

"It's the way the road meanders through my property. Probably closer to a half mile as the crow flies."

He slipped his arm around her shoulder, and Misty snuggled in closer as they walked. "If we're going to ride later, I should get back to help Dori, don't you think?"

"Good idea."

***

Misty hurried inside and found Dori ready to remove the turkey from the oven. Misty quickly washed her hands and put on an apron.

"Hold the platter, and I'll lift the turkey out of the pan," Dori instructed.

She slid the bird onto the platter and then set it on the counter. The heat of the oven rushed over her, as Misty stepped up to put the biscuits in the empty oven and set the timer. The two ladies stood back to admire the glistening brown bird. Dori wiped her hands on the apron covering her dress.

"You did a wonderful job with the meal, Dori." Misty blew a scraggly hair out of her face and dabbed her forehead with a paper towel.

"It's my job, but a big meal like Thanksgiving is also fun."

"How so?"

"Mr. Jenkins doesn't eat much, and there's not much to prepare since Jenny—." Dori's face clouded. "I'm sorry."

"I know what you mean. Don't apologize." She twisted a dish towel in her hand and studied Dori at the stove. "May I ask you something?"

"Sure." She stopped mashing the potatoes and faced Misty.

"Why do you call Adam 'Mr. Jenkins' and me 'Ms. Stephens?' Does Adam require that?"

Dori wiped her hands on a dish towel, then draped it over her shoulder. "Makes things easier. It was my idea."

"I don't follow."

"If he has business associates over or even you, for instance, what would you've thought if I'd walked in calling him Adam?"

Misty tilted her head and considered. "I see what you mean."

Dori smiled then lifted the pot of potatoes off the stove and quickly scooped them into a serving bowl. She dropped a dollop of butter into the center of the vegetables. "If you'll start taking the serving dishes to the dining room, I think we're about ready to eat."

Adam pushed open the kitchen door and stuck his head in. "Need any help in here, ladies?"

"Just in time." Misty motioned to the turkey. Adam followed her into the dining room carrying the turkey platter. Once everything was placed on the table, Dori removed her apron and stepped into the living room to get James.

Everyone gathered around the table. Adam reached for Misty's hand. He cleared his throat.

"It seems a little empty this year," he said gruffly. "But take a hand, and I'll ask the blessing."

Misty's heart swelled with emotion as she took Dori's hand in her other hand, and James completed the circle. They bowed their heads.

"Heavenly Father," Adam began, "We ask your blessing on this food and on our lives in the coming year. Though our hearts are heavy with those missing, we're very grateful we have each other. Thank you for the people you've brought into our lives this year. Strengthen our bodies and our spirits for Your service. In Your Son's name, we pray."

"Amen," they chorused.

Adam squeezed Misty's hand before releasing it, and she smiled. Jenny's empty spot had to be unbearable for Adam. Misty prayed God would give him and his family extra comfort to carry them through the holiday.

Adam carved the turkey as the others passed the serving dishes around. They took turns handing their plates to him, and he placed slices of steaming hot turkey on them.

"It smells delicious." James spooned gravy onto his potatoes. "You've outdone yourself this year, Dori."

Dori's cheeks flushed. "Thank you, James."

Misty glanced from James to Dori, who displayed a shy smile. Misty could hardly wait to get Dori alone to find out what that was all about. She grinned.

Adam caught her eye. "What's so amusing?"

"Oh, nothing." Misty lifted a forkful of dressing to her mouth to avoid having to say anything more.

Adam turned his attention to his housekeeper. "Dori, do you have plans this afternoon?"

"I'll call my sister in California, then settle in to read a good book that's been sitting on my desk for a while now."

Adam gave her a reassuring smile. "Sounds like a pleasant afternoon. What about you, James?"

"Nothing much for an old bachelor to do by himself on a holiday," he replied. "Stores are mostly closed. Too early for Christmas shopping, anyway, in my opinion."

Adam chuckled. He forked another slice of turkey onto his plate and added a scoop of cranberry sauce.

"It's a shame you'll be alone," Misty chimed in.

"Oh, I don't mind, Ms. Stephens. Been that way for so long, it's hard to think of something different." He glanced at Dori before he picked up his glass of tea and took a drink.

"Seems to me—" Misty felt herself being poked with a sharp object under the table. Her eyes widened when she realized it was Dori's fork. She covered her mouth with her napkin to keep the giggles from erupting.

"What's that you were saying?" Adam winked at her.

So, everyone was aware of Dori's crush—except for the object of the crush, it would seem. Though given his wistful look, surely it wouldn't take much for James to be made aware.

"Just that I hope everyone enjoys their afternoon off." Misty reached for her glass. "You both work so hard for Adam that you deserve it."

"Are the horses ready for our ride?" Adam asked James.

"Yes, I checked them this morning. They've been fed and watered."

Adam set his fork down and wiped his mouth. "Dori, that was a delicious meal."

Dori beamed. "Thank you, Mr. Jenkins. Ms. Stephens was a lot of help."

Misty shook her head. "Very little compared to your hard work."

"Thanks." Dori stood to clear the table. "How 'bout some pie?"

"Might have room for a piece of pumpkin." Adam rubbed his stomach.

Misty laughed. "I'll take a small piece of apple."

"I'll help you." James tossed his napkin on the table and reached for the turkey platter.

Dori's cheeks reddened. She stacked the empty dinner plates, and James followed her into the kitchen.

Misty squeezed Adam's arm. "Ooh, did you see that?" she squealed softly.

"You've got quite a grip there." Adam winced playfully. "Yeah, I've known Dori has a crush on him. Seems he's finally starting to figure it out."

Misty rubbed her hands together. "It's exciting, don't you think?"

"Romance is definitely exciting, Missy." He leaned over and kissed her.

"It can be." Misty put her arms around his neck, drew him closer, and kissed him again. "Seriously, though, wouldn't it be great if they got together? Dori seems lonely."

Adam frowned. "She does. I can never get her to talk about her life. She's closed up tighter than a clam." He paused. "It seems odd she doesn't appear to have any family, none that she speaks of, anyway. That makes me think she's had some heartache—probably something fairly deep."

Before Misty could wonder what Dori's heartache might have been, the kitchen door opened. Dori carried a tray filled with slices of apple and pumpkin pie. James followed close behind with a pot of coffee.

"You read my mind." Adam reached for the coffee pot.

They drank their coffee and ate the pie at a leisurely pace. No one wanted the dinner to end. The kitchen needed to be cleaned and put in order before the long ride Adam had promised. The time was nearing two o'clock, and sunset came early. Misty roused herself.

"Dori, I'll help you with the dishes."

"Thank you."

Misty piled plates on the empty tray. Adam and James grabbed the cups and followed the ladies into the kitchen. As Misty and Dori loaded the dishwasher, the men brought the rest of the food into the kitchen and began putting it into containers. Half an hour later, with the kitchen in order, the men excused themselves.

Dori stacked the last of the dishes into the dishwasher, then wiped her hands on the dish towel.

"I guess that about does it." She draped the towel over the drawer handle. "Do you need anything else before I leave?"

Misty considered for a moment. "No. I think we'll be fine. Thank you for all the hard work you put in today."

Dori smiled. "My pleasure."

They hung their aprons on the hook by the door. Misty followed Dori to the living room where James and Adam were discussing ranch business and watching football.

Adam stood. "All finished?"

"Yes," Dori said. "I'm leaving now, if that's okay."

"Sure." Adam pulled two envelopes from his pocket and handed one to Dori and the other to James. "I appreciate your diligence. It's nice to have two trusted employees. This has been a rough year, and unlike some, you've gone out of your way to make my life easier."

Dori's eyes misted. "Thank you." She tucked the envelope into her pocket and hugged Adam.

James shook his hand. "I appreciate it."

"No problem." Adam put his arm around Misty's shoulder. She clasped her hands in front of her.

"I'll see you out," James said to Dori as he helped her put on her coat.

"Thank you, James."

Misty nudged Adam, who grinned back at her. Once the other two were safely out of earshot, Misty squealed. "Oh, I hope they get together. They're both lonely."

Adam pulled her into his arms. "What about me?"

Misty shot him a glance. "You look pretty satisfied to me."

"It's the lunch."

Giggling, Misty allowed herself to be drawn closer. He stroked her hair. She smiled. Life couldn't get any better than this. Marriage or not, what she had with Adam far exceeded her marriage to Ryan. Despite their spat over Hope House funds, she was comfortable with their relationship. She looked into Adam's eyes. God would work out her trust issues in His perfect timing.

"Penny for your thoughts."

She leaned back. "Just thinking about how fortunate we are and how happy I am with our relationship. Life's pretty good, huh?"

His eyebrows arched before a smile settled on his lips. "It is."

Was that disappointment that flashed across his face?

"Are you ready for that ride now?" Adam locked the front door and switched off the foyer light.

"Lead the way."

Chapter Thirty-One

Adam held Bella's reins and offered his hand for Misty to swing herself into the saddle. He mounted the other horse, a three-year-old stallion, sure-footed and steady. Although he'd been to this part of the ranch numerous times, it had been months since he'd ridden this path. He'd meant to check it out prior to today, but between ranch business and Hope House, time had gotten away from him.

Adam gave a command, and the stallion started trotting. Bella fell in line behind him.

With the sun halfway across the afternoon sky, it would likely be dark before they returned. He needn't worry. The horses were sure-footed and could find their way home once back on level ground. The moon would be full. He'd given Misty a heavy jacket to wear. Water canteens hung from their saddles. He'd pocketed a sturdy flashlight and insisted Misty carry a smaller one.

Adam understood Misty's attraction to riding. More than once he'd sought the refuge of the wide expanse of the ranch when life had overwhelmed him. It brought him closer to God and away from his problems. Now, if he could only figure out how to get her and their relationship to the next level. She'd grown way too comfortable with the boyfriend-girlfriend routine.

When the path widened, he motioned for her to pull alongside him. The smile beaming from her face spoke volumes about her mood.

"Having a good time?"

"Incredible," she gushed. "I never tire of riding this beautiful horse." Misty rubbed Bella's neck and she whinnied in response.

He laughed. "Well, I can see you two are inseparable."

"Bella's a good horse. Sure-footed."

"You'll appreciate that in a few minutes."

Misty frowned. "That bad?"

"No, a little rocky. Nothing we can't handle." He urged his horse on at a faster pace. Bella matched his step. She wasn't going to be outdone by the stallion. Misty smiled at the horse's antics.

The terrain grew rockier. Adam tightened his reins to allow his horse time to gain its footing.

"You weren't kidding." Misty clutched her reins tighter. "I had no idea your ranch had land like this."

Adam stopped. "All of this is hidden from the ranch proper." He swept his arm toward the south from where they'd ridden. "We'll plateau out in a minute, and it'll be a nice break from the rough terrain. The last break, I should add."

Misty turned to look. The ranch had disappeared from sight. "Wow, it's really isolated out here."

Adam flashed a smile. "Which is a good thing. Let's enjoy the quiet before the busy week begins."

"You're right." Misty urged Bella on as they hit a patch of ground that was wide open pasture. She broke into a trot. Adam's horse matched her stride until they came upon a stream.

"Bella doesn't care for water, so be careful crossing." Adam grabbed Bella's bridle, and Misty spoke to her as they crossed the shallow water. The horse whinnied in protest, but Misty kept rubbing her neck.

"The rest of the way should be fine." Adam released the bridle. "We've had some storms, but I've never had problems up here."

Misty looked around at the rocky terrain intermixed with oaks, elms, and pines. Although the oaks and elms were almost leafless, the pines still had their green needles. She gently guided her horse straight up the hilly path and followed closely behind Adam.

"Are you ready for a break?"

"Sure."

He tied his horse to a tree and helped her down. They walked hand in hand across the ridge and looked at the creek below. The sound of trickling water combined with the trees rustling.

"This is relaxing." Misty couldn't think of a better way to spend

Thanksgiving afternoon. It'd been the best one she'd had in years. She hoped it was the beginning of more to come.

"If you squint, you can see the top of the ranch house down there." Adam pointed in the direction they'd ridden from.

She shaded her eyes with her hands. "Wow, we've ridden quite a distance."

He glanced at the sun low on the horizon. "Yes, and there's still more to see. Next time, we'll start earlier so we can linger and enjoy the scenery. Let's go up the trail a ways then head back." His brow crinkled. "I don't want to be caught up here after dark. I'd feel better if we were closer to the ranch when dusk settles."

Misty searched his face. She trusted his instincts, though sensed no danger herself. It had been a beautiful, sunny day with no hint of storms or clouds that could roll in and block the moon when it rose. They remounted and rode in silence as the horses trotted.

"Around this next bend is a beautiful view of Hope House and my orchards," Adam called back over his shoulder.

Misty pushed Bella to keep pace with Adam's horse. As they rounded the bend, he carefully navigated around a small drop-off. Misty followed closely. He led her to a tiny clearing and they dismounted. Misty tied Bella next to Adam's horse.

"Oh, this is beautiful." Misty pulled her sunglasses from atop her head and put them on. "This is a bird's eye view of your entire property."

"Jenny loved it up here." His gaze surveyed the outlying property.

Misty squeezed his hand. "I thought all the other spots on the ranch were beautiful, but I think this is my favorite. Too bad it's difficult to reach. I see why you don't come here often."

"It's a full afternoon's ride, for sure." He whisked one of the canteens off the horse and handed it to her.

Misty took a long drink of the cool, refreshing water before recapping the canteen. Adam did the same with the other one.

"We have so much to look forward to, Misty." He slipped his arms around her from behind. She grasped his arms and leaned against his chest.

"Hope House opens in a little over a month." She tingled with excitement. "I'm starting to get butterflies."

"Me, too. It'll be a huge responsibility to process women and children through on a daily basis."

"I'm glad the funding fell into place."

"Mostly, thanks to Mr. Duncan."

Misty no longer cringed at the man's name. "He's been very generous."

"Indeed. You'll be here for Christmas?"

She turned to him. "I wouldn't miss it. Am I helping Dori again?"

Adam's brow crinkled. "Actually, she always takes Christmas week off. Obviously, I want her to take the holidays and spend them with her family, but like I said, I'm not sure if she has any, at least not around here. She's very flexible, but not about Christmas. It was a condition of her employment."

"That's odd." Misty considered what he said. "Not that she'd want Christmas off. I can see that, but why so adamant? Do you think there's anything wrong?"

He shrugged. "I don't pry. She's such a good employee. She's open and friendly, but she's entitled to her privacy. After all, I'm her employer."

Misty nodded. "What do you do for food?"

Adam's laughter echoed through the valley. "There are stores, and I can cook."

"You?"

"That's right. Actually, I'm even better with a phone than a stove. I order a meal and pick it up from a local restaurant."

Misty smiled. "I'm impressed."

"What? That I can drive or that I can pick up food?"

She laughed. "You're terrible, you know that?"

"I know." He grew serious. "I'm self-sufficient but not so much that I can take care of the housecleaning and cooking duties for this ranch and run Jenkins Enterprises at the same time."

A rustling in the grass caught Misty's attention. She recoiled from the noise, expecting a snake to slither out of the brush. She grabbed Adam's arm and pulled him in front of her.

Adam chuckled. "It's probably just a chipmunk rustling for food."

"Nevertheless, I'll stay here until I'm sure." She peered around Adam just as a little ball of fur scurried out of the brush and disappeared into the woods.

"Bella doesn't like snakes, either. Good thing it wasn't one." He untied the reins and handed Bella's to Misty. He swung onto his horse's back and pulled him sideways.

"Thanks for the info." Misty mounted, spoke to Bella, and fell in line behind Adam again. The terrain grew rockier as they climbed higher along the trail. She was amazed to see the neighboring farm and, beyond that, the slim line of a highway.

"We'll turn around in that flat spot up ahead." Adam pointed. "Be careful, the path gets narrow."

Rocks crumbled from the path as the horses climbed the last few feet. Adam navigated the turnaround, but before Misty could follow, chunks of rock slid from under his horse. The stallion screamed in terror. Adam sawed the reins back and forth to gain control. He spoke to the horse, his voice calmer than Misty felt as he tried to steady the horse. She looked over her shoulder and began to coax Bella back. She felt the hysteria transferring from Adam's horse to hers.

"Easy girl, it's okay."

Bella yanked her head in protest, but Misty continued to speak and rub her neck. Frustrated they weren't making progress to get out of Adam's way, she prayed. They couldn't stay on the small ridge indefinitely. More ground gave way under the horse's pounding up and down, back and forth in an effort to escape. Misty's pulse raced as Adam wrestled with the animal.

Sweat poured from his face. Misty's throat choked with fear.

"I can't hold him," Adam yelled.

"Get off!" she screamed.

"I'm trying," was the last thing she heard before the horse tumbled down the crevice, Adam still in the saddle.

Misty jumped out of her saddle and ran to the edge where Adam went down. She dropped to her knees, then onto her belly, and hung over the side.

Was that Adam's body at the bottom? She couldn't be sure. "Adam!" Her voice echoed through the air and faded unanswered.

Her body trembled with horrible thoughts of possible injuries racing through her mind. "Oh, God! Please don't let him be dead."

Misty strained to get a better look. His horse lay twisted on its side halfway down. She retched as bile hit the back of her throat. "God help me," she cried. "What am I going to do?" Her cell phone! She jumped up and felt her pocket. Yes, it was still there. She pulled it out and looked at the screen. No coverage.

"Rats!"

She shoved it back into her jacket pocket. Shadows settled around her as the sun sank lower on the horizon. Certain she could pick her way down the hilly countryside with the help of her flashlight once dusk fell and Bella's sure-footedness, Misty considered her options. The closer she got to the ranch, the more likely she was to get cell phone coverage. Although Adam needed immediate medical help, if he were still alive, she couldn't risk climbing down to him and getting stuck. Leaving was his best chance for survival.

"Easy, girl," Misty spoke gently to the mare and attempted to grab her reins. Bella stomped the ground in protest. Still rattled by the other horse's scream and the avalanche, she wanted no part of Misty's soothing talk.

"Come on, girl." Again, Misty reached for the reins, but Bella tossed her head.

Misty looked around. The mare had her pinned in. "I have to get on better ground than this."

The ground shifted underneath Misty's feet. She felt her pockets for the carrot she'd snatched earlier. Extending the carrot toward Bella, Misty eased forward. Bella whinnied, stomped her foot, and shook her head up and down.

"Come on, girl, one more step," Misty begged. The grounded

shifted more, rocks slid underfoot, and Misty lost her balance. She clawed for Bella's reins, just out of reach. As the ground gave way, Misty's screams filled the air. She desperately grabbed for something, anything to hold onto as she half fell, half slid down the hillside, rocks and branches scraping her arms and face. Dust flew up, choking her throat and blinding her vision. Pain seared her head when it struck something hard. A warm, wet trickle of blood oozed from the side of her head before everything went black.

Chapter Thirty-Two

Misty sucked in her breath, struggling to regain her senses. Groggy from hitting her head, she tried to sit up but sank back. She'd had the wind knocked out of her. She focused on short, shallow breaths and attempted to sit up again. Stars danced in front of her eyes.

Where was Adam? The whinnying cry of her horse in the distance told her Bella was okay and still on the ridge. Somehow Misty had to get back up there. She rolled onto her knees and gently stood. The pounding in her head made her stomach churn with nausea.

Once steady, she scanned the horizon.

Adam's red-checkered shirt!

A cry escaped her throat as she ran, then stumbled across the rocky terrain. When she reached him, she dropped to her knees beside his crumpled body. She tucked her two fingers in the crook of his neck. To her relief, his heartbeat pulsated through her fingertips. Carefully, she checked his extremities and his neck, then thoroughly checked his head.

He didn't appear to have a neck injury. What about his spine? The possibility of a fracture existed. She weighed the risks and decided rolling him onto his back would be worth risking further injury. A complete assessment of his wounds had to be made before she could decide her next step.

Misty smoothed the ground next to Adam and gently rolled him over, careful to keep his head, neck, and back aligned the best she could. Superficial lacerations covered his face and neck. Further inspection of his arm confirmed her fears. Broken. She felt along the dislocation of his shoulder, and from the position he lay, she suspected he had broken ribs. She didn't dare probe too hard. From his uneven and labored breathing, one of his lungs could be collapsed. Obviously, he had a head injury. He was out cold. Her own injuries paled in comparison.

The last glimpse of sunlight faded behind the trees. The risk of shock setting in increased with the darkening sky and the cool night air. Misty fished her cell phone from her pocket and checked it again. Dead. Could this get any worse? She shoved the phone back into her pocket.

No one would be likely to miss them before morning when Dori or James came to work. For once, Adam's generosity would work against him. Surveying the top of the ravine, Misty estimated the climb back up to be a couple hundred yards the least rocky way. She couldn't go back up the way they came down, though it was less than twenty-five feet they'd fallen. She wouldn't even entertain the idea of going back up the jagged incline. If she fell again, they might both die before they were missed and help arrived.

She shrugged out of the heavy jacket and shivered against the cool breeze. Spreading it as best she could over Adam's upper body, she tucked the arms around him to create a cocoon effect. The more heat trapped, the better chance to fend off shock. Her hand ran over something small and hard in the jacket pocket. She reached in and pulled out a lighter.

"Praise the Lord!" It wasn't a flashlight, but it was a light. The canteens had been lost with Adam's horse. She had no idea where her flashlight had fallen.

Misty looked above at the fading sky. "God, please watch over Adam." She surveyed the side of the ravine. "And please keep me safe."

"Adam, I know you can't hear me, but I'm going for help." She leaned across his body and kissed him gently on the cheek. "I love you." She hesitated. "And if we ever get out of here—I'm going to tell you the truth—and then, if you'll still have me, I'm going to marry you. Do you hear me? You better not die on me."

The night air grew cooler by the minute, and Misty shivered. Nothing could be done about it. She tucked the lighter into her pocket. The ravine jutted in front of her. She crisscrossed the rocky terrain, carefully choosing her step. Rapidly, the terrain grew steeper, and she used her hands to climb.

"You are the God of the universe," she prayed aloud. "Guide my steps, direct my paths." She had to reach the top before dusk faded into total darkness. Grateful there would be a full moon, Misty still didn't want to make her ascent in the dark.

She clawed at the dirt and wrenched her feet into strongholds as she scaled the side of the hill. Twice she slid backwards and chastised herself for losing ground. She prayed there weren't snakes, scorpions, or spiders she might accidentally put her hand on. Adam's injuries mounted in her mind, and she tried not to lose hope. Every time she slipped, it meant more time he lay on his back unconscious.

Bella whinnied directly overhead.

"Oh, thank you, God." Misty hastened her pace. She clawed and stepped almost in rhythm now, gaining ground steadily. Once, she stopped and wiped her forehead. She craned her neck to get a glimpse of Bella on the ridge but couldn't see the horse.

Misty would have given anything for one of the canteens, but the detour wasn't worth it. Nor was getting near that dead horse, even if she could be certain the canteens were still with it. She shuddered.

Grasping the large rock in front of her, Misty hoisted herself up and plopped down for a moment. She pulled her cell phone out again and attempted to reboot it to no avail. Pocketing it, she took a deep breath and looked up. She was two-thirds of the way back to the ridge. Bella had been quiet for several minutes.

"Please God, don't let Bella wander off." Misty groped in the darkness for something to grab onto but nothing felt solid. She couldn't risk a fall. She reached into her pocket for the lighter and flicked it. Holding it up, she surveyed the terrain. She'd have to cross more to her left to finish her ascent, which would take more time. "Rats."

She tucked the lighter back in her pocket and scooted to her left. Her mind ruminated over Adam's injuries. Her life and what Adam meant to her came into clear focus with each step toward the cliff. She'd been a fool to put him off. Her fears and insecurities seemed miniscule compared to her fear of losing Adam now.

Bella's whinny sounded softly above her again. Misty laughed and cried at the same time. "Hold on, girl," she called out. "I'm almost there."

Sweat poured from Misty's face and drenched her back, making her clothes sticky with the dust embedded in them. Pain seared through her jaw. Fearing a fracture, she pushed the thought aside as she grasped the ridge ledge.

Spent, Misty prayed for strength. She tried to swing herself up onto the ledge. The effort took two more tries before she flung her leg over the side and hoisted herself up. She lay face down for a moment, panting and gasping for air. Then she rolled over and sat.

"Bella, here girl." Under the full moon, Misty looked around. No horse. Standing, she brushed the debris from her jeans and glanced at the sky. She had a good sense of direction. Although she'd gotten disoriented with the fall, she was fairly certain of the direction of the ranch. None of the terrain looked familiar, but the dark combined with the fact she'd climbed up a different way than they'd fallen contributed to her confusion.

Scanning the horizon for Bella while she walked, Misty sensed the horse was nearby. She'd been overhead the whole time Misty climbed. If Bella were going to run off, she would have right away.

Misty picked her way carefully down the path. Periodically, she pulled her cell phone from her pocket, hoping it had rebooted.

Suddenly, to her left, a whoosh of breath stopped her. She turned. Bella's eyes blinked in the moonlight. The horse was less than twenty feet away.

"Thank you, God." Not wanting to spook the animal, Misty decided not to approach but give Bella a chance to come to her.

Bella flicked her tail. Misty took a couple of steps down the path and the horse matched her step. When Misty stopped, Bella did, too.

"Oh, is that the way it's going to be?" Misty walked fifty feet and stopped. Bella stopped. Misty faced her. She made a clucking sound with her mouth and extended her hand. Bella took one step toward her and stopped.

"Come on, girl, I need you."

Bella slowly crossed the ground between her and Misty. Misty held her breath until the horse's reins were close enough to grab. She buried her face in Bella's mane and wept. Snuffling down a final sob, Misty swung herself onto Bella's back.

She pressed her heels into Bella's side. The horse lurched forward. Misty trusted Bella's sure-footedness, but with the deliberate seesawing back and forth, Misty wanted to scream for her to go faster. It would be foolhardy to urge Bella into a trot.

Misty peered into the starry sky above. God's overwhelming presence enveloped her.

"Is this what You've been trying to tell me?" she whispered into the stillness. "I don't have to know what the result of the next step is—I simply have to take the step."

Tears slipped down her cheeks. Her mind traced through the short time she had with Jenny and the grief she and Adam shared over losing her. The months of building Hope House. Adam now lay at the bottom of the ravine, crushed, his life possibly slipping away.

"God, please protect Adam," Misty prayed aloud. "I love him. I don't want to lose him." She pressed her heels into Bella's sides again and urged her to move faster. Shivering against the cold night, her mind retreated to the day when she handed the ring back to Adam and the pain in his eyes.

How could I have been so stupid?

She understood now what God had been trying to teach her. Her life didn't depend on her strength or her ability to outwit or outmaneuver a powerful man—whether physical strength, financial, or whatever. Her life depended on God.

She looked into the heavens. "God, help me to trust You completely. I surrender my life to You—my marriage to Adam, if he lives, and our future together."

Her breath caught. She could become Adam's wife. Not only did she trust God to protect her—she trusted Adam not to hurt her.

"Oh, if we can only get back to the ranch in time," she wailed to

Bella. As if sensing Misty's despair, Bella began to trot. Misty tightened her grip on the reins. Bella kept a good pace over the rough surface. The ground leveled off as they reached open pasture.

Misty again resisted pressing Bella into a full run. She let the horse set the pace and carefully studied the path ahead under the moonlight. In the distance, a faint glow of two lights appeared.

Misty craned her neck and blinked her eyes to make sure the lights were real. "Oh, thank you, God." She laughed and cried at the same time. As the lights brightened, the Mule came into view with Dori at the wheel. *How did she know?*

Misty spurred Bella into a full run and shortened the distance between her and Dori. She reined the horse in and slipped out of the saddle a few feet from the Mule.

"Oh, Dori, I'm so glad to see you," Misty gasped. "Adam's hurt."

Dori's mouth tightened into a grim line. "What happened?"

"Do you have a cell phone on you? Mine's dead."

"Of course." Dori jumped out of the Mule, pulled the phone from her pocket, and handed it to Misty. "What happened?" she repeated.

"Hold on." Misty punched 911 into the keypad. When emergency services answered, she gave directions to the ranch and details of Adam's injuries.

Handing the phone back to Dori, Misty burst into tears. "It was horrible. Adam's horse threw such a fit. The next thing I knew, they both tumbled down the side of the ravine."

Dori put her arms around Misty. "Shhh, it's okay now."

"No, Adam is still at the bottom of that ravine." Misty stepped back and stifled a sob. She grabbed Bella's reins. "I've got to go back."

"Oh, no, you don't." Dori jerked the reins.

Her forcefulness stunned Misty. "I have to."

Dori shook her head. "We'll wait for EMS. You're not going back down into that ravine. Adam would be angry if I allowed you to risk your life." She tied Bella to a tree.

Misty paced. "What is taking so long?"

Dori didn't reply. Her head bowed and her lips moved slightly.

Biting her lip, Misty added her own prayers for the first responders to hurry. A rumbling sounded in the distance, followed by the wail of sirens.

Dori jumped from the utility vehicle.

Misty ran toward the ambulance coming up the path. She was at the driver's door as soon as he came to a stop. "I'm a nurse. There's an injured man in a ravine about a mile from here."

"Get in," the driver said. "A fire truck's en route. Should be behind us momentarily." He lurched forward.

She looked back. Dori jumped in the Mule and started up the path, a safe distance behind the ambulance.

Within sixty seconds, the fire truck's siren pierced the air and appeared in the side mirror. Misty's stomach flopped. "It's very remote. We won't be able to get to Adam by vehicle."

The driver glanced at her. "You'd be surprised at how close we can get. We'll hike in the rest of the way."

Misty wished she could echo his confidence, but she'd spent precious time picking her way down the path. She prayed he was right.

The path grew more treacherous, but the ambulance lumbered along. Dori had long since fallen behind, the Mule's dim headlights fading in the distance.

"This is where we stop." The driver parked. The fire truck stopped behind him. The emergency personnel gathered their bags and flashlights, and Misty led the way.

When they reached the place where Adam went over the edge, Misty pointed to the spot in the ravine where she remembered leaving him. The emergency technician shined his spotlight on the area. After securing rappelling lines, the firemen began their descent. They alternated between rappelling and climbing through the overgrowth of vines and bushes on the steep hillside. Misty prayed for them to go faster. Time seemed to stand still with each methodical movement they made. She turned at the hum of the Mule. Dori arrived on the scene and jumped out.

"Any luck?" Dori leaned over to take a look.

"Not yet," Misty almost whispered. No point in voicing her fears—that Adam could be dead. She couldn't wrap her mind around the fact she might not have the chance to marry him—if he still wanted her.

Dori slipped an arm around her and pulled her close. "It'll be okay."

Hot tears coursed down Misty's cheeks. Her body began to shake. "I can't lose him."

"Shhh," Dori tried to soothe her. "We have to pray he's still alive—and as long as he's alive, there's hope."

"We've found him," a shout came from below.

Misty and Dori leaned over the edge again. Misty couldn't force her voice to form the question in her mind. An eternity seemed to pass while they waited for word on Adam's condition.

Finally, Dori shouted over the edge, "How is he?"

"He's alive!"

Misty sat back and cried. "He's alive, Dori. He's alive."

The two women hugged each other then moved back from the edge in anticipation of Adam being brought up. Within minutes, a pulley system was rigged with the firemen at the top. Adam was lifted out strapped to a backboard in an emergency stretcher basket. With the personnel at the bottom guiding the basket, Adam came into view, still unconscious but alive. That's all Misty cared about. She would move heaven and earth to pull him through whatever the next few hours, weeks, or months held for him.

"Thank you, God," she whispered her praise.

After Adam was unloaded from the basket and placed on a stretcher, Misty squeezed his hand and kissed him on the forehead. "Hang on, Adam. You're going to be all right." She paused and leaned closer. "I love you."

"Ma'am, we've got to move out," a firefighter spoke. "His vital signs don't look good."

Misty released Adam's hand. He stirred slightly. The emergency personnel pushed the stretcher into the ambulance. Misty felt Dori by her side.

"I'll drive you to the hospital," she said.

Misty nodded. The next twenty-four hours would be critical in Adam's condition. He had to survive his injuries, possibly surgery, before she could think recovery. Even then, the unknowns nagged at her mind. Moments later, she pushed aside her thoughts as she untied Bella and wearily swung into the saddle, then followed Dori back to the ranch.

Chapter Thirty-Three

"We've prayed. Now we'll leave Mr. Jenkins in God's hands." Dori handed Misty a cup of coffee and sat beside her in the surgical waiting room. Except for an occasional orderly who passed through, the room was empty.

Misty smiled. "Thanks, Dori. Not only for the coffee but your encouragement. I don't know what I'd do, if you weren't here."

"You'd be okay, but I'm glad to help."

Misty ran her hand along her aching jaw, relieved it wasn't broken. The emergency room staff had X-rayed it after they tended to her scrapes and the laceration on her head. Thanksgiving Day—the fellowship and food shared around Adam's table—seemed like a distant memory. Suddenly, she remembered Dori wasn't due to return to the ranch until the following day. "Why did you come back to the ranch?"

Dori's cheeks flushed. "Well, I got sidetracked when I left earlier."

"By James?" Misty nudged her playfully.

"Yes, if you must know. I get a little flustered around him. It's supposed to get bitterly cold over the next couple of days. My heavy coat was in the hall closet at the ranch from last winter. We had a warm spell and I just never took it home. I meant to grab it this afternoon before I left but forgot. I almost didn't come back because it was late."

Misty drew a long breath then released it. "Whew! I'm thankful you did."

"Me, too." Dori sipped her coffee. "When I found the house unlocked with no one around, I became alarmed. The horses were not in the stalls, so I got the Mule and started looking."

"An answered prayer, for sure."

Dori smiled her agreement.

Misty stood and paced, stopping occasionally to compare the clock on the wall to her cell phone, which to her relief had finally rebooted. Exasperated, she dropped back into a chair and picked up her coffee.

"The endless waiting drives me nuts." Misty twirled the coffee straw between her fingers.

"Yes, it does." Dori's voice trailed off.

Misty mulled over her next thought before voicing it. After all, she didn't know Dori that well. The older woman's countenance reflected something brewing beneath the surface. Deep within her, a wall had been built around her emotions designed to keep people out. Something pierced her soul.

Steam rose from the coffee cup. Misty took a sip before setting it on the table. She inhaled and summoned her courage.

"Dori, may I ask you something?"

"Sure."

"I hope you won't think this is too forward."

Dori's face tensed. "Go ahead."

"Where's your family? I mean, do you have any family?"

Setting her cup down methodically, as if biding time, pain tightened the lines around Dori's eyes. She met Misty's gaze. "Everyone has family, Misty."

Misty kicked herself mentally for stumbling around something she sensed was serious. Her face grew hot. "What I meant to say—"

Dori raised her hand. "It's okay. I know what you meant. I might as well tell you." The corners of her mouth edged up slightly. "I haven't even told Mr. Jenkins. Actually, I haven't shared this with a soul. I've successfully dodged every situation where anyone could ask. Until now."

Misty shifted in her chair. Why had she forced the issue? To satisfy her curiosity? No. She'd connected with Dori—apart from her relationship with Adam.

"I had a daughter. Amy. She was five." Dori exhaled and looked at her hands before continuing. "My husband took her to get ice cream. It was supposed to be a little excursion, to give me a chance to take a nap. I was recovering from the flu." She pinched at the side of the

Styrofoam cup.

Her voice barely audible, she continued. "Another driver ran a red light and T-boned our car. Killed them instantly."

Misty's hand flew to her mouth. "Oh, Dori, I had no idea. I'm sorry for asking you."

Tears coursed down Dori's cheeks. She stared straight ahead, almost in a trance. "Of course, the other driver survived." Sarcasm dripped from her last statement.

Misty felt Dori's frustration. Always the innocent being hurt. Of course, she knew Dori well enough to know she didn't wish death on anyone else, regardless of her own loss. Misty tried to swallow against the ache tightening her throat. When would human suffering ever stop? Not this side of heaven, she was sure.

Dori reached for a tissue, wiped her eyes, and then looked at the tissue she twisted in her hands, her tears still falling freely.

Misty put her arm around her, her own tears mixing with Dori's. "I'm sorry," she whispered as she held her friend. "For the accident—for making you relive it."

"I've relived it a thousand times. It was time to voice it." Dori pulled away, blew her nose, and tossed the tissue into the garbage. "I've kept it bottled up inside of me for too long."

"Did this happen at Christmas?"

Dori's eyes widened. "How did you know?"

"Adam said you always took time off at Christmas, but he didn't know why. That it was a condition of your employment. I would've never asked, if I'd known how badly you've been hurt." Misty's hardships paled in comparison to what her friend had suffered. Dori's situation put her own life in perspective. "I'm sorry."

Dori shook her head. "You know—I'm glad you asked. I feel better having confided in you." She placed her hand over Misty's clasped in her lap.

Tears pressed at the corners of Misty's eyes again, but she refused to let the them spill over. She swallowed hard. "Then I'm glad you shared with me."

"I've finally reached the point where it's not the first thing I think of when I awaken each morning." A tremble rippled through her. "Almost twenty years later."

"I can only imagine." Misty felt inadequate to say anything else. Silently, she sent up a prayer.

"Enough about me." Dori blew her nose one last time then looked at Misty. "Now, turnabout is fair play."

Misty groaned. "What do you want to know? After your admission, I'm an open book."

A slight smile hinted at the corners of Dori's mouth. "Why aren't you engaged to Mr. Jenkins anymore?"

Misty dropped her head into her hands. "Ugh. I've been so stupid."

"How?"

Misty lifted her head. "Adam's fighting for his life. We could've been married by now. Instead, I've wasted all this time."

Dori's face clouded. "But you still haven't answered my question."

"No, I guess I haven't." Misty stood and paced the empty waiting room. "I have major trust issues. I stepped out on a limb and trusted Adam, accepted his proposal, and then—"

"Yes?"

"I was at the ranch one day and overheard Adam firing his foreman," she confessed. "It wigged me out—no, actually it terrified me."

Dori's forehead crinkled. "I don't understand. Mr. Jenkins is one of the nicest men I know."

Misty dropped back into the chair beside Dori. "I was married before, also. Only my husband was abusive and tried to kill me—more than once. The last time we got into an altercation, the police shot and killed him."

"Oh, Misty, I'm sorry." Dori reached for her hand. "Now I'm beginning to connect the dots. In a way, it's like what I went through."

"What do you mean?"

Dori stared quietly across the room. "I refused to grow past the point when I lost my little girl, my husband." A leftover sob escaped her throat. "I spent years grieving, refusing to let anyone in."

Misty's heart ached at Dori's admission, but she waited for her to continue.

"Loneliness is unbearable. I'm sure you know." Dori's voice broke. She looked down at her hands for a moment before continuing. "But it was almost like a punishment I felt I deserved. After all, how could I move on with my life and be happy, when they were gone?

"I became entrenched in this way of thinking—punishing myself instead of letting God heal me." She paused again, her voice reduced to a whisper. "But I'm still alive. I deserved happiness."

"It's not too late." Misty smiled. "What about James?"

Dori flushed pink. "We'll see. But I'm too old to have children. I threw away a lot of years. You're wasting time you could be happy together."

"You're right. God dealt with my heart when I climbed out of the ravine and trekked down the hillside. I trust Him with my life, and I trust Adam not to hurt me." Misty glanced at the clock on the wall. "Now if we could get some word from the doctors."

As if on cue, Dr. McCarthy and a nurse came through the surgical waiting room door. Dori and Misty leapt to their feet.

Dr. McCarthy swiped his surgical cap off his head. "He came through fine, Misty. He has a concussion, of course. I set his shoulder. It was dislocated and broken. As long as he takes care of it and rehabs, it'll be good as new in a few months."

"Thank you, sir." Misty shook his hand before introducing Dori.

"The most important thing is watching for pneumonia," Dr. McCarthy continued. "One of his lungs collapsed, and he has a couple of broken ribs. It didn't help that he lay in the cold night air for so long." He paused and smiled. "But I have it on good authority he'll have one of the best nurses in the hospital taking care of him."

Misty's cheeks flushed.

Dr. McCarthy patted her arm. "You can go in to see him now for a few minutes."

"Thank you, doctor," Misty said.

"I'll wait out here." Dori reached for Misty's purse and coat. "Give him my best."

Misty followed the nurse into the recovery room and peeked around the curtain surrounding Adam's bed. Her breath caught. The cool, steely resolve that got her through the toughest cases did little to prepare her for the sight of Adam lying with tubes and wires protruding from his body. Trembling, her throat tightened with each step she took toward him.

Easing onto the side of his bed to sit down, she leaned over and kissed his forehead. "Adam," she whispered.

His eyes fluttered then shut again.

"It's okay. Rest. I'll sit with you." She caressed his hand. "You scared me to death when you went over the side of the ravine. I thought I'd lost you for good."

Adam stirred. Misty glanced at his monitors. All seemed to be in order. *What would I do, if I lost you?* She cringed. It wasn't something she ever wanted to find out.

"I love you." She brought his hand up to her cheek and kissed it.

Adam's eyes struggled to open. Finally, they seemed to focus on her face. "I—love—you."

Misty mustered up more bravado than she felt. "You're going to be fine." She squeezed his hand. She'd be his strength until he regained his own. "We've got business to take care of. Hope House opens in a month."

"Jenny." Worry filled Adam's face, his forehead crinkling.

Misty frowned. Did his concussion make him forget that Jenny was gone? She wouldn't address it until she was sure. Instead, she said, "Jenny will be proud of what you've done for her."

Adam closed his eyes. After a moment, he opened them, again. "I thought for a minute she was still here."

Misty held his hand between hers as he drifted back to sleep. It would be hours before the anesthesia wore off. His chest rose and fell with each respiration. She prayed his body would heal and there wouldn't be any lasting effects from the concussion.

Adam's ranch and Hope House meant everything to him. Though

she knew nothing of his ranch functions, James and Dori did. Misty made a quick decision. As much as she didn't want to leave Adam right now, his business interests were important. He'd taken his eye off the business when Jenny died and got taken advantage of. She draped his hand on his chest and pulled his covers in closer.

"I'll be back," she whispered. She tiptoed to the door, then glanced back.

Why did this have to happen now?

Chapter Thirty-Four

Outside in the hallway, Dori's face appeared when Misty pushed through the recovery room doors. She wiped the tears stinging the corners of her eyes. Dori gathered her into her arms.

Misty embraced her, then pulled back. She didn't have time for more tears. Not now. "He's banged up pretty bad, but he'll mend. As much as I don't want to leave, we have to get to the ranch and make sure everything's fine there."

"I've already called James." Confusion etched Dori's face. "Why don't you stay here?"

Misty shook her head. "No, there's Hope House business to take care of. I'll ride with you back to the ranch so I can pick up my car. I know I'm not Adam's wife—yet—but I want to talk to James and kind of keep an eye on things for Adam. I think he would want that."

Dori nodded. Misty hoped she hadn't appeared to question Dori's loyalty. Dori was the last person Misty wanted to hurt, but thoughts of the trust Adam had placed in Ted nagged her mind. She had to be eyes and ears for Adam, until he was well enough to take the reins back. First would be to call Max Bowen and see what contingency plans, if any, Adam had put into place in case of his debilitation.

Misty smiled. "How about an early lunch at the deli across the street, and then we'll go back to the ranch? My stomach just reminded me I haven't eaten in almost twenty-four hours."

Dori winced. "It hasn't been that long for me, but now that you mention it, I'm famished. And Misty—" She paused. "I understand completely what you're trying to do for Mr. Jenkins."

Misty exhaled. "Thank you for saying that. I didn't want to offend you. I have no intention of taking over. I've worked with Mr. Bowen, Adam's attorney, on Hope House business. I'll get him to kind of look over things, okay?"

Dori waved her hand in the air as if to erase Misty's words. "No offense taken. That sounds like a good plan. Now, let's eat."

Misty's stomach churned from anxiety more than hunger. She had one more call to make—to Adam's parents—and she wasn't looking forward to it.

***

Misty pulled the covers closer against the chill in her condo. She'd failed to put the heat on before she went to bed the night before. Now she dreaded climbing out to take a shower, but she had a busy day ahead.

The past two weeks had flown by at lightning speed. She'd scaled back to part-time hours at the hospital to keep Hope House on schedule and get to the ranch a couple of times a week to look over the operation there. Max Bowen had managed the financial end and James managed the ranch itself. With Beth working part time for her, Misty tracked Beth's progress in her college classes and still managed to squeeze in an hour on Saturday mornings to play with the children at the shelter.

She'd reassured Adam's parents he was on the mend. He'd insisted they not make the trip when they'd be coming for Hope House's opening after Christmas.

Christmas was a little over two weeks away. Adam would be released from the hospital in the next few days. Misty mulled over her plans. First on her agenda was to stop by her parents' house en route to the hospital. They'd surprised her by returning from Europe, despite her assurance she'd survived the accident with minor injuries and Adam was on the mend. Her mom had called last night, insistent she stop by first thing.

Misty threw back the covers, showered, and ate a quick breakfast. Did she dare hope whatever troubled her mother wouldn't take all morning to unravel?

Her hopes were dashed thirty minutes later when Mother greeted her at the front door and said they would talk after Misty had taken care of a "little chore" for her. Sighing, Misty followed her down the hallway and into the master bedroom. Clothing boxes were askew on the bed. *Well, the sooner she went through her mother's ritual, the sooner she'd be out of here.*

"Hand me those sweaters, Misty." Her mother exchanged her armload of lighter autumn wear for the sweaters Misty had pulled from the storage boxes. "I can't believe how cold it has gotten already."

She looked at the taut lines on Mother's face. Something was agitating her—more than usual. And it wasn't the weather. "Yeah, that's one thing we haven't been able to do—slow down time. But it is December."

Mother's face softened briefly then tightened again. "Age catches up with all of us eventually." She stepped back to assess the sweater arrangement on her closest shelf. "I think that about does it."

Misty stacked the wardrobe boxes in a corner for Papa to carry back to the attic later. "Is something wrong? You didn't call me over here to chat about your clothes. You certainly didn't need my help for this 'little chore.'"

Her mother dismissed the comment with a pat on her arm as she walked past. "Nothing really."

Misty drew a deep breath. So, it was going to be twenty questions. Unraveling Mother's thoughts was harder than digging a pearl from an oyster. And they rarely yielded anything jewel-like. "Why don't I pour us some tea, and you can tell me all about it?"

Mother dropped into a chair at the kitchen table and brushed a hair back from her face. Misty stole an occasional glance while she poured the hot tea into cups and placed them on a tray with some butter cookies.

"Here we are." She set the tray on the table and handed Mother a cup. Misty pulled out the chair beside her and sat. She spooned sugar into the cup and stirred, then waited while Mother did the same.

Wrapping her hands around the cup, Misty enjoyed the warmth of the steam rising between her hands. "Are you returning to Europe for Christmas?"

A smile spread across Mother's face. "In a couple of days. Savannah will meet us in London on the twenty-second."

"I don't know why you felt the need to rush home in the middle of your trip, especially when you plan to be here for Hope House opening. But I'm glad you're getting this time together." Misty's heart ached that she'd not be with her folks for the holidays.

The smile faded. "You could go with us."

Misty set her cup down hard. "Are you asking me to go?" Her mother had never invited her on a trip.

"You're welcome, if you'd like." Mother pinched at the edge of a cookie.

Misty's stomach churned. Unsure of what to say—how to voice her feelings, she left her thoughts unsaid. The invitation was a left-handed approach, but at least Mother had extended it. "I'd love to accompany you and Papa, but I've got obligations here. I'd never get my passport up to date and make the arrangements in time—even if I wanted to leave Adam, which I don't. Not while he's still hospitalized." Her voice fizzled with her reasons. There really was only one reason. She hadn't been invited in time to go. She shifted in her chair, praying Mother would change the subject.

Mother shrugged. "Maybe next time."

Misty swallowed hard against the tightness in her throat. "Sure, I'd love to."

"What are your plans for the holidays?"

"I'll spend them with Adam." Her cheeks grew warm. "Out at his ranch. He'll be released any day now."

"I see." Her mother stirred her tea then lifted the cup to her lips.

What did she see? Will I have to drag it out of her?

"When do we get to meet this Adam?"

"I'm planning a dinner," Misty said. "He's important to me." She waited for her mother's reproach.

"Please do. We'd love to get to know him better."

What? Had someone kidnapped her mother and left this woman in her place?

"O-kay." Misty twisted her napkin in her hand. "Mother, what's wrong?" she blurted out. "You don't seem yourself today." She glanced at the time on her phone. "I'm sorry, but I have to get to the hospital. If there's something the matter …"

Mother didn't answer. Instead, she stood, walked over to her desk, and retrieved a small envelope. She hesitated and then slipped a photo from the envelope. Her hand shook as she sat in front of Misty. "We should've taken care of this long ago. Your accident. Adam's brush with death. Well, I don't want to leave the country again with loose ends. We're too old." She leveled her eyes to meet Misty's. "Besides, you deserve to know."

Misty's pulse raced. Nothing good had ever come from Mother's melodrama, despite how much she insisted she despised it in others.

Tears seeped from the corners of her mother's eyes. Insane fear gripped Misty as she reached for her hand.

"What is it?" Her breath caught when Mother placed the photo in her hand. The woman in the photo staring back at Misty had strawberry-blonde hair and hazel eyes. *Like looking in a mirror.*

Chapter Thirty-Five

"Who is this?" The boldness echoing in Misty's ears surprised her. Raising her voice would only garner reproach, but she felt like she'd been kicked in the gut, and she didn't know why. Her gaze flew from the photo to her mother's eyes. "Who is it, Mother? An aunt I don't know about? Maybe a relative from Ireland?"

"Misty, I never wanted to keep this from you." Mother's voice hovered above a whisper. "Papa should've told you long ago."

The photo fell from Misty's hand. She grasped her mother's arms. "What should he have told me?"

"She's—your—mother," her voice broke off with a sob at the end. "Your biological mother."

"No." Misty sobbed, tears streaming down her cheeks. "Is this some kind of a sick joke? You're my mother."

Misty's mother swiped at her own tears. "Of course I am, in every sense of the word—except biology." She reached down and picked the photo from the floor. "She gave birth to you. She was your father's first wife, but she abandoned him—." Regret etched her face.

"And me." Misty finished her sentence.

Mother shook her head. "Not like that."

Fire burned in Misty's chest and threatened to engulf her. "How then?"

Her mother stood and began to pace. "It's your father's story to tell."

"Where is he?" Misty's fists clenched for reasons she couldn't count. Anger. Betrayal. Outcast.

"He's upstairs in his study." Her mother waved toward the stairs.

"Does he know you're telling me this?" Misty was incredulous. Her mother dropped a bombshell, and Papa sat up there—what—reading?

"No."

Misty ran to the stairs. She took them two at a time. Reaching the top, her lungs felt like they would explode. She rapped on his study door but didn't wait for an answer.

"Papa, how could you?"

Her father's face said it all. The secret was out. She dropped to the floor at his feet and sobbed.

Papa patted the chair next to him. "Sit up here, lass. I'll tell you the whole story."

Misty climbed into the chair and wiped her face with the tissue he offered. "Who is she?"

"I met her when I worked in New York City as a delivery boy. She was an aspiring actress." Papa paused and rubbed his chin. "Beautiful but headstrong. A lot like you." He patted her hand.

Misty felt the sting of his comment. *How could I be anything like a woman I've never met?*

"We married too quickly. Before we knew it, you were on the way." Papa smiled. "'Twas a wonderful discovery."

"Did she think so?"

Papa's face clouded. "You're too smart for your own good, lass." He cleared his throat.

Misty twisted the tissue between her fingers. Her mother didn't want her. That much was obvious.

"We tried to make it work, but we were too different. She had ambitions and dreams. I wanted a home and a wife."

"She left?"

"In the middle of the night." He snapped his fingers. "Never saw her again. She sent me a telegram from California saying she couldn't stay anymore, felt choked off."

"Just like that?"

Papa nodded. "I heard from her again a couple of years later when the divorce was final. She'd grown tired of the West Coast, missed the big city." Papa grunted his disapproval. "Wishy-washy she could be at times. She returned to New York, but I'd left for South Carolina at that point."

"Where you met Mother?"

Papa's eyes glistened. "The best thing that ever happened to me—and you." His voice barely a whisper, he continued. "Your mother loves you very much, Misty."

Misty sobbed at his admission. Did Mother love her—like she did Savannah? Her head pounded with confused thoughts racing around. Memories flooded back that made her entire life suspect.

Would she ever really know if her mother loved her? The woman who raised her, that was. Obviously, her biological mother hadn't.

A knock at the door preceded Misty's mother opening and sticking her head inside. "May I come in?"

Misty clutched Papa's hand tighter as Mother dropped into the chair beside her. She began to weep again when Mother reached for her other hand.

"Misty, I never wanted to keep this a secret. I sensed it would hurt you if—when it came out." She frowned at Papa. "But I agreed because in the beginning you were little, and honestly, as time went on, I didn't think about the fact that you came into my life differently than Savannah. It just became easier to keep hidden and at the same more difficult to figure out how and when we would tell you. But just so we're clear, I ..." Her voice broke.

Misty lifted her head and through her tear-filled eyes, looked at the only mother she'd ever known. "What, Mother? You what?"

Her mother shifted and cleared her throat. "I love you the same as if I had given birth to you."

Misty threw her arms around her mother. She'd heard the words she'd spent her whole life longing to hear. Mother held her close and let Misty cry out her pain. Stroking her hair, Mother shushed her after a moment.

"You're going to make yourself sick," Mother scolded.

Misty lifted her head and looked into her mother's eyes. "Like mother, like daughter."

"Well." The corners of Mother's mouth edged up.

"Will you forgive me, lass?" Papa wiped tears from his cheeks.

"Yes, Papa, but please don't keep any more secrets from me, okay?" A feeling of horror flooded her. "There aren't any other secrets, are there?"

He patted her hand. "No. Wasn't that one enough?"

***

Misty unlocked her front door, tossed the keys onto the coffee table, and collapsed onto the overstuffed sofa cushions. She couldn't face anyone, much less Adam right now. Her whole life felt like a fraud. She rubbed the tightness in the back of her neck, and then fished her cell phone from her pocket and clicked on the number to the hospital.

"Hi, Sandra." Misty recognized the nurse's voice who answered. "Has Adam Jenkins left for physical therapy yet?"

"A few minutes ago. He mentioned you were supposed to come by this morning. Is there a problem?"

Misty rubbed her forehead. "Not really. I got delayed by family business. Would you let him know I've decided to go to Hope House for the day? I'll be by later this evening."

"Sure."

Misty said good-bye and pushed up from the sofa. Immersing herself in her work would be easier than reliving the morning by sharing her news with Adam. Until she'd processed her parents' revelation, she couldn't bring herself to talk about it. Besides, Hope House would open in less than two weeks, and much remained to be done.

She foraged in her fridge for a bottle of water and grabbed a bowl of cantaloupe she'd cut up the night before. Sitting at the bar, she forked the fruit out and stared into space. Where was her biological mother? Had she really cared so little as to leave and not look back? There had to be more to the story than what Misty had been told. A cold chill ran through her. Was she ready to learn whatever the rest of the story might be?

The only thing to do was to go to Hope House and stay busy. It wouldn't be difficult, given that they were behind schedule. She placed a call to Dori and asked to meet her there. Beth should already be on site.

Misty grabbed her purse and, within fifteen minutes, pulled into the parking lot. The landscaping still needed to be completed. She made a note to have James take a ride over to push that along. Nothing much was going on at the ranch right now, so he'd have time.

"Dori," Misty greeted her friend from across the parking lot. She waited for Dori to catch up to her.

"How's Mr. Jenkins this morning?"

Misty dropped her keys into her purse and avoided eye contact with Dori. The lady was astute enough to sense a problem. And the best thing she could do was bury her feelings for now. "Actually, I didn't get by the hospital. My parents needed something, and I never made it over. He's in physical therapy now."

Dori cinched her purse over her shoulder. "What can I do to help?"

"Let's take a look." Misty followed her through the door and surveyed the building, still empty of furniture. The flooring had been installed since she'd been there last. The walls had been painted a beautiful earth-tone combination of cornflower, soft green, and wheat colors. Stretching her neck, she could see into the gym. The mural of a mother and child had yet to be painted on the gym wall. Beth hurried out from the inner offices.

"I saw you on the security monitor." A smile spread across Beth's face. "What do you think about the floor? Isn't it gorgeous?"

Misty glanced at the floor again. "They did a beautiful job. I can't wait until the whole place is finished, though. I'm anxious to open our doors."

"I agree," Beth replied. "Dori, do you want to work on the menu for the dedication ceremony?"

"Sure." Dori hung up her coat.

"Did you need anything, Misty?" Beth turned back to her.

"Not really. Keep the menu simple, heavy hors d'oeuvres and drinks. We need to bring the celebration in under budget." She looked at Dori. "I've lined up some interviews for you to conduct for potential kitchen help. They'll also act as attendants during the ceremony. We're not using a catering company. I want you to prepare the food, but I don't expect you to work yourself to death."

Dori beamed. "Sure thing. I'd love to be in charge of the food."

Misty squeezed her arm. "I'm glad I can count on you two. I've got to make a few calls. I want to make sure the furniture is on its way." She started to walk away and then checked her step. "Beth, why hasn't the mural been painted in the gym?"

"The artist will be here tomorrow."

Misty flashed a smile. "Thank you for handling that, as well."

The two ladies walked back to the offices, chatting as they went.

The homey atmosphere in the cavernous building enveloped Misty. No matter what fell apart outside these walls, Hope House had become her safe haven. She twirled the end of her ponytail between her fingertips and considered the irony of her feelings. Was she retreating?

By early afternoon, exhausted, she'd crossed the last item off her to-do list. The stack of valances for the windows still sat in a pile in the corner. The maintenance men had hung the blinds and rods, then left for the day.

Beth and Dori emerged from the inner offices.

Misty smiled. "Finished?"

Beth handed her some paperwork. "A tentative menu and a rough estimation of cost."

"Wow, you ladies are efficient. Thanks." Misty thumbed through the papers, nodding her approval.

"Dori came up with the figures, and I'll make some calls to double-check prices. We can get most of the items at Costco or Sam's Club." Beth took the paperwork from Misty.

"One last thing to do before I get out of here." Misty pointed to the valances. "Wanna help?"

"Sure," they chimed in.

Misty pulled the valances from their wrappers and stacked them on a table nearby. Beth scooted a stepstool under the first window. She lifted a rod and handed it to Dori, who threaded a valance onto the rod, and handed the ensemble to Beth to be hung.

"These are lovely." Misty ran the blue-and-wheat-colored material through her fingertips.

Dori stepped back and eyed the first two completed windows. "They have a beautiful effect on the room, too. It's amazing how much they spruce up the windows."

"I agree." Beth handed another rod to Dori. "You know, I've been thinking about something else we could do. It'd be nice to have a winter garden out back. What do you think?"

"Sounds like a great idea." Misty unwrapped another stack of valances and laid them on the table. "Maybe you can get James to till up the ground with the ranch tractor." She winked at Dori.

Dori blushed bright pink to her hairline.

"What am I missing?" Beth stepped down from the stool.

"Nothing, I assure you." Dori frowned at Misty and then busied herself with the next rod and valance set. "You better step back up there. This one's almost done."

"Not so fast." Beth giggled. "What's this about James?"

"Just that he'd be more than happy to assist us." Misty nudged Dori. "Right?"

Dori flicked the valance she'd been holding in her hand at Misty. She stepped back to dodge the material.

Beth squealed. "Ooh, are you two an item?"

"No, we're not 'an item.'" Dori slipped the valance onto another rod and stepped onto the stool. "I'll hang these myself."

Misty couldn't contain her laughter anymore. Before long, the other two laughed with her. "This is the most fun I've had in a long time." She leaned against the table and wiped her eyes.

"Maybe there'll be a double wedding," Beth suggested with a gleam in her eye.

"Now that would be counting two chickens before they're hatched," Misty pointed out. "Adam's still in the hospital, and—he'll have to ask me again. What are the chances of that?"

"Pretty good," Dori and Beth chorused.

Misty shot them a pointed look. "We'll see. Now let's get back to work. I wanna get out of here sometime today."

When they were finished with the task, Misty was pleased with the work accomplished in one day. Not only did she have the menu, along with an estimate of costs, they'd hung almost twenty valances throughout the buildings.

Dori and Beth emerged from the office with their coats and purses.

"Well, ladies, you should be proud of the hard work you put in today."

"My pleasure." Beth hugged her on the way out.

Dori echoed her sentiments as she slipped into her coat. "Are you going to the hospital?"

"Not sure. I'll call Adam and see how his day went." After saying good-bye, Misty locked the door behind them, then watched through the windows until they'd climbed into their cars.

She grabbed her water bottle and took a sip. Should she go to the hospital? Maybe Adam could get by one night without seeing her. She'd successfully worked hard enough to fill almost every inch of her mind during the day. The other parts, Dori and Beth filled.

Hope radiated inside her. The three of them had come so far in the past month. Dori had emerged from her shell and fit right in, as if they'd been friends forever. Ultimately, that's what life was about. Not Misty's past, nor her mistakes. Only what lay in front of her.

Including Mother, Papa, and Savannah.

Misty frowned. Could they go forward as if nothing had changed?

Maybe the uneasiness between she and her mother all these years hinged on her mother's angst about the secret. Misty sucked in a breath. For the first time, she had another feeling—anger toward her father.

How could he have done this to both of them?

Chapter Thirty-Six

Misty retreated to her office, grabbed her Bible, and dropped into the chair behind the desk. Flipping the book open to Galatians, she began reading where she'd left off the night before. At the end of the third chapter, her back straightened. She reread the verse.

"So in Christ Jesus you are all children of God through faith …"

Her fingers traced the words. She'd read something similar in another of Paul's letters. Where? She flipped over to Ephesians and began to read. Her spirit soared when she got to the fifth verse in the first chapter.

"In love he predestined us for adoption to sonship through Jesus Christ …"

She clasped the Bible shut and clutched it to her chest. "God," she whispered. "I'm yours, not only because you created me—not just due to biology—but because you chose me, and then I chose you." Her tears spilled freely down her cheeks. "I get it now. I do fit in—with your family. Don't let me forget that as I try to process this—craziness in my earthly family."

The feeling of her mother holding her close lingered in her soul. "Mother chose me, too." Regardless of how they moved forward as a family, Misty had a different perspective now about her mother. For now, she'd give her anger to God and move forward. If she'd learned nothing else in the past few years, she understood it was unhealthy to fixate on something you couldn't change. She knew she'd have to grieve the loss of what she thought she'd had—just like she had her marriage. More importantly, her parents loved her. Her dad, in his own mixed-up way, thought he was protecting her…and likely he was.

But maybe, just maybe, in time, her parents' revelation would work out to be a good thing. She could hope, anyway.

After she spent another few minutes praying, she reached for the phone. The only thing she wanted was to go home, fall into bed, and get a good night's sleep. But she had to call Adam first.

Exhaustion laced Adam's voice when he answered the phone. "Hello."

"Rough day?"

"Better now, but yeah, they're killing me in physical therapy." A groan punctuated his words.

Misty laughed. "You're supposed to feel that way after therapy." She sobered. "Listen, I've had a pretty busy day myself. Do you mind if I come first thing in the morning instead of this evening? I still have to run by the dry cleaners and pay a few bills."

"Are you avoiding me?" He covered the phone and coughed.

"You're not getting rid of me that easy."

"Seriously, I'm exhausted, too. I won't be good company tonight."

Misty frowned. Adam had been in overall good physical condition before the accident. She shrugged off her concern. Even the fittest person complained after therapy. The therapists weren't doing their job if the patient didn't complain.

"Are you sure you're feeling okay, otherwise?"

"Yes, Nurse Stephens, I'm fine."

Misty let out the breath she'd been holding. If he was well enough to banter, he was fine. Her overactive imagination needed to be put to rest. "Then I'll be by first thing in the morning and bring you breakfast."

"Now that's something to look forward to." Amusement edged his voice. "How did it go with your parents?"

"Could've been better." Misty had tried to push their conversation from her mind. As long as she stayed busy, she'd managed. Her time spent with God in prayer and Bible study had renewed her soul, but she knew from previous upheavals, she'd go through various emotional stages before her mind adjusted to her parents' news. Now wasn't the time to have a discussion with Adam. She wasn't sure if she could voice what she felt right now, anyway. "I'll tell you about it tomorrow, okay?"

"I'll be waiting."

She chuckled. "As if you were going anywhere, right?"

His laugh came through the line again. "Something like that."

***

Misty's cell phone buzzed on the nightstand. She wrapped her wet hair in a towel, cinched her bathrobe around her, and crossed the bedroom to see who'd left a message. The hospital's number flashed across the screen. Putting the phone on speaker, she listened for the message while toweling her hair.

"Misty," Dr. McCarthy's voice came through the speaker. "Adam's condition has worsened. I won't be available for the next hour, but I'll try to catch up with you later."

Worsened? What did that mean?

Misty punched the number to the hospital into her phone. "Come on, pick up." She leaned into the closet and pulled out the first shirt her hand touched and grabbed a pair of jeans from her dresser. She recognized the voice of the charge nurse who answered.

"This is Misty Stephens. I'm calling for an update on Adam Jenkins. Dr. McCarthy left a message on my voice mail that Adam's condition has worsened."

"Pneumonia set in overnight. Antibiotics were started a couple of hours ago, but his vitals have steadily declined."

Misty's heart sank. "I'll be there in ten minutes." She thanked the nurse and hung up the phone. She typed out a quick message to Dori and Beth, promising to update them when she knew more.

God, I can't lose him.

She covered the miles as fast as the law allowed and then some. When she pulled into the parking lot ten minutes later, Misty continued to pray. She'd always trusted God's plan for her life, through her awful marriage, Ryan's death, and then Jenny. Losing Adam would be a blow from which she didn't think she'd recover.

Making her way through the hospital, Misty ran over the protocol in her mind for Adam's treatment. She'd check every IV line, sterile procedure, and medication to make sure nothing was left wanting in his care.

"Misty."

She turned to see Leah walking toward her. "What are you doing on this floor?"

"Just a quick meeting with the charge nurse." Leah hugged her. "How's Adam?"

Misty frowned. "Not good. His condition deteriorated overnight. I'm on my way in right now to see what I can do."

Concern etching her face, Leah touched Misty's arm. "Let me know if I can help."

"Thanks." Misty didn't want to seem rude after everything Leah had done for her, but Adam was top priority. "Can I catch up with you later?"

Leah smiled. "Keep me posted."

Misty hurried to Adam's room. A thin oxygen tube lay across his upper lip leading into his nose. Her gaze quickly went to the monitors. His heart rate was steady, but his face was gray. She checked his chart and noted the strong dose of potent antibiotics. He was getting the best.

"Adam." Misty leaned close to him. "I'm here." She ran her trembling fingers along his cheek, and he stirred.

His eyes fluttered slightly and then closed again.

"You're gonna be okay." Misty's heart pounded. Did she believe that? When it came to people dying, it happened sometimes despite the best treatment.

God, please don't take him.

She laid the stethoscope end on his chest and listened. Both lung bases sounded diminished but worse on the side of his collapsed lung. Crackles were clearly audible on that side, also.

Misty rose up and draped the stethoscope around her neck. She hurried back to the nurses' station.

"Hi, Tracy," Misty spoke to the nurse behind the desk. "When do you expect the doctor again?"

"He's running behind. Probably not before ten o'clock."

"Page me when he shows up, if I'm not back first." Misty grabbed a Post-It pad and scribbled her pager number on it.

Tracy reached for the piece of paper. "Will do."

Misty hurried down the hall. She had agreed to take her parents to the airport that afternoon. Ducking into the business center, she was relieved to find it almost empty. Quickly, she scrolled through her apps and selected a car service. Once she called and arranged the pickup, she carefully constructed a text to her mom and pressed send. Her mother would have an absolute fit with the change of plans, but it couldn't be helped. She didn't have time for Mother's twenty questions.

Her stomach in knots, Misty headed for the cafeteria. Almost nine o'clock, and she'd not eaten since the evening before. She'd go back upstairs to eat in Adam's room while she waited on the doctor. Ten minutes later, with a takeout container filled with a croissant and fruit, Misty gripped a Styrofoam cup of coffee, weaved through the breakfast crowd, and got in line at a cash register.

Dr. McCarthy strolled across the cafeteria talking with two other doctors. Misty paid for her food and hurried to catch up with him.

"Dr. McCarthy," she called out when she drew nearer.

He turned. "Misty." He said something inaudible to the other doctors, then broke away, and walked toward her.

"I came from Adam's room." She swallowed hard. "His vitals appear stable, but I don't like the way his lungs sounded."

Dr. McCarthy's jaw had a grim set to it. "Acquiring pneumonia was the last thing Adam needed. The germs in here are sometimes worse than one could be exposed to on the outside."

"You're right." Misty pushed down the fear of losing Adam. Worry hampered her ability to function, and she didn't want to miss something in Adam's care.

Dr. McCarthy touched her arm. "As you know, the next few hours are the most critical, but we jumped on this pretty quick and loaded him with strong antibiotics. Keep a close eye on him, and page me if anything changes."

Tears stung the corners of her eyes. "Thank you." She hurried back to Adam's room.

Settling into the chair next to his bed, Misty popped open her container. If only life would settle into an even keel. Whatever that meant. In the quiet of the room, she prayed.

God, I want to be Adam's wife, have his children. Most of all, I want him to live.

The drip of Adam's IV and whoosh of his oxygen were the only semblance of life. She pushed aside the takeout box and coffee and caressed his hand. Strong and steady, this hand had guided her through the last few months. Lifting his hand to her cheek, she closed her eyes and prayed.

Please heal him. I can't do this again.

Adam stirred. Misty jumped to her feet and leaned in. "Adam?"

Chapter Thirty-Seven

Adam grew still, his breathing shallow again. Misty stroked his face but got no response. Disappointed, she sank back into the chair and pulled the book of Psalms from her purse. Flipping through the pages, she read from one passage and then another.

The LORD is my light and my salvation—whom shall I fear? ... To you, O LORD, I lift up my soul; in you I trust, O my God ... Hear my cry, O God; listen to my prayer. From the ends of the earth I call to you ... lead me to the rock that is higher than I.

Her cell phone buzzed in her pocket. She fished it out and looked at the screen. Mother. She read the text. Mother and Papa were at the airport getting ready to board. Misty smiled at the three words that seemed to flow easier from her mother. "We love you."

She laughed through her tears. Maybe they'd rounded a corner in their relationship, after all.

She texted them a brief message and pocketed the phone. If only her sister were here to lean on. Savannah had been gone the better part of five years. She'd come home for Ryan's funeral, but her stay had been brief.

Savannah worked hard to reach lost souls and give humanitarian aid. Misty swallowed against the ache in her throat. Of course, that's where her sister should be. She rubbed her temples to relieve the stress setting in.

She grasped Adam's hand. "One day all this will be behind us, and we'll be together."

Misty laid her head against Adam's bed and listened to his labored breathing. To her surprise, the door pushed open, and the second shift nurse entered the room. She glanced at the clock on the wall.

"Hi, Misty." The nurse greeted her, then focused on Adam's chart.

"Hi, Sandra. I didn't realize how late it had gotten. No change since I've been here."

"Give it a little more time." Sandra flashed an encouraging smile.

Misty attempted a smile. "I'm finding that patience is not a strong suit for me."

"It never is when you're on that side of the crisis."

After Sandra left, Misty reached for her fruit. Picking over it, she managed to eat a few bites before setting it aside again. She scrolled through the radio channels until she found her favorite Christian station, then leaned back in her chair. Her eyelids grew heavy. She couldn't fight the weariness in her body. Sleep overcame her.

Scenes of the accident and Adam plunging over the side of the cliff startled her awake. The clock showed she'd been asleep for more than an hour. She roused herself. Adam hadn't stirred. She checked his vitals, tossed her wilted leftovers in the garbage, then left the room.

Sandra looked up as Misty approached the nurses' station. "How's our patient?"

"Unchanged. Look, I have a couple of calls to make."

"I'll let you know if anything changes."

Misty smiled. "Thanks."

Farther down the hallway, Misty tapped the ranch's number on her phone and waited for Dori to answer.

"Hi, Dori."

"Misty!" Dori's voice came through the line. "How's Mr. Jenkins?"

"No change. It may take twenty-four to forty-eight hours to start seeing a turnaround. Keep praying."

"You know I am."

"How're things there? Did James give you a list of supplies?" Misty pulled a notepad from her purse that held a checklist for the ranch.

"Yes. The purchase order is sitting on Adam's desk, like you asked."

"Good. I'll try to get away later on and take care it."

"James said no rush." Dori paused. "Everything's fine here, Misty."

Misty winced at Dori's tone. She'd tried not to step on anyone's feelings, but she sensed a defensiveness building in Dori and James.

She'd intended for things to run more smoothly by helping out during Adam's absence. "Thanks for all you do, Dori. Adam relies so much on you. There's no way I could've handled any of this without you."

"I'm glad to help, Misty. Sorry if I sounded a little edgy. It's the time of year."

"No apology necessary. I'm here for you. We're in this together."

"Thanks."

Misty pocketed her phone and hurried back to Adam's room.

***

The next morning, Misty expected to see an improvement in Adam's condition. More than twenty-four hours had passed since antibiotics had been started. She ran through his vitals and listened to his chest. She moved the stethoscope and tried again. A low, raspy breath escaped his lips.

She draped the stethoscope around her neck, dropped into the bedside chair, and reached for his hand. "I don't know what else to do but wait—and continue to pray."

Adam had portrayed his accident to his parents as minor, despite Misty's urgings to do otherwise. Jenny's death had been a blow to them, and he hadn't wanted to worry them when he expected a full recovery. They were due to arrive for the Hope House dedication in a couple of weeks. Should she call them? What would she say? Misty lifted Adam's hand to her cheek. She didn't trust her own judgment on what was the right thing to do anymore, for either of them.

If only he'd wake up.

Time dragged along at an infuriatingly slow pace.

"Okay, I can't keep sitting here. It's making me nuts." She adjusted the radio channel to soft classical music and then crossed the room to open his blinds. Letting in a small amount of light would make the room more cheery, should he wake.

Outside in the hallway, Misty stopped the floor nurse.

"I'm going to the chapel for a little while. You have my cell number. If you can't reach me, send someone down. I want to know the minute he awakens."

"Will do." The nurse jotted the info on her notepad. "I'll put this in his chart as soon as I get back to the desk." She squeezed Misty's arm. "He'll be fine."

From your lips to God's ear.

Misty stepped into the elevator and rode to the first floor. Weaving through the flow of staff and visitors, she made her way to the chapel.

She pushed open the door. Dark and quiet, the room seemed to beckon her. Misty's eyes adjusted to the candlelit room. She softly stepped down the small aisle and knelt on the altar cushions at the front. Crossing her hands in front of her on the altar railing, she soaked in the chapel's tranquility. Memories from the past year flooded her mind, and an overwhelming sadness enveloped her. The year Ryan died had been tough. She couldn't know the hard times that would follow.

Despair gnawed at her with fears of the unknown. There were no assurances she and Adam would marry, even if he pulled through. And what about her parents and sister? What was her role in the family now? Did Savannah know? If she didn't, would they tell her?

Misty's head throbbed with questions and no answers. "God," she pleaded. "I'm helpless to control any of this. The only thing I have control over is my commitment to you." She laid her head on top of her hands and closed her eyes. "That hasn't changed, but my heart is slipping away. I'm afraid like I've never been afraid before." Tears seeped from her eyes and dripped down her hands.

"My life has been turned upside down. Ryan's death—well, I don't know what to feel about that anymore." She lifted her head. "Mother isn't really my mother."

No, that wasn't right. Not exactly. "I can't think straight either, apparently."

Misty peered at the stained-glass window behind the crucifix. "Watching Adam go over that cliff. I was helpless." She blew out a breath. "I am helpless."

"I need you," she whispered.

The smallest spark of hope flickered somewhere deep inside. It was as if God had spoken aloud. "I'm here." Warmth flooded her and buoyed her spirit.

Misty looked around. She wiped the tears from her cheeks with her fingertips. For the first time in weeks, she had renewed strength and the fortitude to face whatever unknown waited. She could do this, with God's help.

"Thank you," she offered a final prayer and turned toward the door. Startled when it cracked open, she froze.

Dr. McCarthy stuck his head inside.

"What's wrong?" she croaked.

A smile spread across the doctor's face. "He's awake and asking for you."

Misty ran to the door and pushed past Dr. McCarthy. She charged down the hallway, praising God in her soul.

When Misty stepped into his room moments later, Adam rolled his head toward her. "Hey."

"Hey, yourself." She laughed before bending over to kiss his cheek. "What's the idea of relapsing when I had my back turned?"

"That'll teach you—to not pay—attention to me," Adam tried to tease. He coughed in spasms and then closed his eyes.

"Shhh, you're not out of the woods yet." Misty adjusted his IV tube and reached for the thermometer. She inserted the tip into his ear and then looked at the reading. "Still low grade, but the meds have kicked in."

She sat on the bed next to him and held his hand. "We have a lot to catch up on when you get stronger."

"How long?" Adam's eyes fluttered shut again for a moment before he opened them again. "How long have I been in here?"

"A couple of weeks."

"Christmas?"

"No, remember the accident happened on Thanksgiving." She caressed his hand and then lifted it to her cheek. "Don't worry. You'll be out in time for Christmas. We'll celebrate it together. Just the two of us."

A smile crept across Adam's face and then his eyebrows crinkled. "Hope House."

She laid a finger across his mouth. "It's on schedule. Everything's been taken care of. Beth, Dori, and James have been a great help."

His eyes closed and soon his breathing deepened. His vitals traced across the monitor, even and regular. Misty breathed a prayer of thanksgiving. Hope had returned.

***

Misty's stomach churned as she walked through the hospital halls a week later en route to Adam's room. Leah had given her a job when she desperately needed it, and now Misty had given her notice. Her plan to work part time wouldn't work out—at least not now. She wasn't the first to walk away. It was the nature of healthcare. Overworked staff often equated to high turnover. Misty had been spread too thin trying to keep everyone happy. She took a deep breath and exhaled, allowing the tension to leave her body.

She pushed open the door to Adam's room. "Well, now. Who's ready to go home?"

A smile stretched across his face. "I'm going to breakfast first—if you'll take me."

Misty chuckled. "I kind of figured that would be priority this morning." She pulled a wheelchair from the hall and parked it in front of Adam's bed. "We'll stop off at Subway and get a breakfast sandwich filled with lots of fresh vegetables."

"I don't think so."

"Why not?"

"Try IHOP. I'm talking about a real breakfast, after this hospital food for the last three weeks." Adam's chin had a firm set to it. There would be no changing his mind.

Misty grimaced and plopped down on the bed beside him. "Ugh. That's such unhealthy food."

He leaned over, kissed her cheek, and nestled closer. "I'll have blueberries on my pancakes, okay?"

She giggled as he pulled her into his embrace. "You're silly, you know that?"

"I think you've mentioned it before."

The easy banter between them encouraged her. Trekking through the dark the night of Adam's accident, she'd made a lot of promises to herself and to God. Somehow, she would screw up her courage and confess overhearing the conversation between him and Ted, which led to her not trusting him completely. Now wasn't the time, though. "I'll step out so you can finish dressing."

Adam threw back the covers. "I'm dressed and ready to go."

Misty clapped her hand over her mouth before saying, "Adam Jenkins, you are one crazy guy."

He jumped out of bed and into the wheelchair. He leaned back to pop a wheelie with his one good arm. "I've gotten pretty good with this thing over the last week."

She crossed her arms in front of her chest. "I see that. You know, I think you've broken every hospital rule there is."

Adam couldn't hide his glee. "Probably."

"Let's go."

After gathering his discharge paperwork and wheeling Adam to the car, Misty climbed into the driver's seat. He reached for her hand.

"It's good to be out of that place. I don't know how you stand working there."

She had heard similar remarks before. "You have to look past the place and see the people, their pain, their needs."

He nodded. "You have a heart for people, for sure."

Fifteen minutes later, they pulled into the IHOP restaurant parking lot. Adam refused her help to climb from the car.

"I had three weeks to convalesce, about two weeks too long, if you ask me," he grumbled. "Time for the roles to be reversed."

She resisted helping him up the sidewalk. Inside, they took a seat in a secluded booth in the back and placed their orders.

"How do we stand with the dedication ceremony?" Adam asked.

"Everything's on schedule. I've asked the mayor to say a few words and hired a band."

Adam's eyes widened. "The mayor? Wow, you've got pull."

"He was happy to be a part of the opening." Misty stirred sugar into her coffee. "I found him to be very supportive. The schedule is at the office, and we can go over it as soon as you're up to working."

Adam reached for her hand. "Christmas is in three days. Do you want to do anything special?"

"Something low-key. We had enough excitement at Thanksgiving." Memories of that awful moment when Adam plunged into the ravine pressed at her. God had been good in restoring them both.

"Dori won't be joining us. Nor James." Adam's eyes danced with mischief. "He's taking her to Sullivan's downtown."

"Ooh, Sullivan's. How swanky."

Adam smirked. "Well, you got your wish, it seems."

"It would seem." Misty's heart overflowed with joy that Dori had finally opened the door of her heart to James. She prayed things would work out between them.

The waiter returned with their plates. After Adam said grace, they spent the next thirty minutes eating and making small talk. Misty purposely kept the conversation light, but now that he was out of the hospital, they would have a serious talk—soon.

Much had happened the night he'd been injured. Demons had been put to rest, and she intended to straighten things out. She'd made peace with whatever might happen afterwards.

Chapter Thirty-Eight

"That was about the best Christmas dinner I've ever eaten." Misty snuggled onto the couch beside Adam a few days later.

He put his arm around her. "Not very fancy, but it's kind of nice, the two of us." His smile faded as he grew serious. "Although I'd like your parents to join us one day soon for dinner."

Misty grinned. "We'll do that. But I like the quiet. In case you haven't figured it out, I'm not a fancy kinda girl."

"Do tell." He snuggled closer. "Do you like your new cowboy boots?"

She snickered. "Definitely something I didn't have."

He frowned. "You don't like them?" He sounded hurt.

"Oh, no, I love them." She kissed him. "Now we match."

Adam groaned. "That wasn't exactly what I was aiming for."

"Men."

"What's that supposed to mean?" He pulled her even closer and nestled into her hair, causing her to giggle harder. She pressed her hands against his chest. It would be too easy to get carried away.

"Thank you again for the bracelet. It's beautiful." She swirled the gold and diamond bracelet around her wrist.

"Too bad I didn't know you weren't fancy before I bought it."

Misty cut her eyes at him. "You."

Adam grew serious. "Life is good."

"Hmmm." She settled in close again.

He traced the outline of her hand with his finger and then kissed the back of her hand. "If only the good didn't come out of such tragedy."

"Hope House?"

"Uh-huh."

"Jenny would be proud of you."

The light dimmed in his eyes. "She'd be glad I didn't wallow in self-pity. That women like her will have a place to escape."

Misty straightened and held his gaze. Her pulse raced. She'd made a decision the night of Adam's accident. No matter what, they had to get their relationship out in the open and quit dancing around her lack of trust. It stood in the way of everything. Their dreams. Their future together.

She cleared her throat. "Jenny's death taught me something, Adam. Not to waste time. I'd failed miserably, though, until your accident."

His brow creased. "I don't follow."

"I've already told you about my parents' confession—that I have a biological mother out there somewhere."

Adam nodded. "It doesn't change anything—not with us anyway. And like I told you, I'll do whatever it takes to find her—if you choose to do so."

She clasped her hands and inhaled deeply to try to dissipate her anxiety. "I appreciate that, but now I have something to confess. Remember the day here on the ranch, not long after we were engaged?"

He rubbed his chin and considered. "Can't say as I do."

"The day you fired Ted."

"Ah, yes. That day." Adam leaned against the cushions. "He's fortunate I controlled myself that day."

An uneasy tension stirred inside of Misty. "What do you mean?"

"Just that he's fortunate," Adam restated matter-of-factly. "A lot of men wouldn't have handled the situation that lightly."

The familiar anger Misty had worked hard to rid her soul of came rushing back. Had her first reaction been the right one? No, she'd already settled this. Her head pounded with her confused thoughts.

"But what does that have to do with anything?"

Misty forced herself to smile through her consternation. There was no easy way to say it. "I was here and overheard your conversation with Ted."

"I still don't follow."

"I arrived early for our riding date. Since you were busy, I decided to go to the restroom so I'd be ready to ride when you finished." She took a deep breath. "I heard you fire Ted."

"Is that what's been bothering you?" Adam straightened, eyes wide and his mouth agape. He slouched back against the couch cushion, as the events and their significance from the last few months seemed to fall into place in his mind. "You gave me the ring back right after that."

She resisted lowering her gaze, as the old Misty would've done. Instead, she braced herself for the chastisement that might follow, along with his anger. After all, she had eavesdropped and then covered it up.

He reached for her hand. "What did I say that scared you?" His voice soothed, without condemnation.

How did he know she'd been scared? She cleared her throat and looked at her hands. "Adam, I'm sorry I brought this up now. Actually, it's embarrassing."

"Misty, don't pull away." He lifted her chin with the crook of his finger then cupped her cheek with his hand. "Please."

She fidgeted. "You said you were the boss and you would decide when someone packed their bags."

"That scared you?"

Her throat constricted. "It was your tone."

"But I was angry. Ted had embezzled money from me when I was distracted and grieving." His jaw muscle tightened then twitched. "My anger was reasonable."

Misty nodded. "I understand that—now."

Adam stood, walked over to the window, his back to her. Finally, he turned, his voice tight. "I don't understand why you didn't wait around and tell me it upset you. I'm not a tyrant."

This was going worse than she'd anticipated. Why had she been so foolish in letting the problem fester? She had to try to explain—somehow salvage things. She couldn't lose Adam now—not when she'd finally found her courage to trust. Somehow, she had to make him understand.

"You're the farthest thing from a tyrant I know," Misty whispered.

"But I have to tell you, Adam, your voice sounded like Ryan's." Tears trickled down her face. "His words kept ringing in my ears, 'I'm the boss!' It wigged me out. I'm sorry."

Adam gathered her into his arms. "Shhh, it's okay."

She leaned against his chest, savoring the strength of his arms around her. "Can you forgive me?"

"There's nothing to forgive. I love you. I'll never hurt you like Ryan did." He lifted his head and looked her in the eyes. "You're a treasure to me. I wish you'd believe that."

She sniffed. "I do, Adam. I finally do. The night of the accident made a lot of things clear to me."

His eyes gleamed. "Well, then, I guess plunging into a ravine was worth it."

Misty shook her head. "You're crazy, you know?"

"Someone told me that once." His smile faded. "Please promise me you'll tell me when I do things to upset you. Our relationship will never work, if you don't."

"I promise." She reached for a tissue and wiped her eyes.

"And one other thing." Adam stepped back, his face indicating he wanted his words to sink in. "I'll get angry in the future. You will, too. We may even raise our voices some. We're fallible humans."

Her breath caught as she exhaled. "I know. My reaction was unreasonable. Fortunately, I've grown past that. As long as we can talk things out when you get angry—give me a chance to communicate back."

Adam smiled. "Absolutely." He glanced out the window. "The weather is beautiful today. A little chilly, but sunny. Wanna take a walk down to the stables?"

Misty gulped back the last of her tears and mustered a smile. "No horseback riding, though."

"Oh, come on." Adam reached for his jacket as Misty slipped into hers. "Just a little ride. The horses are getting stir-crazy."

"I happen to know James has been exercising them regularly." She followed Adam through the terrace door and caught his hand in hers.

The crisp cool winter air stung her nose and eyes, and she huddled next to him. "Besides, it's too cold."

Adam's laugh echoed through the hills around them as they neared the horse barn. "It's never too cold to ride."

"I'd rather not." Misty couldn't explain her feelings, but she feared getting back on Bella. More than that, she wasn't ready to see Adam on horseback.

He stepped into the stables and held the door for her to follow. They crossed the room, and Misty grabbed carrots from the barrel next to the stalls.

Adam's eyes searched her face. "We have to get back in the saddle eventually," he said quietly.

Misty held the carrot up to Bella and waited while she pulled it in with her lips, chomping as she went. "But not now. It's too soon."

He nodded. "You're probably right."

"I'll be honest. I am scared, but it's also too soon for either of us to take another fall." She attempted a laugh. "And if I've learned nothing else this year, it's that anything's possible."

Adam rubbed her back. "I think we've both learned that. Okay, no riding. Let's take a walk instead."

They strolled down the path toward the apple groves and stood on the hill facing Hope House across the valley. The trees were bare, and the countryside spread out around them. The view had changed incredibly in the last nine months.

"A dream realized." Adam's voice was barely audible.

Misty slipped her arm around him and snuggled close. "Less than a week now until the dedication ceremony."

"I couldn't have done it without you." He looked into her eyes. "I wouldn't have wanted to do it without you."

She let him pull her into a full embrace. "I'm glad I could help."

"More than you'll ever know." The warmth of his breath flowed over her neck. He kissed her cheeks as he stroked her chin with his fingertips, sending a tingling sensation down her spine.

She lifted her face, seeking his lips with hers. The intensity of his kiss sent shivers through her. How much longer could she endure a courtship?

***

Adam lifted his head. "Let's take one of the Kawasaki Mules and go over there. I want to look around one last time to make sure everything is in order."

They'd walked through the compound before Christmas, but he didn't want any last-minute glitches. Besides, he felt connected to Jenny every time he set foot in the building.

"Good idea." Misty followed him to the garage. Within moments, they were lumbering over the hilly terrain toward Hope House.

"You ladies did a remarkable job with the daycare center. I love the animal murals on the walls, especially the colts." He reached for her hand once they'd parked and climbed out.

"I thought Jenny's Place should reflect her interests. I gave the artist a photo of Willow and her colt."

He squeezed her hand. "Brilliant idea."

Inside, he switched on the lights and soaked in the beautiful colors of the main building.

Misty's eyes roved over the spacious interior. "Will you be okay here for a minute? I want to check on the food menu one last time. Dori was supposed to leave it on my desk."

"Go ahead. I'm going to wander around." Adam gave her a smile as she left. The sound of her step on the hardwoods faded as she rounded the corner to the offices.

He rubbed his neck. His prayer preceding Thanksgiving had plagued his thoughts since the accident. He'd wanted God to intervene—to speed things up so he and Misty could marry. At first, he believed the accident was providential—God had answered his prayer. Misty's confession confused him. Were they ready for marriage?

God, show me which path to take with Misty.

Adam strolled back to his office that adjoined Misty's and dropped into the desk chair. As he waited for the computer to boot up, rustlings from her office filled him with warmth. They would be working side by side in less than a week.

His gaze drawn to the screen, he clicked through the icons until he reached the Hope House bank account. Perilously low. He thumped a pencil on the desktop.

Misty stuck her head in the door. "Decide to do some work?"

He smiled. "Just thinking."

"Finances?"

"Yep." He leaned against the headrest. "Until we actually have women and children coming through here, it's difficult to gauge the exact need."

Misty sat in the chair in front of his desk. "Donations have picked up with it being the last month of the year. People are looking for tax breaks."

"It'll all be gone by March."

Her forehead furrowed. "You're right."

"Well." He stood and forced a smile. "God has provided so far. He'll continue to do so. We have to trust Him."

Misty came around the desk and slipped into his outstretched arms. "Wanna walk over to Jenny's Place or have you had enough exercise for one day?"

He leaned his chin against the top of her head. "I think it's time to go home."

She leaned back, concern lacing her face. "Are you all right?"

"Yeah, I have a lot on my mind right now." He couldn't tell her his fears for the future—their future. Would it be right to ask her to marry him again when he had all this financial responsibility? He'd be asking her to shoulder a great deal in taking on Jenkins Enterprises and Hope House. JE had always been solid, but now it was linked to Hope House whether he liked it or not. Hope House couldn't fail. He saw no other way in the foreseeable future to support it but through JE's additional funding. But that was an issue for another day.

He smiled. "Let's go home."

Chapter Thirty-Nine

New Year's Day had finally arrived. Misty hummed as she wriggled into her evening gown then stepped into her sequined black heels. After a quiet evening last night, she was ready for a party. The year had been long and difficult. Joy and happiness were at the top of her resolutions for the New Year.

Misty felt better after her discussion with Adam the week before. Though she was glad to have the air cleared between them, his reaction wasn't exactly what she'd hoped. Sure, he'd not truly gotten angry— more like frustrated. And he seemed to get over the feeling rather quickly. But she'd expected more from the discussion.

Like a proposal.

Instead, he continued as though he were very comfortable with their relationship.

She ran the brush through her hair a final time and smoothed her hands over her dress. The fundraising ball had been formal, but she'd chosen a more subtle black evening dress with off-the-shoulder sleeves for the opening of Hope House.

She sighed. Who could blame Adam for not producing the ring again? After all, she'd shattered his heart months before. And he'd been through a lot in the last month. For that matter, the last year. Maybe he'd finally embraced the idea of a long courtship. Misty glanced at the clock. Where had the time gone? She grabbed her clutch purse and took one last look in the mirror. Surely Adam wouldn't be late on such an important night.

Her gaze caught the little white envelope from Mr. Duncan's attorney lying on the foyer table. She picked it up. She could smile now at her memories of caring for the elderly man. Mr. Duncan had passed shortly before Christmas and insisted on no funeral. His attorney had sent the note indicating his estate would be divided among a few charities, but the bulk of it would go to Hope House. Her chest ached when she recalled her insistence that he not leave her a dime. Had she hurt him? She would take flowers to the cemetery later in the week. She chuckled. What would he say if he knew a bouquet adorned his grave?

The doorbell rang as if on cue. She tucked the edge of the envelope under the flower vase. She rushed to answer the door.

"Perfect timing," she exclaimed when she opened the door.

Adam beamed. "You are beautiful. Stunning, actually."

Her face grew warm. "Thank you. You don't look so bad yourself." She leaned in and kissed his cheek. He slid his hands around her waist and pulled her closer. His lips met hers in a lingering kiss.

"Hmmm, I could get used to that," Misty murmured.

"I'm counting on it." Adam stepped toward the door. "Ready?"

Misty grabbed her black clutch purse. "Yes, if we don't hurry, we'll be late."

"Don't want to keep the masses waiting on the most important night of the year."

Misty paused. Their hard work over the last several months had brought Hope House into a reality. Adam's eyes reflected back the somberness that suddenly washed over her. "Are you okay?"

"Yeah, hard not to think of Jenny. Wishing she were here."

"Me, too." She patted his arm. "She's with us in spirit. I can feel her."

A smile spread across Adam's face. "I can, too."

Twenty minutes later, they parked in front of Hope House. After climbing from the car, they stood hand in hand and looked at the sign at the entrance of the building.

"It's really true," Misty whispered. "A place where women can feel safe." She looked at Adam. "A place to start over."

He squeezed her hand. "We've come a long way in the last year."

She swiped at the tears that flowed easily. "Yes, we have. Now, let's go have some fun."

He handed her his handkerchief. "It's what Jenny would've wanted." He brushed a kiss against her cheek and opened the door.

Though Misty had been there the day before, the effect of the live band and the work Dori and Beth had put into the evening's setup changed the atmosphere. Heart-shaped red and pink helium balloons floated near the ceiling with streamers dancing beneath. Multicolored spotlights shone on the stage, reflecting a backdrop of enlarged photos of women and children. White linen-covered circular tables adorned with candles lined the periphery of the room. A dance floor accented the middle. Hors d'oeuvre tables were set up in the back.

Misty's breath caught. "Oh, Adam, it's beautiful."

"You did a fantastic job." With his hand to her back, Adam guided her through the crowd. A cheer went up as first one person then another recognized the couple. Adam shook a few hands and nodded to people he recognized.

Misty hugged Leah, Danielle, and the other nurses from the hospital who came to lend support. "I'm glad you could get the time off to come." Misty stepped back. "Who's minding the store?"

They laughed. "Don't worry. I'm headed to the hospital as soon as we're finished here," Leah assured her. "I'm so proud of you—for this." She motioned toward the stage.

"Thanks, Leah." Misty hugged her again. "I'll see you later."

Tanya and Jackie from the women's shelter waved across the room to her. Misty made a mental note to greet them after Adam's speech. Right now, Adam motioned for her to join him and his family.

He slipped his arm around her when she reached his side. "Misty, this is my mom and dad, Jennifer and Austin Jenkins."

Misty shook hands with his parents. "I see where Jenny got her beautiful name."

His mom wore a sad smile. "Thank you—and thank you for helping Adam with Hope House."

"I've enjoyed it. Jenny was a very special young lady." Misty didn't have a chance to say anything else before a rugged man bearing a strong resemblance to Adam stepped forward and extended his hand.

"Seems my brother forgot about me. Colton Jenkins." He nudged Adam with his other arm.

Misty smiled, glanced at Adam, and back to Colton. She shook his hand. "You don't seem like someone easily forgotten."

Adam burst out laughing. "Gotcha there, little brother."

Colton grinned wider, his perfect white teeth flashing from his tanned face. "No, Adam's the forgettable one."

"Whoa, now, boys." Jennifer stepped between them. "No competition tonight."

Misty's face flushed, but she laughed along with them. She was glad for the rescue, and equally glad when Adam drew her closer.

"Adam, my parents are here. Oh, and Savannah's with them." Misty spoke to Adam's family. "I hope you don't mind."

"No, go ahead." Jennifer touched her arm. "So nice to finally meet you."

"And you, too."

Misty rushed to greet her parents and sister with Adam close behind. She threw her arms around Savannah and hugged her.

"Wow, you've got quite a bear hug there, sis." Savannah finally stepped back.

"How did you manage to get some time to come home?" Misty's heart felt like it would burst from joy. She squeezed her sister's hand.

"My furlough became permanent."

"I don't follow."

"I'll tell you all about it later. My situation in China became," Savannah's voice caught, "compromised, so the mission board brought me home."

Misty sobered. "I'm sorry. I know how much being there meant to you."

"It's God's will. He has another plan for me. I have to believe that." Savannah cleared her throat and flashed a smile. "Tonight's about Hope House. We have plenty of time to catch up later."

"Okay." Misty leaned in. "I have someone for you to meet." She turned and slipped her hand into the crook of Adam's arm as she motioned him forward.

Savannah's smile widened.

"Mom, Dad, Savannah, this is Adam." Misty held her amusement as Papa scrutinized Adam. "Adam, these are my parents, Jack and Sophia Callahan."

"Good to meet you." Adam shook hands with her dad and gently hugged her mom. He nodded to her sister. "Savannah."

"Nice to meet you." Savannah gripped his hand.

"I'm thrilled you made it back from Europe in time for the dedication." Misty's chest ached from happiness as her parents and Adam chatted. The only empty spot was Jenny. Misty ignored the guilt of having her own sister present when Adam's wasn't. She pulled her focus back to the merriment of the evening.

She sensed Colton's presence before she saw him. He sidled up to the group with the swagger and confidence she'd already come to expect from him. She introduced him to her parents. They shook hands, but his focus zoned in on Savannah.

What's going on here? If Colton were drawn to Savannah, no way would she return his interest—nor would he stay interested long when he learned of her occupation.

Misty motioned to Savannah. "This is my sister, Savannah. She's on furlough from her mission work in China."

Was it her imagination, or did Colton's face sag slightly?

"Nice to meet you." He shook her hand. "Better get back to Mom and Dad." He clapped his hand on Adam's shoulder. "See you later."

"I think it's about that time." Adam gestured toward the stage. "If you'll excuse us—"

"Certainly," Misty's dad replied. "We'll see you later, lass."

Misty squeezed her dad before following Adam to the front of the room. She spotted Dori and Beth and signaled the ladies to join them onstage. As they made their way forward, Misty whispered to Adam, "Should your family join us?"

"I already asked. They don't want to be in the spotlight."

"I can relate." Misty smiled.

Adam reached for a microphone. "I'd like to welcome everyone to the festivities tonight. There are a couple of things I'd like to share, then you're welcome to enjoy the hors d'oeuvres, drinks, and good music."

He motioned toward Misty. "First, I'd like to thank Misty Stephens, the director of Hope House, her administrative assistant, Beth Matthews, and my assistant, Dori Branson, for all their hard work in pulling this evening together. As many of you know, I was in an accident, and Hope House would have never opened on time, if it hadn't been for them."

Thunderous applause filled the room. Adam applauded the three ladies along with the crowd. Beth and Dori's faces beamed. Misty's heart filled with appreciation for what these two women had become to her. They weren't just co-workers. They were friends.

"Ms. Stephens and Ms. Matthews have worked tirelessly to keep the construction of Hope House on schedule and secure funding. In doing so, they've made my dream—this shelter—a reality.

"Hope House is in memory of my sister, Jenny, an abuse victim," Adam continued. "With millions of women battered each year across the US, we hope to do our part in providing a safe place to rebuild their lives."

Adam paused. The crowd applauded again. He glanced at Misty and smiled. She touched his arm and nodded her encouragement.

"I'd like to thank the donors who made this possible. Almost everyone in this room has contributed toward Hope House in one way or another, either with time, talent, or money." He reached into his pocket and pulled out a check. "I received notice this afternoon that Mr. Charles Duncan, one of our benefactors, bequeathed an endowment in his will to Hope House in the amount of one million dollars."

Gasps, followed by applause, filled the air.

Misty's heart thumped. A million dollars? Had she heard right? She realized her mouth gaped open. She snapped it shut then leaned over and whispered to Adam, "Are you serious?"

He grinned and covered the microphone. "The first check is right here," he whispered.

She looked at the zeroes behind the first digit and gasped. Hope House's funding was secure now. She breathed a prayer of blessing for this man who'd been at the root of so much evil—who now stood in the presence of his Savior.

Adam put up his hand to quiet the crowd. "I want everyone to enjoy themselves. There's plenty of food and drink, but first—I've got one final announcement to make." He pulled a small jewel box from his pocket, opened it, and slipped out a diamond engagement ring.

Misty's pulse raced. *Right here in front of everyone?*

"I tried to put this on Misty's finger a few months ago, but it didn't stay."

Laughter laced the air. The warmth from Misty's chest rushed to her cheeks.

Adam turned to her. "I'm going to ask you in front of witnesses this time." His eyes sparkled.

She took a step toward him and extended her left hand. Thunderous applause rocked the auditorium, reverberating so she could barely hear his words. She leaned forward as he slipped the ring onto her finger.

"I said, are you sure?" he repeated himself.

"Oh, Adam, I've never been so sure of anything in my life."

Adam took Misty in his arms and kissed her. The applause grew louder. When he lifted his head, she looked into the eyes of the man she knew God had ordained for her. Her past was just that—her past. Her future stood in front of her.

THE END

Also from
Laura Hodges Poole

The Award-winning
Return to Walhalla

Available from ShopLPC.com
and your favorite retailer